The Cave

By

Sam McGowan

To My Buddy Al,

Best Wishes,

Sam McG

ISBN: 1-4033-0243-X Ebook
ISBN: 1-4033-0244-8 Softcover

This book is printed on acid free paper.

1stBooks - rev. 05/08/02

Prelude - 1956

"I'm scared," the little boy called over his shoulder into the inky blackness behind his outstretched body.

"Go on, Toby. You can get through all right. If you find anything, I'll dig it out and follow you."

"But what if I get stuck, like Floyd Collins did?"

"You won't. But even if you did, I'd get to you. The bottom is river gravel and the roof's solid rock. I'd go ahead and dig it out if I was by myself or with someone bigger than you are. But you're small enough to get through without digging. If it goes, we'll dig it out later."

"Well, okay. But promise that you'll be right here and you'll come get me if I get stuck."

"Son, I'll be right here. I'm not going anywhere."

The ten-year old boy took a deep breath, then pushed off, slithering his way over golf-ball sized pebbles that made up the creek bed. The waterway was just like any of the dozens of other shallow streams which wound their way through the hills on either side of the Tennessee River - with one exception. This stream bed was fifty feet underground!

The limestone roof over Toby Carter's head was low, barely eight inches above the gravel, too low to allow Uncle Bob Carter to get through. For a ten-year old boy, the crawl-way was easy enough to get through, although for an adult it would have been impossible without some enlargement. Fortunately, it was at least ten feet wide. Many cave passages are as narrow as they are low. Looking ahead in the soft, warm glow of the light of the carbide lamp, Toby saw that the passage made a bend to the right, away from the aboveground stream bed in the middle of the valley. He hollered back over his shoulder, "It bends to the right."

"That's a good sign. Go on as far as you can, but don't take chances. By the way, you're already further than anybody has ever been before. You're in virgin cave, son."

Virgin cave! Those words would have stilled the fear in the heart of an older person and changed it to excitement, but Toby Carter was only ten. To him, the fact that he was in a crawl-way where no person had ever gone before meant only that he was getting further and further away from his Uncle Bobby. Uncle Bob; folks said he was crazy for wanting to spend all his free time exploring the cracks and crevices in the limestone along the Tennessee. In 1956 Tennessee and Kentucky the ordeal of Floyd Collins was still real in the minds of a lot of people. Many adults remembered the newspaper headlines and Skeets Miller's pathos-filled stories about the Kentucky farmer-turned-cave-explorer who was pinned by falling rock in a

iii

cave not far from Mammoth Cave, then died of starvation and exposure before rescuers could get him out.

Bob Carter was an oddity in an area where most men found their peace out in the woods with a rifle or on the river with a fishing rod in hand. Not that Bob wasn't an outdoorsman - he hunted and fished as much as anyone else. It was just that the underground world had a strange hold on him. He was a Twentieth Century explorer, drawn into the underground water conduits in the Tennessee limestone by the many sights and wonders which few eyes had ever seen - or ever will.

Young Toby gritted his teeth and kept crawling up the low passageway, even though he would just as soon have been somewhere else. Out on the river maybe, or up in the woods trying to outsmart a bushy-tail. Even though he was only ten, Toby Carter could hit a squirrel in the eye from fifty feet with a .22, thanks to the tutelage of his father and the same Uncle Bob who was waiting in the passage for his report. He wouldn't even have minded being back in the large walking passage they had come through to get back to this tiny crawl-way.

He wondered just what it was that drove Uncle Bob to want to seek out new cave passages. His own father wasn't adverse to caving - had he been, he wouldn't have allowed Toby to go with Bob - but on the other hand, caves held no particular fascination for him. Toby was like Bob, though. He liked caves as much as hunting and fishing, but to him it was just something unusual to do. This low, crawly passage spooked him. Fear welled up in his throat as he continued pushing with his feet and pulling with his elbows, wriggling his way through the underground creek bed. But even as he felt scared almost out of his wits, an excitement such as he had never known in his young life slowly caught the boy in its grasp.

What was this?! He could raise his head; it had been on its side. He had reached a joint, the limestone had eroded away just enough that the passage was about a foot high. Up ahead the ceiling looked even lower than what he had crawled under so far. Yet he continued on, even as he felt solid rock pressing on his back as he crawled, while the river gravel pressed into his chest, sternum and abdomen. There was no way Uncle Bob would get through this squeeze, not without a lot of digging.

After working his way through the low squeeze, Toby saw that the ceiling was getting higher and the passage beginning to widen. This was fortunate for him; a pool of water nearly blocked his way. He managed to squeeze himself along the side of the shallow pool, avoiding the water and keeping his clothes reasonably dry. Even though he was only a boy, Toby knew that wet clothes in a cave meant misery, and could mean death under certain circumstances. Temperatures in caves remain constant, at the mean temperature for the region. This one was cool; fifty-eight degrees. While this was warm enough as long as one was dry, a person soaked to the skin in wet clothes could develop hypothermia and die.

Now that he was out of the squeeze and into more comfortable passage, Toby felt a sense of relief. He was no longer afraid, his fear replaced by anticipation. Water in the passage had to come from somewhere; the cave must go on. He stopped crawling and listened. Was that someone laughing? No, he recognized the sound - water, falling water. The flame of the carbide lamp flickered. Was it about to go out? No, it shouldn't be. They had changed carbide and filled the water compartment in their lamps just before he went into the passage. Still, Toby felt more secure knowing he had a flashlight and candles in the cave pack dragging behind him. Then he felt something, and realized he had been feeling it all along. A faint breeze was beginning to increase. That meant one thing, larger cave passage up ahead.

"I think I'm going to break through," the boy shouted into the darkness behind him.

"What was that? Are you okay?" He heard Uncle Bob's voice faintly. He must be two hundred feet or more behind him. "I...THINK...I'M GOING...TO...BREAK...THROUGH. I...FEEL...A...BREEZE." He shouted the words slowly. Then he continued crawling, not waiting for his uncle's reply.

There was no doubt but that the breeze was increasing in strength, and the ceiling was starting to rise. He could raise his head. Up ahead it appeared that he might be able to get up on hands and knees. Toby crawled faster. There was no doubt that the ceiling was considerably higher then it had been.

"I see formations. Bacon rind. And soda straws. Hey, a stalactite!" He called back to his uncle, forgetting to speak slowly. He was now on hands and knees, requiring less effort than the belly crawl he had come through. The helmet and lamp were back on his head; his efforts were less awkward. The breeze was stronger. Then, suddenly, the ceiling went up, way up. He had crawled into a large cave passage - or was it a room?

Toby got to his feet. He directed the beam of the carbide lamp first one way and then another, the flame illuminating the total darkness where no light had ever penetrated. Toby Carter was awestruck at the sight. From the ceiling, some twenty feet over-head, hung stalactites of massive proportion. Similar sized stalagmites reached up from the floor while hundreds of more modest-sized formations protruded from both floor and ceiling. He counted at least a dozen columns, stalactites and stalagmites which had grown together over centuries of solution action as acid-charged waters worked their way through the limestone above his head. Flow-stone bacon rinds decorated the walls where water dripped down the sides of the dome - for he

v

realized that was what he had found instead of a large, trunk cave passage. But what a dome! It must be fifty feet across! Such sights were enough to generate awe in even the most experienced cave explorer. The most magnificent sights of all were the gypsum flowers and helectites, which reached out from the walls of the room.

Air movement in the room was slight, but there was enough for him to know that there had to be another entrance. He knew that from listening to Uncle Bob. His previously-felt fear had been totally replaced by a new sensation; Toby now realized what it was that made his uncle thirst to find new caves and new sights. With his excitement at its highest peak, Toby looked around the huge room, searching for the other entrance he knew had to be there. He exhaled mightily, then watched as the vapor drifted toward the tiny passage through which he had just come. He made his way in the opposite direction, exhaling each minute or so and watching the drifting mist. By this time he was well out of earshot from Uncle Bob. No point in yelling to try and tell what he had found, even though he wanted to reveal his discovery to someone. There would be plenty of time for that later. Uncle Bob would want to dig a way in here; that was certain.

His light probed the walls of the room as he looked for the opening that had to be there. Several places looked promising, but turned out to be small grottos, indentations in the rock without the hoped-for lead. But he knew it had to be there, the air movement told him that. How long had he been in the room? Without a watch, it was impossible to tell. Five minutes? Ten? He was going to have to start back before Uncle Bob became concerned and started trying to dig his way in. That would take hours of pushing sand and gravel out to one side to make a trench so a larger person could get through.

Toby noticed a tiny stream of water coming from under the wall of the cave. It emitted from a resurgence that would allow a cave rat to pass through, but that was about all. There was no way even a ten-year old boy would ever get through that hole, not without a lot of digging and probably even some blasting. Uncle Bob hadn't used dynamite in caves much - he never had too - but Toby knew that some cave explorers would blast their way through a promising lead and destroy anything in the way if they thought they could find something on the other side. The water was trickling into a rather large, but very shallow pool. Toby waded along the edge; on the opposite end water was flowing - really a trickle - out of it. He followed the tiny stream to where it disappeared into what looked like another grotto.

Toby crawled into the grotto, if that was what it was. It was about three feet wide, with a sloping ceiling that seemed to stop about two feet above the gravel floor. This one appeared deeper than the others he had found; there were formations in it, including a large flow-stone drapery at the very back. The water disappeared under the drapery. Toby dropped onto his belly and peered under the flow-stone. He felt a rush of cold air on his face. He listened. What was that? It sounded like running water, a lot of running water. But then, sounds were magnified considerably in the hollow recesses of a cave. The passageway seemed to be no smaller than the one through which he had crawled to discover the room - he was already thinking of it as "Toby's Room." He knew Uncle Bob would be starting to worry. He would just go a little way, then come back. Toby started into the tiny passage.

To his surprise, he only had to crawl ten feet, then he was on his feet again, in another large hollow in the rock. This was no room! He was in cave; there was no doubt about that. The walls were smooth, with scallops. Water had flown through this passage over the years, a lot of water! No formations decorated the passage and the floor was solid rock, with a steadily flowing stream running to his left. If his sense of direction was correct - he had no compass with him - it flowed toward the Tennessee River. According to local legend, when TVA dammed the river the waters filled a huge cave entrance. Also according to legend that cave had once served as shelter to the early settlers in the region, and to countless Indians for thousands of years before that. Bob had long thought there should be another way into the cave, one which would allow its exploration even though Kentucky Lake waters now filled the entrance. Had he found a way into the huge cavern Uncle Bob suspected ran along the Tennessee Valley?

Toby's emotions were divided. One sense told him it was time to go back, to keep Uncle Bob from worrying; the other told him to press on, to see what lay up ahead. What would Uncle Bob do? He would probably start trying to dig his way into the passage. Toby decided to go on a little ways, then come back. He studied the walls for landmarks to help him find the fissure through which he had come, then realized that the water coming out of the side of the wall would be an identifying mark. He wouldn't have to make a marker.

Toby made his way downstream. Up ahead he could hear the sound of more water. The stream he was following must be flowing into another. There could be dozens of underground streams flowing into the creek. Every creek bed in the area was dry; every stream was a sinking stream that disappeared into its bottom as soon as it reached the level of the limestone. Not a single one emerged again on the surface. That was why Uncle Bob knew there had to be a really large underground waterway in the region. Now Toby had found it! He was certain of it.

Should he go on? He was by himself, God only knew how far beneath the Tennessee hills. Common sense told him the best thing to do was turn around, then come back with Uncle Bob. Toby had never heard of the National Spelological Society's rule, "Never cave alone," but he knew that going ahead was not the best thing to do. What if he fell? No one would know where to look for him. But the passage was basically unhindered by rocks. The floor was smooth from the constantly running water. He decided to go on a little further.

Just when Toby was ready to turn around, he realized the burbling sound of the water was increasing in intensity. It sounded like a waterfall, or rapids in a stream. He felt a strong breeze on his face as his carbide flame flickered again. He was going to have to change carbide before he started out, but he knew this flickering was from the breeze. He hurried on.

Five minutes later Toby's passage came to an end as it intersected another passage; a large one. The new passage was some fifteen feet below the level of the one he was in. That accounted for the sound he had been hearing; the stream he had been following fell into a pool fifteen feet below. He had discovered an underground waterfall. Without either ropes or a ladder, there was no way to get to the lower level. It was time to turn back.

It took Toby half an hour to make his way back to the low crawl-way through which he had come. As he entered the passage, he could hear sounds - someone grunting, something scraping. Uncle Bob was trying to dig the passage out.

"Uncle Bob," Toby shouted into the crawl-way.

"Tobe! Boy, I was beginning to worry about you. You've been gone an hour and a half!"

An hour and a half? Surely not. He couldn't have been gone more than half an hour. "What did you find?"

"Beautiful...columns...big cave," Toby's words were indecipherable to Bob Carter, who had only made two body lengths travel into the passage.

"Did you say 'big cave?"

Toby heard his uncle, but didn't answer. He was too busy negotiating the low squeeze which almost caused him to panic during his trip into the new discovery. Up ahead he could see the light from Bob's lamp. To his surprise, the trip out of the low, tight passage was much easier - and less time consuming - then the one going in.

Once out of the crawl, the little boy stood up in the trunk passage where Bob had backed up to wait for his nephew.

"Well, what did you find?" Bob's curiosity was almost more than he could bear.

"You're not going to believe me. You'll think I'm making it up."

"Under other circumstances I might. But not here. You had to be someplace, and I don't think you just crawled into a crack somewhere and hid."

"Okay. The passage bends to the left and gets lower, but just for a little ways. Then it gets bigger - I was able to get up on hands and knees. Then I came out into a huge room, with stalactites, columns and those things that grow on the walls in some caves."

"You mean helectites - gypsum flowers."

"Yeah, those."

"Damn! Helectiites! I haven't seen any of those since I was in Kentucky! That's some find, Toby. We'll have to dig it out so I can get back in there."

"There's more."

"More. What do you mean, more?"

"I found a lead out of the room. It goes into another trunk with large, walking passage. A stream flows through it, to the west, toward the river."

"Toward the river? You're kidding, now aren't you?"

"I said you wouldn't believe me."

"I believe you! I believe you! Go on. How far did you go?"

"Til it came out in another really big passage and fell into a huge stream. The floor of the other one is as high as the barn loft. We'd have to have a rope or ladder to get down into it. There's a waterfall there."

"A waterfall! Boy, Toby. It sounds like you've really found something. What we've been looking for. I can't wait to dig it out. But you must be tired. We'll come back tomorrow. Let's go on out of the cave."

The man and boy left the low passage which led Toby Carter to the discovery of a lifetime. They did come back again the next day, and dug out the passage enough for Bob to squeeze his way through.   Under the waterfall they found an underground river, one which undoubtedly came out in the Tennessee, although the TVA dams had raised the water levels so the entrance must be underwater. Even though they could not penetrate the waters which filled the passage nearer to Kentucky Lake, they knew that Toby had found the upper reaches of the cave the old-timers use to talk about. After that day, Toby Carter would never again be scared in a cave.

Chapter One

"Break right! Break right!" Even as the warning came through his headset, Captain Steve Danson spun the control wheel to the right and pulled back on the yoke. Captain Bob Preston warned his crew, "Hang on in back!"

Toby Carter grabbed onto the braces in the cargo door and held on, at the same time pushing down on the flares beneath his feet to keep them from floating out of the aluminum chute in which they rested. The other three loadmasters each held on as best he could while the force of gravity, magnified three times over, attempted to force them to their knees. A hundred and ten thousand pounds of airplane responded instantly to the control inputs, pitching over on its right wing and around into a tight right turn. Six rounds of 37-MM cannon fire floated through the airspace where the airplane would have been without the turn.

"That was close, BAT TWO. That's pretty nimble work for a trash hauler."

"Thanks, DAGO One. That's why they call this thing the Fabulous Four-Engine Fighter. You get his position?"

"Watch this." The F-4 was invisible in the darkness but the North Vietnamese radar-aimed gun was tracking the fighter as it wheeled into position. Danson had pulled the airplane just out of range of the gun; the crew could see the whole show as it unfolded six thousand feet beneath them. A line of red tracers arced up from below, this time directed at the fighter pilot who had given warning to the C-130 flareship crew seconds before.

Suddenly, the ground around the spot from which the fire originated burst with hundreds of tiny winking lights. They looked like a child's sparkler - but they meant death. No more cherry-red fireballs arced from the muzzle of the automatic antiaircraft cannon; the crew all lay dead or dying after being caught in a hail of deadly explosive projectiles as the cluster-bomb burst. "Nice work, DAGO One. We owe you one." Preston congratulated the fighter pilot for taking out the gun.

"No sweat, BLIND BAT. You can buy us a drink at the club tonight when you get back."

"You can bet on it."

"That's the last of our ordinance. We're RTB. Have fun and watch those guns, hey?"

"No sweat, man. See you in the stag bar."

"Hey, man. All the bars are stag!"

"Don't I know it, we'll see you!"

1

The two-ship flight of Phantoms wheeled away and began a steep climb for the rarefied air of the higher altitudes, where their fuel consumption would be reduced. Their night's work was over; for the crew of the "BLIND BAT" C-130 flareship, it was just beginning.

Tobe Carter thought it somewhat ironic that a caver was part of a military mission named after the one animal most prevalent in caves. He knew the name was a misnomer; bats are hardly blind. The sonar system with which the airborne mammals seek out their flying prey was far more efficient than that given flareship crews in 1966 - a pair of binoculars and, if they were lucky, a hand-held Starlite Scope.

It was also ironic that when they were fragged over Laos, Toby was flying over one of the world's most prominent areas where caves are found. His survival map showed one huge area marked simply "karst," a geologic term derived from a region in Yugoslavia where sinkholes, disappearing streams and numerous known caves are prevalent. The enemy made use of the caves below, storing fuel and other supplies inside their entrances and taking shelter inside when bombers appeared overhead. One particularly notorious antiaircraft gun near the Laotion town of Tchepone was mounted on railway tracks and hidden inside a cave. When American aircraft appeared overhead, it was wheeled out, then put back inside whenever flak destroyers attempted to take it out. Hidden inside the huge cave entrance, the gun was impervious even to B-52 strikes. It had taken its toll on the American "air pirates."

"Hey, Tobe. Do you ever wish we had guns on this mother?" Mike Kelly stood by the flare chute, waiting to replace the flares under Toby's feet when Preston called for their release. Kelly was using Carter's family nickname because there was another Sam on the crew. Samuel Tobin Carter had been called Toby all of his life, until he went into the Air Force. Now everybody called him Sam, naturally, since that was the abbreviation for his first name.

"After an episode like that I do."

"It's sure frustrating - being shot at and not being able to shoot back." Kelly had to shout to be heard over the sounds of the engines and the rush of air through the partially opened rear cargo ramp.

"At least we can call in fighters to take out the guns."

"That's about all they're good for. They sure as hell can't hit anything with bombs."

"Dropping CBU's is like using a shotgun to kill squirrels. But at least it works."

"By the way; what're you going to do on R&R?"

"I don't know. Go to Naha, I guess."

"Why don't you come to Bangkok with Willy and Sam and me?"

"Bangkok? I've been there probably a dozen times. Naha's got the shuttle. We'll be going there again."

"Yeah, but this is different. We'll have a week to just screw around. And I mean 'screw.' Besides, there's nothing at Naha that won't wait until we get back in six weeks."

"You might be right. I'll think about it. How are you going to get there?"

"We can catch a pax flight, or hop a cargo mission on our ACM orders."

"Hey, loads," the pilot's voice came over the intercom, "get ready to drop four. Set 'em for ten seconds."

Carter motioned to Kelly. "Set for ten seconds." Kelly reached down and reset the fuses on the magnesium flares from "six" to "ten". Up forward on the modular pallet holding the flare bin, Willy Cavendish got ready to reload the tray. Sam McDonald, the other Sam on the crew, was on the loadmaster's long cord, forward of the load, ready to jettison everything if the load caught fire.

"Fuses set, sir."1

"Standby to drop." Ten seconds passed. "Drop one...drop two...drop three...drop four." Carter raised his feet, reached down and pushed each flare out as Preston called for it. As each aluminum canister left the tray, a wire lanyard was pulled out of the flare, starting the ejection and illumination sequence. Ten seconds later the canister blew off the flare, deploying the nylon parachute. As the parachute deployed, the flare ignited and burst into brilliance. Three seconds later another, then another, until all four flares were strung out for more than a mile. Night was turned into day in the flare light.

In the cockpit Preston and the navigator, Lt. Dick Benjamin, peered intently out the window with binoculars, scrutinizing the landscape below for signs of movement. Some six thousand feet beneath the belly of their green and brown C-130 lay the main Communist supply artery leading into South Vietnam. Hundreds of little Oriental men and women moved beneath the jungle canopy - but not a sign of them could be seen in the flare light. Any trucks in the area had been pulled off the road and hidden under camouflage. For all practical purposes, there was not a thing below.

"Clean as a hound's tooth."

"Let's pull in the chute and look for lights."

"What do you say we move out of the area for awhile? Give Charlie a chance to get moving again. Maybe we can find something when we come back."

"That might work. Hey load, you guys stow your flare chute for awhile. We're going to do a little recon up the road a ways. Try to stay awake, though. If we got hit, you might not wake up to get out."

Carter motioned to Kelly, "Safety the flares. We're going to cruise around for a bit. He wants us to bring the chute in and close the door."

Kelly inserted the safety pins in each of the four flares Carter was holding in place with his feet, then took them out of the dispenser and placed them back on the wooden tray used to roll the flares from their bin. Toby climbed down off the door. Cavendish came back to help as they unhooked the nylon security straps holding the flare chute in place. He pumped the cargo door open; Carter and Kelly pulled the aluminum flare chute back into the airplane. Cavendish used utility system hydraulics to close and lock the ramp and door. It was much quieter, though still noisy enough, inside the Lockheed Hercules.

With the flare chute in, Toby Carter and the other three loadmasters had nothing to do. This would be a good time to go up front and help the pilots watch for lights. He mounted the cockpit stairs and climbed into the darkened green-house which housed the rest of the crew. Even though the cargo compartment lights were on red, giving minimal light, the cockpit seemed much darker, lit only by the glow of the instrument lights. His pupils had dilated; the red-lighted cargo compartment seemed as bright as with normal white lights. Toby plugged into the flight mechanic's spare headset and stood behind the pilot, peering over his shoulder out the cockpit side windows. On his right sat the flight mechanic, TSgt Don Salts, silently monitoring hydraulic pressures, electrical amperage and voltage, fuel distribution and pressures; all the systems which kept the Herkybird in the air and operating safely.

Toby wondered about the caves he knew were in the hills beneath him. Eastern Laos is generally mountainous, with large areas of exposed limestone reaching upward as tall karst towers. With that much limestone, there had to be some large cave systems in the region beneath their airplane's wings. He had heard there were large fruit-eating bats in Southeast Asian caves, and beautiful formations. Were they as pretty as those found in Tennessee and Kentucky caves? He wondered. Would he ever have a chance to find out? Not likely. Not with the entire area in hostile hands. Perhaps after the war was over - if it ever ended.

Toby Carter was prepared for the Laotian caves in the event he happened to find himself on the ground. He wore the usual issue survival vest under his parachute harness; flareship loadmasters wore chest packs and stowed the packs until they needed them. Hopefully, they never would. In his vest he had survival rations, a water bag, first aid kit, compass, signal mirror, survival radio and extra batteries, pen-gun pistol and flares, survival flares, strobe light with shield, tracer and ball ammunition for his .38 Combat Masterpiece revolver, the revolver itself, a pocket knife and his

4

issue survival knife and sharpening stone. And a flashlight. But Tony had another - special - survival kit he had made up.

Borrowing from the cave packs he had used when exploring the caverns back home, Toby had rigged a pack which could be clipped to his parachute harness, then slung over the shoulder once he was on the ground. In the pack he carried two extra clips and four boxes of ammunition for his M-16, a second GI flashlight and batteries, a canteen of water, extra rations - and a carbide lantern along with three plastic baby bottles filled with carbide. Toby was the only aircrew member in the United States Air Force who carried a carbide lamp in his survival kit!

The lamp was more of a security blanket than anything else, a link with his past before he joined the Air Force and went on flying status as an aircrew loadmaster. Still, in the - hopefully unlikely - event he ever went down over Southeast Asia, Toby Carter had a plan. A simple one, really. He would find a cave and hide in it until the rescue choppers could get close enough to pick him up. A cave, whether along the banks of the Tennessee River or in the mountains of Southeast Asia, was home to Toby Carter.

That old Justrite miner's cap light was Toby's most prized possession; he had been using it that day when Uncle Bobby sent him up that miserable little crawl-way which led into the largest and most beautifully decorated cave west of Nashville. He knew it could come in handy on the ground even if he didn't find a cave. It would be a source of heat to warm the beanie weenies and pork and beans in his pack, and it would provide a softer light than an electric flashlight, a light the gooks just might not be able to see so well.

Next to the carbide lamp, his M-16 was the other item he most wanted to have with him on the ground. Ordinarily Air Force flight crews were armed only with pistols, but at Naha all loadmasters and flight mechanics were required to check out an M-16 when going in-country. Originally the policy had been so crews would be armed in the event they were forced to spend a night at a remote airfield in South Vietnam. Toby wanted the rifle with him because it was a much more formidable weapon than the .38 pistol. He knew he could hit anything with it he could see. Country boys in Tennessee learn to shoot almost as soon as they learn to walk, a lesson the British painfully learned at New Orleans and the Germans in the Argonne. Northerners had learned the same lesson at Shiloh; the only reason the Union had won the Civil War was because the Confederates ran out of ammunition and supplies before the Union ran out of men.

Toby kept the pack - he thought of it as his "cave pack" - and the M-16 hanging with his chest pack on a litter stanchion just forward of the left paratrooper door. He had rehearsed time after time what he would do - clip on the chute pack, hook the cave pack to his harness and strap the rifle to his leg. The guys in the fabric shop at Naha had balked when Toby went to them and asked for special straps and a pack, but a couple of bottles of Seagram's Seven will work wonders. He had gotten his pack and two straps to secure the rifle to him for an emergency bailout.

For nearly an hour Preston orbited high over Laos, while his crew kept close watch on the deep valley through which the Trail ran. In spite of the certain presence of Communists troops, they saw not a thing on the ground. Then, when they were beginning to think their efforts were completely futile, Lt. Benjamin saw a light.

"Hey, look there! Lights! About mid-way down the valley."

"Yeah, I see them. I'll call MOONBEAM. Dick, check the coordinates. Make sure they're in an a clear zone." Preston began issuing orders, preparing for a strike. "Carter, go on in back and get the chute out. Be ready to drop flares in five minutes."

"Yes sir." Carter unplugged his headset and made his way down the cockpit ladder to the cargo compartment. Cavendish was on headsets in back. He had already notified the other two loadmaster/flare kickers that it was time to get back to work.

Toby had had his turn on the door. Now it was Cavendish's time while he, Toby, would take his turn on headsets forward of the load. Kelly was on the bin, loading the tray, while red-headed McDonald would be loading the chute for the Jovial little Irishman from Philadelphia. Toby watched as McDonald and Cavendish put the flare chute back in place, while Kelly pumped up the hydraulic pressure to hold the cargo door down on it. Willy climbed onto the door and plugged into the headset cord Mike offered him.

"Flare kickers ready."

"Roger that," Preston's voice came over the interphone. "Load four, set 'em for ten seconds."

While the loadmasters loaded the flares, copilot Steve Danson maneuvered the C-130 through the night sky, bringing the airplane around to line up for a flare drop. A flight of Navy A-4's was on their way across the mountains, diverted by MOONBEAM from a planned attack on a suspected ford just north of the Mu Gia Pass. Vehicles were a much more solid target than a "suspected ford" that the North Vietnamese would repair the next day, using nothing but baskets, picks and shovels.

"Stand by to drop flares."

"Roger." Cavendish acknowledged the aircraft commander's instructions.

"Drop one...drop two...drop three...drop four." As Preston said the words, Cavendish launched one of the aluminum canisters into the darkness.

"Four flares gone, sir."

"Okay, load four more. Set for ten and stand-by."

Kelly quickly took first one, then another flare from the wooden tray and placed them in the aluminum chute where Cavendish held them in place with his feet. He ripped the plastic covers from the end of each flare and tossed the discs into the night, then pulled out the wire lanyards and placed the loop over the attachment point on the aluminum chute. When four flares were in the door, he reached down and set the dials of the timers to "10."

Eager to see the action below, Carter looked out a side window forward of the left wheel well. His visibility was limited by the small size of the round window. He could see only off to one side. Whatever was directly below would be out of his field of vision.

"Look a there, folks." Preston's East Texas accent came through in his excitement. "Look at the little bastards. Six pretty little maids all lined up in a row! Where the hell are those swabbies?"

Benjamin answered, he had been working the UHF with MOONBEAM. "Their ETA is in three minutes. MOONBEAM should be turning them over to us any time."

A voice crackled over the headsets in the cockpit; Carter and Cavendish could not hear the radio conversations.

"BAT TWO, this is SEA HORSE. Flight of two. We're ETA your position one minute, thirty seconds. We've got your flares. How about a light?"

"Roger that, SEA HORSE." Preston reached up and pushed the toggle switch for the rotating beacon to "On."

"Okay BAT, we've got your light. What have you got for us?"

"A convoy of six, all lined up in a row. What're you carrying?"

"Sixteen HE and two napes each. How do you want them?"

Preston had assumed radio control of the fighters when they reported on freq. "Let's start off with the nape. -,Run-in heading will be two six-five. We'll be at ten grand. Do you need a marker?"

"That's a negatron." The voice of the Navy lead answered, "We've got 'em in sight. Give us some light, then sat back and watch the show."

"We'll do it, SEA HORSE." Then over intercom, "Okay loads, load two more and get ready for a string of six. We've got a hot target and two Navy jocks raring to go."

Danson brought the C-130 back over the target again. On Preston's command, Cavendish launched all six flares at two-second intervals. The flares burst into brilliance as the light of the preceding string was beginning to fade. The two A-4 pilots were right where they were supposed to be. When Preston cleared them onto the target, the two fighters came in low over the convoy, with lead dropping his two napalm tanks on the last truck while his wingman went for the first one. As burning gasoline spread in all directions, the Vietnamese drivers pulled to a halt with nowhere to go.

"Load six morel Set for ten. Be ready to drop in one minute!" Danson maneuvered the Hercules around in a nearly vertical turn to come back over the stranded trucks for another drop. Again the G-forces almost forced Toby to his knees, but, in the excitement of the moment, the pilot wasn't concerned about his loadmasters. The pair of Navy fighter-bombers pulled off the target and climbed upward to position for another pass. "Bomb at your discretion." Preston instructed the fighter pilots to work over the trucks as they liked.

Once again the series was repeated; after the Hercules dispensed a string of flares, the two fighters came in again for another pass. This time they each dropped four high explosive bombs between the fires started by the napalm of their first pass. On the next pass they did likewise.

"Looks like some secondaries on that pass, SEA HORSE. From up here it looks like all six are burning."

"Roger that, Bat. We've still got eight more 500
pounders apiece. What do you want us to do with them?"

"There's a fork in the road about three klicks north, with a grove of trees. Let's put the rest on the fork. Maybe we'll get lucky."

"Sounds good. How about a marker?"

"One marker coming up." To the crew, "Okay guys, get a marker ready."

Kelly reached down and picked up a wooden box-like device about two feet long. He put it in the flare chute and held it until Preston signaled for it's launch.

"Prepare to drop flares and marker, on my command. Drop one…drop two…marker," Kelly pulled the arming lanyard and sent the thermite marker on its way, "drop three…drop four…drop five…drop six."

While the loadmasters worked feverishly to load six more flares, Danson pulled the airplane around into another tight turn. Increasing gravity almost flattened Carter, but he managed to keep his feet. It was worse for Kelly, who struggled with the 27-pound flares, each now weighing three times as much in the 3-G turn. Preston looked for the marker flare on the ground.

"SEA HORSE, you've got your marker. Put your bombs 100 meters north."

"Will do, BLIND BAT. We've got the fork in the road. Keep it lit up and we'll do our work."

As the C-130 passed eight thousand feet over the grove of trees, white flashes of light suddenly burst forth from beneath their branches. Six red cherries erupted from the white muzzle flashes, 37-MM cannon rounds on their way to claw their tormentor from the sky. The burst of flak was wide, missing the left wing by a hundred feet. Now everyone knew the area was hostile.

The two A-4's roared down toward the deadly grove. Instead of dropping half their loads, then coming back around for another pass, the two Navy pilots pickled their remaining bombs as the fork in the road passed beneath the pointed noses of their Skyhawks. Free of their bonds, the tiny A-4's leaped upwards under a burst of power. The sixteen bombs exploded all over the fork of the road, in the grove of trees and beyond. Along with the orange fireballs from the bombs, a larger, more powerful explosion erupted.

"How about that, SEA HORSE! It looks like you got lucky. Take a look at those secondaries. It looks like you got the gun, too. Nice work."

"Thanks a lot, BAT TWO. We've done about all the damage we can. It's time to go home."

"Roger that. You guys can work for us anytime."

After the pair of A-4's left the area, Preston asked MOONBEAM for more assets. From the size and color of the secondaries, there evidently was a fuel dump in the grove of trees. MOONBEAM responded to the request by diverting a NIMROD, a World War II vintage A-26, over to BAT TWO's control.

For the next hour the C-130 and A-26 combination worked over the target. First the twin-engine bomber pilot dropped his high explosives onto the grove, followed by napalm on the next pass. When his bombs were gone the Air Force pilot fired sixteen high-velocity rockets at the target. Then he strafed, the muzzle flashes of his eight.50-caliber machine guns lighting up the night sky with their brilliance. Finally, when nothing else remained, the pilot dropped his own flares onto the target. Then, his ammunition and stores all expended, NIMROD headed home for his base at Nakonphanom.

BAT TWO had dropped string after string of flares during the attacks by the two airplanes. Now only a few - not more than twenty-five - remained in the bin. They had been airborne for almost five hours.

"How's our fuel?"

"We're down to eight thousand pounds. That's barely enough to get home and leave an hour reserve."

"I guess it's about time to call it quits. It'll be daylight by the time we could get back, refuel, reload and get back on station. Okay guys, let's pull in the chute and head for home. Nice job. We've earned our combat pay tonight."

Chapter Two

Heat and unbearable humidity brought Toby Carter out of a fitful slumber. That was one of the worst things about BLIND BAT; crew members were always tired. At least the enlisted men were. The officers slept in air-conditioned dormitories over by the 0 Club, but not so the enlisted swine. Like the other bases in Thailand, Ubon had been built by Red Horse civil engineering teams as a base for fighter-bombers whose lot would be to attack targets in North Vietnam as part of Lyndon Johnson's "Rolling Thunder" campaign. The American facilities at Ubon had been erected to house the 8th TAC Fighter Wing, an F-4C unit. Phantoms were crewed by two men, both officers. No one envisioned that C-130's, with their multi-man crews, would fly out of Ubon on night missions.

Originally, the flare mission had been in Vietnam, operating out of Da Nang. Toby had heard tales of the mission's early days, when the C-130's ranged all over North Vietnam, including the Hanoi-Haiphong area "where the flak was so thick you could walk on it." Almost a year before, in July of 1965, a Viet Cong sapper and mortar attack had wiped out two of the flareships on the ramp at Da Nang. Partly because of the frequent attacks and partly because Da Nang had become so congested, the flare mission moved to Ubon.

After their mission, Toby and the rest of the crew had fallen right to sleep. It was still dark and the temperature cool. But once the sun rose over the horizon and the humidity began increasing, sleeping conditions in the wire-screened hooches were practically nil. It was then that Toby began to have weird, realistic dreams. Such as the one where he was in his bunk, asleep, and VC intruders slipped stealthily in and cut the throats of the occupants one by one. He always woke up with a start, fearful and bathed in sweat.

Even though they were in Thailand, and supposedly "safe" - ground personnel did not get combat pay for duty there - the threat of attack by Communist insurgents was very real. One night the previous week, while Preston's crew was flying, unknown insurgents attempted to probe the base right outside the BLIND BAT enlisted men's hooch. Only the last action of a dying Chinese Nung guard prevented a possible massacre. The man managed to fire his shotgun and give warning even as his throat was being cut. Some of the off-duty crew had been in the hooch; it was well after midnight and the downtown bars had closed. Their weapons were all locked up in the locker on the flight line; no weapons were allowed in quarters. Still, one of the guys, a Scottish immigrant and veteran loadmaster, had a Swedish-K submachine gun in his locker. He had traded a South African mercenary a bottle of Jack Daniels for it in the Congo in 1964. Scotty engaged the intruders with his illegal gun and broke-off the attack before it had really gotten underway.

The base should have been forewarned; after all, only the week before, Bob Preston's crew had been called out of Laos to intercept a pair of mysterious slow-moving aircraft less than ten miles from the base. They had seen nothing. The two intruders had been picked up on radar, leading to the launch of the alert fighters. But when the first F-4 got radar lock-on and fired his Sidewinders, the missiles refused to launch! The ground crew had failed to remove the safety pins that prevented the missiles from accidentally firing on the ground. According to the rumor mill, there was a brand new airman basic on the base, one whose sleeves still bore the marks where his technical sergeant's stripes had been.

Carter lay in the bed for quite some time, futilely trying to go back to sleep while knowing it was a hopeless endeavor. One by one the occupants of the ten bunks in the hooch began to stir, getting out of their beds and making their way to the outside shower house. Toby dreaded the trip; while it was hot as hell outside, the water in the showers was ice cold. No one had bothered to provide the enlisted men at Ubon with the luxury of hot water. Finally, after putting it off as long as he could, Toby swung his feet over the side of the low metal cot and groped for his rubber shower shoes, the "Japanese jump boots" every GI wore in the latrine. Wearing nothing else but boxer shorts (jockey style underwear caused jockey itch in Southeast Asia), he left the hooch and walked down the sidewalk to the shower house and latrine.

Damn, was that water cold! The first burst of water on his skin was made of tiny icicles that penetrated like daggers to his very soul. He always dreaded that initial plunge, but once the shock had worn off it wasn't so bad. Still, he would have given two weeks pay for hot water! It was the same with the base pool. Because the surrounding air was so warm, the waters in the pool felt like ice water. He had only braved the pool one time. But he had to take a bath; otherwise his skin would be crawling with bacteria. He consoled himself by remembering the GI's in the boondocks in Vietnam; they considered any kind of bath to be a luxury!

Kelly came into the shower while he was rinsing the soap he had rubbed all over his body.

"God, I hate this! When I go on R&R, I'm going to spend the first hour just standing under a hot shower."

"I know what you mean. I have to force myself to take the plunge."

"What do you want to do for chow? The mess hall is still open, or do you want to go to the club?"

"Mess hall sounds fine to me. I'm getting tired of fried egg sandwiches. The club menu leaves a bit to be desired."

"Willy and Sam are back at the hooch. They said they'd wait for us. What do you want to do until the sun goes down and it's time to go to the vill'?"

"What is there to do? Besides sit in the barracks and try to stay cool?"

"We could go to the BX. Maybe they've got something new in."

"If they have, the PCS guys will have scarfed it up. I guess that's okay, though. We've got a lot better BX at Naha, and of course there's the big one up at Buckner."

"There's always the club. But if we go and start drinking now, we'll be too looped to go to town."

They had finished their showers. After toweling off, Carter and Kelly walked back to the hooch. Toby pulled on Bermuda shorts and a polo shirt, the unofficial uniform for off-duty personnel in semi-tropical Thailand. Kelly was identically attired, as were Cavendish and McDonald. Don Salts had already dressed and gone to the NCO Club with some of the other engineers and older loadmasters.

The chow hall had thinned out considerably by the time they got there. Only three people were in the chow line ahead of them; airmen who, like them, worked nights and had just gotten out of bed. After paying the mess checker - flight crews were on separate rations - each man picked up a metal serving tray and utensils then entered the serving line. The food was not that bad - roast pork, mashed potatoes, green beans, tossed salad. Drink was a different story. There was plenty of coffee, but who wants to drink coffee when it's ninety-five degrees and ninety per cent humidity? The milk was recombined, with a salty taste that made it almost unpalatable. That left the iced tea and Kool-aid the Thai serving girls carried around in glass pitchers.

"What is that green stuff?" Willy Cavendish wanted to know. "It looks like panther piss; tastes like it too."

"That's another thing I'm going to do on R&R. I'm going to drink a gallon and a half of milk," said Kelly.

'Shoot, the milk in Bangkok is recombined, too," Carter responded.

"Yeah, but it's 'fresh' recombined. This stuff comes out of a can."

"It all comes from Okie. That's one of the worst parts of being in PACAF. No real milk anywhere west of Hawaii."

'I wonder why there isn't a dairy industry in the Far East?'

"Who knows? I guess it's because nobody can afford a cow. Maybe water buffalo don't give milk.'

"It probably has something to do with the heat. Dairy cattle don't like hot weather. Think about it. All of the dairy-producing states in the U.S. are in the north. Wisconsin, Minnesota, Ohio…"

"What kind of cows do they raise in Tennessee, where you come from?"

"We raise beef cattle - black Angus. There's some dairy around but beef cattle do better."

"Personally, I'm a city boy. There ain't no cows in Phillie. I know one thing. I'd love to have a good old American steak."

"That's one thing about Bangkok. Even though the meat is probably water buffalo, it's not that bad. My favorite in the Federal is the barbecued steak."

"Or the filet. That's okay. It's still somewhat tough, though."

"Everything's different over here. Even the women."

"Yeah, that little hump these Thai broads have above their pelvis is weird. When you really get going good, you've gotta watch it or you're liable to get a bruise."

'That's one thing about the neissans on the Rock. They may all be four foot, one, but at least they don't have that hump."

"Hump or not, these Thais have it all kinds of ways over the Okinawans."

"What about Koreans? I was in Osan back in March. Some of those Korean girls are really good looking."

'I've heard the Korean stuff is pretty good."

"My goal is to get some of all of it before I go back to the States. The way I look at it, this is a lifetime opportunity. There's no way I'll ever get back to the Orient once my hitch is up. Might as well take advantage of it."

"You sure as hell don't want to take something back you had just as soon leave."

"That's why the BX sells rubbers. I always take a good piss afterwards. That'll flush out the germs."

"The medics say that works. Take a piss and wash off good with soap and water.

"Hey, Tobe," Willy McDonald looked at Carter, "Are you still carrying that carbide lamp in your pack?"

"I sure am. If we get blasted, I want to be ready."

"Yeah, but what the hell are you planning to do with the thing?"

"You really want to know?"

"Yeah, Tobe. We really want to know," Sam McDonald picked up the conversation.

"If I get forced down, I'm going to find myself a cave and I'm going to hide in it until a helicopter comes."

"You'll be by yourself. Caves give me the spooks." Kelly voiced his disapproval of Carter's plan.

"I don't know. They're interesting enough. My folks took me to Luray Caverns once when we were on vacation in Virginia. It was kind of neat, really. There's some kind of stalactite or something there that they play tunes on," McDonald came to Carter's aid.

"Have you guys ever looked at one of our escape maps? Did you notice where it says 'karst?"

"Karst? What's that?"

"It's a geological term. Means an area where there are a lot of caves. Laos is honeycombed with them, at least according to our maps. I didn't know that when I brought my carbide lamp with me, though. I was thinking more of the caves on Okinawa."

"Those are all off-limits, aren't they? Something about unexploded ammunition left over from the war?"

"Yeah, but I didn't find that out until after I got here. I'd probably have brought the lamp along anyway, just for good luck."

The four young loadmasters prolonged their lunch, talking, eating and drinking tea and Kool-aid. Finally, when the Thai serving girls began to look at them anxiously, they decided it was time to leave. For lack of anything better to do, they went back to their hooch. There they found the other occupants of the hooch, members of another crew from a different squadron.

"Hey, guys. Did you all hear about the 'Goon last night?" Tom Blankenship addressed no one in particular as they came through the door. Blankenship and the other four members of his crew had gone to the Airmen's Club for lunch.

"No, what happened?", Cavendish took the bait.

"Charley got 'em. Shot the poor bastards right out of the sky." "Where was it?"

"Down by Tche Pone. They went in like a rock. Captain Butterworth was working them on the radio. Hell, we'd briefed with them!"

"Was that the guys we met at the club the other night?" Kelly interrupted.

"That's the ones. Real nice guys. Remember, they were telling us what all their mini-guns were going to do to Charley."

"Did anybody get out?"

"Not a soul. At least not that we know of. I guess they've got an SAR out there, looking for survivors."

"That's a damn shame. What got them?"

"Twenty mike-mike. That's the problem with the 'Goons. They have to fly too low." Blankenship was referring to an AC-47 gunship. "At least we fly high enough that the 20-millimeter and .50-caliber can't reach us."

"Have you ever wondered what the old Herkybird would be like with guns?"

"One of those gunship guys said the rumor was that they're going to put guns on Herks. The problem is that there aren't enough of 'em to go around."

"Lockheed's still building them, along with the '141."

"By the way, has anybody ever heard who that crew was that 'Star and Stripes' listed as being shot-down over the North last week?"

"Nope. Not a thing. I can't figure that one out. As far as anyone knows, we're the only C-130's operating out of country, at least on a regular basis."

"I can't figure what they were doing up north. I guess the Marines use their refuelers up north, but they are the only ones who go across the fence besides us."

"The paper said this one was Air Force."

"Maybe it was some kind of sneaky-Pete."

"You know how this war is; there's so many classified things going on, nobody can keep up with them."

"Hell, nobody knows about us!"

"Good point. Shoot, we don't know about us!"

For the rest of the afternoon the two crews shot the bull, read and rested. Both crews were off duty that night. It was not a question of whether they would go to town, but rather "What time?" Even that wasn't much of a question, either. They would go as soon as it got dark. And stay until the place closed. By that time they would all be drunk enough they might be able to sleep a while longer the next morning. That is, if they didn't spend the night in town with a Tee-loc-for-the-night.

Early that evening, just after chow, Carter, Kelly, Cavendish and McDonald left their hooch, then stopped by the Airmen's Club where they bought a 40-ounce bottle of Canadian Club. The four would share the bottle, drinking every ounce before they decided it was time to head back to the base, or to a bungalow with one of the Thai flowers who populated the nightclub where they planned to spend the evening. From the club they went to the *main* gate; there they boarded three samolars - bicycle propelled rickshaws - and headed for town.

The large barn-like building was crowded. It was filled with people, young men in their late teens and early twenties, all dressed alike in Thai silk shirts and slacks, either jeans or locally made sharkskin material. All of the men wore their hair cut short, well above the ears in military style, but also the style of the times. Hair length had yet to achieve importance as the youth culture of the late sixties was still developing. Most of the men were white, with deep tans from working on the flight line in the tropical sun. Some were black; others were of American indian descent, still others were Oriental or Latin.

15

Every woman in the place was definitely Oriental, with almond eyes, dark skin, jet-black hair and - mostly but not all - short in stature compared to the men with whom they danced and talked. The women wore Thai silk also, blouses worn with form-fitted slacks or the Chinese "Suzy Wong" tight-fitting dresses that accentuated the breasts and revealed a lot of leg. Every woman in the night club, whether sixteen or thirty-six, was a prostitute. Their official title was "taxi dancer." They were employed by the club to entertain the young American and Australian - there was a Royal Australian Air Force F-86 squadron at Ubon - customers, dancing with them, socializing or soliciting drinks from young men who were possessed of more dollars than sense (although they had converted most of their money into Baht and left the rest on base.) The real "entertainment" took place in the small rooms in the hooches in back of the building, or in bungalows around town where the more affluent of the girls lived.

Some of the girls were with their "tee-loc", or boyfriend, an airman who had sat up housekeeping with one of the women in an off-base bungalow. That way, at least in theory, the young men could have regular access to sex without threat of the many forms of virile venereal diseases which were so prevalent in Southeast Asia. Sometimes a young man would fall in love with his "tee-loc" and decide to take her home to Mamma. Others were already married to girls back home, who supposedly chastely waited for their husbands to return from the war while remaining true to them during the year they were away.

It was getting late, on toward midnight, and most of the men and some of the women were well on their way toward intoxication, oblivious to the fact that just a few hundred miles to the east a war was raging. Young men of their age were fighting and dying in rice paddies on the other side of the Annamite range which separated coastal Vietnam from the rest of indo-China. The same Mekong which flowed lazily only twenty miles away on the border between Thailand and Laos became treacherous as it flowed out of Cambodia and into Vietnam. Most of the men in the room had never even heard of Vietnam, or Thailand for that matter, until after they had graduated from high school and were in uniform.

Now the young men in the Thai nightclub considered themselves fortunate. Instead of waiting to be drafted and given a gun, they had enlisted in the Air Force. Instead of being in Vietnam, toting a rifle through the paddies, they were in torrid Thailand, working as mechanics on the McDonnell-Douglas F-4C's of the 8th TAC Fighter Wing, clerking in an orderly room, filling requisitions in the supply hut, maintaining the vehicles in the motor pool, manning fire trucks or patrolling the base. They were at Ubon Ratchathani, a town in east-central Thailand. While Thailand was, technically at least, not at war, the young men were there because of what was happening on the other side of the mountains - and on this side as well.

The nightclub and the whorehouse a few blocks away were hangouts for the enlisted men. Most of the officers, aircrew and ground pounders alike, did their socializing on the base at the officers' club. That was where they played their fighter-pilot games, at least the fighter pilots did while everybody else watched; eating drink glasses, playing "dead bird", a game where everyone falls to the floor when someone hollers out the words and anyone left standing must buy drinks for the house, or practicing "carrier landings" on a beer-soaked table or part of the bar. The officers had their own whores - Thai girls who were employed on the base as waitresses, house girls, clerks, etc. For a fee, the Thai women served as surrogate wives for men who often had families back in "the world," thirteen thousand miles away.

Even though they were miles away from the war, for Carter and the other three loadmasters on his crew it was still ever-present in the back of their minds, even when the conversation was focused on their upcoming R&R. Tonight they could relax and have a big time, maybe get laid if they wanted, but tomorrow night they would be back over the Trail, or over in one of the Route Packages north of the DMZ. Tonight, while they were enjoying the lazy atmosphere of the Southeast Asian dance hall, their own buddies, young men just like themselves, were out on missions dodging flak and worrying about the possibility of a hung flare just as they would be tomorrow night. But now it was time to party and plan for the future.

"I tell you, Tobe. You ought to come to Bang-pussy with us." Mike Kelly, now more than slightly inebriated, was continuing his urging from the night before.

"Yeah, Toby. Come on with us. We can all get rooms in a hotel and have a ball. You know, there are a lot of round-eyes in Bangkok." Willy Cavendish reinforced Kelly's urging.

"Man, I'd like to get some round-eye. This Thai stuff is okay, but you can't beat that good old American kind - or maybe Aussie." That was McDonald's observation. "Bangkok would be a good place to find some round-eye, a stewardess maybe, or one of the clerks from the Embassy."

"You know, maybe I ought to go down there with you guys. After all, as you said, Naha will still be there five weeks later when we finish our tour." Toby didn't add "if we finish our tour." He only thought the words.

"Hey listen, guys. If we're all going to Bangkok, maybe we ought to set a temporary PCD, starting tonight. If somebody did get lucky, we wouldn't want to give a round-eye a dose of clap."

"I wouldn't want to have a dose of clap if we went down out over the Trail."

17

"If we went down over the Trail, it probably wouldn't make a shit whether you had the clap or not."

"Speaking of shit, that's how that broad with the band sounds."

"All these Thai bands are terrible. They sound like a cross between the Beatles and temple dancers."

"It really is weird. They play electric guitars but it sounds more like cymbals - or gongs."

"Filipino bands are pretty good. There was one at the airman's club at Naha just before we came down here."

"The airman's club? The only reason I go to that place is to cash a check or eat chow. You mean you actually listened to the band?"

"I'd just come back from a trip. I didn't feel like going to Naumenouie. It was getting too close to curfew."

"I guess you can be excused this time, Sam. But don't let it happen again. You know damn well the New York Bar stays open long past curfew - and there's always some of the guys there."

"I guess I just fucked up."

"Do you ever miss the place?'

"Where?"

"Naumenaouie. You've got to admit, it's a lot better than Koza City."

"Koza. Don't talk to me about that place. There's more rip-off joints in that town than in Tijuana."

It was well after midnight when the four airmen left the nightclub. All were smashed out of their minds, each having consumed ten ounces of the forty pounder they had brought with them. On the way back to town they raced their samolars, with Willy Cavendish chanting-on his driver with the words "Bio, lao, muck, muck. Fuck, fuck. Pong, pong, Suzy Wong; Veee Deeeel" When they got back to the hooch, all four fell in bed and dropped off in an alchohol-induced slumber.

Chapter Three

Carter woke up the next morning to the same heat and humidity of the morning before and of the day before that, the day before that and of every Thai day since the beginning of time. His body was bathed in a sticky pool of perspiration; the sheets felt clammy and smelled like they'd been in a basement for a year. At least this time he had slept a little longer than the day before, thanks to the voluminous amount of alcohol they had consumed the night before and the earlier hour he had gone to bed. The same cold water in the shower awaited him when he forced himself to struggle out of bed and down the walkway. Instead of the chow hall, he and the other members of Preston's crew chose the airman's club for lunch - thought it was breakfast for them. There they could get eggs even at mid-morning; Carter chose a ham and egg sandwich.

Once they had eaten, the four young men returned to their hooch to rest and relax until it was time to go to the flight line. The rest of the afternoon was somewhat melancholy, no doubt because they knew were they were going that night. No one said it, but they were all thinking that it was just possible this could be their last afternoon on earth. While no one brought up the subject of the downed SPOOKY, they all knew the doomed gunship crew's fate could just as well be their own.

Late in the day they changed out of the civilian clothes they had been wearing - cut-off jeans, shorts and polo shirts - and into fatigues. No one wore a flight suit; the one-piece cotton poplin coveralls were uncomfortable in the heat. Besides, the survival people recommended flying in cotton fatigues or the special lightweight jungle fatigues developed for the grunts; either would hold up much better in the jungle than the thin cotton summer-weight flying coveralls. Even though it was 90 degrees on the ground, it was downright cold at ten thousand feet, so they all carried their flight jackets to wear against the chill of the open cargo compartment. When they had changed, they made their way once again to the chow hall, then back to the hooch. The sun was sinking low on the horizon when the blue Dodge six-pack pulled up in front of the hooch; they all piled in for the trip to the flight line.

Their first stop was at the collection of Quonset huts that housed the headquarters of the 8th TAC Fighter Wing. The driver waited outside while the five enlisted men filed inside to meet the three officers and go into the briefing room. He would take them on to the flight line when they were dismissed. The briefing was informal, with the whole crew standing around a map of Laos and North Vietnam. The briefing officer, an F-4 pilot from the 8th Tactical Fighter Wing, pointed out the locations of known flak positions along their route of flight. It was good to know there were no known surface-to-air missile sites that far south, although intelligence photos indicated there were some under construction. Tonight they would be LAMPLIGHTER ONE, operating between the Mu Gia Pass on the border between Laos and North Vietnam and the coastal city of Vinh. They were to be on the lookout for river and coastal waters boat traffic, as well as truck convoys on the roads leading into the mountains toward Mu Gia.

After briefing they got their weapons and survival vests out of the supply locker, then climbed back into the truck for the short trip to the flight line. The Thai driver drove past rows of F-4's, where mechanics worked to recover those that had flown day missions and to prepare fighters for the evening's missions. Armorers, avionics specialists, crew chiefs - all worked together to keep the combat birds in the air. Across the tarmac from the F-4 ramp, parked in revetments off of a taxiway, were the C-130's of Blind Bat.

"Damn green garbage cans." Willy Cavendish voiced a grudging admiration that would become legend in the airlift world as they drove up to 55-0475, the airplane they would be flying that night. Toby Carter never ceased to be impressed by the sight of the airplanes as they sat motionless on the ramp. The Hercules is a pretty big airplane when compared to the smaller F-4, or even to other, smaller transports such as the C-47. To those not familiar with the type, a grounded C-130 looks ungainly, almost ugly, sitting low on the ground, the huge wings sticking out from a barrel-shaped fuselage, with two tiny nacelles with huge propellers at the end on each wing. The tail sticks up at least two stories above the fuselage, like a sail on a Clippership. Painted two shades of green and brown with a black belly, the huge assault transports were camouflaged to blend in with the terrain, the general green appearance leading to Willy's observation. The black belly was a concession to their night mission; airlift C-130's normally sported light gray undersides.

A yellow C-26 power generation cart sat by the nose, it's generator putting out twenty-eight volts of direct current, which coursed through hundreds of miles of wiring, bringing life to the various electrical components inside the airplane. That DC electrical system was a mechanic's nightmare; on later models it had been changed to a three-phase, AC system. But the Naha, Okinawa-based 6315th Operations Group flew the A-model, the earliest version of the airplane that would eventually be recognized as the most versatile to ever take to the skies.

Before they could depart on their mission the airplane had to be preflighted, at least partially. Earlier in the day the ground crew had checked beneath every panel, tested every system, scrutinized every nook and cranny. Now Salts would check-out crucial systems such as the flight controls and inspect the dry bays for signs of leaks, while the loadmasters would insure that everything in the rear was ready for flight and especially that the load could be easily jettisoned. If they were hit, that would be their first action - get rid of those flares! Three hundred magnesium-filled tubes would make one heck of a fire, burning through every inch of aluminum, titanium, beryllium and the various alloys that made up the components of the airplane - not to mention the five thousand gallons of JP-4 in the fuel tanks!

The officers remained inside for additional briefings on weather, up-to-date target information, intelligence and other factors the enlisted men were not required to know. After they were through with their mission preparations, Preston, Danson and Benjamin made their own way out to their steed for the night. Salts had already completed the preflight; all the officers had to do was set-up their crew stations and check the 781 for write-ups that might be important to the flight. They had already briefed for the mission inside; the crew knew where they were going and what the bailout plans were. Preston went through a perfunctory crew briefing - "You know your jobs, let's go do it!" - then they climbed into the airplane. Everyone, that is, but Sam McDonald. It was his turn to play loadmaster; he took his place in front of the airplane on the long scanner's cord.

Starting engines on a Hercules is fairly simple. Instead of using an electric starter, the Allison T-56 engines are turned over by pneumatically powered ones, driven by bleed-air from the gas turbine compressor auxiliary power unit to start the first engine, then engine bleed-air after that. Until the engine-driven generators are on the line, electrical power for the other systems comes either from an external power cart or from the air turbine motor powered by the GTC. The GTC is a noisy little machine, as much so as the engines themselves - after all, it was a small turbine engine. As soon as the GTC came on the line, with hydraulic power now available through utility system power, Carter went back to the ramp control panel and closed and locked the ramp and doors. Had they been nosed into the revetment, he would have left them open for taxi. At Ubon the airplanes were always backed into place, either using engine power or pushed back with a tug.

Soon they heard the rising whine of number three engine as it came on speed, a crescendo of noise indicating that the turbine and propeller were turning at one hundred percent. After number three was on line, Preston started number four, then after a pause while McDonald closed the GTC doors and secured them with the screwdriver all loadmasters carried in their pocket, one and two were started. Now the airplane was vibrating from the power of four turboprop engines. Sam came into the cargo compartment and closed and locked the crew entrance door, sealing the eight men into an aluminum world that would be their home for the next five to eight hours - or perhaps for the rest of their lives.

21

"Ubon tower, LAMPLIGHTER ONE ready to taxi," Steve Danson's voice crackled over the UHF frequency. They were operating over the North tonight, hence the LAMPLIGHTER call sign; BLIND BAT missions were over Laos.

"Roger, LAMP ONE; taxi runway two three; winds calm, altimeter two niner, niner seven."

Preston released the brakes; one hundred and twenty-five thousand, two hundred pounds of airplane began waddling across the tarmac in the twilight. Using the nose-wheel steering tiller on his left, the pilot guided the airplane onto the taxi-way. As they taxied, the crew continued running the checklist, completing the many items required before the transport could begin its take-off roll. Generators had to be checked, along with hydraulic quantities and pressures, electrical outputs and loads, fuel pressures, controls for freedom of movement; all had to be checked, the flaps had to be positioned. By the time they reached the end of the runway the crew had completed over a hundred separate actions. Then, as a final action before take-off, Preston ran all four engines to takeoff power and cycled the props. He nodded at Danson.

"LAMP ONE, ready for takeoff."

"LAMP ONE; cleared to go. Right turnout after takeoff approved," came the words of the tower operator.

Preston taxied onto the runway and locked the brakes. He then advanced all four power levers, while Danson backed him up and Salts kept close watch on the engine gauges.

"Pre-takeoff check complete, sir," the engineer signaled that all engine readings were normal.

Preston released the brakes and the Hercules shot out of the chute like a race horse at Churchill Downs, the sudden acceleration forcing the flight crew back against their seats. It wasn't quite as impressive as a fighter, but it was impressive enough. After just over a thousand feet of take-off roll, the airspeed indicator reached rotate speed; Preston eased back on the yoke, the nose wheel came up and the main wheels left the ground. The airplane lifted off against the backdrop of a reddening sky. They were airborne - on their way to the combat zone.

It was over two hundred miles from Ubon to their target area; the flight would be a good forty-five minutes. They would have plenty of time for a short nap, or just to sit back and think. The four loadmasters lay or sat on fold-down seats in the cargo compartment, each lost in his own thoughts.

Toby Carter was feeling slight pangs of homesickness, really more of a case of wondering if he would ever see the low, rolling Tennessee hills again. So far his crew had been at Ubon for a month and a half; they were at the midpoint of their tour and slated to go on R&R in three days. Only one more mission after tonight then they would have a break. They had been shot at numerous times but had yet to be hit. That made their chances of survival very good, much better than those of the F-105 pilots who flew against Hanoi. No C-130's had been lost on the flareship mission even though several had come back to Ubon - or Da Nang before the mission moved - with holes in the wings, tail or fuselage. But there was always that chance, and the nagging thoughts it led to. The enemy gunners could get better; they could bring more guns into Route Package One and Two and Laos; they could start using SAMS. Or a gun crew could just plain get lucky. Or, the navigator could screw-up and let them get too close to one of the newer radar-aimed guns that were just starting to make their appearance in the more southerly Route Packages as more and more guns came into North Vietnam from the Communist bloc nations of Eastern Europe.

He thought about some of the kids he had gone to school with. This was 1966; Toby had been out of high school for only three years. Only one other person out of his graduating class had gone to Southeast Asia. Tony McPherson had been in the first Marine contingent to go to Vietnam from Okinawa the year before. Tony was air-evaced home after falling into a tiger trap. Fortunately, the trap was old. The bamboo poles had broken under his weight; rather than killing him, they had only maimed. Toby wondered if anyone ever thought about him, or even if anyone knew - or cared - that he was in Southeast Asia.

That was another of the frustrating aspects of this mission - no one knew they were there. While the daily strikes against Hanoi were being publicized to some extent, the night interdiction missions were not, especially not those over Laos. Laos was a "secret war," fought far from the prying eyes of the press and media. They weren't even supposed to be there - the Geneva Accords that ended the Laotian Civil War four years before stipulated that "all foreign troops" would leave the country. No reporters ever came to Ubon to fly missions with them. "Stars and Stripes" carried no articles about the intrepid C-130 crews who went out each night looking for trucks on the Ho Chi Minh Trail. As far as the press knew, or the GI's in the South for that matter, C-130's were nothing but "trash-haulers," ferrying cargo and passengers around the combat zone.

The change in pressure in his ears made Toby and the rest of the crew aware that it was time to go to work. Don Salts was de-pressurizing the airplane, bringing the cabin altitude up to the ten thousand feet above sea level that they would be operating at. The outflow valves in the cargo door had opened, allowing the pressurized air in the cabin to escape. At that altitude, they would be out of reach of all but the heavier caliber guns.

"Okay, loads. Let's get the chute out. It's time to go to work," Preston spoke into his interphone to alert his crew that they were nearing their assigned area. Sam McDonald motioned for them to open the door and put the chute out into the slipstream. The airplane was coming up over the Mu Gia Pass, the cut in the mountains through which all road traffic coming out of North Vietnam and into Laos must pass.

"Load four, set 'em for ten seconds." They hurriedly complied with the pilot's directive.

"Drop four." Kelly was on the door; he pushed the four flares out of their chute. They fell a thousand feet then ignited, exploding into a brilliant light that turned the darkness into a semblance of day - or at least like a brightly lit football stadium. Immediately a burst of red tracers arced up at them from somewhere below. A 37-MM flak position had spotted the airplane. Fortunately the gunners' aim was off; the string of tracers missed.

"Welcome to North Vietnam. It looks like it's going to be a lively night," Salts commented on their first brush with the enemy.

Preston continued on the heading they were flying, northeasterly toward Vinh. They would road reccee between the coastal town and Mu Gia, hoping to spot a lucrative target but knowing their chances were identical to those of finding the proverbial needle in a haystack. The Asian truck drivers had a bevy of tricks up their sleeves, ranging from simply driving with their lights out or with shielded headlights, to elaborate dummy truck parks rigged to attract American fighters who would drop their bombs on nothing.

"What time's our first tee, oh, tee?" Preston asked the navigator to confirm the time for their rendezvous with the first flight of fighters they were fragged to support.

"Oh, nine, fifteen Zulu. That's fifteen minutes from right now, at coordinates eighteen degrees fifty minutes north, one, oh, five degrees, thirty-two minutes east. That's just south of Vinh. A flight of A-4's. They should be carrying seven hundred and fifty pounders according to the frag."

"How long will it take us to get there?"

"Eight minutes, thirty-one seconds. Fly heading zero, eight five."

They arrived over the target, a ford across a small stream south of Vinh, and began flaring.

"Nothing, not a damn thing." Danson voiced the whole crew's frustration when the light of their flares revealed the ford to be deserted.

"Our orders call for us to work it over anyway. How far out are the fighters?"

"They should be less than twenty miles away. MOONBEAM should be turning them over to you any second now." No sooner had Benjamin said the words than the voice of the Navy lead came over the radio.

For the next fifteen minutes Preston's crew flared while the flight of A-4's each dropped their entire load of 750-pound bombs in the general area of the ford. A lot of water was tossed about and several trees were knocked down but little else occurred - no secondaries, no sign of any trucks, nothing.

After the A-4's departed, their next mission was an F-4 flight out of Ubon. They were fragged to hit a suspected coastal loading zone, where sampans and other small boats departed with guns, ammunition and other supplies on the long journey south. When the first string of flares popped over the marshland, swamp grass and water was all they saw. But this time the fighters did a little better - secondary explosions followed the primaries of the 1,000-pounders dropped by the lead fighter. The second airplane dropped on top of the fires set by his leader - more secondaries.

For the next three hours the night was eventful enough as flight after flight of attack aircraft arrived to attack fragged targets under the light of LAMPLIGHTER's flares. Some strikes were seemingly productive, as secondary explosions indicated that something had indeed been below. But most of the strikes were probably wasted, with no secondaries to indicate the presence of stored ammunition or fuel. Two thirds of the fighters missed their aiming points entirely, typical of their profession in 1966 when they claimed a whole lot more destruction from their efforts then they actually got.

In the wee hours of the morning there was a lull in activities. No fighters were scheduled into their area for almost an hour. After that it would be nearing the time to go home as their fuel supply would be getting low.

"Let's do a little road reccee. Loads, put six in the chute and set 'em for five seconds." The shorter detonation time would mean the flares would ignite higher, Illuminating more of the countryside below them.

"Holy cow, Batman. Look at that!"

"You're right, Robin. We better notify the Bat Cave."

Preston called MOONBEAM, "MOONBEAM, LAMP ONE has a convoy of twenty-five, coordinates eighteen degrees, thirty-two minutes north; one, oh, five degrees, thirty-two minutes west. What can you send our way?"

The voice of the airborne command post controller sounded distant from his orbit point over Laos, "Stand by, one."

"Roger that, MOONBEAM. Standing by."

"That doesn't sound good."

"This is the best convoy we've seen yet, and they probably haven't got anybody to hit it."

"Yeah, by the time they get fighters here, they'll be in a village somewhere and off limits." Danson and Preston were doing all the talking.

"LAMP ONE, MOONBEAM. It's going to be a least half an hour before we can get anybody in your area," the words of the airborne controller crackled in their headsets.

Preston spoke over the intercom, "Half an hour! The bastards will be long gone by then." Then in the radio, "Roger, MOONBEAM. Understand three zero minutes. We'll keep them in sight."

Danson looked across the pedestal at his boss. "What do you think?"

"I think we've probably missed a chance to take out two dozen trucks. By the time those fighters get here this road will be as clean as a hound's tooth."

"What can we do?"

"Nothing, really. Not as long as we do what we're supposed to do. Of course we can always try some improvisation."

"You mean, go after them ourselves."

"It's been done before."

"Whatever you want to do."

"Okay, pilot to crew. We're going after these bastards. Loads, put twelve in the chute and set the fuses for six seconds. Nav', work us up a CARP at three hundred feet and keep watch on the terrain with the radar. Engineer, keep close watch on the gauges."

In the back Carter climbed onto the door where Mike Kelly already sat. They knew what their crazy pilot was about to do, and whether they liked it or not, adrenaline was pumping into their veins, bringing the "combat rush" that no synthetic chemical could ever produce. Cavendish and McDonald hurriedly loaded eight additional flares into the aluminum chute, putting three flares under each foot of the two men on the door. There was no time for anyone to vocalize their thoughts or voice any misgivings.

Preston turned the C-130 away from the area where the string of flares still glowed and began a rapidly descending half circle. All four power levers were pulled back into flight idle; the turboprop engines were producing minimum thrust. Benjamin peered intently into his radar scope, searching for high terrain that might be more hazardous than even the ground fire they knew was sure to come. Carter and Kelly sat on the door, straining to hold the flares in place, while Cavendish and McDonald clung tenaciously to the sides of the airplane.

The C-130 descended eight thousand feet in less than three minutes while Preston, who had taken the controls from Danson, turned a hundred and eighty degrees to line up with the section of road on which the convoy was slowly moving along. They were in the foothills of the Annamite Range, and the road was beginning to meander as it rose toward the higher elevations of the Mu Gia Pass. He kept the airspeed up; there was no reason to slow to airdrop speeds. At two hundred and thirty knots indicated, the

26

Hercules would present only a fleeting target to any gunners who might get their range. The airplane was blacked out, with all external lights extinguished, including the red rotating beacon on top of the tail. Not a single word was spoken in the cockpit other than those required to complete their intended action.

Using the radar altimeter, Preston leveled the airplane at three hundred feet above the ground and took up a heading to follow the indications of the Doppler computer. Benjamin had hacked the Doppler while over the convoy, before they began the descending turn. The flares were still hanging in the sky, giving further indication of where their target lay, though they were starting to lose their intensity. Soon their glow would die off, they would appear for an instant as tiny sparks, then become fade away as they drifted toward the earth in a once again darkened world. Benjamin had re-tuned the radar to minimum range, hoping to pick up the metal cabs of the trucks in the more intense lower scale.

"I've got 'em! One, two, three, all lined up like ducks in a row!" Excitement intensified the navigator's voice. "Turn right five degrees. That'll take you right over 'em!"

"Stand-by to drop flares, one at a time on my signal."

Surprisingly, no ground fire had yet reached its clawing fingers in their direction. The North Vietnamese hardly expected a C-130 to drop out of the sky and come in on a convoy in a daring low-level attack, especially not so close to the mountains. Alerted by the flares, the guns protecting the road were trained upwards, the gunners scanning the skies for the jet fighters they knew were sure to come. At that altitude the four-engine transport was overhead and gone before the soldiers who guarded the roads could bring their AK-47s to bear.

The first indication the Communist troops had that things were amiss was the banshee roar of a huge flying something passing overhead, followed by the sudden eruption of twelve magnesium incendiary bombs along the length of the convoy. Their bursting light turned night into day. Preston and Benjamin's timing couldn't have been more perfect; the first flare ignited almost on the hood of the lead truck, with the remaining eleven strewn along the length of those remaining. Miraculously, the trucks were spread along the last straight stretch of road on this particular section of the Trail complex. A few more yards and they would have entered the first of a series of switch-backs that would take them up the side of the rapidly rising terrain of the foothills. The lead driver panicked as the burst of brilliance erupted in front of him. He wrecked the truck, blocking the roadway. The trail was too narrow behind him for following trucks to turn around. Preston pulled the Herk into a chandelle to gain altitude and take a look at the results of their work.

"Looks like we stopped 'em. Let's give them another shot. Load twelve more, same setting."

The next pass was from the opposite direction. Alerted by the previous pass, the enemy gunners were waiting. A hail of tracers filled the sky over the fires started along the convoy line, but the Hercules was flying too low and too slow for gunners whose training had been oriented toward hitting fast-moving jets. The cherry-red and green tracers were passing well in front of the black bulbous nose of the transport. With the convoy halted, Preston had accomplished his aim. The twelve additional flares only added more fuel to the fires that were already burning, but they did set the Tail-end Charlie on fire. Now the whole convoy was blocked and could go nowhere. Preston decided he would tempt fate no more; after the second pass he continued at low altitude for a few miles, then pulled the airplane up into a steep climbing turn away from the mountains. Soon they were back at their normal altitude.

A flight of fighters came into the area about ten minutes later. With the convoy stopped and going nowhere, the twenty-five trucks were easy pickings for the A-4's and A-6's from the Seventh Fleet carriers out on Yankee Station. When Salts notified Preston that they had reached bingo fuel and it was time to go home, LAMPLIGHTER ONE turned toward Ubon, leaving the glowing remains of twenty-five trucks behind.

Chapter Four

After the North Vietnam mission Preston's crew flew one more BLIND BAT over Laos, then it was time for R&R. Yielding to the pressure of his buddies, Toby Carter decided to take his leave in Bangkok after all. The four loadmasters hitched a ride to the city on the morning ration run on its return flight to Don Muang.

When they arrived at Don Muang, there was some discussion as to whether they should stay together or split up. Since their stated purpose in coming to Bangkok was to "get some round-eye," they all decided it would be best to go their separate ways, then meet back at Don Muang for the ride back up-country. They believed it would be easier for them to score while flying solo rather than hanging together in a gaggle. Toby elected to stay at one of the smaller hotels not far from the Federal, the hotel contracted by 315th Air Division for its C-130 crews. He knew the area, having spent two weeks there back in '65 and after staying there a couple of other times on the "stage" mission the 6315th Ops Group operated out of Don Muang.

They got into Bangkok fairly early in the day, having managed to get out of Ubon shortly after returning from their night over the Trail. Toby took advantage of the hot water and air conditioning; he spent half an hour in the shower then climbed into bed for the first decent rest he had had since leaving Naha six weeks before. It was late afternoon when he awoke. He hadn't eaten anything since his flight lunch somewhere over Laos the night before. He pulled on his faithful white denim Bermudas and a Thai silk shirt then went outside and down the hall to the elevator.

As he stood by the elevator shaft, a Caucasian girl came out of the room next to his and walked down the hall toward him. He tried not to stare, in spite of the fact that she was the first round-eye he had seen in weeks. She was what he would call "cute" rather than "pretty," a dishwater blonde with a pertness that was reflected in the sun-dress and sandals she wore. He guessed she was about his age, maybe a year or so older. Like most American, European and Australian women in Southeast Asia, she wore no stockings. Her legs were well-tanned, as was the rest of her body, at least what he could see. The girl smiled at him as she came up.

He stood aside and waited for her to enter the elevator.

"Lobby?" Her accent was definitely American. Southern? Perhaps, although probably more mid-western. He nodded. They rode the three floors to the lobby in silence. The woman got off and turned right, toward the dining room. Toby followed a short distance behind her. They stood together in the foyer, waiting for someone to show them to their tables. Partly because of his shyness and partly because of a deference to her

29

femininity, Toby stood slightly behind her. It was after four o'clock; the dining room was empty.

"Good afternoon," the head waiter said in accented English, "table for two?"

The girl looked back at him quizzically, "Why not?" she said. "We both seem to be alone."

"Sure, if you'd like."

"We might as well share a table. It looks like we're the only people in the place. At least we'll have someone to talk too."

The waiter pulled out a chair for the girl; he put them at a table by the window.

She held out her hand, "Sharon Craft."

He looked into her eyes; they were green. "Toby Carter, or Sam, if you prefer. That's what I've been called ever since I went into the service."

"Toby, now that's a different name! It sounds English. I like it."

'It's family, Irish actually, short for Tobin. That was my great-grandfather's name. He was Irish."

"Yes, I guess Toby would be an Irish name. Well, Toby. What would you recommend for a girl's first meal in Bangkok?"

"Well, this is my first meal in this hotel, although I've stayed at the Federal. It's not far from here. There I always liked the filet, or the barbecued steak. It's probably water buffalo. A little tough but not bad."

"I'm sure it'll be better than the chow hall food at Nha Trang."

"Nha Trang? You're from Vietnam?"

"That's right. I'm a nurse."

"Really? I would never in a thousand years have guessed you were from Vietnam. Are you here on R&R?"

"Yep, that's it. What about you? Are you on R&R, too?"

"Yes, in a way, but not from Vietnam."

"Not from Vietnam, then where?"

"Up-country. Ubon. It's sort of strange. Actually, I'm based on Okinawa but I'm TDY in Thailand. Now I'm R&R in Bangkok."

"That's odd; what do you do? You look too young to be a pilot."

"I'm not. But I do fly. I'm an aircrew member, a loadmaster on C-130's."

"That's interesting. I rode from Nha Trang to Tan Son Nhut in a C-130. It sure was noisy."

"They're that all right. And cold too, if you go to high altitudes. How long have you been at Nha Trang?"

"Seven months; five more to go. What about you?"

"I've been in the Pacific now for four and a half months. Okinawa's an eighteen-month tour for unaccompanied. To be honest, I've not even given it much thought."

"Too long to count, huh?"

"No, its not that. It's just that I don't watch time that closely. I guess it comes from caving."

"Caving? What in the world…?"

"Cave exploring. I used to do that a lot in Tennessee where I grew up. There were some caves not too far from home. You lose all track of time in a cave."

"I've never been in a cave, but I've read about them. There aren't many caves in Kansas, at least not where I live."

"You're from Kansas?'

"That's right - corn-fed and Midwest bred, that's me."

"Did you live on a farm?"

"My father raises wheat and pigs. I gather you're a farm boy, huh?"

"We raised pigs, too. But not wheat. Farmers where I'm from raise a lot of cotton, and some corn. We also have a herd of Angus cattle."

"You know something, I really love your accent."

"Really? I thought everybody north of the Mason-Dixon thought it was hickey."

"Not me. I think it's sweet, sort of sexy. By the way, do you know you have interesting eyes?"

He had heard that before, from the bar girls back on Okinawa. They were always talking about his eyes, but he never gave it much thought. He just assumed they were trying to hustle him for more drinks.

"It's probably my indian blood; my great-great grandmother was a full-blooded Cherokee."

"No, it's not that. There's something else. You've got what they call 'bedroom eyes."

Bedroom eyes! He'd never heard them called that before. Was she leading up to something? Before he could answer or she could continue, the waiter came back to take their order. Sharon decided to try the filet; Toby followed her lead.

"Too bad they don't have Aberdeen Angus in Thailand."

"The meat here isn't all that bad. Some of the guys gripe about it, call it tough, but I don't think it's that terrible."

"Have you ever heard of Kobe beef?'

"Is that where they sling cows off the ground and feed them beer and malt, then massage their skin everyday so it will be stringy? I read about it in one of the James Bond books."

"That's the one. One of the girls at the hospital went to Japan on leave. She went to Kobe. She said it was really marvelous."

"Why did you decide to come to Bangkok? You could have gone to Hong Kong or Taipei, even Sidney.'

"Why not Bangkok? I've read about the city. One time a missionary came to our church to speak. She was on leave from here."

"How ironic; we had a missionary from Bangkok in our church as well. What kind of church did you go too?"

"Southern Baptist."

"Me too! I wonder if it was the same lady?"

"Might have been."

"I didn't know there were Southern Baptists in Kansas."

"There are, but my family is actually from Oklahoma. They moved to Kansas just before the war. But I'm not an Okie; I was born in Wichita."

"The only place I've been in Kansas is Topeka. I had an RON at Forbes air force base one night. We stayed off base in a hotel. About all I remember about it is that it snowed the whole time we were there."

"It does that, all right. At least sometimes. Does it snow in Tennessee?"

"Sometimes, but not it like does in Kansas. We might get six inches or so but it usually will melt after a couple of days. Sometimes we just get an inch or two. I remember one winter when we got a layer of ice, then it snowed on top of that. My brothers and I made skis out of bed-slats and went all over the place."

"How many are in your family?"

"Three boys and two girls. I'm the oldest."

"I've got three brothers. My oldest brother is a pilot in the Air Force - stationed in Germany."

"What does he fly?"

"Fighters, F-100s. He's based at Hahn."

"Hahn? I've never been there. I've been to Frankfurt and Weisbaden."

"I wanted to go to Germany. That's why I joined the nurse corps. But they sent me to Vietnam instead."

"How long have you been in the Army?"

"Two years. I was based at Ft. Bragg for a year, then they sent me here."

"You were at Bragg? I was right next door, at Pope Air Force Base. I used to go over to Bragg to the riding club."

"I went to the riding club. Maybe I saw you there."

"I don't know. That was before I went on flying status, back in '64. When did you get there?"

"October, '64. We might have been there at the same time."

"Probably not. After I moved to a flying squadron I didn't go there as much. Besides, I think I would have remembered you."

"Should I take that as a compliment?"

"Sure." Toby had been trying to watch Sharon's face, but his eyes kept wondering down to her bodice. The sundress was rather snug and cut in such a way that more than the barest hint of cleavage was visible. He noticed that she had freckles right down into the beginning of the valley between her breasts. He also noticed that there were small boulders on the tips of the twin mounds beneath the cotton. He felt stirrings of his own masculinity - and felt guilty at the thought. In spite of his recent activities with Okinawan and Thai whores, Toby Carter's Southern Baptist upbringing led him to put women up on a pedestal, especially those of his faith. That a woman might have sexual thoughts of her own were completely foreign to him.

"I think I would have remembered you, too. Especially those eyes. How could a girl forget those eyes?"

Carter didn't know how to respond to that comment. The thought never occurred to him that she might be trying to lead him toward an advance. In his world, women remained on their pedestals, unapproachable. Their waiter's arrival with their food saved him. At first they ate in silence. Finally Sharon spoke.

"Tell me about your cave exploring adventures. Is it fun?"

"You might say that, If you can call getting cold, wet and muddy from head to toe 'fun.' But sometimes its worth it. When I was ten years old my uncle sent me into a low, crawly passage we had never been in before - it was so low he couldn't get through. I was scared half to death."

"I sure would have been."

"I was, but after I'd crawled about a hundred yards I came out into big, walking passage, Then I found another lead - we call places big enough to get into 'leads' - and came out in a stream passage. It turned out the stream emptied into the Tennessee River five miles away. Nobody had ever been there before. Besides that, the first room I came into was beautiful, with stalactites and stalagmites all over the place. They were pristine, completely undisturbed and never before seen by anyone."

"It must have been a thrill. The place sounds simply lovely."

"I was thrilled - and it was lovely. The most beautiful place I've ever seen. After finding that, I lost my fear. The trip back out seemed to last for just a few seconds; going in had seemed like hours."

"They say there are caves in Vietnam."

"There are, lots of them. And in Laos, too. Every time we fly over Laos I think about the caves below." Carter realized he had said something he shouldn't; very few people knew what his unit did. Sharon was smart; she didn't comment on his slip.

"A friend of mine is at Da Nang, stationed at China Beach. She visited some caves near there. Evidently those caves have some kind of religious significance to the Vietnamese."

"I know the ones you're talking about. The National Speleological Society magazine had something about them. Some Vietnamese hero hid out in the caves while fleeing from the Chinese. He managed to escape his pursuers and vowed to build a monument to Buddha in them. They're supposed to be really spectacular; the monuments that is."

"My friend thought so." By this time they had finished eating. Sharon cocked her head and smiled prettily at Toby, "Toby, I came to Bangkok for some R&R. Right now I would like to have a drink, even if it is still kinda early. Would you like to join me for one?"

Toby was enchanted by the creature who sat across from him. He had not really had a conversation with an American woman in some time. "Sure," he replied. "Would you like to have one here, or see if there is a bar in the hotel?"

"Why don't we go into the bar. There is one off the lobby on the other side. It looks kinda cozy. I peeked in there after I checked in."

The bar was "kinda cozy," as she had said. Sharon Craft led the way to a table in a corner. Like the restaurant, the bar was unoccupied except for the Thai bartender and a waitress. Sharon ordered a Whiskey Collins; Toby decided to try a Rum and Coke. They made small talk as they sipped their drinks. The young nurse was animated in her conversation, and in her actions. Toby was fascinated by the way she played with her hair and tugged on her earlobes as she talked. Several times she leaned back in her chair and thrust her pert breasts out toward him as if she was making sure he knew she had them. He felt her foot brush against his leg, momentarily, then come back again for another pass. Then, after a third teasing touch, she put her calf against his and pressed against him.

"Toby, you are a very nice guy and I think I would like to get to know you better. Why don't we see Bangkok together?"

"I might not be good company."

She smiled that same seemingly innocent smile, "Oh, I am sure that you will. But before we head out to see the town, why don't we go somewhere more private. Shall we go back upstairs? We could go to my room. I've got some liquor in my bag. We could get to know each other a little better."

Toby paid their bill, in spite of Sharon's protest. He felt it improper for her to pay for their drinks, especially after she had invited him into her boudoir. He really couldn't believe what was happening. His first day in Bangkok and he had met this cute round-eye and she had invited him to her room. And she was in the room right next to his! He had really had little expectation he would even meet any American girls, much less develop any kind of relationship with one. In spite of their boasts, he had expected to spend some time in one of the piano bars but then go back to his room either by himself or with a Thai girl from one of the bars.

The girl reached for his hand as they strode down the hall to the elevator. They were its sole occupants as they rode to their rooms on the fifth floor. After the door closed, Sharon snuggled closely to the young man. The effects of the liquor caused her inhibitions to lessen.

"Why don't you kiss me? Or are you shy?" she teased.

Toby was shy all right, but he was not slow to accept her invitation. He took her in his arms as she turned toward him. Her lips were like velvet. Kissing her was nothing like kissing an Okinawan or Thai bar girl. It was a sensation he had never experienced. They held their embrace until the elevator reached the floor and the doors began to open. She drew away from him, but took his hand as they stepped through the doorway together. Hand in hand, they made their way to the door to her room. She handed him the key. When they were inside, Sharon Craft turned toward Toby Carter and drew his face to hers. The kiss this time was much more passionate then before, conveying a message that even an innocent Tennessee farm boy like him could understand.

Sensing her desire, Toby needed little urging. Before he really knew what was happening Sharon was out of her sundress and into his arms. She had very little on underneath.

"Toby, I am very horny. I've not had sex since before I left Fort Bragg. Please do not think I am forward or cheap, but with this crazy war, some things are not the same as we were taught in Training Union. Please take me! And hurry!"

Toby was conscious of her charms even as she presented them to him fully. He was especially conscious of her breasts, which, though they were by no means large, were much fuller than those of the Oriental women with which he was familiar. And there was no hump over her pelvis.

She moaned with pleasure as she drew him inside herself. Toby thought for a second of an overnight in Bangkok a few weeks before when the engineer had been on the other side of a cubicle with a Thai woman. Her sighs and moans of pleasure were new to Toby; the prostitutes he had been with in the past were hardly so demonstrative. Now he was hearing the same sounds from the lovely young woman with whom he was entwined.

After Toby had reached his climax they lay for a moment with him still inside, then Sharon realized he was still potent.

"Hey! If you still can…

Toby needed no urging. But this time it was her turn to assume the superior position.

"Ride a little horsey, down to town..." Sharon sang brightly to them both. But then her song turned to sighs, then moans, then words were coming out of her mouth that surprised them both. She rolled off of him, then urged him back onto and into her. "Fuck me, Toby. Please fuck me, as hard as you can." Toby did as she bade, with no more worry that he might not be able to satisfy her. That such words were something he would never have expected from any of the girls he had gone to church with did not occur to him.

Later, when they were both satiated, at least temporarily, they lay beside each other on the crumpled bed sheets.

"Wow! When I said I came to Bangkok to get laid, I never thought it would be so intense. Toby, you were marvelous. That's the first time in my life I was able to make love as long as I wanted too."

Her praise of him stroked his pride, while her confession that she had had other lovers didn't bother him. He had assumed as much.

"What would you like to do tonight?"

She did not hesitate, "Stay here in bed with you."

"I thought you wanted to see Bangkok?"

"I do, but I am in no hurry. But we can do something if you would like?"

"Would you like to go out and see some of Bangkok's famous night life?"

"Not the R&R spots. And I'm not interested in the live sex shows."

"No, no, no. Nothing like that. But I know a couple of quiet places - piano bars - where Westerners from the embassies and such hang out."

"Civilized places, huh? That would be a change from the officer's club at Nha Trang. But I tell you what, let's take a nap first, okay?" They lay in each others arms until their circulation was about to be cut off. Then they rolled over and went to sleep.

When Toby awoke, Sharon was not in the bed. He heard her shower running. He tried the door that connected their adjoining rooms. It was locked, but his room key opened it. He took his clothes and went into his room, leaving the door open. Toby contemplated the day's events, trying to put them in perspective with recent events of the preceding weeks, as he stood under the hot shower. Three nights ago he had been preparing to take-off for a mission over North Vietnam, not knowing whether he would live to see the dawn of the next breaking day. Now here he was in Bangkok, washing away the remnants of the intimacies of an attractive young American woman, an Army officer to boot! A week from now he would be

36

right back at Ubon, heading back into the war. It was hard to comprehend, more like a dream than reality.

"Give me twenty minutes to get ready," Sharon called to him through their mutual doorway when he stepped out of the shower.

"Okay, I'll knock in half an hour."

"Roger that," he saw her wave her arm, then close the door.

When she opened the door to his knock half an hour later, Toby could hardly believe what he saw. Sharon was now fully dressed, her hair was decorated with a white, silk ribbon that went perfectly with the cotton dress she wore. She had on stockings now, and heels. She was as tall as he, maybe a little taller in the heels.

"How do I look?"

"Good enough to eat. Now there's a thought."

"Later, cowboy. We've got all night - four more of them in fact. Right now I want to restore the energy we used up this afternoon. And, by the way. I'm paying for dinner tonight. There's no sense in you spending all of your money on me. I've been saving up for this trip for months. I can't do much with it at Nha Trang."

"Well, if you insist. But I must say that you hardly look like you're suffering from lack of energy."

After dinner they went to the Dew Drop inn, a piano bar not far from the American Embassy. Since it was a week-night, the bar was not overly crowded. Toby felt somewhat flattered when every eye in the place turned to look at Sharon. He couldn't take his own eyes off of her. It was hard to believe that he had already experienced what that dress concealed - and would again when they returned to the hotel. Of that he was certain. She had assured him as much in the taxi on the way to the club.

"Dance with me."

"But I'm not much of a dancer."

"That's okay. I'll teach you. Shoot, all you really do is just move around the floor to this kind of stuff, anyway." The pianist was playing "Moon River." She led him onto the minuscule dance floor where half a dozen other couples already almost filled it. She pressed her body close to him, so close that he could feel every curve. She put her mouth next to his ear. "I want to keep you primed for when we get back to the hotel." She nibbled on his ear lobe.

When they did get back to the hotel it was nearly 2:00 AM. This time they went into his room. Their lovemaking was more relaxed, with more kissing and caressing, and more adventurous. When he finally entered her he did so without the urgency of their first entwining. He was surprised by the long sigh of pleasure the motion elicited.

"Do that again. Come out and back in again. It feels absolutely marvelous." Her voice was breathless. He did as she asked.

They made love for a long time, their bodies bathed in moonlight coming through Toby's window. Their coupling was leisurely, as they experimented with various positions. When they found one that was especially appealing, they remained in it for awhile. Neither tried to dominate, each took their turn initiating or doing the other's bidding. It was well into the wee hours of the morning before they went to sleep.

The next four days were the most blissful of Toby's twenty years of life. Sharon and he were inseparable. They ate together, slept together and sometimes bathed together. A good portion of their time was spent in bed. On the morning of the third day she told him they had already more than equaled her previous sex life. For that matter, they had done the same in regard to his own. She was already a milestone in his life, anyway. Before her, all of his sexual partners had been Oriental prostitutes - Thais, Filipinas, Okinawans, and one Japanese.

They did find time for some sightseeing and shopping. Bangkok is noted for its temples, the royal palace and the klongs, the canals which once had served as streets before the construction of the paved roads which now carried thousands of Japanese and European made automobiles. He bought her a star sapphire pendant; she bought him an elephant-hide wallet.

On Monday morning they rode to the airport together. Sharon was leaving from the civilian side of the field on a commercial flight while Toby was to catch a late afternoon cargo flight from the Air Force side of Don Muang. She told him good-bye in front of the airline terminal.

"Don't say it, Toby. I've enjoyed myself immensely this week. It's been the best week of my life. But we could never work it out. We might meet again, and I'd be glad to spend another week in bed with you if we ever do. But let's don't make any future plans."

"Sharon, I really have enjoyed the week. And I guess you're probably right. Who knows what might happen to either of us. I guess we're just like two ships passing in the night." He said it, but he didn't mean it. Toby was infatuated, if not in love.

"Well, I wouldn't say that. After all, ships don't run into each other. And you've been in my port enough times this week, that's for sure. I got what I wanted, and you got what you wanted. Let's leave it at that. Look, you had better go. That cab driver's meter is running."

"I guess I had better."

"I'll write."

"Me, too."

"Don't be writing any mushy stuff. I guess we've sort of fallen in love this week, but it's the physical kind. I'm too old for you."

"By eighteen months. Big deal."

"That's enough. Besides, I'll be getting out of the Army in less than a year. You've got longer than that to go on Okinawa."

They kissed, even though she was in uniform. He was in his flight suit, so it was not readily apparent that he was enlisted while she was an officer. Toby watched her through the back window of the taxi as it pulled away. She appeared to be crying.

"I do love you, Toby Carter. I really do. But it would never work out." Sharon said the words under her breath, then picked up her bag and went into the terminal. Passing a trash-can, she dropped a crumpled slip of paper into it.

Chapter Five

On the airplane back to Ubon, Toby lay on top of a cargo pallet and thought about the past few days. He was the only additional crewmember on the airplane. After leaving a message for him at C-130 Ops, the other guys had gone back up-country that morning. He took advantage of the time to contemplate the events of the past week.

This whole experience with Sharon had really been strange; strange in that it had exceeded his wildest expectations. The guys would never believe he had spent his whole stay in Bangkok shacked up with an Army nurse. He could hardly believe it himself! But he had the elephant hide wallet she had bought him in his pocket. The sex they had had! Five days and five nights they had been together. It was sort of like a honeymoon, except that they weren't married. No, actually it was something else, something he couldn't think of a word to describe. A tryst, that was it! A five-day tryst of two lovers. It was the first time in his young adult life that he'd had sex without having to pay for it.

They had made love no less than half a dozen times that very day before finally leaving the hotel just barely in time for her to check in for her flight. They had even talked about going AWOL for a few days, but then decided that wasn't a very good idea. He had definitely had enough sex to last him for awhile; no more visits to the rooms behind the dance hall for him! He hadn't realized there were so many ways to make love. Their relationship had been very experimental. On that first night they had discovered the one position Sharon had most enjoyed, from behind with her kneeling like a temple dancer paying homage to Buddha. Toby felt he was almost demeaning her, with her bowing down like she was worshipping him. But she enjoyed the position so much that she insisted they practice it every night. It seemed almost perverse, not only for the pleasure they both derived but from the message she was sending to him, although she may not have realized it - "Here I am, man. I, woman, bow down to you and your dominance, which brings me the utmost pleasure." The fact that she was an Army lieutenant while he was an Air Force enlisted man made the experience even more profound. She would be in tears, her passion was so great. After they had finished she would clutch him to her breast and cover him with wet kisses, then the next thing they knew they would be at it again.

"Hey, Tobe. What happened to you, man? We were beginning to wonder if you'd gotten thrown in the brig." Mike Kelly greeted him when he walked through the door of their hooch that evening. "Press-on was beginning to think you might have gone AWOL." They had started calling their AC "Press-on Preston" after that last mission over the North.

"I overslept. I called Ops and they told me there was going to be a late flight. You guys had already gone."

"Have you heard what happened while we were gone?"

"No. what happened."

"The gooks got one of our birds; one of the crews from the eight seventeenth."

"You're kidding! Who was on it?"

"The loads were Barney Johnson, Fred Dickson, Marve Clanton and Roy Carlton."

"Did they get out?"

"Nobody knows. Funny thing is, they were on a BLIND BAT, working in the panhandle."

"What hit them? A SAM, flak or what?"

"Nobody knows that, either. As far as anyone knows, they were just tooling along when the airplane blew up. A CANDLESTICK was working the next sector. They saw the explosion. Nobody heard anything out of them."

"That's too bad. They were all good guys. Hey, didn't Dickson's wife just have a baby?"

"Yeah. Now the poor little kid will grow up without a daddy. Damn fucking gooks!"

"How was your R&R?"

"Great, man. Just great. How about yours?"

"It was okay. I spent a lot of time in bed, though."

"Yeah, man. Me and Willy ran into a couple of German stews one night. They liked to have fucked our balls off. Sam got hooked up with a Russian girl from their embassy. Do you believe that? A damn Russian! I hope she wasn't a spy, though I guess she probably was. How about you."

Toby decided to tell them, "I met an Army nurse. She had the room right next door to me. We spent a lot of time together."

"A nurse! That's all right, man. Is she stationed in Bangkok?"

"No, she was on R&R from Nha Trang."

"Are you going to the vill' tonight?"

"I don't think so. I need to get some rest. We'll be back at it again tomorrow night."

"Yeah, I know what you mean. I don't think the other guys are planning to go, either. They should be back from the chow hall anytime. I think I might go to the club after awhile. Have you eaten?"

"No, and I'm starved. I haven't eaten anything all day. But after we eat I want to come back and get some rest."

"You know, it's funny. We go off on 'rest and recuperation' and we come back here to get some rest! This is really a strange war."

They did stay in the hooch that night; amazingly they actually got some rest before their mission the following night. It was one of the few times any of the enlisted men from Preston's crew ever got a decent night's sleep at Ubon. They slept as late as they could the next day, until the heat and humidity finally was more than their bodies could handle. As usual, they spent the afternoon around the hooch, listening to the radio, swapping stories about their week in Bangkok and getting ready for the night's mission.

"Gentlemen, our newest threat seems to be an 85-millimeter gun that Charley has put here," the briefing officer pointed at the map, "Just south of Mu Gia. "We have reason to believe it was this gun that got BAT TWO last week, although we cannot say so for sure. An F-4 was shot-down in the vicinity yesterday. The crew ejected and was picked up. They reported they were hit by something big, bigger than fifty-seven mike, mike."

He went on, "The gun is located somewhere in this general area, but we don't know exactly where. We think it is probably mounted so that it is kept hidden in a cave during the day and rolled out at night. This whole area is honeycombed with caves."

Cavendish interrupted, "Hell, major. You ought to send old Toby in there. He's a cave expert." He pointed at Carter. The major looked up from the map.

"Is that right, airman?"

"You might say so, sir. I used to do a lot of caving back in Tennessee, where I grew up."

"In that case maybe we ought to have a chat. Why don't you come by my office tomorrow afternoon, after you get up. Maybe you can help us out. We've been trying to find someone with knowledge of caves. We've even had the National Speleological Society searching their files for someone based in this area. I guess your name didn't come up because you're based on Okinawa. We didn't think about that."

"Yes sir."

"To get on with our briefing," Major Catlin continued, "This is the area in which you will be working tonight. Keep an especially watchful eye out for any signs of eighty-five millimeter firing. If you can, try and pinpoint the location of the gun. I wish I could tell you exactly where it is so you could avoid it. Unfortunately, I can't."

After they left the briefing and were on their way to the flight line, the big gun was the main topic of conversation.

"How about that? The gooks are hiding their guns in caves!" McDonald opened the conversation.

"Is that possible, Tobe?" Kelly looked at Carter.

"It's possible. Some caves are big enough to hid a Herkybird in. Nickajack Cave, on the Tennessee-Alabama line, had an entrance as big as a three-story building. That is, until TVA flooded It back in the fifties. The problem is that even if they did find out where the gun is, if it is in a cave there's probably nothing anybody could do about it. All the bombs in the world wouldn't be able to get to it."

"Couldn't they knock down the side of a hill?'

"Well, they might. But I doubt it. Limestone is really pretty tough stuff. Those caves have been there for thousands of years. It would take a mighty big bomb to make enough rubble to block an entrance big enough for a gun that size to be wheeled in and out of. Even if they did block the entrance, the gooks would probably dig it out again overnight. The biggest bombs being used over here are thousand pounders."

"Yeah, and we all know these fighter jocks can't hit shit!" responded Willy.

"Even if they got lucky and did block the entrance, the gooks would just dig it out again."

"We better hope we don't get close to that mother tonight. We could be in deep kimshee if we do."

"You can say that again, Salts."

"Okay, Sam. We better hope we don't get close to that mother tonight. We could be in deep kimshee if we do." At Salts' joke all four loadmasters cracked up. The tension of the moment had been broken.

Toby took special care with his "cave pack" and M-16 that might, being certain they were in easy reach in the event of a bailout. He had gone through the pack that afternoon, insuring that everything was still serviceable, and changing the water in his canteen. He had even cleaned his carbide lamp and checked it over, even though it was already immaculate. He had scrounged some more M-16 ammo; now he had over two hundred rounds in the pack - ten boxes of cartridges with four clips. He also sharpened his survival knife and rechecked the lashings that attached it to his survival vest.

On the way to their target area Toby thought about Sharon. It was a shame their lives were separated by so many miles. It would be very unlikely that they would ever be able to see each other again, not unless she did take a delay enroute on Okinawa on her way back to the States - and he was fortunate enough to be on the island when she did. He would probably get into Nha Trang, but if he did the only place he would see would be the flight line.

Their night was busy as they worked a flight of A-lE's out of NKP, followed by two A-26 NIMRODs one after the other. The NIMRODs could spend half an hour or more over a target and get off a lot of ordinance. So

43

could the A-l's for that matter. Preston had put the four attack aircraft on to a grove of suspicious-looking trees just off a known artery. His hunch had evidently proved to be correct; secondary explosions had accompanied the detonations of the first A-l's bombs. The grove of trees evidently hid an ammunition and fuel dump.

Flak had been light, as it usually was over Laos. The attack airplanes had reported some small arms fire but nothing larger than 30-caliber. There had been some automatic weapons fire, probably submachine guns or automatic rifles. All in all it was just another night over the Trail.

But then, during a lull between flights of fighters, it happened. Suddenly the sky around them exploded into light as flak rounds began bursting all around them. Almost instantly the right wing burst into flames as a round went off right behind number four engine. Another round burst just below the fuselage; shrapnel erupted through the floor. Only the aluminum cargo pallet on which the flare bins were secured prevented everyone in the rear from being hit. Smoke began curling up through the floor.

"Loadmaster to pilot, We're hit, sir! The flares are smoking. We've got to get rid of the load, fast!" McDonald was on the loadmaster/scanner's long cord.

"Roger that, load. We've taken several hits. Jettison the chute and open the doors. Let me know when you're ready."

Carter and Cavendish undid the nylon straps which held the flare chute on the door. Kelly opened the door and ramp; Toby and Willy pushed the chute off the ramp then ran to either side of the airplane to grab their chest-pack parachutes and get out of the way of the load. They scrambled forward past the flare bin. As soon as they were clear, Sam McDonald pulled the emergency release handle for the cargo locks. On McDonald's signal, Danson pulled back on the yoke and raised the nose. Fortunately, the pallets were not bowed and did not bind. The load rolled out of the airplane and off the ramp, out into the blackness of the night. A cold blast of air whirled into and around the cargo compartment through the open door.

"Load's clear, sir!"

"Thank God. Take a look at the right wing."

"Holy shit! The whole damn wing's on fire," Kelly shouted to McDonald.

"Sir, the wing's on fire. I don't think we're going to make it."

Preston had rung the bailout bell three short rings, the signal to prepare for bailout. Now he reached over and flipped it forward. A long, continuous ringing filled the airplane. Everyone in the cockpit began unfastening their seat harness and securing their positions. Carter motioned for McDonald to give him his headset. As crew loadmaster, his bailout

44

order would be next to last, right before the pilot. He had already buckled on his pack and strapped the M-16 into the special straps on his harness.

In short order the other three loadmasters ran off the end of the ramp and plunged out into the blackness. Benjamin came out of the cockpit and ran down the cargo compartment floor to the open ramp where Carter stood, the chill wind of the night air rustling his fatigues. Salts was right behind him, followed by Danson. Only Captain Preston remained.

"I'm having trouble keeping this thing level, Toby." They were the only people left on the headsets. "I've been trying to get us away from the Trail, but it wants to turn right, back toward where the bad guys are. Don't wait for me. Go ahead and jump when everyone else is gone."

"I can't do that, sir. I'll wait for you to get back here."

"Suit yourself. But don't wait too long. At the first indication I am losing this thing, get the hell out. Is everybody clear?"

"Affirmative, sir. It's just you and me."

"Okay, I'm putting this mother on auto-pilot. But don't wait around too long. As soon as you see me come out of the cockpit, JUMP."

Toby threw down his headset now that it was no longer useful. He waited by the chasm of the open door, his head turned toward the crew ladder. When he saw his aircraft commander come out of the doorway at the 245 bulkhead, he turned and leaped off of the ramp, out into the night.

He could hardly believe the sudden silence. One second he was standing in a tornado of noise and wind; the next he was falling through space. He reached for the D-ring and pulled it out and away from his chest, then dropped the D-ring into the night. There was a rustling sound as the nylon deployed from the pack, followed by a sudden jerk as the nylon filled with air. Then he found himself suspended beneath an array of nylon canopy and line. The only sounds in his immediate vicinity were the rustling of his canopy and the humming of the suspension lines.

He could hear old 475 going off into oblivion. He looked behind him; a glowing meteorite indicated the path of the doomed airplane. Then there was a sudden explosion and a light that lit up the sky as the C-130 blew up in mid-air. He wondered if Captain Preston had gotten out all right. Probably; there seemed to have been enough time.

He looked around. The sky was black again. No sign of anyone else, which was just as well. If he couldn't see anyone, then the people on the ground couldn't either. He had probably fallen about a hundred feet or so before his parachute opened; he'd pulled the ripcord as soon as his feet left the ramp. They had been at 10,000 feet when they were hit. If they hadn't lost any altitude, that meant it could take ten minutes for him to reach the earth. No telling where he would drift in that length of time.

The four-line cut! In every survival class he had attended, the instructor emphasized the cutting of the four marked suspension lines. He had almost forgotten it. He reached into his pocket for the orange survival knife with the hooked blade. Ordinarily it would have been in the leg pocket of his flying suit, but he was wearing jungle fatigues and a flight jacket. Good! It was there. He found the nylon string which attached it to his belt loop. He pulled the knife out, opened the blade and reached up and above him for the tapes that identified the lines. He sure didn't want to cut the wrong ones!

When the four lines were cut, Toby closed the blade and put the knife back into his pocket. He tested the risers, by pulling down on the left front one he could turn left; by doing likewise with the right one he could turn right. The open panel after the four-line cut allowed air to escape from the back of the chute, propelling it forward. At least he now had some control over his destiny - not much, but some.

His body was in good shape. Since no ejection had been involved there had been nothing to cause him possible harm. He had simply jumped up and let the airplane fly out from under him. He checked his equipment. Surprisingly, everything was still there. Even his revolver was in the holster on his survival vest. The M-16 was still strapped to his harness and his cave pack was there too. Not that he would need them. Hopefully he would be picked up in the morning, at first light. He considered pulling out his survival radio and trying to contact someone. CANDLESTICK was probably somewhere around. MOONBEAM would be above him, probably up around flight level 250 and well out of range of any guns. Then there were the various fighters that were on missions here and there. Someone would be sure to hear him. But no, he was liable to drop the radio. Better to wait until he was safe on the ground.

Toby had never jumped from an airplane before, although he had dropped hundreds of paratroopers. As the jumpers exited the airplane, Toby had often wished he could go with them. Now here he was suspended beneath a parachute, listening to the sounds of the wind in the risers. For the time being all he had to do was relax and enjoy the ride.

But Toby knew that the ride down the remaining 4,000 feet or so to the ground was the easy part. He had to land safely and then he had to get out of the parachute harness in one piece. He had practiced parachute landing fall techniques in survival training, but doing them under the watchful eye of an instructor off of a bench was one thing; executing the proper PLF at night, in unfamiliar terrain, was something else entirely. For that matter, there was no guarantee he would even reach the ground. Tall trees - some as high as 300 feet - covered the ridges of Laos. Toby was well aware of that; he had seen the foliage illuminated in the light of their flares through the crack by the side of the flare chute. Then there were the cliffs; they were over limestone country. He knew well enough that where there was limestone, often enough there would be deep gorges with steep cliffs on either side. Even if he was lucky enough to come down in a bare spot, more than likely the ground would be rocky. And while limestone is considered soft in comparison to other rocks, it's still hard enough! It can also be quite jagged, with remnants of the sea shells from which it was made sticking out in all directions. That would be a hell of a note - to die impaled upon a limestone shard!

There was also the question of where he was. He knew Preston had headed the airplane west, trying to get as far from the Trail as possible before they bailed out. He reckoned they were several miles from where they were hit when the other guys jumped. But the airplane had turned of it's own accord after Preston put it on auto-pilot. Like a fool he had waited for the AC to get down out of the cockpit before he had jumped himself! How far back to the east had they gone? Were they back over the Trail? Where was Preston? Had he gotten out? Toby reasoned that he had; the airplane was some distance away when it blew up and he had seen the pilot come out of the cockpit before he leaped out into space. Preston had been wearing his parachute; he was sure of that.

Listen! What's that sound? Good Lord - truck engines! The sound came from somewhere below him. Now he knew full well where he was; they had drifted quite some distance to the east before he got out of the stricken airplane. He was right back over the Trail! He looked down between the toes of his jungle boots but saw nothing; only blackness. But the sounds of the engines were drawing nearer - and they seemed to come from right below. He pulled on his risers to steer the parachute away from the noise. What was that? Lights? Yes, now he could see lights on the ground 1,000 feet below him. He knew what they were; the shaded lights of the truck headlights. Invisible from the altitudes at which they flew, the narrow beams were becoming visible as Toby drifted closer to them. And he heard voices. That was even worse. Evidently there were enemy troops on the ground somewhere beneath him. He pulled harder on the risers until he was moving in the direction he thought was west.

His eyes had gotten used to the darkness. As his parachute carried him closer to the ground, Toby could see the outline of the ridges. The truck lights were in a gorge; he could see the tops of the ridges on either side. His best chance would be to land on top of a ridge. Even a tree landing would be better than touching down in the valley. That's where the North Vietnamese were. If he came down right in the middle of them, he would be dead. Or on his way to the Hanoi Hilton. He temporarily forgot about the trees and the rocks; his main concern now was to avoid the humans who would definitely do him harm.

Could they see him? Did they see him? Was his parachute silhouetted against the sky? There was no moon, but the sky was full of stars. Surely they could not see him. No one was shooting at him, anyway. Besides, they had no real reason to be on the alert for his descent, in spite of the fact that they had just shot him down. The airplane was several miles away when it blew up. They probably thought everyone had gone down with it. At least he certainly hoped that was what they thought!

He was getting closer and closer to the ground. He could see the trucks themselves, now - and the soldiers walking along the trail beside them. Troops heading south to fight the hated Yankee dogs! He seemed to be drifting away from them, toward the top of the ridge that was his target. Yes, he was going to make the ridge. But where would he hit? He only saw the troops in the shaded headlights of the trucks; he could make out no features on the landscape other than the general lay of the land. Were there trees where he was headed? If so, how many? Was the ridge densely covered, or was the vegetation sparse? He reckoned he had about fifteen seconds before he found out. Toby attempted to relax, in spite of the fact that his heart was beating probably 200 times a minute. His legs - he had to be ready to let them bend quickly as soon as his feet touched, to fall on one side and let his body absorb the shock. A broken leg out here would reduce his chances of survival and rescue to next to zero.

And then he felt the ground come up to meet him.

Chapter Six

The dull throbbing of rotor blades cut through the still of the early morning air; JOLLY 101 was on its way to make a pick-up. An A-lE SANDY kept pace on either side with the Sikorsky HH-3E helicopter. SANDY ONE and SANDY TWO would provide air cover for the slow-moving helicopter as it swooped in low to make the pickup of survivors from the C-130 flareship that had gone in some twenty miles west of the Trail last night. Two other A-1's, SANDY THREE and FOUR, were already in the vicinity of the survivors, talking to them on the radio and coordinating the rescue attempt.

Cavendish, McDonald and Kelly had all left the ramp of the doomed C-130 right behind each other. Their descent to earth was practically simultaneous; they all landed within a hundred yards of one another. Benjamin and Salts had come down two miles away while Danson had landed another mile and a half beyond them. As soon as they were on the ground, the six survivors had all managed to make contact with MOONBEAM as well as a CANDLESTICK C-123 that had been working in the area where they bailed out.

Miraculously, all had reached the ground with only minor injuries. Only Benjamin had landed in a tree; he had managed to lower himself to the ground using the nylon cord, which was attached to his parachute harness for just that purpose. Salts had a sprained ankle while McDonald had broken an arm when he threw it out to ward off branches as he fell through a tree.

"Listen! I hear a helicopter!" Kelly alerted his two companions that their deliverance was drawing nigh. He picked up his survival radio, checked that it was set to the discreet frequency, and began calling, "JOLLY, JOLLY, this is BLIND BAT SIX, over."

Welcome words came through the earphone he had plugged in to prevent the radio noise from being heard by those who might be looking for them. So far they had seen no sign of the enemy. "Roger BAT SIX, this is JOLLY 101. Turn on your beeper for ten seconds, then come back up on voice." Kelly switched the radio to the continuous distress code, counted to ten, then switched back to voice.

"BAT SIX, we've got you pegged. How many are in your group?"

"We have three survivors, I say again, three survivors. We are BAT SIX, BAT SEVEN and BAT EIGHT. There's a clearing right in front of our position."

"Roger that, BAT SIX. We will land and pick you up. As soon as we come to a hover, run out and jump on. Have you seen any sign of hostiles?"

"That's negative, JOLLY 101. So far, things have been really quiet."

"Sounds good. Pop smoke when we're within half a mile."

"We'll do it. You sound close. There you are! About a mile away, heading straight for us."

"Get ready with your smoke. What's your condition?"

"BAT SEVEN has a broken arm, but he can make it without help. We're popping smoke." Cavendish pulled the activating lanyard off of a smoke flare, then threw it out into the clearing.

"We have your smoke. We'll land into the wind."

The three ground-bound loadmasters watched the huge helicopter pass overhead, then swing around to turn into the wind. It seemed to be barely moving as the pilot lowered the machine onto the savanna grass and began working it sideways toward them. They could see an open door where a helmeted crewman waited. Another was manning a mini-gun in a window while another was in a similar position on the other side. They broke from their cover and began the 50-yard sprint to the helicopter's open door. Kelly waited for McDonald and Cavendish; the two uninjured men helped their buddy into the door, then felt hands and arms as the crewmembers reached out and pulled them aboard. Then, as soon as Cavendish was half in and half out of the helicopter, the pilot pulled the collective. The HH-3 began moving up, up and away. Cavendish quickly pulled himself aboard.

"We're going to pick up the rest of your crew. Are you guys okay?" The PJ shouted to make himself heard. A second PJ had already taken Sam McDonald in charge and was checking his arm. Cavendish and Kelly strapped themselves into nylon seats on the left side of the helicopter.

Benjamin was picked up by the hoist and rode up on a tree penetrator. He was in a heavily forested area with no clearing around large enough for the helicopter to maneuver low enough to pick him up. "Hey, guys! Fancy running into you here!" The navigator greeted the three loadmasters as the helicopter crew headed their craft to where Salt's beeper was homing them in. Because of Salt's injury, one of the PJ's rode down the hoist to help him get aboard. Then the two were winched back into the helicopter. Five down, three to go.

Danson's position was less than a mile from where Salt's had been picked up. He was waiting by a small clearing. The pilot brought the bird to a hover fifty feet in the air while the winch operator lowered his hoist. As the co-pilot was being winched aboard, the sudden crackling of ground fire signaled the presence of the enemy. The Jolly Green pilot pulled out of hover and began making his run with Danson swinging forty feet below. Manning the mini-guns, the crew chief and one of the PJ's threw covering fire in the direction of the enemy gunners. SANDY ONE peeled off and came over the clearing to drop a pair of napalm canisters. The pilot pointed the nose of the Jolly Green west, toward Nakonphanom, even as the hoist operator was pulling Captain Danson through the open door of the helicopter.

"Hey, what about Toby and Captain Preston?" Cavendish shouted to no one in particular.

"Yeah, Sarge. What about the rest of our crew?" Danson addressed the PJ, a young Staff Sergeant.

"Nobody's heard a word from them; no voice, no beeper, nothing. But believe me, if we hear anything, we'll go get them. If not us, someone will."

They settled down for the ride across Laos to Ubon, their thoughts preoccupied with the whereabouts of the two missing members of their crew.

At Ubon they were met by the Blind Bat commander, Lt. Colonel Powers, along with the 8th Tactical Fighter Wing commander, Colonel Olds, and the intelligence officer, Major Catlin, and a flight surgeon. The flight surgeon checked them over while the two injured men were carried to the hospital. When the flight surgeon gave his okay, Major Catlin and Colonel Powers ushered them into intelligence.

"Well, men. I guess you all had an exciting night."

"You might say that, sir," as second in command, Danson assumed the role of spokesmen for the crew.

Major Catlin continued while Colonel Powers listened, "Our main object right now is to find Captain Preston and Airman Carter. Carter - was he the man with an interest in caves?"

"Yes sir," volunteered Kelly. "Maybe that's where he is right now. He always said he would hide out in a cave if we went down."

"I certainly hope so. What I want you to do is tell me what happened. How were you hit; where, with what?"

Benjamin was the first to respond," We were right here sir," he pointed at the map on Catlin's wall. "Just south of Mu Gia. We were flying along all fat, dumb and happy when suddenly all hell broke loose."

"Do you have any idea what hit you?"

Danson answered, "My guess is it was an eighty five. Or maybe even a hundred mike, mike. Whatever it was, it was big. Our entire right wing was on fire."

"Could it have been a missile?"

"No, I don't think so. A missile would have hit an engine. We were hit in the wing itself. It was definitely a gun."

"What happened after you were hit?"

"First, Captain Preston rang the 'prepare to bailout' alarm. Then he told the loads to get rid of the flares. We headed west, trying to get away from the Trail before we abandoned ship. We were pretty well certain the bird was gone. The fire in the right wing was too intense. All we could hope for was to get as far away from the Trail as possible before we jumped."

'What about the bailout? Who jumped first?"

"We did, sir." As the ranking loadmaster, Kelly answered the question. "Toby - Airman Carter - stood by the ramp and watched us all go. We went out almost together. We could see each other after our parachutes opened. The three of us all came down within a hundred yards of each other."

"What about the people in the cockpit?"

Danson picked up again, "Captain Preston was flying the airplane by hand. The auto-pilot kept wanting to turn right, a direction we didn't want to go because it would take us back over the Trail. He told us to get our chutes and get out. By the time I got down, Salts and Lieutenant Benjamin had already jumped. Carter was still standing by the ramp, waiting for everyone to jump. That was his bail-out position. I imagine he waited for Captain Preston to come out of the cockpit. He's a pretty conscientious kid."

"Did anyone see the airplane go down?"

"We all did, sir. At least we all saw the explosion. It blew up inflight. The funny thing is, when we saw it go off, the airplane had evidently turned back to the east, back toward where we were hit. It was wanting to fly right wing low. Evidently after Captain Preston engaged the auto-pilot, the airplane turned right."

"Did they have enough time to get out?"

"No doubt about it, sir. It was a good five minutes after I jumped before I heard the explosion and saw the flash. Even if Preston didn't get out, Carter should have. He was standing right by the open ramp when I jumped. Unless he went up front for some reason, he should have gotten out."

"Does anyone have anything to add to the report? If not, why don't you go to quarters and get some sleep. We'll talk again tomorrow, after you've had a chance to rest. In the meantime, if we get any word on the rest of your crew, we'll pass it along to Colonel Powers."

The remnants of Preston's crew left the briefing room; Major Catlin and Colonel Powers remained behind.

"Colonel, I didn't want to tell your men, but I don't think Preston and Carter have a prayer. For one thing, there's no real guarantee that they actually got out of the airplane. Even if they did, where it appears they must have gone down is almost smack in the middle of the infiltration complex. Our chances of picking either of them up would be almost nil, even if we did hear something from one of them. Which, so far, we haven't.'

"I was afraid that would be your assessment."

"I just wanted you to know that. However, we will keep looking. Every crew flying anywhere close to that area will be briefed to be listening for beepers."

"In the meantime I'll call their squadron at Naha. Preston's wife is there. Carter is single. Be sure and let me know if you have any indication whatsoever that they may be safe."

"You can rest assured of that, Colonel. As soon as I hear anything, I'll let you know."

In the truck on the way back to the barracks, the four healthy members of the crew pondered the fate of their comrades. "What do you think, Lieutenant Benjamin? Do you think they might have made it?"

"I don't know Willy. I'd like to think so, but then the airplane did blow up; we all saw it. Maybe Carter got out. He would have had the best chance. As for Bob, it's a long way from the cockpit back to the ramp."

Danson picked-up the conversation, "The problem is that the airplane was hard to control. He was still hand-flying when I got out of my seat. Who knows what might have happened when he put it back on auto-pilot."

"But there was a good five minutes from the time we jumped and when we saw the explosion. That should have been plenty of time for them to have gotten out."

"Maybe Carter decided to go up front for some reason. Captain Preston could have been having trouble getting out of his seat. Toby could have gone to the cockpit to try and help him. Who knows?"

"I guess all we can do is hope."

"And pray a little. That sure couldn't hurt."

Morale was pretty low around the Blind Bat hooches and on the flight line. Back at Naha a morose feeling swept the four flying squadrons. The group had lost two airplanes in less than two weeks. Only the news that six out of the eight men aboard the last one had been picked-up brought any reason for rejoicing. And that was tempered by the probable loss of two crewmembers. That Preston was married and the father of two children helped to worsen the loss. Every crewmember's wife on the island felt a mixture of gladness and sadness; gladness that it wasn't their husband, combined with sadness for Patty Preston.

As for Carter, his loss was felt mostly among the guys in the barracks and the few squadron people who had flown with him in the four and a half months he had been with them. Some people couldn't remember just what he looked like." He was that kid from Tennessee. You know, the one who always carried that special survival kit he had made up himself." That was how he was described when someone asked just who he was. For those who had flown with him, the survival kit was the key. For others who had yet to have met him, he was but a name. He had been in the unit too short of a time to have made much of an impression.

Captain Bob Preston, on the other hand, had been a popular figure in the squadron for almost three years. He had been a co-pilot when the 35th first arrived on The Rock back in 1963. Everyone who had been in the unit for at least six months at least knew who he was, while the old heads had all flown with him some time or other. All of the officers knew his wife from functions at the O-Club. His joking manner and skills as a pilot made him a pleasure to fly with, in spite of the certain degree of recklessness he had exhibited.

Word of Preston's recklessness had begun to spread outside of the Blind Bat and squadron circle. He had been recommended for a DFC for an earlier tour when he had swooped down low and dropped flares on a 37-MM gun position. Colonel Powers had not known whether to put him in for a Silver Star or recommend he be disciplined after his latest exploit, the bombing of the truck convoy. Now, at least, that problem had been solved. At least he hadn't been doing something stupid when they were shot down. The Blind Bat commander's first action when he went back to his office was to pull out a Recommendation for Decoration form and write Bob Preston up for a Silver Star. What about the young loadmaster, Carter? He could always put him in for another Air Medal.

A couple of hundred miles east of Ubon, on top of a limestone ridge overlooking a narrow gorge in an area marked on surface maps as "karst," Toby Carter was taking stock of his situation. Events of the preceding night would forever be somewhat hazy in his mind, although he had a very general idea of what had taken place. When the stars began disappearing behind the tree line, he had relaxed his legs to get ready for the impact. When it came, his breath was knocked out of him but that was all.

Miraculously, he had come down in open terrain, missing the tall trees that had been his worst fear. Instinctively, he had reached up and flipped the release handle that released his right riser, thus spilling his parachute. In survival school the instructors had stressed that as the first thing to do. More than one airman had been dragged to death by a wind-driven parachute. He had then begun gathering the canopy up in preparation for burying it. But then it dawned on him; he was standing on solid rock! There was no way he would be able to bury the chute. He would have to find some other way to conceal it.

His first awareness of his surroundings was that it was cool, much cooler than he expected. Compared to Ubon, it was downright cold! He was glad he had been wearing a flight jacket over his fatigues that night. The nylon jacket kept the chill away from his skin. It must be around fifty, good sleeping weather if he had been back home. Home! The thought of home brought a sudden feeling of despair and momentary panic. Would he ever see home again? Right now he sort of doubted it.

And Sharon, what about her? Two nights ago he had been kissing and caressing her lovely body. Now here he was, on top of a ridge somewhere in Laos. But just where? He was a loadmaster; his job was in back of the airplane. He never saw the maps except at the pre-mission briefing. And that was only a casual glance. He had a general idea where he was, but not exactly. All he really knew was that they had been working from south of the Mu Gia Pass all the way down past Tche Pone.

Toby suddenly remembered his survival radio. He felt for it in his survival vest; it was still there. Maybe he ought to activate the beeper. No, he remembered the trucks he had seen during his descent. He was much too close to the Trail. No doubt there were hundreds of communist troops in the area, probably equipped with plenty of automatic weapons. A rescue helicopter would be shot down before it ever got to him. Were they - the communists - coming after him? Hopefully the answer was no. No one had any real reason to suspect he was there. The airplane had exploded some distance away and there had been no moon, only stars. He had been able to see the ground when he neared it, but it was doubtful anyone had seen him. Fortunately, he had remembered to turn off the parachute beeper as soon as the canopy opened.

What should he do? The first thing was to get rid of that parachute. Toby grabbed the canopy and began rolling it into a ball. Then he remembered - shoot, he had packed parachutes back in loadmaster training! He found the pinnacle and pulled the parachute so it lay flat on the ground. Then he began rolling the canopy toward the risers, trying to make as compact a bundle as possible. As he rolled, he remembered what he had been told in survival school - your parachute is your best survival tool. They had been taught how to make shelters from a section or two of parachute canopy, as well as water collection reservoirs, signal panels and dozens of other things. Then there were the hundreds of feet of nylon cord. It could be braided into ropes, used to tie branches together to make hundreds of things, all of which were described in the survival manual that should be in his parachute harness and another in his survival vest. He even had another survival beeper in the pack. Just a beeper, not a communications radio, but it would serve as a backup. No, getting rid of the parachute was a bad idea; he would be better off to keep it.

When he had rolled the parachute and suspension lines into a fairly compact shape, Toby took a piece of line and tied it into a bundle. He un-slung his M-16 from off his shoulder where he had been keeping it ready in case someone appeared in the darkness, then picked up the parachute with the other hand. There seemed to be a tree-line less than a hundred yards away. He could barely make it out in the dim light of the stars. The chalky white of the limestone increased visibility somewhat. He thought about getting his carbide lamp out of the pack, but decided against that idea. Not until he knew just where he was and whether or not anyone was around.

Toby felt somewhat confused and unsure of himself, or of what he should do. There really wasn't much he could do; not in the darkness and not knowing where he was. He had no idea of the terrain. If he wasn't careful, he could fall off a cliff. Now that would be a damned shame, to make it this far without being injured then die or get hurt like that!

As soon as he was in the tree-line, he decided to make his way just a little distance into the woods, then find somewhere to bed down. What about snakes? No, it was too cool for them. They would be down in the valleys, where it was warmer. Then he remembered that there were tigers in Southeast Asia. But he also knew that they would in all likelihood leave him alone. He wished he could use a light. What about the red lens on his angle-head? Yeah! That would work. It was in his cave pack. He unbuckled the fastening strap and pulled it out. Opening his flight jacket, he stuck the flashlight inside and turned it on, using his body to conceal the beam in case anyone might be close enough to see him. Toby unscrewed the end and selected the red lens from the assortment of red, blue, white and diffused lens covers that were hidden there.

With the red beam he could see where he was going. He looked around and saw that he was in an area of evergreens. That was a surprise; he had not realized there were evergreens in Laos. But he was used to the tropical rain forest down in Thailand. Here, he was in the mountains. And he knew there was a lot of limestone - and evergreens thrive around limestone.

When he had retreated far enough into the trees that he thought he would be safe, he began looking around for some place to hide. What he needed was some underbrush, but the evergreens were so thick there wasn't any that he could see. There were rocks, though. Limestone slabs and boulders were scattered here and there. He found a pile that looked large enough that he might be able to conceal himself between the rocks. This would have to do. All he could really hope for was that they weren't looking for him. When it was daylight and he could have a better idea of just where he was, he would take stock of his situation and figure out just what he should do. Maybe he would be in a place where he could call in a rescue force. Maybe he would be lucky.

Toby settled himself on the parachute; there was no doubt now, he would keep it with him. He lay back and looked up at a patch of stars through an opening in the trees above him. He thought about Sharon, and their lovemaking back in Bangkok. It seemed so long ago. But it had been only a little over a week ago that he had first seen her come out of the room next to his and walk down the hall to where he waited by the elevator. Less than thirty-six hours ago he had kissed her good-bye at the airline terminal. Well, there was one thing he could say. Even if he did die in a combat zone, at least he had had one good fling with a round-eye! That was more than a lot of guys could say, no doubt about that.

Thinking of Sharon and their nights in Bangkok helped Toby to take his mind off his present plight. The cool mountain air and cold rocks penetrated his fatigues. He wrapped a panel of the parachute around him; the nylon was an effective insulator. Finally he drifted off to sleep.

Chapter Seven

Toby awoke the next morning with a start; a heavy machine gun was firing somewhere not very far away. Had he been found? Then the gunfire was drowned out by the high-pitched whine of jet engines. He recognized the sound of an F-4 - he had heard them so many times at Ubon. The Phantom's whine grew louder, than momentarily became muffled, then was loud again. There was a series of explosions, the noise sounding as if it came from somewhere very far away. He realized what he was hearing; an air-strike against something down in the gorge below the ridge. The guns were firing from the opposite side of the gorge. He was thankful none seemed to be on his ridge.

"Welcome to the war, Toby," Carter thought to himself as he rolled out of the parachute paneling. Before he peered over the top of the boulders by which he had slept, he reached out and picked up his loaded M-16. Cautiously, he peered around first one side and then the other. Something stirred within his vision. A man? No; relief swept over him when he saw a doe and fawn browsing among the pine needles not fifty feet away. If the deer were there, then there must not be any humans close enough for them to smell. His own scent lay between the rocks, close to the ground, and had yet to reach their nostrils. He raised himself out of his nook and stepped from behind the boulder. The deer raised her head, took a whiff, then whirled on her hind legs and galloped away. Her fawn followed behind on spindly legs.

He was hungry. It had been close to eight hours since he had eaten anything. There were some cereal bars in the survival packet in his vest. No - he might need those later. He decided instead to settle for one of the candy bars he had stashed in his jacket pocket. He pulled out a Three Musketeers. While he ate the candy, he thought about his situation.

There was one thing for sure; the presence of the antiaircraft guns across the valley ruled out a possible early rescue from where he was. No helicopter would be able to get in during daylight and pick him up. And he knew that rescue missions just weren't flown at night. He would have to move. The question was - where too? His survival vest contained maps of Southeast Asia and a compass. Before he did anything, he needed to find out where he was.

First, he needed to find out on which side of the valley was his ridge. To his dismay, when he took out the compass the needle pointed to the right. The valley was in front of him; he was on the east side. That meant the Annamite mountains were behind him. On the other side was South Vietnam, but no telling how many North Vietnamese troops lay between him and friendly forces even if he were able to cross the mountains. He wished he had landed on the opposite side, even if that was where the guns were. At least he would have been able to start making his way west toward the Thai border. When he was far enough from the Trail, then he could call in a rescue force. That is, if his radio was working. It had been the last time he checked it, but that was before he had hit the ground so hard.

Toby pulled the radio from its pouch on the vest. He extended the antenna and turned the switch to "receive" then put it to his ear. There was the welcome sound of static. At least his batteries were okay. The one in the radio should last for several days as long as he used it sparingly. And there was a spare in the vest and the beeper in the parachute harness.

He took stock of his situation. He was in Laos somewhere south of Mu Gia and north of Tche Pone and on the east side of a valley. So far, that was all he knew. Looking at his map, he reckoned the stream in the valley was possibly a tributary of the Xe Bongfai. There was an abandoned airfield not far from the village of B Phanop. Rats! If he was near there, it meant that North Vietnam lay on the other side of the mountains! He was further north than he had thought. To get to South Vietnam would mean traveling south, then east. He had better come up with some other plan.

He looked at the map again. Suddenly, a word on the map leaped out at him - k-a-r-s-t. Shoot, why hadn't he seen that sooner? He was smack in the middle of a Laotian karst region! The rock he had landed on last night was limestone, as had been the pile of boulders he had spent the night in. There were probably caves nearby - big ones too, since he knew the region he was in got plenty of rainfall. That was what he had said he would do if he went down; find a cave and hide in it.

Let's see; what did he have with him in the way of survival equipment? What would help him in a cave? He knew his carbide lamp was in his pack, along with more than two pounds of carbide. That would last for several days, as long as he used it sparingly. He had an old cloth cap with a mount for the lamp in his pack; that would free his hands for other uses. There was a flashlight and four spare batteries in his cave pack, plus another attached to his vest. There was a packet of candles in his bag and two packets of waterproof matches. In the survival vest was another box of matches in a metal container. What he didn't have was coveralls and dry clothes; but, he had his parachute. The nylon would be useful for many things.

For weapons, he had an M-16 and .38. The vest had a couple of pouches filled with spare pistol cartridges and he had two hundred rounds of .223 ammo in his cave pack. Then he had his issue survival knife; it was strapped to the front of his vest. There was also a pocket knife and small sharpening stone; he could use that to start fires when his supply of matches ran out. What about food? in the vest he knew there was a can of survival rations; they had gone over the contents during the various survival courses he had taken. There were a couple of high-energy candy bars, a couple of meat bars and the cereal bars, all sealed in a metal container. He would save that for a last resort. Then there was the canned food he had in his cave pack. There were even a couple of cans of Sterno he had picked up in the BX. And he had a full canteen of water, although that shouldn't be a problem. It rained nearly every day this time of year. There should be water purification tablets in his vest. For signaling purposes there was a mirror, along with the pen-gun flares and regular flares as well. There were six tracer rounds in his vest, separate from the other pistol cartridges, though right now they were useless.

The sight of the deer was encouraging; there probably were other animals around as well and maybe fish in the streams, if there were any streams. After all, this was karst, a region where streams tend to disappear and flow underground. There should be berries and other fruits around, although he wasn't sure just what varieties grew this far into the mountains.

Toby carefully repacked the parachute into its pack. His parachute was a chest pack, a new innovation with Blind Bat crews because the loadmasters had to move around so much in the back of the airplane. Wearing a regular backpack made loading flares a real chore, especially when the pilot was jinking around to avoid flak. The damn things tripled in weight then, making them weigh close to a hundred pounds! That was why Chuck Loomis in the 817th suggested Blind Bat crews be issued chest packs; the loadmasters could wear the harness and stow the packs where they could reach them. The new harnesses were easier to modify for his cave pack. Even though the canopy was somewhat smaller - that was one reason he hit the ground so hard - it weighed less than the backpack canopies. He appreciated that now that he planned to take the parachute with him.

After binding the pack with a piece of nylon 550-cord cut from one of the suspension lines, Toby clipped it to the harness and slung it over his shoulder. He slung the cave pack over his other shoulder, took the M-16 in his right hand and prepared to move out. But before he went too far, he wanted to take a look into the gorge. He doubted that anyone would see him; no one knew he was there. At least he hoped not. He skirted the edge of the open area in which he had landed - he saw that it was solid limestone, just as he had thought. Taking advantage of the shadows of the pines, he made his way to the edge of the cliff, venturing just close enough that he could see into the valley below.

Smoke was still rising from craters left by the bombs the fighters had dropped less than an hour before, but already he could see construction crews working to fill the holes. He saw what they had been bombing. A road crossed over the rather large river that flowed through the gorge. He estimated the gorge to be half a mile wide, maybe more. It looked closer, but then distances were deceiving in the mountains. He scanned the opposite ridge.

Hold it! What was that? Right at the crest of the ridge he could see figures. Damn! They were gun crews! He could see at least four separate positions. He wished he had a 30/06 with a scope. He could pick off the gun crews one by one and they would never know what hit them. He thought about taking a shot with his M-16 but realized that would be a futile move. The M-16 was a fine rifle, but not for long shots. What had they said about it back at Pope when he first qualified with it? That it was designed to pack a lot of power at close ranges and for rapid fire. He would just have to make note of where the guns were located and let the intelligence people know about them when he got back - **if** he got back!

What time is it? He looked at his watch; the big hand was on eleven and the little hand was on ten. It was almost ten o'clock, but that was Ubon time. There was a one-hour time difference between Thailand and Vietnam. It was probably 0850 where he was. What difference did it really make, anyway? Toby set off down the ridge line. The cool, nighttime temperatures had given way to the heat of a Southeast Asian day. Soon, Toby's fatigues were dripping wet with sweat.

As he got further away from the cliff the rocks were covered by humus. Here and there was exposed limestone. The terrain reminded him of the limestone along the Tennessee River at home, except the hills here were more like East Tennessee then the rolling ones in West Tennessee where he had grown up. Home! A sudden sadness overcame him at the thought of home. Would he ever see those Tennessee hills again? Right now his prospects were somewhat dim, especially since he was right in the midst of the North Vietnamese infiltration routes. Were he anywhere in Laos but where he was, a helicopter rescue would be almost immediate. But not here, not with so many antiaircraft guns and NVA troops around, not to mention the Pathet Lao.

The thought of the Pathet Lao made him shiver. The Laotian breed of communists were noted for ruthlessness that surpassed even the Viet Cong. He had heard stories of downed airmen who fell into their hands. One rescued pilot came back with tales of hearing his back-seater being skinned alive! At least the North Vietnamese would send their prisoners north to Hanoi. The Pathet Lao were unpredictable. They might turn any man they captured over to the NVA - or they might just as soon torture him to death. No, he definitely did not want to be captured by the Pathet Lao, that was certain.

Toby was deep in the forest, under tall, spreading trees that stretched a hundred feet and more into the air. They reminded him of the huge white oak, hickory nut and beech trees under which he had spent so many boyhood hours hunting squirrels. Suddenly a realization dawned upon him: Sure, he was thirteen thousand miles away from home, but in a way he was home. He was in the forest, a different kind of forest to be sure, but still a forest. Toby Carter had spent most of his life in the woods. If there was any place where he was home, it was in the woods. Had he been in the rice paddies of Vietnam or the swamplands along the Mekong he might have felt he was in an alien land. But he was in the Laotian highlands in almost the exact same kind of terrain he had known as far back as he could remember. He thought about the line from the Davy Crockett song, about being raised in the woods and knowing all the trees; that was him. And like Crockett, Toby Carter was a Tennessean.

A loud noise almost directly overhead made him start. An explosion? What was that rustling noise? Then he knew - it was the sound of thunder, followed by rain starting to hit the leaves high above him. The rising temperatures had caused the moisture to rise up the slopes of the mountains, forming cumulous clouds over the ridges. The clouds were developing into tropical thunderstorms. Soon the drops would reach him on the ground. It was the rainy season in Laos, when it rained every day without fail. More than two hours had passed since he set off down the ridge; it was mid-day, time for the daily buildup of thunderboomers over the mountains. He had been in the shade of the forest canopy and hadn't realized that clouds had obscured the sun. Where could he find shelter? Then he remembered the parachute; a panel stretched between two trees could keep the rain off of him.

Quickly, he cut a length of 550-cord from a suspension line, then tied it between two trees. Over the taut nylon cord Toby threw a section of parachute cloth. The rain was already beginning to reach the ground through openings in the forest canopy. The young airman fastened the four corners of the piece of cloth to other trees with pieces of suspension cord. Now he had a rude tent, but one that would at least protect him from the rain. His gear was under the tent. He crawled beneath the nylon canopy and lay down on another piece of nylon.

For his shelter, Toby had used one of the olive green sections of nylon. It would blend in with his surroundings better than the orange and white panels. Many downed airmen would probably have tried to get rid of the parachute entirely - Toby's first thoughts had been to do just that. Now he reasoned that it was very doubtful that the communists patrolled the ridges where he was. There were gun crews on the opposite ridge, but they were right on the edge of the cliff overlooking the roadways in the gorge. He was far enough from the gorge now that there was little danger from being discovered. He had seen no sign of any human anywhere.

The rain lasted for over an hour. It poured down onto the trees in torrents, but the canopy above kept much of the water up in the trees. Still, the ground was covered with rivulets of water. He had chosen to make his shelter over a nearly flat boulder, which allowed him to remain above the rain-soaked ground. Moving through the forest and staying dry after the rain ended would be a problem he would have to deal with. He looked up at the nylon shelter over his head. Hey! That was it. He pulled out a section of dry nylon - another greenish brown panel - and began fashioning a poncho from it. It would be impossible to stay entirely dry, but at least he could avoid getting soaking wet.

After the rain stopped, Toby remained in his shelter for a time - until the drip from the leaves overhead began to decrease in volume and intensity. Now wearing his improvised pancho, Toby took down his shelter after shaking the nylon so most of the water would be thrown off. He set out through the forest again. Water ran everywhere in streams of varying size. The streams ran into each other and became larger as the water followed its natural course of taking the path of least resistance. Then his ears detected a new sound above the dripping from overhead and the rippling streams. He knew the sound - falling water. Was he nearer the edge of the cliff than he thought? Curious, he followed the sound as it grew louder in his ears. All of the streams seemed to be flowing in the same direction. They all flowed together into a creek that was now filled to overflowing. The rushing waters of the creek were running toward the falling water sound which first caught his attention.

Toby followed the creek; he judged the distance to be about a hundred yards. Then he came to the source of the sound. The rushing muddy waters of the rain-swollen creek disappeared into a crevice in a limestone slab, then fell an unknown distance to splash onto rocks somewhere far beneath the surface of the earth. A cave! There was a cave beneath him! But the problem was that there was no way to get into it. If he had enough rope and some rock-climbing gear...but no, the opening wasn't large enough. He could tell that much just by looking at it. Even if he had rappelling equipment and could get into the hole, there was no way he would go into it when there was this much water pouring in. A person would drown before reaching the bottom, or be so wet then they got there that hypothermia would kill them in the cool air of the cave. But if there was a cave beneath him - and there definitely was - it might be possible to find another way into it that would not be so wet. He would have to do some poking around to see what he could find - and hope the enemy didn't find him in the meantime. Toby sat down on a rock and watched the flowing waters as they disappeared into the crevasse.

Now, where would be the best place to find a way into the cave? For a moment he forgot where he was, that he was a downed airman in a war on the other side of the world from his natural home. He pondered the problem. He was on top of a ridge. More than likely the whole ridge was limestone; it was probably one giant honeycomb with caverns leading everywhere, especially if it rained like it just had every day during the rainy season. The cave beneath him would be huge, probably as big or bigger than any he had even seen. Maybe even bigger than Flint Ridge! How long was Flint Ridge now? Let's see, what had he read about the huge cave system that lay just across a valley from Mammoth Cave? Fifty miles and still growing? Some people thought it was at least a hundred miles long, and possibly even longer.

He would have to look for another insurgence, an opening where a surface stream flowed underground. Any water that went in would doubtlessly make its way toward the valley floor, or maybe even to the water table beneath the valley. The geology of the region was a mystery to him, other than that his maps labeled the area as karst. That term alone told him there was a lot of limestone, with disappearing streams, sinkholes and caverns. No doubt about the disappearing streams! He was looking at one.

What time is it? Toby looked at his watch. It was late afternoon, 1630 hours local time. He reckoned he had spent close to two hours in his shelter during the rain and waiting for the dripping to slow. Then he had hiked for close to an hour. When did it get dark in this region? He probably had another two hours of daylight, then maybe half an hour or so of twilight, if that. He needed to find some place to spend the night, a place where he would be able to rest without worrying about discovery. He could look for cave entrances tomorrow.

Toby walked south along the ridge, away from Mu Gia and in the direction of Cambodia. From studying his map he knew there were valleys to the south that led east, through the mountains toward South Vietnam. He knew also that those were the routes the NVA troops and supply convoys took as they made their way into South Vietnam. His chances of making his way to safety along those routes were not too good. But now that he knew there was probably a cave system beneath him, he felt somewhat better. Perhaps he could even find a way across the valley. If he could get on the other side, then he might be able to move far enough away from the infiltration routes to call in a helicopter.

It was almost nightfall before he found a dry place in which to spend the night. A limestone bluff rose above the forest floor. A rock outcropping had kept the rain away from the rocks beneath it. He wouldn't need to put up a shelter in case it did rain; the rock above would keep him dry.

He was hungry again. There had been no sign whatsoever of the presence of any other humans on the ridge - any that were there would be his enemy. Maybe it would be safe to light one of the Sterno cans and heat up a can of beanie weenies or something. The Sterno burned with a tiny blue flame; he would have little trouble concealing it so it wouldn't be detectable. He could heat some water as well. There was a packet of tea bags in his pack, along with some instant coffee.

Food would be a major problem if he weren't rescued pretty soon. There was probably enough stuff in his pack and in the survival kit for him to get by for a week - maybe longer. If only he weren't in the middle of a combat zone! And in a "secret" war to boot. As far as the Air Force was concerned, he wasn't even there. What would they tell his parents? No doubt by this time they had been notified that he was missing. But then again, maybe not. He had been on the ground now for less than twenty-four hours.

Back to the subject of food: There seemed to be plenty of game around - deer, squirrels, monkeys and birds. It would have been simple enough to have shot the doe this morning. But the sound of a gunshot was sure to attract attention of a kind he did not want. Maybe he could take advantage of an air strike - kill a deer while the antiaircraft guns on the opposite side of the valley were going off. No, the noise of the jets and firing would probably spook the game. That doe this morning hadn't seemed disturbed, though. He hadn't seen her until after the F-4's had departed the area. It was a thought, after all.

The beans and Vienna sausages were tasty to someone with an empty stomach. Their warmth made his belly feel good. He heated water in the canteen cup while he ate. Gosh!! The sun had gone down and there was a definite chill in the air. While the cool air was a definite relief compared to the heat and humidity of Thailand - and South Vietnam for that matter - his clothing was not designed for cold weather. He was glad he still had the parachute to wrap up in.

At least the cool air meant there was little likelihood of encountering snakes this high up in the mountains. Toby hated snakes; he always had. There had been copperheads all over the place when he was growing up. His father had taught the children to avoid any and all snakes so they would not be attracted to a poisonous variety. Southeast Asia teemed with snakes of every kind in the lower lying regions. Thailand was known as the Land of the King Cobra, after all! But that was down around Thakli, at least three hundred miles away. There were also Kraits in Southeast Asia, but they were a creature of the cane fields, not of the highland forests.

What was that? A faint droning sound reached his ear drums. He knew instantly what it was; he had heard that same distinctive sound dozens of times. The droning of four turboprop engines identified the source of the noise as a C-130, an A-model from the sound. Toby realized it must be the nightly Blind Bat mission approaching its target area along the Ho Chi Minh Trail - the same area Preston's crew had been assigned last night. The sound grew louder; the airplane was approaching his position. Soon the sky would light up as the crew began dispensing flares in what he now knew to be a futile attempt to detect communist traffic on the Trail below. He wished he were up there, knowing clean sheets awaited him back at Ubon, rather than here where his bed would be a slab of limestone.

Where were the other guys? Had they all been picked up this morning at first light? They certainly should have been; everyone except him and Preston had gotten out of the airplane at least twenty miles from the NVA-infested infiltration routes. And what about the pilot? Preston had been out of the cockpit and on his way toward the ramp when Toby jumped, and only then when he saw his aircraft commander motioning to him to get the hell out of the airplane. Preston had to have jumped right behind him. He would have come down in the same general area. Was he somewhere on this same ridge as he, trying to determine the best plan of action for getting far enough away to call in a helicopter? Or had he had the misfortune to land in the gorge, as Toby almost did? The pilot could have been captured - or killed. Or he might have gotten lucky and landed on the other ridge beyond the enemy positions. Captain Preston might be making his way west, away from the Trail, just as Toby hoped to soon be able to do himself.

A sudden glare through an open spot in the forest canopy caught his eye. He knew instantly what it was; the flareship crew had dropped their first string of flares. From his position under three hundred feet of foliage, the glare of the flares came only as an occasional glimpse. That was good; at least he would be able to sleep. What about the damn fighters? They would be coming soon, no doubt about that. Every night at least three flights would be fragged to this section of the Trail. The problem was that the F-4 crews couldn't hit the side of a barn with a baseball bat! At night, they were as liable to drop their bombs on the ridge as in the valley. He could be a victim of bombs dropped by his own side! That thought was even more disturbing than the possibility of death itself.

He wrapped himself in the parachute canopy and lay down on the limestone slab. The pack would serve as his pillow. The M-16 was by his side; his right arm was through the sling. He ran his left arm through one opening of the survival vest. It was not the most comfortable way in the world to sleep, but he wanted to be sure he had the rifle and vest where he could get to them quickly in the event he had to make a hasty departure. Had he been able, he would have kept the vest on. But the pistol holster was in back; the .38 would have been digging into his back all night. Toby wished he had been wearing a web belt instead. But then again, if he had he might have lost the whole thing when he jumped - pistol, canteen, knife and ammunition. As it was, the canteen was in his cave pack and the pistol and knife were attached to the nylon vest.

Sharon. He hadn't thought of her since leaving his makeshift shelter after the rain had stopped. She would be back on her shift at Nha Trang by now. "Maybe I'll see you at Kadena." Those had been her parting words. She was considering asking for a delay enroute on Okinawa when she left Vietnam for "the world." If she did, she would spend a week on the Rock. He would take leave and they would spend the time shacked up in a hotel in Koza, a repeat of their R&R in Bangkok. She had given him her DEROS, 1 November, his birthday. "I'll give you a birthday present you'll never forget." That had been her reply when he mentioned that she would be leaving Vietnam on his birthday. Now he wondered if he would ever get back to Okinawa at all, let alone in time to put in for leave for that week if she decided to do it.

The sounds of an air strike came to him through the forest. Good. From the sounds, the target was some distance away. Far enough that perhaps he would be immune to the possibility of any stray bombs falling on his head. He did hear something hitting leaves overhead occasionally. At first he thought it was rain but then he realized what he was hearing. Shrapnel from spent antiaircraft shells falling back to earth after exploding two miles in the air. With that knowledge, and thoughts of his Bangkok orgy with Sharon Craft in his mind, Toby Carter feel asleep for the second time in the remote mountains of a little known land called Laos.

Chapter Eight

Toby Carter spent a restless first full night on the ground in the heart of enemy-occupied Laos. His sleep was frequently interrupted by air strikes against the infiltration routes in the valley. He had not realized the tremendous amount of noise generated by the various elements involved in combat - the belching roar of the antiaircraft guns, the whining screams of the fighters, the explosions of the bombs and rockets. The din was almost unbearable, even from his position at least three miles from the gorge where the fighters vented their fury.

One of Toby's main concerns during the night was that one of the fighters would drop its load well wide of the target and hit his ridge. He was acutely aware of the almost total lack of accuracy exhibited by the fighter pilots. Maybe they could hit targets in daytime but, at night, under the light of flares, the pilots were lucky if they came close enough to a target to throw dirt on it when the bombs went off. There were some exceptions, like the Navy A-4 and A-6 crews from the carriers out on Yankee Station. As for the Air Force jet jocks, especially the F-4 drivers, anything they hit was strictly by accident.

Occasionally, the attacking aircraft would be accompanied by the throaty roar of reciprocating engines and large propellers. When he heard those sounds he could go back to sleep without worry. He knew the A-26 and A-1 pilots knew their stuff; he had no fear that one would get excited and pickle his load three miles from the target. But most of the attacking aircraft were jets, and the knowledge of their almost complete lack of accuracy kept him awake during their attacks. Toby's night was practically sleepless. "How does Charley stand this crap?" he wondered.

Finally, some three hours after midnight, there was a lull in the battle. For about four or five hours he was able to rest virtually undisturbed. It was midmorning when the sounds of the jungle - birds singing, monkeys howling and chirping, deer snorting - roused him from his slumber. He awoke with a start, momentarily confused by his surroundings, followed by a profound feeling of sadness that overcame him when he remembered where he was. The hills of Tennessee seemed not just thousands of miles, but centuries away from the Laotian ridge on which he was virtually trapped.

There had been no rain during the night but the foliage was wet from dew and mist. Traces of fog floated among the trees, remnants of the mist that had filled the valley and covered the ridges during the early morning hours and prevented further air strikes. Now it was beginning to burn off as the sun's rays penetrated through the top of low-lying clouds, causing them to dissipate, revealing a turquoise sky. The jungle came alive as the sun made its presence known. Toby was amazed at the many life forms around him - everything from tiny insects to deer. What about tigers? He remembered that there were big cats in the mountains. No, if there was a cat around, the animals would let each other know.

What was his plan of action for today? Basing his assumptions on the previous day, he reckoned that he had about three hours before the daily deluge commenced. It would rain for an hour or two and drip for a couple more, then things would begin to dry. He needed to get his show on the road, to begin searching for a cave entrance, sink-holes or other signs, then find someplace to erect his shelter at the first indication of the gathering storm. Carter reached into his pack and pulled out a cereal bar; he ate it just as it was. There wasn't time to boil it in water and make a gruel.

Toby decided that since it was apparent he would never be able to cross the gorge and it was highly unlikely that he would be able to walk down and across the mountains to South Vietnam, his only hope lay in finding some way to get across the valley without being seen. That the valley teemed with hundreds of North Vietnamese ruled out the possibility of crossing on the surface, at least in daylight. Road traffic at night meant that a night crossing would be equally difficult. The one possibility was that of a subterranean route. His map showed the area where he was as karst; he had seen evidence of caves beneath the ridge already. He had his light - thank God he hadn't quit carrying it as he had thought to do numerous times! If he came across a cave -and there was now no doubt but that he would - he had the means and the experience to venture into it.

Having studied everything he could find about caves since he was old enough to read, Toby knew that his best chances of finding an entrance would be to get down into the valley and find the resurgence where the underground waters emerged. But he couldn't get into the valley; it was filled with North Vietnamese soldiers! His next option was to find an insurgence, an upstream entrance where a stream began its underground passage. He had already found one, but it wasn't large enough for him to get into. Even if he found one, there was the ever-present danger of flooding from the daily cloudbursts. Caves are made by water action and serve as underground water conduits. Just as surface streams flood, caves do likewise, often becoming completely filled with raging torrents of cold water that can kill a person by either drowning or hypothermia. His hope was that the cavern he was certain to find would be big enough that it could handle the runoff from the daily thunderstorms without flooding.

He would search for a wash, a natural depression on the ridge through which runoff waters would follow their natural path of least resistance toward the water table beneath the earth. The stream in such a valley would either run down the side of the hill to the valley floor, drop over a cliff as a waterfall or disappear into the reaches of a cave. That the ridge was largely limestone was apparent; an insurgence into a cave was almost a certainty. Toby packed his parachute and other gear, slung it over his shoulder and continued moving south along the ridge.

As he made his way slowly down the ridge, Toby saw evidence of caves. Sinks - depressions in the surface - were everywhere. Some had openings at the bottom that led into the earth. He checked several for air currents flowing either in or out, a sure sign of a cave below. But there was no air movement; all appeared to be "blind" pits. Had he been back in Tennessee and on an outing with some of the cavers he had met, he no doubt would have climbed down into some of the pits just to check them out, to see where they went. But he lacked the proper equipment, had no buddy to keep an eye on him and was short on a most important element - time.

The elevation of the ridge-line seemed to be lowering. Without an altimeter he couldn't be sure, but it seemed to be. That could be good and it could be bad; he might be coming to a valley on the ridge or he might be dropping down into the main river valley along which the infiltration route ran. His map wasn't drawn to a small enough scale to show the true topography of the land. He could only draw a general idea. It seemed that the ridge he was on would follow the river valley for quite some distance, but then he couldn't be sure until he had walked it.

It was around noon when Toby came to a large depression on the top of the ridge. He knew what he had found - a sink. If there was any indication that there might be cave below, this was it. He began searching for holes that might lead into the depths below. He found nothing. In spite of his failure, the presence of a sink was encouraging. Water ran in but didn't run out; it had to seep into the rock and down into the limestone that made up the ridge. That meant there had to be cave below. He almost forgot where he was; in his mind he was transported across thirteen thousand miles of ocean and land and placed back in the hills along the Tennessee River.

Maybe he ought to drop lower on the ridge. He was some distance above the cliffs that made up the walls of the gorge. Or maybe he ought to check the side away from the gorge. That was it! The cave probably started on the east side of the ridge and ran down toward the river - or hopefully under the valley. If it did, then maybe he could find another cavern coming in from the opposite ridge. But first he had to get into the valley and, before that, he had to find a way into the cave that had to be beneath his feet.

There were more sinks on the top of the ridge, even some open pits. He wasn't looking for pits, though. Toby wanted to find a more or less horizontal entrance that wouldn't require a lot of climbing. If all else failed, then he might have to check out some of the pits. But a pit could be a one-way street without a partner to keep watch above and help him out when the time came - or go for help if he needed it. Here, he was alone; as alone as one could ever be.

His map indicated that it was some distance to the next river valley to the east. That meant the streams all flowed underground, a sure sign of a cave below. He came across more sinks, and more exposed limestone. Then he came to a place where there were no trees, only solid limestone with no earth covering. "A helicopter could get in here," he said to himself aloud. But no, he was still too close to the gorge and the hundreds of communist troops and workers along the Trail. Any helicopter crew who came to get him would have to either fly across the Trail from the west or across North Vietnam to the east. Either way would be almost certain death for the low and slow-flying Jolly Greens. Even if they did manage to get in and pick him up, they would have to run the same gauntlet of guns on the way out. There was one other rescue possibility, but then he wasn't even sure if that capability even existed in Vietnam.

Toby Carter suddenly forgot all about rescue possibilities; below him a hundred feet or so was another sink, but this one had an ominous black shadow on one side. He was too far away to tell for sure, but it looked like an obvious cave entrance from where he was. At any other place and any other time, he would have quickly scrambled down the side of the hill and into the sink, but not here. He had seen no one, but there was always the ever-present possibility that Charley might be on the ridge. He knew that the VC in the south sometimes hid in caves and there were reports of guns in cave entrances. He would have to approach with extreme caution.

What about snakes? He had yet to see one and he didn't think there were any this high up, but there was always that possibility as well. In this part of the world, the leg-less kind could be as dangerous as the two-legged snake. He un-slung his M-16 and brought it to a ready position where it would be ready to fire no matter what he happened to encounter. A shadow fell across the sun. He looked up and saw the gathering clouds of the daily thundershower. He didn't want to venture into an unknown cave when it was threatening an imminent rainstorm. Drowning was just as sure a form of death as a bullet or snakebite. Maybe he had better wait a while before going into the cave; the cave he was sure was there.

Toby pulled out a parachute panel, an orange one this time, and stretched it between two trees, facing it so he could watch the sinkhole from inside. He wanted to see how much rainwater ran into the sink. A peal of thunder rolled across the hills; the first drops of rain began to fall as he was putting the finishing touches on the shelter. "Just in time," he spoke out loud to himself. There was no one else to talk too.

The rain came down in sheets, just as it had yesterday. But today he was more in the open; yesterday he had been in the forest with three-hundred foot trees and their canopy of leaves between the rain and him. Visibility dropped to less than half a mile as the rain came down in veritable torrents. If it rained like this every day in the mountains, there should be sizable caverns beneath the ground. He looked for the sink, hoping to determine just how much water was going into the cave -: if there was a cave entrance there. Sheets of rain made a veil that totally obscured his vision.

Just as suddenly as it had begun, the rain stopped. One minute the sky was black and angry, pouring reservoirs of water onto the earth; the next the sun was peeking around a cloud and the only water falling was the droplets from the leaves of the trees under which he had pitched his tent. He looked down into the sinkhole. There was some water running into it but not the huge river he had feared. Most of the runoff seemed to be flowing toward another sinkhole he had not seen before. It was further down the side of the ridge, but probably flowed into the same cave.

He waited in his shelter until the runoff had slowed to a trickle. While he waited, a low-flying F-4 swooped right down the middle of the ridge above him. The sudden appearance of fellow Americans thrilled him, then a feeling of despair came over him as he remembered that they were up there, while he was down here. They could have been on the other side of the world. What were they doing? He had seen no ordinance slung beneath the wings, only two large pylon tanks. Then he remembered; RF-4's made reconnaissance flights over the Trail at all hours of the day. He had seen a recon flight - but what were they doing over the ridge? Looking for guns?

After the sun had been shining for about an hour, Toby decided the flow of water had reduced to the point that he could think about checking out the cave. Quite a bit was still flowing into the other sink, but he was not interested in it at this point. The temperature had climbed with the appearance of the sun; the moisture caused increased humidity. He took all his possessions and climbed down the side of the hill toward the sink. As he neared it the air become cooler; he knew from a lifetime of being around them that cool air (except in winter, then it would be warm) was a sure sign of a cave. When he came to the side of the collapsed limestone that made up the sinkhole, there was no longer any doubt. There was definitely a cave entrance here. A gaping blackness under a limestone ledge attracted him like a powerful magnet.

Toby reached into his pack and brought out his old Justrite light. The bottom was already filled with carbide; he put the top under a rivulet of water. In no more than a second the tiny compartment was full. He reached back into the pack for the special cap he had been carrying along with the lamp for almost two years now. On the front of the cap was a bracket for attaching a carbide lamp just like the one he had in his hand. He wished he had a miner's helmet, but the hard hats were too large and bulky to fit in his pack. At one time he had thought about putting a bracket on the front of his flight helmet; transport crews wore a special lightweight one instead of the more familiar helmet worn by jet jocks. Then he remembered the soft cap and picked one up at a local hardware store in Sanford, the next town up the road from Spring Lake and Ft. Bragg. That was before he got orders to Okinawa, while he was still at Pope. While it wouldn't protect his head, at least it would leave his hands free for climbing.

A sound of tumbling water came from inside the cave entrance. Probably the water coming in through the other sink, he reckoned. Cool air was coming out of the entrance. After putting the cap on his head, Toby gripped the lamp with his left hand and held his right over the reflector. Acetylene gas built up under his hand. He quickly pulled his palm across the striker. A loud "boom" gave notice that the lamp had ignited. "Have to watch that," he spoke under his breath to himself. He had forgotten about the noise that sometimes accompanied the lamp's ignition. A blue and yellow flame erupted from the tip of the lamp. It well should have; he had been cleaning it religiously without using it for two years. And for years before that when he did use it almost every week.

The flame flickered in the considerable breeze that came out of the mouth of the cave. Air movement in the cave entrance was another sign of a considerable cavern inside. As he stepped into the entrance, a feeling of excitement came over him. He always felt that way when going into a new passage where he had never been before. Come to think of it, he'd felt the same way the first time he had ventured into Sharon. They had joked about it later. For a moment he thought about her; she would be back at Nha Trang, probably sleeping or sunbathing before her shift that night. He had no time to dwell on her right now, not if he ever wanted to see her again - or anyone else for that matter.

It took a moment for his eyes to become accustomed to the dim light inside the cave. He was in what is known as the twilight zone, an area where outside light illuminates the first few feet of a cavern. Technically, he was not inside the cave as yet; according to the speleologist, a true cave must contain total darkness. As the retina of his eyes opened and allowed him to see, he looked around. The entrance way was large enough to stand up in. To his surprise, the floor was mostly dry, although there was a small stream off to one side where the water that had flowed into the sink came in. From up ahead came the sound of rippling water, an indication of a sizable stream flowing into the cave. Should he take his weapon and parachute with him? There were plenty of places to stow them here. No, he had better take everything further inside. Someone just might decide to start poking around in the cave and find it.

He rounded a corner and saw that the ceiling was lowering. The stream flowed in one direction but a dryer passage led off to one side. He opted for the dry one; if he had to crawl, at least he wanted to stay as dry as he could. Maybe he ought to think about making some kind of outer garment from the parachute, one that would help to keep him dry and at the same time conserve his body heat. It was cool in the cave, as cool as the night air. Without a thermometer it was hard to tell, but he estimated the temperature at somewhere around 55 degrees.

Toby had slung the M-16 over his back; now he pushed the rolled-up parachute and pack in front of him. He was still wearing the harness over his survival vest, as he had been doing ever since he bailed out. Fortunately, the passage was high enough that he could stay pretty much on hands and knees. He wished for knee-pads. That was something else he might be able to make from parts of the parachute.

In spite of the military equipment he was wearing, Toby felt just as he had back under the Tennessee ridges. The yellow glow of his carbide lamp brought a feeling of warmth over the damp place as it penetrated the darkness. Here and there he saw stalactites and flow-stone, indications that this passage did not flood. That was good; he had been worried that he might not be able to stay in the cave for long periods because of the daily thunderstorms.

He continued crawling for about three body lengths until he came to an intersection. One passage led to the right, the other continued on ahead. He exhaled and watched his breath as it drifted in the direction he was going, then accelerated as the vapor was suddenly wafted along by a stronger breeze from the right. He would go that way; the breeze was coming from inside the cave. The sound of running water was stronger from that direction as well.

His lamp illuminated a small tubular passage, one that could easily accommodate his person - even on hands and knees. Toby crawled into it, still pushing the parachute ahead of him. He crawled for what he guessed to be about fifty feet; the sound of running water became increasingly louder every foot he crawled. The airflow in the passage was strong, causing his lamp to flicker. He thought back to when he had discovered the new passage in Catamount Hollow Cave. Someone had named the hollow when they killed a panther in it back in pioneer times. When the entrance to the cave was found, it was naturally named after the hollow.

There was something unusual about the light field in front of him. The lamp was illuminating the sides of the tunnel, but there was a core of blackness ahead. That could be an indication that the passage was widening. Suddenly the ceiling rose and the walls opened up - he had come out into another passage! He climbed to his feet; the ceiling was a good twenty feet or more above him. His light barely reached the opposite wall. A stream of rushing water ran down the middle of the passage. Toby reached down and picked up his parachute, then slung it over one shoulder. This was some cave! It appeared even larger than he had expected. He set off downstream, following the water. Eventually he expected to either come out into another passage or the river would sump as the water rose to the roof of the cave, and be impassable. Or he could come to an entrance.

He was aware that the floor of the cave seemed to be sloping. He pulled the compass from its pouch on his vest; the stream was running at an angle with the main valley as it had appeared on his map. Here and there, other passages came into the main trunk from both directions. Some carried water while others - those on the opposite side - seemed to be dry. One particularly large passage led off from across the stream, yet it carried no water. What was it? An old stream passage from before the valley eroded away? Perhaps. If it was, it probably came out on the side of the gorge. That would explain how the cave entrances he had seen on the opposite side of the valley had formed. There were probably passages all along the ridge.

The stream grew larger downstream, swelled by other streams that came in. He reckoned he had come more than a mile when the unmistakable roar of a waterfall alerted him that something happened up ahead. A hundred yards further down the passage the stream ran over a brink and into a pit; the passage he was following continued on ahead without the stream. He peered into the pit. The drop appeared not to be more than about ten feet, then the stream cascaded over boulders as it made its way into another passage somewhere below. It looked like a fairly easy climb down to where the water hit the rocks, but below that he couldn't tell. The roar of the falling water was almost deafening; maybe there was another fall on down below his field of vision. He wished he had a rope. Then he remembered; he could make one from 550 cord. All he would have to do would be braid the nylon lines together. He would do just that before attempting the climb.

After ruling the climb temporarily out of the question, Toby decided to continue his exploration on the same level where he was. Now that the stream had dropped to a lower level, he was in dry cave passage. He noticed that there were bats clinging to the ceiling, rather large ones, almost as big as crows. Were they vampires? Probably not, there was no blood on the floor; they were more likely to be fruit bats. Fortunately, their numbers were not that great; had there been a large colony the cave floor would have been covered with guano. At least the passage was large enough he wouldn't have had to crawl through it if it were there.

Toby noticed that his breath was moving ahead of him again. There was evidently an opening to the surface somewhere up ahead. Since the elevation of the cave had dropped down somewhat since he first entered but the water had dropped even lower, he guessed that the entrance would be somewhere on the hillside, probably on the side of the gorge. At one time the stream had probably flowed out of the cave, before centuries of erosion cut the valley floor to its present depth. He could see light up ahead, even though he knew that by this time it would be dark outside. The darkness of a cave is much blacker than that of even a dark night. It is absolutely total darkness, of a sort found nowhere else in the environs of the earth.

Soon he looked up and saw stars; he was at the entrance. Sure enough, he was on the side of the hill. The cave entrance was on a wide ledge; boulders and evidence of a former stream led down the hill in the light from his lamp. The walls were not the steep, solid limestone he had seen at the place where he landed. There were trees beneath the cave entrance.

What was that? He heard ominous rumbling sounds, the noise of engines - truck engines. They came from somewhere below him. He was definitely over the valley floor, that much was certain. But how far below were the trucks? Was he over a strong point, or just a section of trail? Did the troops who guarded the trail know about this particular cave entrance, or was it high enough and well enough hidden that they had missed it? He reasoned that his best avenue would be to spend the night somewhere near the entrance to the cave and wait for morning and daylight to investigate.

He looked at his watch before he doused the carbide lamp; it was nearly nine o'clock. He had been in the cave for almost six hours. He'd gone through two carbide fills. How much more did he have? There were four baby bottles full in his pack - or there had been. Now one was only about two thirds full. He was going to have to conserve it. The same goes for food. He had about two weeks worth with him when he jumped, not counting whatever was in the survival ration tin. And that was only by scrimping, eating only twice a day and not very much at that. Those two items would be his main worry. There was one possibility for food, though. It was very possible he might be able to find an enemy food dump somewhere. He assumed that the Vietnamese probably used the caves to hide their supplies. They were a good place for storage - out of the weather and almost impervious to air strike. More than likely any such supply dumps would be closer to the valley floor than he reasoned that he was.

Then he heard it, the unmistakable droning of a C-130, an A-model by the sound. Blind Bat was out again tonight; soon their flares would be bursting into brilliance over the Trail. He thought about calling on his survival radio but decided against it. There might be someone close enough to hear the static. It would have been better if the radios were equipped with some kind of headset, but as they were designed a survivor held the receiver to his ear and spoke directly into a microphone. Besides, what could he tell them? That he was still alive, but that was about all. He was on the wrong side of the valley for helicopter rescue. He was beginning to wonder if there was any way he could get out. Maybe he ought to just surrender. No, at least he was still free. As long as he was, there was always that single slim chance that he might be able to find a way!

Chapter Nine

It was 0900 at Udorn Royal Thai Air Force Base; Airman Second Class Roy Westerbrook had just begun his shift in the photo interpretation section. As one of a handful of specially trained experts, Westerbrook's job was to interpret the data found on the miles and miles of film taken each day by the RF-4C's of the 11th Tactical Reconnaissance Squadron and the RF-101's from the 20th TRS. As he worked, Roy Westerbrook was thinking about Pong, the seventeen-year old Thai girl who was his "tee-loc" and with whom he shared a bungalow off-base. He thought about how soft her body was and how that girl enjoyed making love! Westerbrook was only twenty himself, the same age as most of the other enlisted men on the base. Roy had been at Udorn now for all of three months, since the 11th TRS arrived from the States.

While Thailand was hardly Indianapolis, it was still better than Vietnam. He had a buddy at Tan Son Nhut. In his letters Dan Manahan described the night life downtown. It sounded nice, almost as good as Bangkok, but there was the constant threat of terrorism to deal with, as well as the frequent mortar attacks on the base. Here, no one was shooting at the GI's and while the Thai girls might have brown skin and a peculiar hump to their pelvis, they had everything that counted. "LBFM's, little brown fornicating machines," that was what the older NCO's called the Thai girls. And there was no doubt but that the title was well deserved; Westerbrook could attest to that. He and Pong made love at least three times every day, twice at night and once in the morning before he went off to work. On his days off, they sometimes lay in bed all day.

Westerbrook was like a lot of other GI' s in that he had a girlfriend back in the States to whom he wrote long, passionate "I love you and I really miss you" letters and who sent him perfumed letters in return. "What she doesn't know won't kill her;" that was how he reconciled his relationship with Pong with the one with the Indiana girl back home. What he didn't know was that Sarah Ann thought the same way; she was humping her blonde, cheerleader butt off in the back seat of a Chevy Impala nearly every Saturday night with one of the football players at indiana U. where she was enrolled as a sociology major. George Washington Jackson was big, black and dumb, like most of the players. But the in-thing at I.U. for a white coed was to be sleeping with - not just dating - a negro, especially a member of the football team. And while Washington might be dumb, he could really give a girl a good ride, much better than anything Roy had ever done. Sarah Ann's letters to Roy were as made up as his were to her.

Westerbrook was one of three airmen in the room. All sat at well-lit tables with a stack of aerial photos on either side of their viewing area. Master Sergeant Jones, the shift leader, sat at his own desk off to one side of the room. Jones was there to assist his charges with their interpretations.

Roy scrutinized the photos under a large magnifying glass, looking for anything that might indicate the presence of enemy troops, vehicles or a supply dump. He knew that what he might find could lead to an air strike so he tried to be darned certain that he didn't miss something that might be carefully hidden. This particular strip was from a low-altitude run the afternoon before by an RF-4 down a ridge just east of the Ho Chi Minh Trail. He had been told to look particularly for any signs that might indicate the presence of someone on the ridge. A C-130 flareship had gone down not far from there a couple of nights back and two of the crewmembers were still missing.

"Nothing but trees," he thought to himself as he scrutinized the photograph as closely as he possibly could. But, no, there were some open spots on the ridge; they appeared to be almost solid rock. There were some dark spots on the photographs; round, almost circular shadows. He knew from school and experience that they were sink-holes. Laos was full of them; the whole country was one big cave. That was one reason the fighters had so much trouble hitting anything; all the enemy supply dumps were inside cave entrances where they were out of sight and protected from bombs and rockets. Even B-52 strikes did little damage to the limestone. He knew it and so did everyone else in the photo lab as well as in the intelligence section. Hell, this whole interdiction thing was nothing but a waste of time and money! If it wasn't for Pong - or some other Thai beauty - he would have just as soon been back home in Indiana.

Hmmmm, now there were some real sink-holes! There were five of them, almost in a cluster. Between two of them was an open area with only a few trees. He looked closely at the open area, his mind still on Pong and the sex they had had that morning, only two hours before. Suddenly, he started.

"Sergeant Jones! Sergeant Jones! Come here! Look at this!" Westerbrook's excited shout caused everyone in the room to forget what they were doing and rush over to his table.

"What the fuck is going on, Westerbrook? You're going to disturb the Colonel. He's probably having his morning coffee and doughnuts about now. This had better be good." The negro master sergeant was perturbed at Westerbrook's outburst.

"Oh it is, Sarge. It is. Now tell me, what does this look like to you?" Roy Westerbrook pointed at something on the photograph. Jones put his own magnifying glass over the spot. He looked where Roy pointed, then motioned to Glassman and Shuman, the other two photo interpreters who were in the room.

"You guys take a look at this. Tell me what you think."

Jack Shuman looked up, "It looks like a person, someone lying on the ground with some kind of shelter over them."

"The shelter looks like a piece of parachute, Sarge," said Bill Glassman.

"We better call in Captain Jester, sir. He'll want to see this."

"You're right, Shuman. Glassman, go down the hall and see if the captain is in. Bring him back here, on the double."

"What if he doesn't want to come?"

"Tell him it's something big. He'll come."

Captain George Jester was sitting in his office, reading the latest issue of "Playboy" when Glassman opened his door.

"Sir, Sergeant Jones wants you to come down to Photo ASAP. We've found something, something big."

"It had better be big, Glassman, for me to leave this," he held up Miss July. "Have you ever seen tits like these?"

"Not in a long time, sir. These Thai girls don't have them like that."

"Makes you wish you were back in the world, doesn't it? Now just what have you found that's so important?"

"It wasn't me, sir. It was Westerbrook. He came across something on a photo. We all looked at it and agree; it looks like a man lying under a parachute canopy."

"You're shitting me! Where was it taken?"

"On a ridge just south of the Mu Gia Pass."

"But who in their right mind would erect a parachute canopy out in the open in that area?"

"It's not exactly in the open, sir. That part of Laos is mostly mountains with lots of trees. There are sink-holes all over the place. Maybe whoever it is felt he was far enough from the Trail not to fear the enemy."

They came into the room. Jester went straight to the table. Jones began explaining what they had found but the captain held up his hand, "Glassman has already given me the gist of the story." The officer scrutinized the photograph, "Damn, it really does look like someone! I'm not even an interpreter and I can see it. Listen, have a dozen copies made of this immediately. And get a definite fix on the position. I'll notify rescue."

Later that day Captain Jester and Sergeant Jones met with Major Diedrich from the Aerospace Rescue and Recovery Service squadron, Colonel Loveless from the 7/13th Air Division and Colonel Gibson from intelligence. A large blow-up of the picture was pinned to a briefing board. It was obvious that the figure was indeed a person, and that they were lying under a parachute shelter of the type taught to all Air Force aircrew members during survival training. Simply put, it was nothing but a makeshift nylon tent made of a section of parachute thrown over a piece of rope tied between two trees.

"If this is a survivor, why hasn't he contacted someone by radio?" asked Major Diedrich.

"Maybe his radio is out of commission? Just who do we have down in that area, anyway?" Colonel Loveless asked the question.

Colonel Gibson answered, "There are four possibilities, although none of them mesh exactly. First, we lost an F-4 about thirty -five miles north of the position two weeks ago. Neither crewmember was rescued, even though both were seen to get out of the airplane. We had assumed them to have been captured.   Then three nights ago a C-130 flareship was shot down approximately ten miles south of the position - or maybe I should say that was where they were hit. The pilot turned the airplane west and got about twenty-five miles away before ordering his crew to bail-out. Six out of eight crewmembers were rescued more or less unharmed. The pilot and one of the loadmasters are still missing."

"Has there been any contact with either of them?

"No sir, we've not heard a thing from anyone in that area. No voice, no beeper - nothing." Major Diedrich answered Colonel Loveless' question.

"Have we any reason to assume they got out of the airplane?'

"Yes sir. Every reason. The rest of the crew said the airplane was still flying when the last man jumped. Only the loadmaster and pilot were still aboard."

"Why didn't the loadmaster jump? Wouldn't he have been in back?"

"Yes sir, but his bailout order was next to last, right before the pilot. His fellow crewmembers say this kid was really conscientious, that he wouldn't have jumped until the pilot was at least out of the cockpit."

"Could the airplane have blown up with them still aboard?"

"There's that possibility, but the rest of the crew said there was a good five minutes between the time the last one jumped and they saw the airplane explode. That was plenty of time for the two crewmembers to have bailed out."

"Have we found the wreckage?"

"A high-altitude recon photo taken day before yesterday shows what we think is the wreckage. It's located about fifteen miles northwest of where this one was taken and about thirty miles from where the survivors were picked up."

"Could we mount a rescue into this area?" Loveless looked at Diedrich.

"Sir, it would be almost impossible. This photo was taken on a ridge-line just east of the main infiltration route out of the Mu Gia Pass. Any rescue force coming in from Thailand would have to fly right across the Trail."

"What about from the east?"

"That's almost as bad, sir. The position is on the west side of the Anmmite Range; on the other side of the mountains is North Vietnam. It might be possible to get someone in there to pick him up, but a rescue force would have to cross part of North Vietnam or fly up the mountains for over two hundred miles to get there. We're willing to try of course, but we need to have some kind of definite proof that this indeed is a survivor before we would risk a rescue team."

"Hell, man. He's lying under a parachute. Who else would be using a parachute for cover?"

Colonel Gibson spoke, "Don't forget, Dave, there are a lot of parachutes dropped over that area every night. We fly flare missions all over that area on a nightly basis. Even if it's from a personnel chute - and it looks like it is - it could be one that some other downed airman discarded."

"What do you recommend, Major?"

"I'd suggest we schedule another recon flight down the ridge. Look for more evidence that someone's there that we want to rescue. We'll alert all of our rescue crews to be on special lookout for signals from that area. I'll notify our people at Scott to pay close attention to their satellite images from that region."

"What if there is someone there? What then?"

"We could always send in a ground team, or we could mount a helicopter rescue."

"What about a Fulton recovery?"

"We've never done it, sir."

"What about TAC? That new mission from Pope is just about operational, isn't it?"

"Now, that I don't know, sir. You would know more about that than I do. Our job is rescue and recovery. TAC handles special ops. You would have to check with them."

"I see, major. It was just a thought. I'll advise General Momyer of what we've found, and that we plan to run another recon flight over that ridge this afternoon. Captain, I want that film analyzed as soon as possible after that airplane is back on the ground." Two hours later another RF-4 made a pass over the same ridge; this time the opening was void of any sign of human presence. Toby Carter was much further down on the ridge, still near the cave entrance where he had spent the night.

Toby had spent another somewhat restless night at the entrance to the cave, his sleep somewhat disturbed by frequent firing of antiaircraft guns on the opposite side of the valley and the nearly constant noise of air strikes. He wasn't worried about stray bombs and bullets; the cave would protect him just as other caves did the same for the enemy. It was that constant din! His brain could not shut down with all of that noise in his ears. He finally managed to get some rest in the wee hours of the morning after Blind Bat began running low on fuel and headed back to Ubon. The same gray mist filled the valley and hid it from prying eyes of any airmen who might pass overhead until mid-morning.

When he awoke, Toby found that he was indeed at a cave entrance some distance up the side of the hill from the valley below. Immediately below the cave, as well as on the hill above and on either side, were tall Asian pines. He knew it was very unlikely that the cave entrance could be seen from below. The hillside was quite steep, but not so that it would be impossible to climb either down or up. Behind and above the cave was a limestone bluff that reached up some seventy or eighty feet. It was probably roughly the same distance to the floor of the valley. A ledge ran along the base of the cliff; he decided to go exploring, like the bear that went over the mountain, "to see what he could see." He took his M-16 and cave pack but left the parachute and harness inside the cave entrance where it would be out of sight.

Almost immediately Carter discovered that his entrance was hardly the only one, although it very well could have been the main water passage at one time. There were cave entrances all along the base of the cliff. Some were large enough to get into while others were barely big enough to allow a rabbit to squeeze inside - if there were rabbits in Laos. He wasn't sure.

A few hundred yards up the cliff the wall again became almost sheer beneath him, although the ledge continued. He could see other cave entrances along the ridge. There must be a veritable maze behind that limestone face! The whole ridge was nothing but a huge honeycomb; he was certain of that. He would have to be very careful not to get lost.

He looked down toward the valley, now that his view was unhampered by trees. What he saw amazed him; the half-mile wide valley looked like a super highway! All along the gorge men - and women - were moving along both on foot and in vehicles. Many were pushing bicycles laden with supplies. Why couldn't our fighters hit targets like these? He wondered. But then he had the answer.

Suddenly the walls of the gorge reverberated with the sound of an approaching jet. Almost immediately the valley floor became empty as the figures ran clear of the trail and concealed themselves under garments of camouflage material. Within seconds the valley appeared void of any human presence; even the trucks were gone, their drivers had pulled into cave entrances along the valley walls. Any photos would show nothing but an undisturbed valley. It was no wonder they couldn't seem to halt the flow of men and equipment moving south toward South Vietnam!

"If I only had a decent rifle, I could do more damage then the whole Seventh Air Force," he mused to himself under his breath. This was an ideal place for a sniper. The caves would provide cover while the limestone cliffs on either side of the valley would cause the sound of gunshots to echo so much that no one would know from where they had come. His M-16 wasn't suitable for what he had in mind. The lightweight automatic rifle had been designed to allow rapid fire, not accuracy at long ranges. Toby knew he could do a lot of damage if only he had a 30/06 or something similar.

But he had no long-range rifle - and killing North Vietnamese was not his number one problem. The sight of so many people below him made his prospects of rescue even less. There was no way he would be able to get across that valley, not with hundreds of North Vietnamese troops milling around. His only hope lay in finding a way under the valley, but even that was doubtful. A good size stream flowed right through the middle of the valley; it was highly unlikely that any of the cave passages crossed over. He would just have to try, that was all.

He needed to get into the lower passage to continue his exploration, and before he could do that he had to make a rope. There was a length of nylon rope attached to his parachute harness; a special device designed to allow an airman to lower himself to the ground if his parachute became entangled in trees or on a cliff. But that rope was too small to climb back up very well, although it could come in useful if he needed to descend something without planning to return the same way. He had plenty of materials for making a rope, though. Several hundred feet of nylon 550-cord made up the suspension lines of the parachute. He would cut off several and braid them into a rope; he had learned how to do just that at 4-H Club camp when he was nine years old. After that he had won a rope-halter making contest; Toby could braid with the best of them. Making the rope would take his mind off his predicament and give him something to do while passing the time. And there was always the possibility, no matter how remote, that he just might be able to find a way to get to the other side of the valley.

When the inevitable afternoon thunderstorm came, Toby was inside the cave entrance cutting strands of suspension line away from the parachute. He wanted to make a 100-foot rope. After cutting the lines he needed, he again rolled up the remaining lines and canopy into a compact enough package that he could put it inside his pack. Now, more than ever, he was glad he had not discarded the parachute that first night.

Toby sat down on a rock just inside the entrance and began braiding the lines one over the other into a six-strand rope. He had no idea what the actual strength would be, although he knew that each line by itself was stressed at 550 pounds, hence the term "550-cord." Even with the splices he would have to make, the finished product should be strong enough to serve as an assist for his descent into the lower passage and to climb back out again.

There was one thing puzzling him about the caves on this side of the valley. There were no antiaircraft guns anywhere on his side that he knew of, while the other ridge bristled with them. Was it because the walls were so steep? They didn't appear to be any more so than the ones across the valley. Many of the guns over there were at or near the crest of the ridge. Did it have something to do with logistics? He had read about Dienbienphu, and how the Viet Minh had hauled heavy artillery pieces - including antiaircraft guns - across the mountains virtually by hand. There had to be an explanation, but for the moment, at least, it defied him.

He was satisfied with the rope as it took shape under his hand. Maybe it wouldn't win any prizes and it surely would never lead to a contract to be a rope maker, but it would be able to do what he wanted just fine. Since it was nylon it would be flexible, lightweight and easy to carry. He didn't want to be burdened down during his explorations. He would carry only a section or two of parachute along with a coil of extra 550-cord in his cave pack. He could make Prussik knots from strands of 550-cord as a climbing aid. He would wear the survival vest and carry his cave pack and M-16; there was no telling who or what he might run into in the cave, especially on the level near the valley floor.

There was no doubt but that the communists used the caves for shelter and storage. The question was, just how far inside them did they go? He doubted very much if any of them were serious cave explorers. They were familiar with caves by necessity, not by choice. He reasoned that the North Vietnamese would lack the curiosity about caves that caused him to be willing to get wet, muddy and cold while seeking to see what lay up a tiny crawl-way or around the next bend in a long, strenuous rock-strewn trunk passage.

It was nightfall by the time he had finished the rope. But it was dark in a cave all the time, day or night. Now was as good a time as any to try and get into the lower level and see where it would take him. He lit his lamp and put the cap back on his head. A small crevice made a safe and secret hiding place for his parachute. Slinging the newly-made rope over his chest and shoulder and carrying the rifle, he set off to descend into the lower passage. Except for the presence of the rifle, he could have been back in Tennessee setting out on another caving adventure.

There was still a lot of water coming down the stream passage and tumbling over the brink of the falls. But there appeared to be room for him to climb down one side and stay far enough away from the water that he could stay reasonably dry. He was wearing his flight jacket over his fatigues and he did have on the new jungle fatigues. They would dry out quickly when they did get wet. That much was in his favor. Getting soaked to the skin in a cave was almost as dangerous a prospect as falling or drowning.

Toby tied one end of the rope around a boulder; he could have free-climbed down the waterfall but this would give him an assist he might need when he came back up. And he had every intention of coming back up, even if he should find a means of getting across the valley. This was just a recon trip; he intended only to find out where the stream passage ran. He dropped into the slot for the climb.

After descending to the level where the water impacted on boulders, he found that he was at one end of a very large chamber. The stream cascaded along a sloping wall, then fell again to another sloping wall. He estimated that it was fifty feet or more to where the underground stream hit the passage floor. There it flowed into another even larger stream, a veritable underground river that came from somewhere up the ridge. He realized that the cave he had found was probably one of the most impressive in the world, yet it was very likely that no one in the international caving community would ever know of its existence.

With the aid of the rope, the descent to the floor of the cave was not unduly difficult. Nor should the climb back to the upper level be all that hard, either - although for an instant he wished he had brought the parachute with him in case he decided not to come back. He would explore in the direction the water was flowing; that would no doubt take him to the valley floor. The size of the cavern almost overwhelmed him. The passages were larger than those of Mammoth Cave. But what did you expect, in a land where it rained nearly every day for months at a time?

In a cavern this large the walking was rather easy, although he was well aware that on his return trip he would be moving constantly uphill. But the slope was gradual rather than steep; he should have no problem making his way back. The noise of the river was deafening, it was white water all the way and the current was very swift since the stream was flowing downhill. He was thankful that the cavern was plenty wide enough that he could stay on dry ground out of the water.

He explored for more than three hours, making his way through what he estimated to be more than two miles of cave. After a time the waters began to flow more slowly as the floor of the cavern became more or less level. The noise began to subside to that of a rippling stream rather than rushing river. He reckoned that he must be nearing the entrance; he must be wary from here on out. Then up ahead, he saw the glow of a light at just about the same time he heard the chug, chug, chug of a gasoline powered generator.

It was time to turn back.

Chapter Ten

"Well, Captain. What have you found?" Colonel Loveless opened the meeting. The same principles were there - the 7/13th representative, Colonel Gibson from intelligence, Major Diedrich from rescue and the photo interpretation and intelligence officer.

Captain Jester looked around the room at his seniors before he replied, "Sir, I'm afraid we didn't pick up anything at all yesterday. The spot where we saw him in the photo from the day before is empty. Here, I've had it blown up." He put an 11x14 blow-up of the rock slab and the two trees on the briefing board. "Here is the one from yesterday. You can see it's the same spot."

"It sure looks the same, Captain. But can you be absolutely sure?"

"Unless the targeting information in the aircraft was out of kilter, and there happens to be an identical spot on the same ridge. I have no doubt sir, this is definitely it."

"Well, where could he have gone? Major Diedrich?"

"Who knows sir? Maybe he moved further down the ridge. A survivor would hardly want to stay in the same place that close to the Trail. Not unless he's very dumb - and neither one of the two men from that C-130 are dumb. Just the opposite, in fact."

"Just what do we know about them?"

"Captain Preston is an Academy graduate, class of '61. He finished in the middle of his class, was captain of the lacrosse team and a member of the debating team. He finished near the top of his pilot training class."

"Why isn't he in fighters?"

"Good question, Sir. It seems that his class advisor at the Academy had been in C-130's at Ardmore. He told his students that the C-130 mission was one of the best in the Air Force, that the airplane flew like a fighter and you could move around in it. Preston asked for C-130's, as did two thirds of the guys who were counseled by that same advisor."

"Who was the advisor?"

"A Major Radcliff, Sir. Or he was then. Now he's a Lieutenant Colonel. He commands a C-130 squadron at Pope, a special operations unit."

"The Sky Hooks?"

"That's the one, Sir."

"What about the airman, what's his name - Carter?"

"Airman First Class Carter. That's right, Sir. Airman Carter is something else. His scores on his Airman Qualification Tests were quite high, but his intelligence tests are even higher. Airman First Class Tobin S.

Carter is probably one of the most intelligent enlisted men in the Air Force, according to his tests. His IQ is higher than that of most officers. But you would never know it. He's a country boy, from Tennessee. And there is something else about Carter that could have some bearing on this situation."

"And what is that, Captain?"

"I talked to Major Catlin, the intelligence officer at Ubon. He briefed Preston's crew the night they were shot down. During the briefing he mentioned the 100-MM gun in the cave south of Mu Gia and north of Tche Pone. The cave is less than five miles from where this photo was taken. One of the other crewmembers put in a jibe about Carter and the fact that he is an experienced cave explorer. It seems that Carter always carried a special survival pack - he called it his 'cave pack' - and that he had told the other enlisted men on his crew that if he was ever shot down over Laos, he would find a cave and hide in it."

"What point are you trying to make?"

"Look at this, sir," Jester put an enlarged copy of the photograph on the board. He pointed at a dark spot in the picture, an object down the hill a hundred feet or so from the figure under the parachute.

"I see what you're pointing at; what the hell is it?"

"That sir, is a sink-hole. Laos is pock-marked with them." He put another photograph on the board, an enlargement of a shot of the same scene taken the afternoon before. "We blew up this shot of the same sink-hole. Look here, down near the bottom. See that dark area?"

"I see it, but what are we looking at?"

"One of our photo interpreters is from indiana. He doesn't have anywhere near the experience with caves our boy Carter has, but he has been in a few. He says we are looking at an entrance to a cave."

"Get to the point, Jester."

"Well, sir, here's the way I see it. We have a picture of a man lying under a parachute within a hundred feet - we've checked the distance - of a cave. One of the people we're looking for just happens to have a background in cave exploration. We know for a fact that he had with him his special pack, included in which was a carbide lamp, I might add, when he jumped. The other loadmasters saw him pick it up and put it on when the pilot rang the bailout bell. He also had an M-16 strapped to him; he had the fabric shop make special straps for both the pack and the rifle. In short, we have a man who was prepared to hide out in a cave if he had too. I think this is Airman Carter in the photo and the reason we found no evidence of him the next day is that, one, he was captured, two, he has moved on down the ridge or, three, he is inside that cave."

"Why was he lying out in the open when the first picture was taken?"

89

"He wasn't exactly in the open. Actually he is between two trees; it just so happens that the angle was exactly right for our recon ship to pick him up. After all, he wasn't worried about being spotted from the air, quite the contrary. But to answer your question, I talked to the crew who took the picture. They came down that ridge just after a fairly large thunderstorm had moved through the area. Westerbrook, the photo interpreter from indiana - and the man who found the figure, by the way - thinks he might have been waiting for the rain to stop before going into the cave. Caves carry water and can fill up rather quickly, so I'm told.

"Here's the scenario we came up with: Carter, whom we assume the figure to be, was walking down the ridge when he came across the cave entrance. He's been on the ground now for two full days; he knows it rains every day at mid-day this time of year. It's rained in that area for the last two months every day including the last three days. He decides to wait out the inevitable thunderstorm, so he erects a shelter to keep dry. Then he went into the cave and that is where he is now."

"That is definitely an interesting scenario, Captain Jester. I commend you and your men for developing it. What do we do now? Major Diedrich, rescue is your bailiwick. What do you think?"

"Sir, there really isn't anything we can do until we get a definite confirmation that the survivor is there. I guess theoretically we could send in a couple of PJ's and have them search the cave. But our men aren't trained for that. Then there is the question of getting them back out, or getting them in for that matter."

"What about Special Forces, or Navy SEALS?"

"I don't think either of those groups include cave warfare in their training. For that matter, we don't know for sure he is in the cave, nor do we know how big it is. You know, some caves are quite large. Mammoth Cave is rumored to be more than a hundred and fifty miles long. He could get in there and get lost and never be found; even worse, a rescue team could get lost. If we could just get a definite contact with him, rescue would be willing to try and get him out. But right now we just don't have enough to go on."

"I see, major. Colonel Gibson, just what does intelligence know about caves in Laos?"

"Colonel, all we know for sure is that there are hundreds - maybe thousands -of them in the country - in Vietnam, too. As for this particular area, we know there seem to be several down in the valley. That area is one of our most difficult targets. It's the one place where the Ho Chi Minh Trail runs right out in the open, yet we can't ever seem to find anyone there. Still, we bomb it all the time. There are a lot of guns on the west ridge, but none on the east for some reason. Fortunately, that is the ridge where our man

90

was seen. Photos of the valley show a number of cave openings along both sides; we believe the Charlies are using the caves to hide in during the daytime as well as for truck repairs, storage - that kind of thing."

"Hmmmm, if the North Vietnamese are using the caves, that could mean Carter - if this definitely was him - could run into someone in the cave. He could be killed or captured, is that right?"

"He very well could. I don't know what he hopes to gain by hiding in a cave, other than using them for shelter. It looks like he would let us know if he was ready to be rescued. Maybe his radio is broken."

"There are other means of signaling. If he was as well prepared as Captain Jester thinks he was, he would be able to signal us some way. I guess the only thing we can do is keep an eye on the area, watch for some sign. Advise all of our aircraft to be on the lookout for anything on the ground that might be a signal; strobe-lights, mirrors, tracers fired in a pattern - anything.

"Captain Jester, I want you to keep an eye on this. We'll schedule a photo-run down that valley every day. Tell the crews to try and get shots from all angles. Also, stay in touch with the intelligence officer at Ubon. Have him interview everyone who knows this kid, and Captain Preston, too for that matter."

"What about the people on Okinawa. That's where the flareship crews are based, you know."

"That's right, I'd forgotten about that. Get in touch with the people in his unit there. We might even think about going to his last stateside squadron; maybe even send someone to talk to his relatives and friends if the need arises. In the meantime, keep your fingers crossed."

Toby Carter was back at the cliff-side cave entrance. After seeing light up ahead and hearing the sounds of a gasoline engine, he had decided it was time to turn around and head back. There was no way he was going to be able to get out of the cave that way. He didn't check to see who was using the light. There was no need for that; he was well aware it would be someone whom he did not want to meet.

It had taken him almost three hours to get to where he saw the lights; it took only two to get back to the rope. Scaling the breakdown-strewn slope was fairly uncomplicated, with the aid of the hand-braided line. He used the rope primarily to stabilize himself as he walked up the sloping wall. Thank God it wasn't sheer! He wasn't sure if he would have been able to climb out with Prussik knots or not. Using rope knots to climb a manufactured rope was one thing, working them up a braided nylon line - and a hastily made one at that - was another.

It was still dark when he reached the cliff-side entrance where he had spent the previous night, his third night on the ridge. It was nearing morning after his fourth night on the ground in Laos. He didn't want to sleep in the cave, knowing that to do so would cause him to lose all track of time. He remembered reading about the Crystal Cave expedition up in Kentucky when he was eleven. A large group of cavers had gone into the cave the legendary and ill-fated Floyd Collins had discovered, planning to spend two full weeks without returning to the surface. After only a couple of days the cavers began to show strain from being isolated in a realm of total darkness. But, his situation was different from theirs. They had been in the cave by choice, for the sole purpose of exploring the cave. He was in this one for another, far more motivational reason - survival. If he had to, he would, but as long as he could remain out of sight yet still be outside the cave, that was how he wanted to at least spend his sleeping hours.

Toby awoke around noon when a low-flying F-4 made a pass down the valley. There had been no bombs dropped and very little firing. "Must have been a recon," he muttered under his breath. "Well, it's time for breakfast. Let's see now, yesterday we had scrambled eggs and ham, I guess today we'll have ham and scrambled eggs." He had begun talking out loud to himself during the night. It had been almost five days now since he had spoken to another human being.

"At least I can eat a hot meal." That was one luxury he knew most survivors never had. He had several small cans of Sterno in his cave pack along with some packets of heat capsules he had scrounged from supply. Since he was well above the "communist hordes" - he remembered the term from GI Joe comic books - there was no reason to fear detection from his fire. Both the Sterno and the heat capsules burned with a blue flame; neither gave off any smoke. Water was the least of his worries; there was plenty in the cave.

His physical condition was deteriorating slightly, but not as much as it would have under other conditions. His bowels were loose, but not diarrheaic. For the past three days his crotch had been red with jungle rot from lack of personal hygiene. He had considered bathing in the stream in the cave but the waters were much too cold. At least his feet were in pretty good shape, except that they were itching because he had to keep his boots on most of the time. One thing he had remembered to keep in his cave pack was extra socks. "I should have brought a change of underwear and some baking powder." Those two items would have probably alleviated the crotch rot. He did have a bar of soap and a green GI towel. Some washing with rain water did manage to keep the fungus from becoming any worse.

He had gone to sleep under a black cloud of despair, the result of his discovery that the mouth of the cave - at least he thought it was the mouth -

was occupied by enemy troops. There went his chances of getting across the valley undetected! He had also given up on the possibility of a passage leading under the valley to a cave on the other side. No, it looked like this was it. His only hope of rescue lay in leaving the cave and working his way further down the ridge and away from the infiltration routes. But in the cave he was in familiar surroundings, the same kind of environment in which he had spent so much time throughout his growing-up years. He was reluctant to leave what seemed almost like his mother's womb.

There was one thing he could do to pass the time - weave more rope. He left the 100-foot length tied by the waterfall so he wouldn't have to lug it around. There were some side passages on the upper level that he wanted to check out. He suspected that they led to the entrances on the side of the cliff. While he was well aware that exploring them would accomplish little, at least it was something to do, something to take his mind off of where he was and what he was doing - and his probably inevitable fate.

Maybe he ought to just go back to the sink-hole and call for a chopper. He knew they would probably come in for him if he called; the Jolly Green crews were already building a reputation for their courage and willingness to go in and pick up survivors from right out of the jaws of the enemy. But he hated to expose a five-man chopper crew to the gauntlet of fire he knew they would have to run to bring him out. It wasn't like he was a fighter pilot with a lot of classified information in his head and a couple of million dollars worth of training behind him. He was just Toby Carter, an enlisted swine who could easily be replaced. Hell, there were people standing in line for his job all over the Air Force! And all that was required was to be able to pass an eighth-grade math test and a flight physical.

Flying status was a big deal - you wore the sexy flight suits (A guy back at Pope had had an affair with a non-flying sergeant's wife; she had always wanted him to come over wearing a flight suit with no underwear. "Everything is right there!" she had told the guy.), drew flight pay, combat pay and received an income tax exemption. A fat lot of good the extra pay and tax exemption did him now!

As he worked on the length of rope, Toby's mind wandered back to high school. Where were his classmates now? As far as he knew, only three guys had gone into the military - and he was one of the three. The other two were the McBrayer brothers, Tony and Billy. Tony had gone in the Navy and Billy into the Marines the same week that he went into the Air Force. Sammy Gillison had gotten married when JFK announced that anyone married after October 1, 1963 would be subject to the draft. A lot of guys had rushed into marriage then; his mom had told him about them. Some were already divorced, but their ruse had worked as they won draft exemptions.

He thought about Maxine Milligan. Gosh, had he had a crush on that girl! But she had never known he existed. Let's see, she would have graduated the year before last, with the class of '64. She was two years behind him. Then there were Alliene Silvers and Sandy Bradshaw. Alliene and Sandy were first cousins. He had known them as long as he could remember. They went to church and school together; he saw them six days of every week, including twice on Sunday. The only day he didn't see them was Saturday. They were both good-looking girls, but they had considered him as "a friend," not a potential lover.

Stephanie Smith was also in his Sunday School class. Like Alliene and Sandy, she was an attractive girl. But his relationship with her had been somewhat different. They had dated a few times. One night they had parked at his grandfather's old place. They had gotten into some rather heavy petting; ironically it had been the first time he had kissed anyone. She had let him caress her breasts and even kiss her nipples. There had been no doubt that she was getting aroused and was ready to go all the way. But when he put his hand on her crotch, she had broken out in tears. They had driven home in silence. After that they hardly spoke. He had heard that she was engaged to a preacher boy who went to the Baptist school in Jackson. Toby knew him; he had preached at their church on Youth Sunday. A real drip, one with a deferment because he was in college and an ordained minister.

He wondered about his family. Would he ever see them again? The thought brought tears to his eyes. He had hoped to take a "mod bird" back to the States right after Christmas. Now it looked like he would never go home. They probably knew he was missing by now. How would they take it? His mother would be praying for him constantly. Daddy might feel guilty for signing the papers so he could enlist at seventeen. No matter; he would have enlisted when he was eighteen anyway. In fact, he probably would have gone into the Army and tried for flight school.

What about his brothers and sisters? Matt was a freshman in high school this year, or would be when school resumed in the fall. Peter was almost seven years old; he would be in second grade. Petey was the member of the family he missed most. Every time he had thought about his little brother when he was in basic training, tears would well up in his eyes - just like they were doing now. They would both be getting excited about the opening day of squirrel season; it was only about a month away. His youngest sister, Sarah, was ten now. She would be in fifth grade at Lavinia School. His other sister, Cathy, would be in her second year in college. She went to Union University in Jackson, the same school that Stephanie attended. Shoot, she would be in her senior year this year!

94

He would have been a senior at the Academy had he gotten the appointment his last year in high school. Up until now he had felt that he actually would have missed out on some things by going to the Academy as he had planned. After all, the past three years had been rather exciting, what with Dragon Rouge and all, then flying in Southeast Asia. But now it looked like his career might be coming to an end. And he wasn't even old enough to vote!

At twilight he decided it was time to do some exploring; at least he could change his dismal train of thought. He wouldn't go far, just check out some of the leads along the cliff. There was a passage just inside the entrance that undoubtedly connected with one of the other caves on the side of the hill.

Sure enough, the passage continued for about a hundred feet then intersected another one that led to an outside entrance. He peered over the side into the valley, being careful to stay well enough concealed that anyone below or on the other side of the valley would not see him. Why would anyone be looking up this way, anyway?

What he saw below made his heart stand still; a truck convoy was making its way down the valley. It stretched for at least a mile! He could see the narrow slits of their headlights from this angle. From the altitudes at which the flareships worked, the lights would be invisible. He doubted that the trucks could even be seen under flare light. Not unless the flares happened to be right over the middle of the valley. Darn! If only he had a heavier caliber rifle! His M-16 wouldn't reach that far with any power. With a powerful enough rifle he probably could put a round right through the engine block on every truck in the line. The slitted lights made a perfect aiming point. He was tempted to try with the M-16 but decided against it. Wasting ammunition; that was all he would be doing. That and tipping off the gooks to his presence for no good reason.

Frustrated, he went back into the cave and continued his explorations. He was right; a veritable maze of interconnecting passages lay behind the limestone cliff. Before he decided it was time to head back to where he had made his camp, he had explored an even dozen entrances. For an inexperienced caver, finding the way back to where he had started would have been an awesome task with so many passages to choose from. But Toby was not inexperienced; he had been careful to look behind him and file away in his memory a description of each passage that he left. He had no trouble making his way back.

It was still rather early, shortly after midnight, when he got back to the entrance behind the trees. A flareship was working overhead; the light from the flares illuminated both walls of the valley - but not the floor below. The pilot was working fighters on a target somewhere downstream; the antiaircraft guns on the opposite ridge were raising quite a din as they threw lead at the attacking fighters when one came in range. Occasionally a CBU-carrying fighter would make a run on the guns, but they were well protected. Unless a canister happened to break apart right inside a gun pit, the tiny bomblets would sail harmlessly over the heads of the gunners. A lot of tax-payers' money was being thrown into that valley, and all to no avail.

Well, he was in the war but not of the war. There wasn't a blooming thing he could do. There was no way he would be able to go to sleep with all that racket; might as well do a little more exploring. There were some other leads near the entrance that he hadn't checked. If he was going to die here, at least he could find out as much about the cave as he could before he went.

Some of the leads were quite interesting. They led into large dome pits that evidently opened to the surface some fifty feet above his head. At least they had better; if not, then someone had painted stars on the ceiling with luminous paint! Toby crawled into one lead that seemed to go on and on at hands and knees level. He estimated that he had crawled for more than two hundred feet when suddenly his light reflected off of something. His heart missed a beat; this was not right! The reflection came from something that had to be metal. Maybe it was a drop of water. But no, there it was again, about twenty-five feet ahead of him. He continued crawling toward the unidentified sitting object. Then he came out into another pit.

It couldn't be! Toby Carter, you're going nuts! You've been down here too long. His eyes had to be playing tricks on him because the reflection was from a metal D-ring on a piece of nylon and cotton webbing. He knew full well what he was looking at; he had been involved with similar materials for more than two years. An airdrop container! But, not one that was still in use. This particular type hadn't been used for years, not since Korea. His father had bought some at a surplus store, to use for the Lord only knew what. They were nylon and cotton on the outside and padded with fiberglass. But how had this particular bundle gotten here?

Then he knew. The parachute was still attached to the bundle. The risers and suspension lines reached upwards into a chute that came into the dome at an angle. Someone - sometime - had dropped the bundle and it had fallen into a pit on the surface. Whoever was the recipient of the drop had not known how - or had not bothered - to retrieve it. Or maybe it was supposed to fall into the valley, but had drifted over the ridge as he had. Who had dropped it? The French? As far as he knew, they had conducted most of their operations further north, on the Plain of Jars and up by Dienbienphu, which was a good two hundred miles away. He poked at the bundle, turning it over. It was heavy. There on the side were the words "U.S. Army Air Forces." World War II? Maybe, but the fact that the Army

Air Forces had become the United States Air Force in 1947 didn't necessarily mean the bundle had been here that long.

What was inside? His spirits suddenly rose. The contents of that bundle just might be something he could use! Shoot, the C-rations they were issuing now had been made in 1943, the date was stamped on the side of the cartons! They were almost twenty-five years old and still good. The bundle was in pretty good shape with no evidence of water damage. He tugged at the straps, fumbling in his excitement.

When he finally got the carton open, his heart leaped for joy when he saw that there were indeed C-rations in the bundle - eight cases of them. But the other contents made him even more excited. Individually wrapped in oil cloth were the outlines of several weapons. By their length he judged that three were rifles of some kind. One was a bit longer - perhaps a BAR? There were some shorter weapons as well; from their length he assumed they were probably carbines or maybe even Thompson submachine guns.

And there was ammunition. Some was packed in bandoleers. He looked at one - .30 caliber. There were several metal ammunition containers marked " .30- caliber, U.S. Army" on the outside. There were some smaller containers marked "alcohol." (What were they dropping alcohol for?) He did a little dance on the floor of the pit as he realized what he had found. Here was a veritable treasure-trove, almost everything he needed. The only thing missing was carbide. What was he thinking? Alcohol burns. He could rig up some kind of lamp out of C-ration cans and conserve his remaining carbide for when he really needed it. There were even some GI blankets in the container, still wrapped in plastic and exuding that new woolen smell. Had the bundle been lost outside, everything would probably have been ruined, but a cave has a constant environment. The position of the bundle was such that it was clear of water that fell in from the surface when it rained. The parachute had diverted the falling waters so they fell to one side. And the pit was close enough to the entrance that the room was generally dry.

For the next two hours, Toby worked almost feverishly moving the contents of the bundle to the cave entrance where he had made his camp. He brought everything out, including the container. He left the parachute and risers; he had one of his own and it appeared to be hung on some protrusion in the pit through which it had fallen. Evidently only the weight of the bundle had prevented the whole thing from being hung up somewhere between the bottom of the pit and the surface. His labor had made him tired. He would check out the weapons and inventory his stock in the morning.

Chapter Eleven

Exhausted by the effort of moving all of his recently discovered booty, Toby Carter slept like a played-out baby. It was mid-afternoon by the time he awoke. He looked at his watch; it read 1435. "That can't be right," he said to himself. "I can't have been asleep for almost ten hours!" Then he remembered what he had been doing during the early morning hours. Excitement again consumed him as he thought of what he had found.

Before he began investigating the condition of his find, he told himself not to be too disappointed if the things in the bundle turned out to be to old to be useable. The C-rations would probably be all right; they were canned goods and would be impervious to moisture and just about anything else. His main concern was over the ammunition and the weapons. While the interior of a cave is more or less stable, the bundle had been at the bottom of a shaft that led to the surface. Some rainwater would have run through the shaft and onto the bundle, even though it looked to be in pretty good shape. There was some fungal growth on the container, but only on the outside.

"I guess the first thing to do is inventory this stuff." Toby began laying the various items side by side to determine just what he had found. There were eight cases of C-rations, a one-gallon metal container of alcohol, four cans of .30-caliber rifle cartridges, two of .30-caliber pistol cartridges - no doubt for the carbines - one container of .45-caliber pistol cartridges and eight weapons, along with two bandoleers filled with .30 caliber cartridges packaged in five-round clips. The bandoleers were wrapped in oil-soaked cloth, as were each of the weapons. That was a good sign; the oil would have prevented rust. There was also a wooden case marked "Grenade - Fragmentation."

Toby unwrapped and inspected each of the weapons in turn, beginning with the one he believed to be a Thompson submachine gun. Sure enough, it was. Also wrapped in the package were two full clips, each loaded with.45 ammunition. Surprisingly, the gun seemed to be unharmed, even after falling at least sixty feet through an open shaft. But then again, the container had been packaged to be dropped from an airplane. He laid the wicked-looking weapon and the clips on top of the oil-soaked rags in which they had been packed.

Next he turned his attention to the two smaller packages; they were indeed M-1 carbines. Again, there were four loaded clips packed with the rifles. Both weapons were brand new; each was still covered with Cosmoline. There was one package that was longer and heavier than the others - the one Toby had guessed to be a Browning Automatic Rifle. It was, indeed, a BAR; again there were loaded clips packed with It, four this time.

That could be a handy weapon, if the ammunition worked. He then turned his attention to the last four packages, expecting them to turn out to be M-1 Garand rifles, the standard military issue automatic rifle of World War II.

When Toby opened the first package he was at first dismayed to find that what he had were old bolt-action rifles of World War I vintage. But then he took another look; these were bolt-action rifles all right, but they were 30/06 Springfields, the famous 1903A-3, one of the most accurate rifles ever issued to military forces. Almost immediately he thought of a fellow Tennesseean, the one played by Gary Cooper in an Academy Award-winning movie. Sergeant Alvin C. York had used a rifle just like this to kill and capture an entire company of German soldiers during the Meuse-Argonne offensive. York had gone up against a machine gun nest with nothing but a rifle and a .45 automatic pistol. His amazing accuracy so overwhelmed the German commander that he surrendered the rest of his men to a single soldier after twenty had been slain.

Toby Carter lifted the Springfield rifle. He picked up the olive drap towel and cut off a piece with his knife. Then, using the swath of terry cloth, he wiped the Cosmoline from the stock, barrel and action. When the rifle was clean, he raised it to his shoulder and sighted through the peep sights. The stock fit his shoulder just like it had been custom made for him. Now here was a rifle! The black plastic M-16 seemed so futuristic, but the Springfield represented the quality of a bygone age.

What about the barrel? Had the packers included a cleaning kit? There were still some smaller packages that he had yet to inspect. One turned out to contain four bayonets but another was what he was looking for - a canvas case for a three-piece metal rod and two steel brushes, along with a small metal box filled with cotton patches, solvent and oil. He screwed the three pieces together and inserted a patch. The tiny patch went through a slot on the end of the last rod. Using the rod, Toby cleaned the barrel of all traces of Cosmoline, leaving it clean and shiny. The rifle was just like new.

There were three more Springfields; Toby laid them alongside the other weapons. Then he took stock of what he had. Each ammo can held 500 rounds; there were four. He had 2,000 rounds of .30-caliber in the cans, plus another 200 in the bandoleers. There was another thousand rounds for the carbine, plus a thousand for the Thompson. The question was, would the ammunition still fire? If it would, then he had weapons enough for a small war, not to mention fifty hand grenades. What was he going to do with this stuff if it did work? Then he turned his head toward the valley below.

It would be easy enough to see if the ammunition was still serviceable. All he had to do was fire off a couple of rounds. The cartridges were still shiny; they looked brand new, even though they had to be as old as he, if not older. He could toss a grenade off the side of the cliff. But if he did, then anyone below would know there was someone up there. Wait a minute - all he had to do was wait until the next air strike! He could fire one of the rifles while the machine guns on the other side of the valley were firing. No one would hear a single shot among the din of the automatic weapons. He could flip a grenade out when an airplane flew over; the gooks would think it was some sort of small bomb.

Toby took one of the Springfields, the one he had cleaned up, and set off up the side of the cliff. The daily rain had stopped; doubtlessly there would soon be an air strike or a recon flight. It would be futile to begin planning what to do with the weapons if the ammunition wouldn't fire. There was a rock outcropping about two hundred feet from the cave entrance. From there he could see the valley, but couldn't be seen himself. The next time the guns began firing, he would fire off a few rounds himself. Even if his shots were heard, they would be taken for those of just another exuberant soldier taking pot-shots at the aircraft and hoping to get lucky. When he reached the overhanging rock, Toby sat down to wait.

While he waited, Toby began pondering the possibilities if the ammunition proved serviceable. He was very optimistic about the cartridges, even those in the bandoleers, but the grenades were another story. His experience with grenades of any sort was nil, but his father had kept a supply of cartridges at home for years after having brought them home from the service. They still fired after twenty years.

Even though his discovery brought him no nearer to rescue, at least it was an encouragement. Counting the remnants of his supply, he now had enough food to last for more than a month. As for the weapons, what they might do was enable him to begin waging war on his own. For over a week now, he had been watching the fruitless results of the fighter attacks on the gorge. So far, he had not seen a single truck destroyed. As for damage to the roadways, there was none. The valley floor was solid rock, limestone for the most part, and the bombs being dropped over the region had little impact on it. Even the tremendous explosive power of a B-52 strike could do little damage to solid rock cliffs and valley floors. Yet, while five hundred pounds, or even a thousand, of high explosive would barely dent the surface of the rock, hundreds of years of slow solution action by acid-charged waters had cut miles and miles of caverns beneath the cliffs, and pockmarked the valley until it looked like the surface of the moon.

Toby had never really studied the geology of the valley before, partly because most of his observations had been at night. Now he saw that the valley beneath him was filled with craggy limestone formations - "karst towers" - that reached up from the valley floor. Some were almost as high as the ledge where he waited for the inevitable air strike that was probably on its way right now. If it wasn't, no doubt preparations were being made for one at Ubon, or maybe Udorn or NKP, perhaps even Da Nang. Crews were being briefed, checking weather and filing flight plans even while mechanics and armorers worked to prepare the airborne steeds for the modern day knights whose lot was to ride out and do battle with the North Vietnamese dragon.

It was not long until darkness would fall across the land. That meant that the guys at Ubon were getting ready for the night's missions over the Trail and up north. No doubt everyone knew he was missing, probably presumed dead. What about the others - Mike, Willy, Sam, Don? He knew they had bailed out, along with Lieutenant Benjamin and Captain Danson. Everybody had gotten out of the airplane before him, with the exception of Captain Preston. What about Preston? He was on the his way to the back when Toby jumped. Surely the pilot had come to earth somewhere close to where he had landed. Was he wandering around this same ridge somewhere? Or had he fallen on the opposite ridge? Maybe he had been captured and sent north to Hanoi? Worse still, maybe he had been severely injured and then died a slow, agonizing death with no one to comfort him or even to know that he had died.

Thinking about the possibility of Preston lying somewhere dead - or dying - from injuries made Toby morose. His own prospects were not that good, but at least he was not injured. About the best he could hope for would be to evade capture for as long as he could. Maybe he would hold out here for years. Japanese soldiers were still being found on islands in the Pacific, even though the war had been over for twenty-one years! God, he hoped he wouldn't have to live in these hills for that long! Or even for a year. He liked being out in the woods and he loved caves, but he wasn't adverse to people, either. Especially people like Sharon.

Sharon - dear, sweet Sharon. (Sweet? Firey was a better word.) He had been thinking about her less and less the longer he was on the ridge. He had thought he was in love with her when they left Bangkok, but now he knew that their relationship had been more passion than love. She was right; there was no way they could have anything more than a fling, not with her being in Vietnam and him on Okinawa. Even if she was based on The Rock, a relationship would have been very difficult because of the thing about rank. Officers were not supposed to "fraternize" with enlisted men. Sharon had joked a lot about that during those days and nights in Bangkok. "Hey, Toby. Do you want to fraternize a little?" "Boy, Tobe. You do a good job of fraternizing," she would say.

It was starting to get dark. He hoped an air strike came soon because he would like to test-fire this rifle in the daylight. He'd picked out a target on one of the karst towers, a lightly shaded piece of limestone that stood out against the darker gray. The idea of just firing a rifle into the air ran against his grain. His father had always told him never to shoot unless he had something to shoot at and never to point a gun at anything you didn't mean to kill.

He was looking down the valley when suddenly a dark shape materialized just above the tops of the cliffs. An F-4 - it looked like an RF-4C - was making a pass down the valley. Quickly he aimed the rifle at the target he had chosen, then waited for the guns on the other side to start firing and the noise of the jet to reach him. As the first wave of jet noise resounded off the valley wall, Toby squeezed off his first shot - the cartridge fired!

The recoil felt good against his shoulder, no worse than a 12-gauge shotgun. A puff of dust rose from the center of the white patch of limestone. Hey, this rifle is pretty well already sighted in! Quickly, he worked the bolt and fired again, then again and again until all five shots had been fired. What about the grenade? Shoot! He had forgotten about it. But then his plans did not directly involve the use of the grenades, anyway.

Toby felt good about the way each bullet's impact had been within the white patch. Still, he would like to make a more accurate analysis of just how the rifle shot. How he could he do that? One way would be to bore-sight it, to put the rifle in a vice and sight through the barrel at a target, making adjustments to the sights so that the sight picture and the view through the gun barrel matched. He probably could anchor the rifle with rocks but he still wouldn't know exactly where it shot unless he fired several rounds with the gun still anchored. No, he was going to have to shoot it. And the only place where he could do that and be able to check where the bullets hit would be back up on the ridge. He would have to make his way back to the sinkhole during the night. He could sight in the rifle first thing in the morning, then come back through the cave to his camp.

One of his main concerns now was light. He was down now to just a little more than two bottles of carbide, enough to last for about forty-eight hours of constant burning. He still had his flashlight and extra batteries; they should definitely be conserved. There was a gallon of alcohol in the booty from the cave; he would have to jury-rig some kind of lamp. Perhaps he could come up with something using empty C-ration cans. It wouldn't have to be elaborate, just functional.

When he got back to his camp site, Toby retrieved some tin cans from his garbage stash. He didn't have any tools to work with, but he did have a survival knife and one of the tiny half-moon P-38 can openers that were in C-ration boxes. And he had the multi-functional knife from the survival vest, the one with the screwdriver, leather punch and can opener blades in addition to a conventional knife-blade. The flame from the carbide lamp should be hot enough to weld the metal cans.

It took some thought and experimentation, but eventually Toby came up with a workable lamp. He used a ham and lima beans can for a reservoir and a turkey loaf can for a reflector. A part of his towel made a wick, as he stuffed it into the reservoir can and pulled a corner through the bottom of the top can. He could light it with the cigarette lighter that was in his cave pack, along with a can of lighter fluid. As a lamp, it left a bit to be desired, but at least it was an acceptable source of light that would allow him to get through the cave without using his now-precious carbide supply.

Toby left the entrance shortly before morning, after hiding his stash in a side passage where it would be safe from detection by anyone who might accidentally happen to wander into the cave. It was more than a mile to the sink-hole; Toby covered the distance in a little over an hour. Finding his way back was relatively simple; he followed the stream until he found the crawl-way. He was traveling light, carrying only his vest, the M-16 and the Springfield; along with his ever-present cave pack.

Light coming through the sink-hole entrance told him that dawn had broken. Cautiously, he made his way out of the entrance then up the hill to the open area. He reckoned that he was far enough from the valley that his shots would probably not be heard by the troops in the gorge. Still, he wanted to fire the rifle, make any needed corrections, then get out of sight as quickly as possible.

For a target, Toby brought a piece of cardboard from one of the C-ration cartons. He hung it on a tree on one side of the rocky area, using a piece of spring from his parachute harness as a nail, then paced off the distance to the other side of the clearing. He wanted to be as far from the target as possible. Then he lay down in the prone position, steadied the rifle with his left arm, and fired five shots at the center of the cardboard. After firing the last shot, Toby reloaded the rifle, then got up and trotted across the clearing to check the results.

He was pleased with the group; no more shots would be required to sight the rifle in. Someone had evidently zeroed it prior to packing it in the container. That was logical, the weapons had probably been intended for immediate combat use. He put the cardboard back in his pack, took the rifle and other gear and climbed back into the sink-hole. Within an hour, he was back at his campsite. He lay down on the bough bed he had constructed under a rock overhang just outside the cave entrance and went to sleep. He wanted to be well rested before he put his plan into action.

Toby awoke to a peal of thunder from the daily monsoon shower. He looked at his watch; he'd been asleep for five and a half hours. Now was as good a time as any to get into position so he could put his plans into action, but first he wanted to eat a hot meal and drink something warm. It might be a long time before he had a chance to eat again. There was still some Sterno left; he heated a can of beefsteak and a canteen cup full of water. Toby dined on steak and washed It down with hot tea before moving out.

Toby entered a side passage, the one that led to the labyrinth of cliff-side caves. There was one particular place that he wanted to go, a cave just across the valley from an automatic antiaircraft gun position. He had lain at the entrance of the cave and watched the gun crew as they fired at one of the recon flights as it came down the valley. Excitement welled in his breast as he made his way through the cave; the feeling was exactly the same as that he had felt as a thirteen-year old boy sneaking up on a bushy-tail squirrel in a shaggy-bark hickory tree.

When he looked out the cave entrance, Toby saw that the rain had stopped. The storm had moved further west. Ironically, he could see a rainbow behind the other ridge. It was centered almost exactly over the gun position just across the valley! Had he been superstitious, Toby might have taken the rainbow for a sign. He was religious, but his religion was that of the Baptists, not the Pentacostals or Charismatics. Neither were his beliefs in common with those of the Quakers or Jehovah's Witnesses. For Toby Carter, there was no religious prohibition against killing another human being in time of war.

He could see the North Vietnamese gun crew behind their gun just below the base of the opposite ridge. Like him, the North Vietnamese were cloistered in the mouth of a cave. There were at least five people in the gun pit that he could see. No traffic was passing below at the time; he could hear their voices floating across the valley as they jabbered away in Vietnamese. He guessed the range to be about five hundred yards; he set the elevation control on his leaf sight accordingly. Toby lay down on the ground behind a boulder. It was just right for a gun rest. Then he settled down to wait.

Several times he heard the whine of turbine engines high overhead, F-105's returning from missions to the Red River Valley, but no aircraft came close enough for the gunners on the opposite cliff to begin firing. That was what he was waiting for; Toby was not yet ready to openly reveal that there was a man with a gun on the ridge. He could see the gun crew plainly; they had no reason to keep hidden. Whenever the sound of approaching aircraft reached their ears, the five Vietnamese would take their stations by the gun. After the fighters had passed over and the whistling sound of their engines had faded away, they would return to whatever they had been doing. They evidently had a transistor radio; the sound of music - American rock - came across the valley to Toby's ears. The gooks were listening to AFRTS! That was almost too much for him to comprehend.

So NVA troops liked rock music, huh? It shouldn't have surprised him; everywhere he'd been it seemed that younger people ran around with Japanese transistors tuned to rock stations. Toby wasn't a rock fan; Hank Snow, Lester Flatt and Earl Scruggs and Merle Travis were more his style. And Chet Atkins, mustn't forget him! Toby had been trying for years to learn to play like Chet. Thinking of Hank Snow reminded Toby of a song that had been on one of his albums, a song that fit his own situation. Actually, Bobby Bare had recorded it first, about a Waycross, Georgia man who killed somebody then took refuge in Miller's Cave. The last words had been something to the effect that the singer was lost and doomed forever in Miller's Cave. Toby felt a little bit that way himself because it certainly appeared that this Laotian cave would be his final home on earth. At least it sure looked that way, unless something changed.

Hey! What's this? The barrel of the gun across the valley was moving. Something had alerted the crew; maybe they had a telephone link-up with someone. No doubt they did. Before the crew had manned the gun, but had not traversed it; apparently they now were getting ready to shoot. Toby put the front sight squarely on the gunner's head and lined it up through the leaf sight on the rear.

"Come on, you mother-fucker. I just dare you to start shooting that cannon!" His finger tightened on the trigger. Then he heard the sound of a fighter, down low and coming fast.

Suddenly, without warning, the muzzle of the gun across the valley flashed fire. Almost as soon as it did, Toby Carter squeezed the trigger on the Springfield. His aim was a little bit off. He was trying to hit the gunner in the forehead; instead the one hundred and eighty grain steel-jacketed bullet broke the bridge of the man's nose, penetrated his brain and blew out the back of his skull.

Working the bolt as fast at he could, Toby picked off each of the remaining four members of the gun crew while the shock of seeing their comrade die before their eyes had them momentarily confused. He shot every one of them in the head. It was a force of habit with him; he had learned to shoot squirrels in the head with a .22 to avoid spoiling the meat. At this distance, hitting a man in the head was about the same as hitting a squirrel in the same extremity at one hundred feet. The F-4 flashed overhead as he was firing. A few seconds later he heard its bombs exploding somewhere down the valley, followed by the booming of afterburners as the pilot pulled up into a steep climb to get away from the flak from the guns along the ridge. After it had gone, the transistor was still blaring from the gun pit across the valley.

Toby patted the stock of the rifle. He had always heard that the Springfield was the best American rifle ever made. Now he had seen the evidence for himself. He reached behind the mesh of his survival vest and pulled out the piece of cardboard he had used to zero the weapon. About an eighth of an inch below and to the left of the center was a single hole about the size of a dime - with five scalloped edges.

Toby reached into his jacket pocket and pulled out another five-round clip. Opening the bolt, he pushed the five cartridges into the magazine and put the clip back into his pocket. He moved a little closer to the cave's entrance, now that the people directly across the valley were no longer capable of seeing. From his new position he could see another gun crew a little further down the valley. He was above them slightly and could see into their pit. They were traversing their gun back around to face the direction from which the attacking fighter had come. Evidently there was another one around somewhere, either that or the first one was coming back in for a second pass. Why did they do that? Making successive runs from the same direction seemed like a standing invitation for trouble.

The gunner was depressing the barrel of the 37-MM gun, evidently lining his sights on something. Toby heard the loud booming of an F-4's twin GE engines. He didn't wait for the gunner to open fire before shooting him (or was the gunner a girl?) right beneath his helmet. Again he worked the bolt and fired as fast as he could aim. Five shots, five dead NVA. Within two minutes, Toby Carter had wiped out two NVA gun crews. The North Vietnamese were in the process of learning the lesson the Germans had learned in the Argonne Forest, the Mexicans at the Alamo and the British had learned at New Orleans, not to mention the Yankees at Shiloh, Chickamauga and dozens of other places - there's nothing more dangerous than a Tennessee boy with a rifle in his hands!

After killing the second gun crew, Toby decided it was time to vacate that particular position. He doubted that anyone was aware of his presence, but a change of tactics was probably in order. He went back into the cave and scrambled down to a lower level. His next position was further down the valley, where he had a good view of a spot where the road ran right between two karst towers. Light was beginning to fade; it would soon be dark.

About an hour after sunset, when darkness was settling on the land, Toby spotted the first convoy of the night as the drivers were forming up for their run through the valley. He waited until the lights of the first vehicle had passed well beyond the karst towers before he put a round right between the slitted headlights, bursting the engine block. The second round went through the gas tank, sending a shower of gasoline onto a hot exhaust pipe. Using the light from the fire, Toby quickly disabled the next three trucks in the convoy, then set them afire with another clip. Then he sat back to watch the show as a flight of A-4s brought in by Blind Bat systematically destroyed the first convoy they had ever managed to catch along this particular section of road.

Chapter Twelve

"Colonel, I thought you should know about this." Captain Jester was in Colonel Loveless' office at Udorn. He handed the 7/13th intelligence officer a deciphered message. "We just got it from Security Service. It seems one of their snoop planes picked up a rather frantic message from a North Vietnamese station in Laos."

"What does it mean?"

"Well, sir. The message was in the clear. Evidently a sniper has been killing their gun crews and construction workers on the Trail. The guy must really be a crack shot; every single one of his victims has been hit in the head. The Charlies have been jabbering about it for hours."

"Probably a Special Forces Trail-watch team."

"We've checked. They don't have anyone in that part of Laos. Too risky, they say."

"What does this have to do with us?"

"The area where the sniping has been occurring is along the gorge below where our illusive survivor was photographed."

*You've got to be shitting me, Captain! Surely, you don't think one of those missing C-130 people is doing this, do you?"

"I don't know sir, but there's more."

"What?"

"I talked to Major Catlin, the intelligence officer at Ubon. It seems that one of the Blind Bat crews reported something rather strange a few nights back."

"And what was that, Jester?"

"They were working the same area where Captain Preston was shot down, right over this same gorge. All of a sudden they saw flames on the ground. They scoped the area with binoculars and saw it was a truck. Then another one burst into flames, then another. From the light of the fires, they saw a whole convoy blocked by the ones that were burning. A flight of Navy A-4's was enroute to them. They ran them onto the convoy and knocked out the whole thing - fifty-three trucks. It was the biggest truck kill of the whole war so far. And it's really ironic."

"Ironic? What do you mean?"

"Just this, sir, we've dropped hundreds of tons of bombs on that valley but until now no one had ever seen a truck, an elephant or even a coolie. It's because the gorge is so narrow and deep at this point there's always a shadow. No one would have seen this convoy had not that truck burst into flames right before their eyes."

"Do you think this has something to do with this guy Carter?"

"I don't know sir. The shooting could have been. We know he had an M-16, although I don't know how anyone could make kills like the Charlies are reporting with an M-16. They're made to throw a lot of bullets in a hurry, not for accuracy. Besides, these shots are being made from almost a thousand yards in some cases. You'd have to have a scope for that kind of shooting. Still, it's a rather odd coincidence."

"Maybe the guy in the photo is someone else - CIA maybe. Perhaps its not Carter."

"But he was definitely under an Air Force personnel parachute. No one else uses multicolored parachutes, just flight crews. And then there are the other pictures, the ones of the cave entrance on the cliff."

"You mean the ones that show what looks like a cave entrance behind a grove of trees?"

"That's the ones. We have several shots, all taken at different times, that have images in them that appear to be a person. One shows someone by a large cave entrance on the side of a hill. Another strip has what looks like a person on a ledge some distance down the side of the cliff from the entrance."

"There has to be an explanation. Maybe one of the survivors from the flareship is hiding out in the cave. But how would he be able to do all that damage? From what you've told me, it sounds like there is more than one person doing the shooting. Even if it is this Airman Carter - or Captain Preston, we can't rule him out - there's nothing we can do until he makes contact with someone. You remember what Major Deidrich said."

"Yes, sir. I remember what the major said. I just wanted to keep you up to date on what we've found."

"I appreciate that, Jester. And I will see that the information is passed on to Seventh. I know General Momyer has been watching the developments. He'll be interested in your assessment. Stay in contact with Security Service. Let me know if anything else interesting turns up on their tapes. You're dismissed."

After his first action against the NVA, Toby decided it might be prudent to move his camp back to the top of the ridge. It was only a matter of time before the enemy would realize someone on the ground was killing their troops, and not fighters. When they did, surely they would find a way to scale the cliffs and begin searching the cave entrances. Of course they would probably search the top of the ridge as well, but they were more likely to go to where the shots were coming from first.

During his explorations, Toby had discovered that the many cliff-side entrances were all water passages made when the water table was much higher, before centuries of erosion had cut the gorge and left the tall karst towers. A huge labyrinth of cave passages honeycombed the limestone ridge. Some were huge, "bore-hole" passages while others were narrow canyons. Still others were "hands and knees" crawling and there were some that could only be classified as belly crawls, barely passable by anything bigger than a rabbit. In spite of the complexity of the caves, he had discovered that some passages were fairly straight, leading almost in a straight line from the stream passage to the side of the hill.

Rather than carry everything back to the sink-hole, Toby decided to establish a main supply base in one of the side passages leading off of the main trunk that carried the underground streams from the ridge down to the lower level. He would keep only enough supplies for his immediate needs at his new camp; replenishment would be easy enough. He re-stocked his cave pack with food and ammunition for the Springfield and M-16.

Carter took all day to move the stock from the entrance to his new supply base. After he had finished, he went back for one last look at the camp and to police the refuse of his stay. Using a piece of parachute cloth, Toby gathered up the C-ration cans and cartons and put the whole mess in one of the dozens of alcoves just inside the entrance. His latrine would present another problem; had he been thinking, he would have been using parachute cloth as a crapper. All he would have to do would be bundle the stuff up and shove it into a crevice. As it was, he had to cover up the evidence of his presence with rocks.

When he was satisfied that he had completely erased all evidence of his former presence, Toby left the area that had been his home for the past ten days. From now on he would maintain a roving camp, sleeping at a different place every night. He spent that first night just inside the sink-hole entrance, close enough that he could see from light coming in from the surface, but far enough inside that a casual searcher would be unlikely to see him.

When he awoke, it was daylight outside. Rather than go back to the caves from where he had been shooting the previous day, he decided to do a little exploring. He would investigate the ridge south of the sinkhole. Not only could he get a better feel for the land, he might find more targets. There seemed to be more air activity in the vicinity today, particularly reconnaissance flights. Perhaps it was due to the improved weather. The usual midday thunderstorm was not gathering. The annual monsoon period was in its last days; the dry season would soon start. Every time a fighter or reconnaissance bird swooped over, the flak guns in the valley and on the ridge would open up. He wondered if the gooks had manned the gun positions he had taken out the day before. It was a shame he couldn't destroy the guns; all he could do was kill the gunners.

Listen! What was that? A new sound had joined the crescendo of automatic weapons fire - a deep boom. When a flight of F-105's passed over at fairly high altitude, he saw them suddenly scatter as flak began bursting right in their path. That had to be something big; 85-MM or better. Could it be the same gun that had brought them down? The "big gun in a cave?" There was no doubt but that the lights he had seen had been in this direction; maybe the gun was in the mouth of his cave.

Sunlight coming from the west side of the forest indicated that he was near the gorge. Why not take a look; maybe he could see something worth taking a shot at. When Toby got to the edge of the woods, to his surprise he found that it overlooked the exact same spot where he had done his successful shooting. From his perch on the edge of the cliff, Tobin Carter could see just about the entire valley, except for the parts behind the karst towers. And there were targets - dozens of them.

Both of the gun-pits where he had killed the crews were again occupied. He could see into other positions at well. There was an even more lucrative target down below; a construction crew was working to remove the burned-out hulks of the convoy from where they blocked the road. The A-4's had done a very good job; not a truck had escaped. Chalk one up for the Navy! But what was even better than the destruction of the convoy was that the Trail was temporarily blocked. At least a hundred workers were struggling with the blackened remains of the vehicles.

"Those guys look like they're having a really boring day. Why don't we liven things up a bit for them?" Toby was talking to the Springfield. "Now who wants to be first?"

Over to one side of the group, in a small cluster, a handful of people in khaki uniforms seemed to be having a conference. Officers, no doubt; trying to figure out just what would be the best way to get the trucks off of the road. There was only one piece of equipment down there that would be of any use; a bulldozer. It sat idling a hundred feet or so from the conferring group. He was surprised to see them out in the open like that. Were they not yet aware that someone on the ground had killed the gun crews, and that he might just still be lurking in the vicinity? Well, if they didn't know, they were about to find out! Toby shot the bulldozer driver right between the eyes.

His next shot was aimed at one of the officers in the group. A man at three hundred yards is just as big a target as a squirrel at twenty-five. Toby didn't miss. The rest of the group scattered and dove for cover, but did not reach it until his third shot nailed an NVA sergeant. The bulldozer still sat, its engine idling and the dead driver slumped in his seat. Toby knew where the fuel tank should be; his fourth round exploded diesel fuel all over the hot engine. Ten seconds later it erupted into flames. One round left to fire, then he would have to reload.

At the sound of his first shot, the antiaircraft gunners ran to their guns. Evidently they had been told to fire at the ridge-line if anything happened again. But they had no idea where to fire; each report from the Springfield echoed through the valley, reverberating off the limestone walls, sounding like a hundred rifles fired one right after the other. Toby drew a bead on the gunner in the nearest pit. He squeezed the trigger, "Just like Daddy taught me," he thought to himself. The gun fell silent.

Toby kept the gun crew in view as he drew a second clip from his pocket and loaded the five cartridges into the magazine. Two of the gunners were pulling the body of their slain comrade from the gunner's chair while the gunner in the other chair reached across to help them. The fifth person in the pit was talking frantically into a field telephone. Toby shot him next, then killed each of the others in turn. Rather than turning his attention to the next gun crew, who were still firing randomly at the cave entrances below him, he decided to try and blow up the ammunition piled beside the gun. His third shot did the trick; dirt, smoke and debris erupted from the cave entrance that served as their gun pit.

Before reloading, with two shots still left in the rifle, Toby turned his attention to the other gun crew. They were still firing at the wall below him, traversing their barrel back and forth, walking the shells along the cliff wall, trying to put rounds in the mouth of each cave. The firing stopped when Toby killed the two gunners who were operating the gun. He reloaded, then killed the other three.

"God save us from these Americans, they shoot like devils." So had a German soldier written in his dairy during the Meuse-Argonne Offensive in World War I. The Americans the German soldier was writing about had been using the same Springfield rifle that Toby had just used with such effectiveness. Doubtlessly, the North Vietnamese had never read those words. But even if they had not, their thoughts were probably something along those same lines.

Other gun crews further down the valley were still in action, the noise of their firing making quite a din. Toby took advantage of the echoing gunfire and confusion to pick-off five members of the construction crew. All had taken cover, but from his vantage point atop the ridge, he could see an arm here, a head there, a leg sticking out over there. Even if he couldn't kill everyone he shot at, he could wound. And wounding was just as effective out here as a clean shot through the head.

By now Toby was aware that some of the people he had killed were women. One of the antiaircraft gunner's long hair had come floating out of her helmet as she fell backwards when his bullet hit her. For an instant he thought about Sharon, Stephanie, Ailene, Maxine or Sandy. What if one of them were out here and someone was trying to kill them? But the thought quickly passed as he drew a bead on his next victim. "That's war," so the saying goes. If the North Vietnamese wanted to put women into combat, then they were as subject to being shot as the men. Any other time and any other place and he might have had second thoughts about killing women, but not here and not now.

Now that he had formally announced his presence - no fighters had been zooming around when he fired his first shots - Toby decided it might be prudent to move back from the ridge. He was convinced he was not going to get away from this place alive, but he wanted to prolong the final reckoning as long as he could - and do as much damage as one man could possibly inflict on an enemy in the interim. Flak gunners all down the valley were shooting the hell out of the ridge, but they were wasting their shells as surely as did the American fighter pilots every night. Which was more costly? No doubt the bombs cost more in terms of money, but the shells cost time and energy just to get them this far south on the Trail. The results were the same in both cases - zero return on the investment.

What about the grenades? He suddenly remembered that he had yet to test one. Might as well be now as any other time. He pulled one from his pocket, pulled the pin and tossed it over the side of the cliff. He began counting; one thousand, two thousand, three thousand...He had gotten all the way to ten thousand before he heard the loud boom followed by the reverberation of the explosion off the valley walls. Once again the flak positions began firing.

After moving back into the woods, Toby resumed his course down the ridge. Looking at his watch, he reckoned that he had perhaps another hour before it would be time to start back. He wanted to get back to the sink-hole before nightfall. Once again he would spend the night in the cave. Tomorrow he would try something else. He was willing to do anything to harass the NVA and alleviate his own frustrations at being in an ultimately impossible situation. No doubt the gooks would be looking for him after his latest disruption of their day. It was only a matter of time before they sent a squad to search the ridge. No doubt they were already trying to scale the walls and get into the caves. He would have to be very careful from now on.

He was about two miles further down the ridge - and perhaps four miles from the sinkhole - when a pair of Navy A-6 intruders swooped low over the valley. As they were climbing steeply to get into position for a dive-bombing run, the big gun he had heard before opened up on them. From the sound, it appeared that the gun was right below him. He moved to the brink of the ridge. While he could see nothing beneath his position on the ridge -

the gun was too close to the base of the ridge - it was evident by the smoke and noise that it must be almost right below. If that was true and his calculations were right, then the gun must be at or near the mouth of the cave. He could see that the river in the valley suddenly got larger just below him, even though he couldn't see the nearest bank. The gorge must be nearly five hundred feet deep at this point. There was no way he could see the floor immediately beneath him, especially since he had a natural fear of falling and could not get too close to the edge.

It was strange, his acrophobia. The thought of standing at the edge of a five- hundred foot cliff made chills go up and down his back, yet he could stand at the edge of an open C-130 ramp at twelve hundred feet and not fear a thing. He had found that other men who flew seemed to be fellow acrophobia sufferers. Back at the other place, when he was sniping at the gun and construction crews, he had been lying flat on his belly. Besides, the excitement of battle had had his adrenaline up; the natural "combat high" is a conqueror of all fear. He looked at his watch; time to start back to the sink-hole. While on the way back, he thought about the gun below and the cave. The more he thought about it, the more he became convinced that the resurgence of the cave had been below him and that it was in the cave mouth that the NVA hid the reclusive gun which had been causing so much trouble for crews operating over Laos. So far that gun had gotten two C-130 flareships, along with an F-4, two A-1's, an A-26 and an F-105. The F-105 pilot had been zooming along at 16,000 feet, blissfully on his way back to Thakli after a mission in Route Package One, when the gun opened up and shot him out of the sky. He had thought he was out of danger once he crossed the Annamite Range. He had been wrong.

Maybe he could take out that gun! The sudden thought caused him to shiver with excitement. It just might be possible. He could come up on the crew from the darkness of the cave. They would have no idea that he was even there until he started shooting. The Springfield wouldn't work in this instance. He would have to use something that would throw a lot of bullets in a hurry. The M-16? What about the Thompsons? He hadn't even fired them, but so far every round of 30/06 had gone off just like advertised. Not a misfire in the bunch, which was pretty good for ammunition that had been manufactured before he was even born. The rifle was even older, probably almost as old as his dad - and he was fifty years old!

Rather than taking out through the cave with killing on his mind, he would do a reconnaissance and make sure that the gun definitely was in the mouth of the cave. A good time to probably find it inside would be first thing in the morning. Or at least before noon. Most of the crew would probably be asleep then; maintenance people would be checking the gun over after the night's firing. He probably should lie low tomorrow, then

114

make his recon the next morning. If everything worked out, he would go back the next day - or the day after that - and take out the crew. Maybe he could even spike the barrel with a grenade. Blow the breech, anyway.

He was almost to the sink-hole when he heard voices. Oh, shit! Not so soon! How many were there? Had they found any sign that he had been there? The rain would have washed away evidence of his earlier camps, but had they been into the sink-hole? Where had they come from? Were there others? He took shelter behind a rock, un-slinging the Springfield even as he moved. Now would be a good time for the M-16; too bad he had left it in the cave. Were they looking for him? Foolish question; sure they were! He just hadn't expected them so soon.

Silently, trying to be as quiet as possible, he opened the bolt and slipped a single round into the barrel, leaving the five rounds in the magazine intact. He now had six rounds, plus another six in his revolver, that he could fire without reloading. Another clip was strapped to the butt of the rifle with one of the rubber bands from inside his parachute pack, one of the ones that held the suspension lines in place prior to deployment. He peered stealthily around the side of the rock.

One, two, three…there were at least a dozen. That was not good. It looked like he would be in for a gun battle anyway you looked at it. He had to kill every single one of them; he couldn't afford to have any get away to bring reinforcements. Hell, here he was with twelve-to-one odds against him, and he was worrying about someone getting away! Maybe he ought to be worrying about getting away himself! "Take no counsel of your fears," so had written George Patton in 1942, three years before Toby was born. Oh well, it might at well be here as anywhere! The grenades could be a help; he still had two of them in his cave pack. Hopefully, they weren't duds.

The platoon of NVA troops was drawing nearer. They were in a line abreast formation, checking every rock, every fallen tree, every clump of bushes. It would be only a matter of time before they found him. They were spread apart, with about ten feet between them. That was going to make it hard. Every one of them was carrying an AK-47, an automatic rifle; that made it even harder! He was facing an even dozen men armed with semiautomatic rifles and here he was with a fifty-year old bolt action and a revolver - and two hand grenades that might or might not go off. Oh yeah, he had a knife. He had forgotten about the knife.

The knife - maybe it would give him the edge, the element of surprise he needed. Good Lord! Hadn't he spent hour after hour chucking knives at that old English walnut tree in the back yard, the smokehouse and just about anything else into which a knife blade would stick? The smokehouse had so many cuts in it from knife blades that the wall was beginning to come apart even before he left home. The problem was that he had to judge the distance just right in order to guarantee that the knife would hit blade-first. And he hadn't thrown a knife in years now. Besides that, he had never thrown the survival knife, although from the construction, it would probably make a good throwing knife - with practice. He didn't have time to practice.

What the hell? He pulled the knife from its scabbard on his vest, flipped it around and caught the blade between two fingers. One of the soldiers had spied his rock; he started in Toby's direction. Toby threw the knife, then without watching to see what happened, snapped up the Springfield and shot the next nearest in the chest; no time for head shots here! Then he dropped another even as he saw the first one start to crumble to the ground, the leather-covered hilt of Toby's knife sticking from his chest. Another soldier swung his AK-47 in Toby's direction and got off one burst before the ground-bound airman killed him with a shot to the forehead. Three down, nine to go. With his right hand, Toby reached for one of the grenades in his pack. He pulled the pin, drew back and threw the grenade in the direction where he had seen two others disappear in the underbrush. For a second he thought it was a dud, but then a blast of dirt, smoke and debris signaled that it still worked, after all these years. A scream pierced the air, a high-pitched scream, almost like that of a woman.

A radio? Had any of them been carrying a radio? He didn't remember seeing one, but surely they had some means of communications with whoever had sent them. Bezinnnngggg! A round knocked a chip off his rock. One of the zipperheads knew where he was, or thought he did. Toby held his fire, waiting for one to show himself. There was no point in just tossing bullets around with a bolt-action Springfield.

What was that? Movement! A burst from an AK-47 flew in his direction. The bastards were trying to rush him! We'll have none of that shit! They were in the open, running toward him. He dropped three soldiers dead in their tracks and the others dropped to the ground. One round left in the gun. One of the uninjured North Vietnamese was still visible. Toby shot him in the thigh, then opened the bolt and pushed a clip into the magazine. So that's how Sergeant York did it? There were still five left, and one was wounded. And it would soon be night.

The remaining NVA were being very cautious now. Probably they were green troops, on their way south. Someone had detailed them up here to look for him.

"Hey, GI! You surrender now? Okay?" One of the bastards could speak English! Toby was tempted to shout back, "Fuck you!" but kept silent. They were probably trying to sneak up on him, to surround him, just like the Indians did Custer. Only at the Little Bighorn there had been two thousand Indians and about three hundred white men. His odds weren't quite that bad. All he had to do was see 'em, then he could hit 'em.

He caught movement out of the corner of his eye. Slowly he swung the barrel of his rifle around in that direction, just like he used to do when he caught a glimpse of a squirrel high in a hickory tree. Okay, you bastard. Just move one time and you're going to be a dead mother-fucker. There it was! Now! Toby fired at a patch of khaki. One more down, four to go.

He guessed that one or more of them was pretty close to his rock. Maybe it was time for the other grenade. He pulled the pin and flipped it about thirty feet on the other side of the rock. When it went off, he scrambled out from behind the rock and dove behind a tree some twenty feet away. One of the zips rushed toward the rock. Bad move - he was dead before he hit the ground. Three to go, unless the grenade had gotten one. There were still three rounds in the rifle.

Wait a minute! Now there's a change in the odds! Right in front of him, within arm's reach, was an AK-47. There, just a few feet away, was the body of the first NVA, the one who had happened to get in the way of his lucky throw with the knife. Did the others know where he was? He lay as close to the ground as he could get and reached out one arm. His fingers closed on the cold steel of the barrel. No searing pain went through his arm, no one had shot at him. He pulled the AK-47 toward him. He cradled it in his arms and slung the Springfield over a shoulder. Okay, you bastards. Now the odds are getting even better!

Somebody shouted something in Vietnamese. The three remaining troops were on their feet, firing their AK's and rushing his rock. Hey guys! Over here! He fired half a dozen rounds as quickly as he could pull the trigger. All three North Vietnamese fell to the earth, mortally wounded. Twelve out of twelve, not bad for a country boy. Or rather, maybe that was to be expected.

Chapter Thirteen

It was a beautiful late summer Tennessee day. The leaves were starting to turn yellow with brownish tips, a sure sign of lack of rain. Through the windshield of the Air Force blue sedan - "you take the blue of the sky, and a pretty girl's eye" - Major Dan Oberlin could see a turquoise sky, as clear as a bell and not a cloud in sight. There certainly was no sign of rain today.

Dan Oberlin loved driving down the Tennessee highways, like the section of US 70 he was on today. He would soon be coming out of the Middle Tennessee hills and crossing the river at New Johnsonville, passing over into the part of his adopted state that natives called West - never "western" - Tennessee. Oberlin had lived in Tennessee now off and on for almost fifteen years, since he had first come to Sewart Air Force Base as a C-119 navigator fresh out of flight school back in 1951. He had met his wife there; she'd worked in the Base Exchange, in the men's clothing department. She was only nineteen at the time, fresh out of high school at Franklin. But he was only eighteen months older himself. They'd taken one look at each other and fallen in love on the spot. What he hadn't realized at the time was that not only had a Tennessee girl won his Minnesota heart, but her state had captured him as well!

Ever since he and Jan had gotten married after his return from a tour with the wing in Japan, no matter where they had gone on orders from Uncle Sam they had always ended up back at Sewart. They had gone to France in 1958 when the first '130s went to Europe. After three years there they had come right back to Tennessee. Then it was back overseas again, this time to the Far East, to Okinawa. That was in 1963. Then they had come back to Sewart again. When his promotion to Major came through, the wing gave him a new job, with wing intelligence. "Military intelligence, now that was a contradiction in terms," that was the first thought that came to his mind when he got the orders taking him out of the 62nd TCS and reassigning him to wing headquarters. He still flew with the 62nd - when they were not off TDY somewhere - but only enough to stay current and maintain his qualifications for flight pay. At least now he didn't have to spend six months out of the year off TDY somewhere. And since he had just come back from overseas only a few months before, his number was not due to come up anytime soon for another tour in the Pacific.

Oberlin had his radio tuned to WSM but about the time he crossed the river into Benton County the signal began to fade. He spun the dial, looking for another station that wasn't fading in and out. He found WDXI, in Jackson, "1310 on your radio dial," the announcer was saying. West Tennessee, it was a part of the state that was unfamiliar to him from the ground, but not from the air. He knew all the towns - Parsons, Camden, Huntington, Milan, McKenzie, Paris, Union City - all had served as landmarks on his map during the low-level training missions that were a regular part of troop carrier life. At least the terrain in this part of the state was less rolling; the old Herkybird didn't bounce around so much in the summertime heat at 300 feet as it did on missions into the mountains of East Tennessee.

But today he wasn't sitting at the navigator's table on an E-model; rather he was behind the wheel of a Ford sedan, a Falcon no less. And he was seeing West Tennessee from a different angle, horizontal instead of vertical or nearly so. He had followed U.S. 70 west before, but always in the air.

As he drove, Oberlin thought about his mission. He was on his way to talk to a Tennessee farm family about their son, a boy about the same age he had been when he first arrived at Sewart. This boy was listed as MIA, missing in action, but today he just might have some good news for them, depending on what he found out during his visit. He didn't know this Airman First Class Samuel Tobin Carter, at least he didn't think he did. The name didn't ring a bell though Oberlin knew that Carter was stationed at Naha, Okinawa, the same base he and his family had left less than a year before. But then it did sound somewhat familiar; maybe he had seen the name on some crew orders when he was pulling a tour at TMC at Clark. A lot of TAC C-130 crews had passed through there; from what he had been told about this kid, Carter, he had been TDY to Mactan last year about the same time he was at Clark at the Transportation Movement Coordinator office. That had been his last TDY before coming back to Sewart.

At a wide place in the road called Hickory Flat, he left U.S.70. From there it was only a couple of miles down one road and about a mile down another to the Carter family home. He drove down a gravel road across a wooden bridge to an unpainted wooden house. He estimated its age; probably over fifty years old. The yard was shaded by several huge white oaks; they were probably twice as old as the house, maybe three times. An old roadbed ran through the edge of the yard, the remains of a road that had once served armies, settlers heading west, adventurers and travelers on their way to see the sights on the other side of the Mississippi. The Frenchman, Alexander de Toucqville, had traveled this road, as had Andrew Jackson and Nathan Bedford Forrest; so had Grant's armies as they headed South toward Shiloh.

"Mr. Carter? I'm Major Oberlin, from Sewart."

"How do you do, Major?" Sam Carter shook Oberlin's hand. "So you're from Smyrna? I got out of the Army there, back in '45."

"You were based there? Well, how about that? What did you do in the service?"

"Flight engineer, on B-24s. When I was at Sewart I was a ground instructor. Taught hydraulics to new pilots and flight engineers. Come on up on the porch. It'll be cooler there than in the house."

"It really is cool here in this valley." His use of the word "valley" instead of "hollow" gave him away.

"Where're you from, Major?"

"I was born in Minnesota, but I call Tennessee home now. My wife is from Franklin. That's where we live now."

Frances Carter came out on the porch. She was a somewhat plump woman in her early forties; her husband looked to be a few years older, fifty maybe. After the introductions, she addressed the Air Force officer, "I understand you have some word about Toby?"

"Maybe you could call it that. At least we think we do. We - that is, the Air Force - think there is reason to believe he is not only still alive, but he has so far managed to evade capture. But there are some things we need to know, that's why I'm here today. I'm with the intelligence office at Sewart. The people who keep track of survivors in Southeast Asia need to find out some things about your son."

"What kind of things?"

"Several things, Mrs. Carter. Why don't we get started by the two of you telling me everything about him you can think of. Just what kind of person is he? That's what we want to know."

"Well, Toby was always a good boy. He hardly ever gave us any trouble, except that he was sometimes argumentative." Mrs. Carter did most of the talking while her husband sat and listened.

"What kind of student was he? Did he get good grades?"

"Not as good as he could have. Toby is a very smart kid, but he's lazy. He never studied; we hardly ever saw him bring a book home from school, unless it was a library book."

"What about girls? Does he have a girl friend?"

"No, not that anyone knows about. He rarely dated when he was at home."

"What did he do? Was he active in sports?"

"He went out for basketball in grade school, but hardly ever played. In high school he was on the baseball team but never played there much either. What he did do was spend a lot of time in the woods. He was a hunter, all three of our boys are, even the youngest. Toby started hunting when he was nine years old. From the time he killed his first squirrel there probably wasn't a day during hunting season when he didn't go out into the woods or the fields hunting something. Squirrels, rabbits, birds, you name it and Toby hunted it."

"I assume he was a good shot."

"Is' a good shot. All of my boys are good shots; they ought to be, as many cartridges as they've shot up," Sam Carter got into the conversation. "Let me show you something." He got up and walked off the porch, at the same time motioning for Oberlin to follow.

"Look at this." He pointed toward an English walnut tree. The bark was chipped away. "Those boys did this; they put their targets on this tree. There's enough lead in that tree to make a boat anchor. And come over here, look at this." He pointed to the side of an outbuilding. The unpainted boards were cracked and weathered; Oberlin could see where the point of a knife blade - several knife blades - had penetrated the boards hundreds of times. "That Toby would spend hour after hour throwing his Scout knife into this tree; if not his Scout knife, then a butcher knife."

"That's interesting. Just how good of a shot is he, anyway?"

"I think I've got something in the house that will answer that question. Come on." Sam Carter led Oberlin through the back door. He reached atop a cabinet and pulled down a rolled up piece of brownish paper. "Take a look at this."

Oberlin unrolled the paper; it was a target. The target was shot full of holes, or rather there was one hole right in the middle. Most of the bulls eye had been shot away. Not a single other hole was in the paper. In one corner were the words, written in a boyish scrawl, Toby Carter - 1957. That was nine years ago, Oberline thought. Toby would have been eleven years old!

"That answers one question, now what about his fascination with caves? There aren't any caves around here, are there?"

"Not here. They're up by the river. That was my brother's doing. Bobby was stationed up at Fort Campbell. He and some of his buddies got to going into some of the caves up there. After he got out of the Army, he started looking for caves down in this area. He lives up by Camden, now. He was the one that got Toby into the cave thing. Me and his mother were both worried silly, especially after we found out about the time Bobby sent him into some place no higher than that second rung on that chair over there in the corner. Not a whole lot wider, either. I think Toby took his old carbide lamp with him when he went back to the service after his first leave."

"Mr. Carter, you've answered the two questions I was sent here to ask. I wish I could tell you some more news beyond what I've already told you. Maybe I'll be able to come back with something good to tell you in a few days."

They walked through the house and onto the front porch.

"Mrs. Carter, it was a pleasure to meet both of you. Like I told your husband, I hope I can come back with some good news in a few days. In the meantime, I'd begin praying even harder for him. He needs all the help he can get."

"Don't worry, Major. I'm praying for him all the time. So's everybody in our church, and I guess everybody here and in Milan, too."

"That is really fine, Mrs. Carter. And I believe those prayers are being answered." With those words Major Oberlin took his leave of the Carter family and headed back up the road to Sewart.

Several days later Captain Jester was again in Loveless' office at Udorn. "Sir, we just got the report from the intelligence officer at Sewart. He went to Carter's home and interviewed his parents. Would you like to read the report, or have me give you the highlights?" Captain Jester queried Colonel Loveless.

"I would like to read the report, but first why don't you give me the highlights."

"Yes, sir. Basically, it seems that Airman Carter has always been somewhat of a loner. He spent a lot of time out in the woods. His cave exploration background goes back to when he was ten years old; his uncle, a former paratrooper by the way, started taking him into caves after he got out of the service."

"That pretty much goes along with what we had already been able to find out."

"There's one other thing, sir."

"Let's have it."

"Airman Carter is a crack shot; the interrogating officer was shown an old target Carter had shot at when he was at 4-H Club camp at age eleven. Every bullet was in the bulls-eye, in a group you could cover with a dime. In fact, everyone of them - ten shots - went through the same hole!" Colonel Loveless looked up from the report in front of him; he peered at the younger man over his bifocals.

"What you're telling me, Captain, is that we have a survivor on the ground in Laos who is; one, an outdoorsman; two, a crack shot and three, an experienced cave explorer in a country that is full of them?"

"That's just about it, sir. In a nutshell."

"I guess your scenario would explain who the person is in the picture and who is raising so much havoc with our friends on the Trail. But I still don't understand how he could be doing such shooting with an M-16. Hell, from these reports from Security Service, the gooks are claiming this guy is making shots at a thousand yards, and hitting everything he shoots at. The

Army and Marine snipers are nowhere near that good, and they're using specially designed sniper rifles."

"You have to remember, sir. Carter wasn't trained by the military. He's been shooting since he was old enough to walk. Besides that, he's from Tennessee."

"What the hell does that have to do with anything? A lot of people are from Tennessee."

"That's right sir, people like Davy Crockett, Sergeant York, Nathan Bedford Forrest and his raiders. In fact, most of Forrest's men came from the same general area that Carter grew up in. For that matter, every one of the men who went to the Alamo with Crockett were from within that same region. Are you familiar with Sergeant York, sir?"

"That he won the Medal of Honor in World War I, but that's about it."

"He won that medal because he could shoot. York killed two dozen Germans and captured what was left of a machine gun company; about a hundred and fifty of them - all by himself. He went up against machine guns with a bolt-action rifle - and won."

"I see your point. You think that Carter got hold of a Springfield rifle?"

"I don't know, sir. But I'm ninety-nine percent certain that Airman First Class Samuel Tobin Carter is hiding out in that cave and killing more VC than our air strikes. He's doing more damage to the infiltration routes than our bombing campaign and the White Star teams all rolled into one. And the most important thing is that the North Vietnamese are scared shit-less of him."

"I guess so, after he's killed how many now, close to fifty?"

"More than that now, sir. Our latest intercept message involved a patrol the North Vietnamese sent out especially to kill or capture the sniper. Not a single man came back."

"No shit?"

"No shit, sir. The North Vietnamese think their men are being killed by a ghost."

"A ghost!"

"Yes, sir. That's what they're telling the people in Hanoi. That may just be the way they're trying to explain why they can't take the sniper out, but then you have to remember, the Vietnamese are quite superstitious and so are the Lao. Evidently this particular cave is sacred; they think they have offended God or something, now He's punishing them."

"I thought the communists were atheist."

"The communists are, but you have to remember that probably two thirds of those coming down the Trail have no idea what communism is. Most are just rural Vietnamese, simple people with little sophistication. To them, they're fighting the Americans because we've taken the place of the French."

"Don't start sounding like a dove on me, Jester."

"It's true, sir. Ho Chi Minh has convinced his people that they're fighting a war that is a continuation of the war with the French. We've known that for months, ever since the North Vietnamese started sending troops to the south. The average North Vietnamese soldier is not from Hanoi, but from some village out in the boondocks. In a way the North Vietnamese are just like us; they send farm boys to South Vietnam while the United States does the same thing. You know the saying; the war in Vietnam is being fought by the hicks, spicks and niggers while everyone else stays home and makes a buck."

"Carter is a hick, isn't he?"

"You might say that, sir. He's a farm boy, and he never went to any school beyond high school."

"He's like all the rest of the soldiers, sailors and airmen fighting this war - and all the other wars the U.S. has fought for that matter. From what we know about him, he seems to be a good kid. You know what, Captain?"

"No sir."

"We've got to get him out of there, but I'm damned if I know how we can do it without risking a lot of people."

"Yes, sir. I agree with you. There has to be a way to get him out, but how?"

"Come to think of it, there is a way. I just thought of it. But first he has to make contact with us somehow. Captain, I thank you for your report. And I believe your assessment of our intelligence is excellent. Are you a praying man?"

"Yes, sir. I believe in God. It's been a while since I went to church, but I pray."

"Me, too. Like a lot of us, I suppose. We need to be praying that this kid will make contact with us - soon. I guess we should pray that he has the means of making contact with us."

"Should we notify the chaplain, sir?"

"That might not be a bad idea, Captain Jester. It sure might not."

After Toby's battle with the NVA squad, he had some cleaning up to do. He couldn't leave the bodies where they lay; someone might come along and find them, then his sink-hole. Besides, the bodies would start to decompose in a few hours. He didn't want to have to smell them. Burying the bodies was out of the question. For one thing, he didn't have a shovel. Besides, the task would be too time-consuming, especially since he was on top of a solid rock ridge. Then he remembered; there was a pit about five hundred yards away, on the opposite side of the ridge from the gorge - and from his cave entrance. He didn't want to dump a bunch of dead bodies into his cave, and he didn't want to dump them into the valley where they would be sure to be discovered. It was nearing nightfall; he would have to hurry to get all of the bodies located and disposed off before it was too dark to see.

Finding the pit was not as hard as he thought it might be; he walked straight to it. But then he had to find all twelve gooks, then drag each one in turn across nearly a quarter mile then dump him in the pit. Fortunately, the Vietnamese were small. Each weighed no more than a hundred and twenty-five pounds; several were smaller. Seeing the results of his work up close made him feel uncomfortable. Even though he had already killed more than fifty of their fellows, these were the first enemy troops he had been close enough too to really have a good look.

He was surprised that they looked so young, even younger than he was at twenty. They were probably older than they looked, but he doubted that any were much older than he. Getting them to the pit and throwing them in was not as difficult as he had thought it might be, but the sound of the bodies crashing off the limestone walls was disconcerting, especially the "thud" they made when they hit the bottom. The pit must have been close to a hundred feet deep. Pulling his knife from the chest of the first man he killed was the worst experience of the lot. The knife was buried to the hilt, and the blade was covered with the dead Vietnamese' blood when he finally pulled it free. Toby wiped the blood on the soldier's khaki uniform.

Before dragging each body to the pit, Toby removed the packs and ammunition and retrieved each of the unfortunate soldier's rifles. Everyone was carrying an automatic AK-47, the new weapon that North Vietnamese soldiers were being issued. He collected the captured booty by the sink-hole. From there he would carry it into the cave and add it too his stash.

After he had finished the gruesome task of hiding the evidence of his battle, Toby retreated into the sanctuary of his cave for the night. He had settled on one of the dry side passages leading to the cliff side as a base; he didn't want to go to sleep in a part of the cave that was subject to flooding. The particular passage was one that led to an opening on the cliff wall, one of the old stream exits from the early years of the cave's existence. At the entrance he could sleep outside the cave, yet still be secure from detection. He could even watch the fireworks from the nightly air strikes, and even join in himself if he wanted too. Ever since that night when he had stopped the convoy in the valley and the fighters had come in and destroyed it, it seemed that the valley by the karst towers was a favorite target of the strike aircraft. Tons and tons of bombs had been dumped into that valley in the past several days; unfortunately, they did little damage.

Before he went to sleep, he began planning the next day's activities. He would travel light, taking only his M-16, the survival vest and pistol, his cave pack and a few grenades. The rope to the lower level was still in place; he could carry another link anyway, along with a section of parachute cloth in case he decided to sleep before coming back up to the upper level. Tomorrow would be a reconnaissance mission; he would find out what waited below, then come back for a more potent weapons package after he had determined just what he was going to be up against. A gun as big as the one he thought was in the mouth of the cave would probably have a large crew, maybe as many as two dozen men - or women?

He was grateful that none of the squad he had battled had been women. There was no doubt but that some of his sniper targets had been, he had seen their long hair fly when their helmets came off as they fell. But they had been on the other side of the valley, too far away to see the damage that had been done to them. To Toby, women were not for war, not even Orientals. While he definitely preferred the Caucasian beauty of someone like Sharon Craft, the Vietnamese and Thai women had a beauty of their own. He had always been impressed by the delicate features of the young Vietnamese women he had seen on the streets of Saigon, and the rounded curves of their bodies beneath the clingy Aoa Dais that they wore.

What about Sharon? Where was she tonight? What was she doing? Did she still think of him, or had she really written off their trysting in Bangkok as just that, a fleeting love affair that was but a part of one's life? He would like to see her again, but now he knew that would never be. Nor would he ever see his folks again, not his parents, not his brothers or his sisters. He would never see the people he had gone to school with for most of his young life. At least not in this life. What would happen to him when the NVA bullet finally found its way into his body? Would he feel the pain? After that, then what? Toby believed in God, and he believed the soul lived on after death. He had every reason to believe he would go to Heaven when he died. He had grown up in the Baptist faith, with the belief that confession of Jesus Christ as the Son of God and the Savior brought eternal life. He had learned the words to John 3:16 so long ago that he didn't remember not knowing them, "For God so loved the world, that He sent His only begotten Son, that whosoever believeth in Him should not perish, but have eternal life." Toby believed in Him. He remembered that Sunday morning, a week before Easter, when he had realized that Jesus had died for him.

Thinking about Jesus made him remember Sunday School, and the girls in his class. Every Sunday morning he had sat in the intermediate Sunday School class with them, then on Sunday evenings he had gone back to Training Union. Most of the time he was the only boy in the class; one guy with anywhere from three to about a dozen girls. Just before he left to go into the Air Force, they had had a party for him and he was the only boy there. That party had signaled the end of his childhood innocence. The next milestone in his life had been the barking of the drill sergeants who met the plane bringing his group of recruits to the San Antonio airport from Memphis. Actually they had gone through Dallas, where the Memphis contingent had boarded another plane that was filled to the gunnels with recruits from all over the country.

Those five weeks at Lackland had definitely been a formidable obstacle. But now he realized that the training instructors were from a different world, that of the support side of the Air Force, not the operations side. None of them had ever experienced combat and none ever would; not the civil engineers, supply clerks, air police, motor pool and other job specialties the TI's represented. Even the mechanics were in support functions, it was only the operations people - the pilots, navigators, flight mechanics and loadmasters - that saw real combat. Even SAC's finest, the boom operators and gunners on the KC-135's and B-52's, were well removed from any danger in the present war. They flew too high to be threatened by the guns of Laos and they never operated over North Vietnam.

Only the fighter pilots and the trash haulers got close enough to the war to see what it was really like, them and the helicopter crews. The trash-haulers got a much closer look than even the fighter pilots. While both faced danger every day, the airlifters worked with grunts who were out in the paddles facing the illusive enemy. But no one in the Air Force was seeing the war like he was; "right down amongst 'em," as old Cuzzie Seavers used to say.

Chapter Fourteen

The next morning Toby gathered his equipment and sat off into the depths of the cave. When he got to the drop to the lower level, the young survivor found the rope still intact and coiled by the waterfall where he had left it. He had been a little worried that the Viets might have ventured into the cave looking for him and found it. But he had seen no sign that anyone had been in the upper levels of the cave. Maybe they thought the shooting had all been coming from the top of the ridge.

Using his hand-woven rope more as a safety line than anything else, Carter climbed down the breakdown to the lower level of the cave. The water was up a little in the stream-bed below from what it had been the first time he had ventured down the climb. But the stream was running clear, giving no evidence of flooding. There had been no rain for several days now; the monsoon season was apparently over. Now the region would be entering the dry season, the time when the North Vietnamese would begin pouring supplies down their pipeline to their troops in the south. The flareships and fighters would be working overtime, trying to find the trucks, then stop them before they got their loads close enough to South Vietnam to aid the enemy war effort there. That was why the destruction of that gun was so important. There was no way any air strike could take It out. And no one else would ever be able to find it. Special Forces had no cave warfare troops, after all!

Although he tried not to think about it, in the back of his mind Toby knew that his own chances of knocking out the gun were about the same as being rescued. Picking-off gun crews and repair workers from long range with a rifle was one thing, his victims had had no idea where the bullets came from that killed them. In fact, they had never known what hit them! At least not those who had fallen to his first shots. The gun crews had known someone had a bead on them, but who and from where was something they never figured out.

Going up against a gun in a cave was going to be different. There was always the remote possibility he might be able to find some way to snipe at them from long range, but he doubted it. This would more than likely have to be a commando style operation, one where he suddenly threw a lot of firepower at those he was attacking and knocked them out before they came to their senses and started shooting back. Maybe his grenades would come in handy. As for the knife, that incident on the hill had been nothing but pure, blind luck.

Retrieving his knife from the body of the dead NVA soldier had been probably the worst part of his ordeal on the ridge. It had been covered with warm, sticky blood. A gooshy, sucking sound had emitted from the soldier's chest when he pulled it out. At least he had had the presence of mind to wipe the blood on the Vietnamese' own uniform and not on his! Then there was the one he had hit in the thigh and only wounded. The young soldier had more or less committed suicide; he had raised his gun and tried to shoot Toby. His .38 had taken care of that one. What would he have done if the man had surrendered? He was in no position to take prisoners, but did he have the coldness of heart to shoot a wounded man after he had surrendered? That would make him as bad as the VC!

The size of the lower passageway was truly impressive. With ceilings almost a hundred feet high and a full-fledged river running in a trunk passage that was equally as wide, the cave was equal too or perhaps even greater than Carlsbad, at least from what he had read about the New Mexican caverns. He had never been there himself; only vicariously through books and articles in the NSS News.

From the breakdown and mud wall where he had climbed down, to where he had seen the lights and heard the voices and generator was probably close to three miles of uninterrupted cave passage. Wouldn't the big-time cavers in the NSS go wild if they could see this! But it would be a long time before any other non-Orientals would ever see this cave. It was probably a completely unexplored cave. He doubted that the Viets had been in the cave very far. There was no reason for them too. The last time any non-Asians had been in the region was before the French defeat twelve years before.

He wondered where the river came from. He had not been upstream past where he had climbed down from above; the water was too deep and too wide for him to cross. Getting soaking wet in a cave that far inside was suicidal; he would die from hypothermia before he could get outside. And that was what one would need to do, unless they were wearing diver's wet suits or some other special clothing designed to prevent loss of body heat. One of the exposure suits they carried on over-water flights would have come in handy. There had been some on the airplane, but that was one item he hadn't thought to include in his bag of survival tricks. Maybe next time - no, this was a once-in-a-lifetime experience - there would never be a "next time!"

This far upstream the water seemed almost still, though he knew that it was moving quickly toward the entrance. Because the waters were so still, he knew they were deep, even if he could see rocks on the bottom. There was truth to that old saying, the one about still waters always running deep. Noise from the waterfall behind him and rapids somewhere up ahead made the lower chamber a noisy place indeed, a big change from the almost dead silence of the upper part of the cave where he had spent the last several weeks. There, the silence had been almost deafening, broken only by the occasional drip, drip, drip of water falling from the end of a stalactite off somewhere in the inky darkness.

At least the vastness of the cavern made for easy walking. And there were no tight constrictions to crawl through while lugging an M-16 and pushing and pulling the rest of his equipment along. He had been tempted to leave his radio with the stash from the airdrop bundle. That radio was his one link with the outside world. Even though he could hardly use it in the cave - and would be very unlikely to do so in the valley - he could scarcely afford its loss. That was why he was wearing the vest, with the survival and signaling equipment that there was always the off-hand chance he might have a chance to use even yet.

He had been following the river for almost two hours when he glimpsed a light up ahead. But this light was more subdued than before, and he heard no sound of generators. A glance at his watch told him it was mid-afternoon. The gun crew was probably asleep, resting for their work that evening. At least the cool atmosphere of the cave would make sleeping easy for them, much easier than for the Blind Bat enlisted men back at Ubon! The thought had never crossed his mind before, that the gun crews were better rested than the aircrews with whom they dueled each night. Come to think of it, he'd been sleeping much better at the cave mouth than he ever had at Ubon, or even during his R&R in Bangkok. At Ubon it had been the heat; in Bangkok Sharon had not let him get much sleep. But then he had hardly wanted to sleep, not with someone so lovely, so blonde and so willing as her around!

Toby un-slung his M-16 and checked to see that there was a round in the chamber. From here on, he would have to be careful. Until he got close enough to the entrance and the outside light, all he could really hope for was that no one would be looking back into the cave and see his light. He snuffed out the carbide lamp and pulled the angle-head flashlight from his cave pack. He unscrewed the end and selected a red lens from the assortment inside. The red glow would not be as visible as the warm, yellow glow of the carbide lamp and it would not cast as long a beam. Shining the light directly at the ground in front of his feet, he eased his way stealthily toward the light up ahead.

To conceal himself as best he could, Toby clung as closely as possible to the wall of the cave. There was more breakdown - chunks of limestone that had fallen from the ceiling - the closer he came to the entrance. He could use those boulders as concealment. Fortunately, the rushing of the river over the breakdown boulders near the entrance concealed the sound of his movement. The river's roar was almost deafening. How did the North Vietnamese stand the constant noise? Evidently, they were used to it. He eased his way as close to the light as he dared, then stopped beside a limestone slab as big as a house when he reached a point where the entrance of the cave was visible in the light.

The cave's valley entrance was truly huge, in contrast to the comparatively tiny sink-hole up on the ridge through which he had entered it. The ceiling was at least fifty feet high and the passage three times that wide. On one side the river flowed out into the valley; the other had been cleared of the many rocks and boulders which once had covered the floor. Now the cave entrance was home to the crew of the big gun that was silhouetted in the dim light from outside. A section of rail ran out of the entrance, the rails that allowed the crew to move the gun in and out of the cave whenever they wanted.

It was daytime and the gun was unattended. The members of its crew were asleep, suspended in hammocks slung from wooden racks by the rock wall of the cave. Only three Vietnamese were awake; one was keeping watch while two others tended a cooking fire just outside the entrance. Crates of ammunition for the gun were stacked at the end of the rails, placed so the crew could load the trolley with extra rounds before moving the gun out into the daylight of the outside world; or more likely into the night. There was another structure in the cave, a container that reminded him of the remnants of ancient wooden cribs pioneers had constructed to hold their corn. It was made from saplings lashed together with spaces between almost large enough for a rat to get through. Maybe it was an ammunition container, but if it was, it was empty.

But then he caught movement in the container. His curiosity aroused, Toby left the sanctuary of his slab and inched his way closer to the cage-like structure. The light was so dim that far from the entrance that he could hardly see. Then he realized what he was seeing; it was a cage! And someone - or something - was imprisoned in it. He moved as close to the cage as he dared, but still could not make out who or what was inside. But there was really little doubt; there was a person in the cage and, unless he missed his guess, that person was an American flyer! They were probably holding a prisoner there until a truck came through to take him up north to the Hanoi Hilton.

Toby felt a pang in his heart as he sympathized with whoever was in the cage. At least he was free, even if his own prospects for rescue were nonexistent. This poor guy was penned up like a trapped animal, waiting for an uncertain fate. Who was it? He was too far from the cage and the light was too dim to tell. Could it be someone from his crew? It was possible, although everyone but himself and the pilot, Captain Preston, should have jumped far enough away from the Trail to have been rescued - as long as they got on the ground in one piece. He wished he could get close and let whoever was in the cage know he was there, but there was just no way. Not today. It was too close to where the gun crew members were sleeping.

For more than an hour Toby scrutinized the scene before him. During that time the person in the cage moved around some, but he still couldn't tell for sure if it was an American. The three Vietnamese continued with their cooking and guarding, although the man on guard duty seemed to be mostly bored, like guards everywhere. Then one of those by the cook pot walked over to a metal gong. Picking up a pole, he whacked the gong two good blows. The occupants of the hammocks began to stir, then climbed out of their sleeping racks and began stirring around. He wasn't surprised to see that several of the sleepers were women, girls really, even though they were dressed like the men in khaki uniforms. Their long hair and breasts gave them away. He felt a stirring in his loins at he looked at some of the slim forms; it was the first indication of his masculinity he had had in days.

At the sound of the gong, the occupant of the cage had also stirred, climbing to his feet to cling to the bars. His size alone ruled out any doubts that he was American. The man had to stoop to stand up in the cage. But he was still too far away for Toby to tell who he might be.

Now that the gun crew was awake, Toby decided it was time for him to go. He looked at his watch - 1600 hours. Better make a mental note of the time. When he came back - if he came back - he wanted to be sure and catch the crew asleep. His eyes had grown accustomed to the lack of light in the cave. He was able to find his way much further into the cave than he had been when he extinguished his flashlight when he was coming out. When the darkness finally became so total that he couldn't see the ground in front of his feet, he once again used his flashlight with the red lens until he was far enough away to re-light his carbide lamp. When he did light it, he was careful not to hold his hand over the tip too long waiting for the acetylene to build up; there was no sense in making a big "boom" that might be heard over the sound of the rushing waters!

After two trips from near the entrance to the waterfall, Toby was becoming familiar with the huge trunk passage. It took much less time to make his way back than during the first trip. The hardest part of the entire journey was climbing up the slope by the waterfall back to the upper level. Even with the aid of the rope, the climb was strenuous. Without the rope, it would have been an impossible climb.

Throughout the trip back to the sinkhole, Toby's mind was on what he had seen at the cave entrance. That the gun was there was no longer as important to him as the person in the cage. Then there were the women; several of the Vietnamese had been women - girls really. They were probably not any older than he. Could he kill young women up close as callously as he knew he would have too to wipe out the crew? Even if they were Vietnamese - and communist to boot? What about the prisoner? Now, that was a new twist; something he had never considered. He had planned to make a sort of kamikaze raid on the gun crew, go out in a blaze of glory kind of thing, not that anyone would ever know to give him the glory. But now what?

After reaching the upper level and pulling the rope up behind him, Toby went to the place where he had stashed his weapons and rations. It was in a side passage deep inside the cave, in a dry area away from the stream. He extinguished his lamp, partly to save his dwindling supply of carbide, but mostly to allow the darkness to overtake him.

There is no place on earth as dark or as silent as a cave. Once the flame went out, Toby could see absolutely nothing. Not a single photon penetrated the veil of darkness that was so heavy he could almost feel it. There was complete silence around him, a silence broken only by an intermittent distant drop of water, falling no doubt from the tip of a stalagmite that had been hundreds - even thousands - of years in the making. His own breathing seemed like a roaring lion in the otherwise silent world within which Toby Carter now made his home.

In that black and silent world, Toby pulled the parachute cloth around himself and pushed all thoughts out of his mind except those dealing with the matter at hand. He suddenly felt a sense of tremendous responsibility, as if the whole war was now on his back. He knew where the gun was that had shot down the crew from the 817th, and probably had shot him down as well. That gun would be pulled back outside again tonight; its crew of women would try to knock other Americans out of the night sky. Then there was the prisoner in the cage. Even though he did not know him, Toby felt a responsibility toward the man. He was free, even if he was trapped like a raccoon treed by dogs in a cave, and the prisoner was caged. He ought to try to free the man - but then what? Then there would be two people hiding in the cave, awaiting the inevitable.

Now wait a minute! The chances were that whoever was in that cage was an officer - a pilot, or at least a navigator. While his own life was not that valuable to the military, an officer was another story. It cost the government hundreds of thousands of dollars to train a pilot or navigator, and that was just to get them through flight school. He knew that the Jolly Green crews were more than willing to risk their lives to pluck downed pilots out of the jungle, even when the survivor was surrounded by enemy troops. If he could get this guy out, then maybe they would come for him. Maybe they would pick him up, too - even if he was nothing but a lowly enlisted swine.

What if he did get the guy out of the cage? He would have to get him to the upper level. That climb was bad enough for him, and he'd been eating regularly for the past weeks, even if the food had been twenty-year old rations. The guy in the cage was undoubtedly malnourished and weak. He would never be able to climb up the rope and it was doubtful that Toby could carry him. Even if there was another way to the lower level, there would be a climb involved. This was a problem he was going to have to work on.

The next question was - when? There was no doubt that whatever he did, it would have to be done during the daylight hours when the gun crew was asleep. If he could catch them in their sleeping hammocks, he might be able to get away with it. But if they were awake, he would be so outnumbered they were sure to kill him.

All right, so he would probably take a lot of them with him; his death wouldn't help the plight of the prisoner one bit - and it wouldn't be so good for him, either! From what he had just seen today, timing would take care of that problem. It would have been fairly easy to take out every single one of the gun crew today. Chances were, he would find essentially the same situation if he went back again tomorrow - or the next day, or the day after that.

What about attacking from the entrance? That was an option he had not considered. Or at least escaping that way. He really didn't know what the slope was like on the outside of the cave. Back up where he had done his sniping, the walls had been practically vertical, but by the entrance where he had spent his first few nights there seemed to be more of a slope. And there were trees in front of and below the entrance. They would afford cover as he approached the cave entrance. The more he thought about the idea, the more he liked It. At least he should reconnoiter the area before he made his attack. It would be a shame to get the prisoner out, then not be able to get him up the climb in the cave when all the time there had been an easier way.

That much was settled. He would check out the hillside tomorrow, then decide on a final plan after he knew how the land lay. There was always the possibility that the NVA were not using that area extensively. The road definitely lay closer to the opposite side of the valley.

Toby's thoughts began to turn toward the cave he was in. He had been so busy trying to figure out how he could outwit the North Vietnamese that he hadn't thought much about the cave. He had been aware of its immense presence without really thinking about the cave itself. Ordinarily the cave would have occupied all of his attention, but ordinarily his life wouldn't depend on the sanctuary it offered. That the cavern was immense was obvious; he had explored several miles of passage and there was probably much more that he had not seen. Wouldn't the exploration crowd in the NSS go wild if they saw this thing! The Cave Research Foundation would be trying to work out a deal with the NVA allowing them sole access to the place, just like they had done with the National Park Service at Mammoth.

It was strange, but the cave was the only part of this whole nightmare that was familiar to him. Killing people was not part of his life; crawling through caves was. Yet it seemed he had entered a new world, one where what was familiar to the teenager or young adult was something he could barely remember. He could hardly even visualize the cargo compartment of the Herkybird in which his most recent life had been spent. Here he was in the middle of the Vietnam War, yet he wasn't even in Vietnam, but in the mountains of a country most Americans didn't even know existed and those who did couldn't pronounce the name. "Laos, It rhymes with louse," that's how the news commentators had told their viewers how to pronounce the name of the tiny mountainous country where President Kennedy had decided to begin his war against communism back in 1961.

Toby had still been in high school then; in 1961 he was just in the tenth grade. A shy, introverted teenager too scared to ask a girl for a date, knowing inside that if he did, he would more than likely be turned down. That was why high school had been such a terror for him, even more than the situation he was now in, at least it had seemed so at the time. At least here he had some control over the situation; then he had been just another victim, what the beautiful people called "nerds." Now the beautiful people were in college or starting out in the business world while the nerds were off fighting the war. It was funny, but he couldn't even remember what most of those he had gone to high school with even looked like. Yet, it has only been three years since he had seen them last.

How long had he been lying here in the blackness of the cave? An hour, two? It must be getting well along into the evening hours, he had heard the wings of bats leaving the cave. There were quite a lot of bats in the cave, some of the largest he had ever seen. Giant fruit bats, some of them. As large as crows. Most of the bats were in the larger passages but there were a few in the smaller side passages like the one he was in. At least it wasn't a "bat cave," filled with millions of the quano-producing creatures whose presence would have caused an awful stench. Here there were a few hundred bats, but they were spread out, not clustered together.

Speaking of bats, it was getting close to time for Blind Bat to make his appearance in the Laotian sky. Soon the four-engine bat-plane would be orbiting seven thousand feet above the Trail, dropping the two-million candlepower wands that would turn night into day - except in the deep shadows of the karst towers, the shadows that prevented the crews from ever seeing most of the trucks below them. So near, yet so far away. No doubt he knew some of the guys on the crew, guys who were much closer to him than anyone in high school had ever been. It was strange that no one ever talked about their buddies from school. Girlfriends, but never buddies. But here guys had buddies who would give their lives for each other, even for the guys who were a bit odd, who didn't fit in. In high school everybody had been split into groups - the athletes, the with-its, the townies, then everybody else, mostly country boys like himself. As for the girls, they had no problem if they were reasonably attractive and had a decent figure. Here everybody had a common bond, one forged by shared experiences and one goal - survival.

Now it was Toby Carter's own survival that was at stake, his and the unknown airman who was pinned in a cage a few miles away at the mouth of the cave. For them to survive, Toby was going to have to put the wheels in motion that would get them out of this place, out of this dark and dreary cave and back into the world of light. He groped for his flashlight. Finding it, he turned it on and shined the beam around the room. The beam fell on the carbide light, the one instrument without which he would never have been able to make this perpetual darkness his sanctuary.

Toby pulled on his survival vest, picked up his M-16 and the Springfield, then pushed-off into the darkness toward the stream passage and the sink-hole.

Captain Jared Stripling's crew was on their third mission over the Trail, and their second as a crew. They had taken off from Ubon shortly after nightfall and headed east toward Laos. Now they were on-station just south of the Mu Gia Pass in eastern Laos. So far the night had been uneventful; they had seen nothing on the ground under their flares. Their first fighters were not due for another half an hour. In the meantime they would continue flaring and searching the ground with binoculars, hoping something worthwhile might appear. If not, they would send the fighters in on that area of deep shadow in the gorge below. The briefing officer had made that clear; unless a positive target had been detected, direct all fighters to drop their ordinance in the gorge.

"BLIND BAT, this is BLIND BAT FIVE," the words came through Stripling's headset on guard. His co-pilot, Captain Tom Boyer heard it too.

"What the fuck was that, Tom?"

"I heard it. What do you think?"

Then the words came again, "BLIND BAT, this is BLIND BAT FIVE."

Stripling tuned his wafer switch to guard channel, then spoke into his boom mike, "This is BLIND BAT. Who are you?"

"Roger, BLIND BAT. This is BLIND BAT FIVE."

"Hey, Jared! I know who it is!" The navigator, Captain Gerald Dickson interrupted, "Remember, the intelligence officer told us to be on the alert for signs of anyone from the crew that was lost in this area six weeks ago."

"You're kidding!"

"No, ask him to identify himself again-"

"Okay, I'll give it a go," then on guard, "BLIND BAT FIVE, this is BLIND BAT. Go ahead with your message."

"Roger BLIND BAT. I need to get out of here. But don't send a chopper. I repeat, do not send a chopper. There are too many guns around me."

"Okay buddy, take it easy. First we have to get some identification on you."

"I understand, but I can't stay on the freq too long. Listen, I need a Sky Hook. Do you understand? Sky Hook."

"Sky Hook? Roger, we have your message." Then to his crew, "What the hell is a sky hook?"

"I don't know. Hey! Maybe he's talking about a rescue one thirty," Boyer responded to his aircraft commander's question.

"I don't think they're using that system, are they?"

"Who knows. Maybe we better call MOONBEAM."

"Okay, BAT FIVE. We'll relay your message. Can you stay on the line?'

"Negative BLIND BAT. Here's what I want. I'll come back on station tomorrow night; same time, same station. Whoever picks me up can verify the information then. But just for your info - my dog's name is Rex, my horse's name is Trixie, my favorite color is Blue and my number is five, five, four, three. Copy?"

Stripling looked at Boyer. "I got them all."

"Okay, BAT FIVE. We've got your idents. We'll pass the information on. Anything else."

"One thing, then I gotta go: Tell the guys hello for me. BAT FIVE, out."

Chapter Fifteen

"We've finally heard from him, sir!" Captain Jester burst into the 13th Air Force intelligence office unannounced.

"What have you got, Captain?" Colonel Loveless recognized his subordinate.

"Last night a Blind Bat flareship picked up a transmission from someone calling themselves BLIND BAT FIVE. That would be Airman Carter's call sign. He then gave several personal identification signs. We've checked them out; they're the very ones on Carter's personnel authenticator card. There's no doubt but that it's him."

"What did he have to say?"

"Not much. He asked for a sky-hook, whatever that means. I guess he was using code for a helicopter pickup. No, the Blind Bat crew said he specifically advised against sending a chopper. Too many guns, he said."

"A sky-hook, did you say?"

"Yes, sir. That's what he said. Does that mean anything to you?"

"You might say it does, Captain. You just might. What squadron did you say this young man is from?"

"The thirty-fifth troop carrier squadron at Naha."

"No, I mean before he went PCS to Naha. Didn't you tell me he was at Pope?"

"Yes sir, that was his first duty station. Let me see, I have his file right here." Jester shuffled through his paperwork. "He was with the seven, seventy-ninth troop carrier squadron."

"That might explain it. Captain, we're going to have to do some coordinating but I think there's a way we can get this boy out, a way with which he might be familiar. He wasn't referring to the Jolly Greens when he mentioned a 'sky-hook.' Have you got your bags packed?"

"My bags? Am I going somewhere?"

"We're going somewhere - to Tan Son Nhut. Go to the BOQ and get enough clothes for a week in Saigon. I have to make some telephone calls. Be back here in an hour."

"Yes, sir." Jester saluted the colonel and backed out of the office.

"Close the door as you leave, captain."

When the door had closed, Loveless picked up his telephone, "Operator, this is Colonel Loveless from intelligence. Get me a secure line to seventh air force. I need to talk to General Momyer."

Toby Carter left the mouth of the cave early the next morning. He hadn't slept well that night; there had been too many things on his mind. He wondered if he had been premature in finally revealing that he was alive to his buddies up in the sky. Had anyone picked up on the "Sky Hook" reference? That had been a real shot in the dark since not that many people were familiar with the mission. Had he not been at Pope in the 779th, he would never have known about it either.

Toby was traveling light, carrying only the cave pack and the Springfield that had proven so worthy of his trust. In his ever-present cave pack he carried extra ammunition and four grenades, along with a C-ration. When he stepped out into the morning light, he put the carbide lamp into the pack as well. He had debated whether to leave the survival vest behind but decided that he should wear it.

The steep walls of the cliff had intimidated him at first, but as he made his way away from the mouth of the cave he discovered that they were less of an obstacle than they seemed. They were not straight up and down although they were steep enough. If a person lost his footing, it would be a long way to the bottom unless a rock or tree happened to block the way.

As he picked his way along the narrow ledges, gradually dropping lower and lower toward the valley floor, he wondered what he was doing. Why didn't he just go on through the cave, ambush the bastards and shoot it out? Chances were, he would be killed, then they would probably shoot whoever the guy was in the cage. He was going to die anyway unless, through some fluke, he managed to pull this whole thing off.

While the hillside was not as steep as it looked, Carter had to be very careful to keep from losing his footing. The lower he got, the more he became convinced that the prisoner would never be able to get back up to the cave mouth by this route. There was just no way he could ever get him back up the side of the hill, especially not if they were being pursued. And if they weren't, he would be shocked. It would be hard enough for him to get back up the side of the hill himself, and he had been getting more or less adequate nourishment, even if it was in the form of ancient combat rations.

It took Toby more than an hour to pick his way down the hillside far enough that he could see the valley floor through the trees. He wasn't sure what kind they were; teak, maybe. Deciding it would be suicide to descend to the valley and the communist troops that were sure to be there, he remained on the hillside, making his way along the slope toward where he thought the mouth of the cave should be. From where he was he had a good view of the valley, yet was at least partially concealed by the tree canopy. He was surprised that there was less evidence of North Vietnamese activity than he had expected. Evidently the road was on the other side of the valley. He took his time, moving like an indian, stopping and listening every few feet while trying to make as little noise as possible. It was nearly mid-day by the time he reckoned he was nearing the mouth of the cave.

A river ran through the middle of the valley floor, weaving its way around the tall karst towers that reached up toward the sky, some almost as high as the tops of the cliffs on either side. He could hear the rush of rapids as the clear, cool water was broken by boulders sticking up from the valley floor. He could have been in West Virginia, East Tennessee, or anywhere in the Appalachians back in the States. Limestone outcroppings poked through the foliage here and there, evidence that the gorge had been cut through solid rock. Perhaps the entire valley had once been one huge cave and the passages under the cliff behind him were once mere side passages.

What was that? He heard voices somewhere up ahead. Toby strained to look but saw nothing. At least no one could see him. He couldn't make out the words but guessed they were Vietnamese, or perhaps Lao. The sounds were coming from somewhere below and ahead of him. They sounded like kids at a party. Wait a minute, those were feminine voices! Un-slinging his Springfield and gripping it in his hands in a semi-port position, Toby made his way stealthily along the side of the hill, being careful to put his toes down first just as his father and Uncle Bobby had taught him years before "so as not to spook the squirrels." He heard splashing water.

About a hundred yards further down the ridge, Toby found the source of the sound. Naked bodies were frolicking in a quiet pool - or it would have been quiet had the waters not been whipped to a froth by the bathers. Naked bottoms and bare breasts told him that he was looking at young women as they were going about their bath. Who were they? Native village girls? Maybe, but he doubted that there were any villagers still left in the valley. Then he caught sight of a male soldier in uniform, rifle in hand as he kept watch. They were Vietnamese women soldiers, or maybe they were from the construction crews. Or they could be antiaircraft gunners.

Toby worked his way as close as he dared to the pool. He must keep himself concealed in the trees. He could hear the gleeful shouts of the girls as they splashed each other in the water. But then he heard another sound, someone moaning; but not n pain. He had heard that sound before. Where? What was it? Then he remembered - it was the same sound he had heard from his flight mechanic's cubicle in Bangkok, the same kind of sighs he had heard Sharon utter when they were making love!

The moaning seemed to be coming from right below him. There! He caught a glimpse of something white through the foliage not twenty yards below him. What he saw startled him. Lying on a blanket on top of a rock, a young Oriental woman was sprawled completely naked. Between her outstretched limbs an Oriental man, also nude, stood with his feet on the ground and his pelvis thrusting against the girl's. Toby could see her face, it was contorted in ecstasy as her lover jousted with her. The girl's breasts - rather large for a Vietnamese - were bouncing in perfect rhythm with the

140

man's movements. The young Tennesseean stood transfixed, watching a live performance by two actors who had no idea they were being observed.

He was surprised by the girl's beauty. He knew that many Vietnamese women were quite pretty, but this one was exceptional, even without makeup. Her cheeks were red with a sexual glow, enhancing her natural beauty. The man looked like any other Vietnamese but from the sounds emitted by the girl and the movements of her body, he must have been an exceptional lover.

Toby started to withdraw into the shadows, but realized any movement on his part might allow the girl to see him. Her face was turned toward him, not more than sixty feet away. He would have to just assume the role of a peeping Tom.

After a few minutes the man seemingly finished. He gave a final thrust, drawing an exceptionally loud sigh from the girl, then stopped his movements. The girl didn't seem to be satisfied, she put her hands on her boyfriend's hips and pulled him toward her. The man said something, then withdrew. But the girl was not to be left hanging. She began stroking her lover, then bent forward to stroke his now-impotent member orally, while at the same time apparently doing something with her hands - stroking his hips perhaps. Toby could see the man return to potency before his very eyes under the girl's ministration. Whatever she was doing with her hands combined with her oral attentions was having the effect she evidently desired. Soon the man was once again capable of giving her the pleasure which she had been denied.

This time the girl assumed a semi-prostrate position as her lover joined her from behind - the same position Sharon Craft had enjoyed so much! With his restored power, the Vietnamese man resumed his stroking of his sweetheart's femininity. She had evidently remained fairly close to her peak, because his first shoving actions seemed to put the girl over the top.

Toby was forced to watch as the Vietnamese couple continued their lovemaking. They went on for an indeterminable time - it seemed like hours to Toby. Finally they collapsed onto their boulder in a heap, giving Toby a chance to discreetly withdraw into the shadows. He crept backwards as stealthily as possible, leaving the lovers once again unobserved by any human.

Now that he had seen the presence of the enemy, Toby was tempted to turn back and leave well enough alone. Who were these people? Members of the gun crew; that was his best guess. If so, then the mouth of the cave must be very near. He sneaked his way along the side of the ridge, after moving a few yards higher. Then he saw it.

His first indication that he was near the cave came when he heard the sound of a roaring river, an even louder noise than that made by the river in the valley. Then he saw white water close to the base of the cliff up ahead. It was coming out of the side of the hill in an open area where there were no more trees. Toby moved as close to the cave entrance as he dared, close enough to finally see the cavernous opening in the side of the hill. The cave entrance was more than a hundred feet high; it was higher than where he was on the side of the hill. Now he could see the railroad tracks leading out of the cave, the tracks on which the gun carriage was moved in and out of its sanctuary by the gunners.

Close to the cave, the ground was scarred - but not pockmarked - from dozens of bombs that had been dropped on the side of the hill and in the valley. The limestone was so tough that there was little damage - the gun had never been in any danger. Nor would it ever be from bombing. Someone had said that the Air Force had even squandered a flight or two of B-52's on the gun, yet it still was a thorn in the side of the American flight crews. This was the same gun that had shot him down! That thought hadn't occurred to him in the cave; maybe it was because caves were almost his natural environment. Suddenly he felt an urge in his heart to kill every one of the gunners, to destroy that terrible gun! Only after he determined in his soul to do just that did he remember the man in the cage.

The guy in the cage. Now that he thought about it, there was something that seemed a skoshy bit familiar about the person. He couldn't put his finger on it, though. Whoever he was, the man was a comrade-in-arms and was no doubt on his way to the Hanoi Hilton unless he could free him. But then what? He had a plan, but would it work?

Toby took in as much of the scene before him as he dared, the yawning mouth of the cave, the roaring river, the pock-marked limestone. The bomb craters - they were really merely dimples in the surface - looked almost like sinkholes. Very shallow ones, perhaps, but sinkholes nevertheless. When he had seen enough, he started back to where he had come down the hill.

As he passed the spot where he had seen the Vietnamese lovers, he decided on a whim to see if they were still there. It had been more than an hour since he had left his hiding place. Damned if they weren't back doing it again! That girl must be insatiable - just like Sharon, he thought to himself. Then it dawned on him, the girl was probably from the gun crew. He would have to kill her. Maybe the guy was too, but he had no qualms about killing him. After all, he was a little jealous. The girl was one of the most attractive Orientals he had ever seen. No, she was one of the most attractive women he had ever seen - period. In fact, she was much prettier than Sharon Craft.

This time he remained in the shadows and did not dally. Better get it while you can! He was thinking about the two lovers as he took his leave and continued on up the hill. The swimmers were out of the water and were dressing. All were wearing khaki uniforms with red collar tabs. They were NVA WACS, there was no doubt about that - if the North Vietnamese called their women WACS. He didn't know about that.

Once he was out of earshot of the swimmers, Toby began hurrying on along the hillside. He wanted to get back to the sanctuary of his cave before dark - for two reasons. One, he didn't want to have to climb the hill in the darkness and possibly be detected and two, the bombers would be out then. There was no telling where their ordinance might fall. He had found where bombs had hit on top of the ridge a good mile from the gorge. The best place to be at night was in the cave, or at least inside one of the entrances. There he would be safe from flying shrapnel.

Climbing down the hill had been fairly easy; getting back up again was a different matter. Toby found himself on hands and knees once he was out of the humus-covered rock and into the limestone. Had he been inside the cave the going would have been easier. For some reason a person tends to tire less easily in a cave, perhaps because the air is moist and temperatures are cool. He had reached the open rock and was almost to the cave when it happened.

Thaannnnnnnnnggggggggg! Something smacked the rock below him and ricocheted away. A bullet! Someone had spotted him. Fortunately, the shooter was not an expert at long range; he had failed to correct for drop. The round had hit at least ten feet beneath him. He could still be in trouble, though. There was a good fifty feet of solid rock with no cover he had to get across before he would be in a position where he would be able to return fire or take cover.

The next five minutes were the longest of Toby's life. All he could do was put one hand and one foot before the other, searching for hand and foot holds. Rounds were impacting all around him as at least three and perhaps as many as half a dozen people were shooting at him. Most of the rounds were hitting well beneath him, but three or four were close enough that limestone shards stung his face and other parts of his body. Deep inside he knew that sooner or later one of the gunners was going to elevate his sights and hit him in the back - or worse still, hit him in a leg or arm and cause him to lose his grip and fall to his death below.

But Toby managed to make his way to the ledge above the cliff- face unharmed, except for some superficial wounds from pieces of flying rock. The ledge was wide enough that he could lie down on it, although there was no cover. At least he could un-sling his rifle and think about returning the fire.

The fire continued unabated, even after he was on the ledge and no longer completely exposed. Toby's eye scanned the opposite cliff; that the shooting was coming from there was obvious. Anyone shooting from below would have been hitting much further below him - if they had been able to even see him from that angle. Then he saw where they were firing from. Across the valley on the opposite cliff were several cave entrances not unlike those above him. At the mouth of one of the caves, he saw three - no, four - figures. Thank God they didn't have a heavy caliber machine gun!

Toby raised his sights, setting them for 600 yards. He wished he had a telescope sight, but he would have to make do with what he had. He propped the rifle with his left arm, using a "hasty sling" to steady it. Toby ignored the rounds that were hitting all around him as he drew a bead on one of the gunners. He took a deep breath, exhaled partially, then held the rest. He very slowly squeezed the trigger; the recoil against his shoulder gave him a feeling of satisfaction as he knew that the bullet had struck right where he was aiming. He worked the bolt to chamber another 30/06 round, then repeated the procedure with a different target. Toby Carter was now in his element, in spite of his somewhat precarious position on the side of the hill. After he dropped the third soldier, the survivor retreated into the cave behind him.

Toby waited for half an hour before deciding to risk exposing himself again. No rounds had been fired after he fired his third shot. When he set off around the ledge, no shots announced the presence of the enemy. It was twilight by the time he reached the cave entrance from which he had departed that morning.

Once in the safety of the cave, Toby sat back in his old camp to contemplate his situation. There was no doubt now that he would have to make his attack through the cave, then escape the same way. That last episode when he was caught out in the open was proof enough that that route would not work, not in the daylight at least. At night it would be impossible because of the precarious terrain. He would go through the cave - and he would do it tomorrow morning if he got the words he wanted to hear from Blind Bat tonight.

Colonel Loveless and Captain Jester departed Udorn at 1100 hours that morning. Two hours later they were in Saigon, at the headquarters of 7th Air Force in the office of the commander, General William Momyer. General Momyer was a fighter pilot; he had been all of his adult life. But the General had a soft spot in his heart for trash-haulers, especially C-130 crews from the tactical commands. He listened attentively as Colonel Loveless explained the situation regarding Carter.

"You say that this young airman has been conducting a small scale war in Laos, huh?"

"That seems to be it, sir. We suspected he might be alive when Captain Jester's men picked out something on a reconnaissance photo. But it wasn't until last night that we were able to make contact with him."

"He asked for 'Sky-Hook'?"

"Yes, sir. Airman Carter was at Pope before coming to PACAF a few months ago. His squadron there went into the program about the time he left. We've checked with TAC Headquarters. He was originally supposed to go into the program with his crew, but then a shortage of loadmasters developed at Naha and he was selected for overseas before being frozen for the program. He knows about 'Sky Hook.'"

"If he wants a Sky-Hook, then I guess we'll have to see about giving him one. Anybody who can do as much damage as you say he's done deserves to be rescued. Why don't you two go on up to Nha Trang. We'll run the mission out of there when the time comes. When is he supposed to make contact with us again?"

"He told the Blind Bat crew he would be back on the horn sometime tonight. I've told the intelligence people at Ubon to brief their crews to be alert for a contact."

"I hope he comes through. In the meantime, I'll set the wheels in motion to get a Sky-Hook mission set up to bring him out."

The two lower ranking officers got up from their chairs, saluted the four-star general and left the room.

Toby decided to wait where he was until he had made contact with Blind Bat, rather than crawling all the way through the cave to the sink-hole entrance. He estimated that the flareship would come on station at around 2000 local. He heard the throbbing turboprops at 1955.

"BLIND BAT, this is BLIND BAT FIVE."

The welcome words of response came through the tiny speaker on the survival radio from his vest.

"Roger, BLIND BAT FIVE. This is BLIND BAT." The voice sounded familiar; maybe it was a 35th crew. The Blind Bat pilot gave no indication of familiarity even though the squadron was probably well aware that he had made contact.

"How about Sky Hook?"

"Roger on Sky Hook. When do you want It?"

"Tomorrow night; how about 0300 hours? Tell them to look for my strobe. When they see it, give me a call." He hoped the NVA weren't monitoring his frequency. He was using the discrete frequency that had been given to them the night he was shot down. Hopefully they didn't have that one yet.

"Roger that, FIVE. We'll pass it on. Anything else?" "One thing - *I may have company.*"

"Say again?"

"Tell them I may have company. Copy?"

"Copy, BAT FIVE. We'll pass it on."

Toby turned off the radio and stowed the antenna. Then he lit his carbide lamp and pushed off into the cave. He would spend the night by his stash. He had a little over twenty-four hours to pull off his mission, then get back to the sink-hole. He hoped that the prisoner would be able to make the trip. What if the man was claustrophobic?

Seeing the fornicating Vietnamese caused Toby to think more of Sharon. He had never watched two people make love before. Toby had never seen a porno film or a live sex show. He had seen strippers in Naumeanua, but all they did was strip off their clothes and dance around in a G-string. The girl had really been ecstatic; so had the man for that matter. He would never have thought about North Vietnamese in that context. He thought about his own experiences with Sharon in Bangkok. She had seemed to be really enjoying herself and had said as much. Now he wanted more than ever to get out of here.

He could probably do it easily enough, getting out of here that is, now that they had evidently made arrangements for a Sky Hook. He didn't have to make a John Wayne show against the gun. But he knew that there was no way that gun would ever be destroyed from the air. There wasn't a bomb in the Air Force inventory big enough to blow down the side of that hill - and that was what it would take. He did have a chance - no matter how remote - of getting in there and out again in one place.

And then there was the prisoner. He would never forgive himself if he abandoned the man. But then he might have been moved by this time. There had been plenty of time for the NVA to move him out since he was there. He would never know until he went back to the mouth of the cave and checked.

He would plan his attack for mid-morning, while the gunners were still asleep. If he could just catch them in their sleeping hammocks, chances were he would be able to take the whole lot before they realized what was going on. If the girls he had seen had been from the gun crew, they probably had just gotten up. But then he had seen nearly everyone in their racks at 3:00 o'clock in the afternoon. Wait, this was Southeast Asia. The gun crews probably got up to bathe and eat lunch, then went back to bed for an afternoon siesta.

He would take his M-16 and one of the Thompsons. The Tommy guns would be the best for the job, especially since the .45 slugs tended to flatten out when they hit something. They would be less likely to ricochet. He would carry several hand grenades. Once the gun crew had been neutralized, he would drop a couple down the barrel of the gun if they would fit; if not, they should at least damage the breech. He looked at his Seiko watch. It was 2200 local. He would get up at 0500; that would give him time to get to the cave mouth by mid-morning, hopefully before the crew got up for lunch. He set the alarm on the wrist watch, thanking God that he had been wearing it when he bailed out. Then he rolled up in the parachute canopy and went to sleep.

Chapter Sixteen

Toby barely slept that night, or so it seemed to him. His mind just would not become inactive; his thoughts were constantly churning as they alternated between what he planned to do the next morning, the Vietnamese lovers and Sharon Craft. He wondered if she was aware that he was missing; probably not. He had only had time to write one letter before they went out on their fatal mission and had never mailed that. It was still in his locker at Ubon when he was shot down. He wondered about the rest of the crew - were they safe? Had they gone back to Naha, or were they still at Ubon with replacement crewmembers? Their tour would have been just about up by this time, then it would have been back to trash-hauling. "Trash-hauling," that was a new word. Willy Cavendish had coined the term one afternoon in the barracks at Ubon. "The Herkybird is a green garbage can and we're nothing but trash-haulers," those had been his words.

He was awakened more by the vibration of the alarm against his wrist than by the sound. The little Sieko - Willy called them "seek-and-fuck-o" - had come in very handy since he bought it in the BX up at Fort Buckner. Of course he hadn't needed the alarm since he had been at Ubon. This was the first time he had set it in months. Toby rolled out of the parachute shroud in which he had been sleeping. Without the folds of parachute cloth around him, sleeping in the cave would have been a chilly proposition. Caves are always cold, except in tropical regions. Laos was a land of mountains and he was in the middle of them, where temperatures were chilly at night, cold enough that the temperature in the caves - always the average temperature of the region - was in the fifties. He lit a candle; the tiny flame seemed like a searchlight in the total darkness of the cavern.

He had laid out the equipment he was to take that morning. A Thompson, with six forty-round clips of ammo; his M-16 and all the ammunition he had for it; six grenades; his survival vest, along with the revolver; radio, knife and his ever-present cave pack. In the pack he had all of his extra ammunition, along with the remaining carbide from his store and the flashlight and batteries. Except during his trip to the entrance, he had been using the jury-rigged alcohol lamp he had made from C-ration cans to conserve carbide.

He ate light that morning; his stomach was too nervous for much of a meal. When he had eaten he picked up his gear and set out for the mouth of the cave. He was allowing four hours to get to the gun, take out the crew and rescue the prisoner - if he was still there. The trek was tedious, as always. At least he was starting from close to the drop-off point; he didn't have to negotiate the crawl-ways from the sink-hole while carrying all of his equipment. He hated that he was going to have to leave most of his treasure behind when he left the cave. It would take too long to move everything to the sink-hole. For that matter, there was no way to retrieve everything. So he had re-wrapped most of the weapons and stashed them in a dry grotto - although he couldn't think of any reason in the world why he went to the trouble to do it. No one had ever been here before and no one was likely to come again, not at least for a very long time.

Toby lowered the weapons and cave pack through the drop-off to the sloping breakdown pile by the waterfall. Then he followed the equipment. The prospect of a climb back up the rocks with the prisoner was not as foreboding a thought as it had been before. Now he knew what an outside route would be like. This was much better. Besides, no one would be shooting at them in the cave - at least he hoped not. The going was much easier in the lower passage. All he had to do was follow the river to the mouth of the cave - and the gun. It was just that the mouth of the cave was at least three miles from where he had dropped into the lower level and the way wound through breakdown piles, tall calcite columns, stalagmites, stalactites, flow-stone and other obstacles that had to be circumnavigated.

When Toby reached the twilight region just inside the cave entrance, he found everything as he had hoped. The gun was inside the cave with the barrel depressed. Two Vietnamese, weapons mechanics no doubt, were working on the breech. Everyone else seemed to be in their sleeping hammocks. What about the cage? There it was! He strained to see if there was anyone inside, but it was too far away for him to tell. There appeared to be someone - or something - inside but who ever or whatever was lying on the floor. There was a guard nearby; evidently the prisoner was still there.

Toby surveyed the scene and began planning for his attack. He would use the Thompson and have the M-16 in reserve, just as he had planned. During his reconnaissance yesterday he had seen no one in the vicinity of the cave other than the girl bathers and a couple of guards - and the stud who had been servicing the Vietnamese maiden. The Thompson was serviceable - he had fired a clip into the gorge during an air strike a few days before to check it out. It was time to launch his attack.

Now that there was no reason to remain concealed, Toby began walking - almost running - toward the cave entrance, the submachine gun cradled in his arms. Only the rock-strewn ground kept him from breaking out into a dead run. He wanted to get as close to the sleeping Vietnamese as possible before opening fire. The roar of the river concealed his footsteps; he had extinguished his lamp and his muddy clothes blended with the darkness of the cavern. The generators were stilled and no lights were on. Only the natural light from outside illuminated the area near the opening; he could see them but they couldn't see him.

When he was as close as he dared, Toby opened fire, killing the guard by the cage with the first burst, then shifting his aim so that the next rounds caught the two weapons mechanics by the gun. He was firing short bursts of no more than five rounds, partly to conserve ammunition and partly to reduce the likelihood of ricochets. To his surprise, the sleepers did not stir immediately when he opened fire. Evidently the river's roar masked the gun's report. He swung toward the sleeping hammocks and opened fire, pointing the muzzle of the gun at the lower tier then allowing the natural muzzle rise to bring the barrel up. He fired until he was out of ammunition.

He quickly changed magazines while watching some of the sleepers sit up, then jump out of their beds. Before the feet of the first one had hit the rock floor of the room, he was back in action. More than half of the sleepers were women, no doubt the same ones he had seen yesterday. He was conscious of the fact even as he continued putting round after round into their soft bodies.

One of the Viets was able to get out of her rack and begin running for the stack of rifles. Toby swung the muzzle of his gun toward her; she was not more than ten feet away. He pulled the trigger; the firing pin clicked on an empty chamber. The girl ran toward the AK-47s; Toby could see her well in the natural light from outside the cave. Her blouse was unbuttoned, revealing firm breasts that bounced in a way that seemed familiar. It was the girl he had seen yesterday, the one with her lover! Her beautiful Asian face was turned toward him as she fumbled with a rifle, trying to pull it off the stack and raise the muzzle to blast him into oblivion.

But Toby was alert while the girl was still groggy from sleep. She had awakened to a nightmare. Now she was confused, although she knew that someone was attacking her crew. As the young woman raised the barrel of her rifle to fire, the butt of Toby's Thompson caught her right beneath the chin. Her head went up in recoil from the blow and she crumpled to the ground like a falling leaf. Toby took the AK-47 from her hands and opened up with it on the sleeping racks.

When the magazine of the AK was empty, he reloaded the Thompson and scrutinized the area. No one was moving. He looked behind him where the girl lay sprawled on her back, her lovely breasts thrusting proudly toward the ceiling. She was still unconscious - or dead? Then he saw her chest move; she was still alive at least. He was tempted to shoot her but couldn't bring himself to do it. She seemed to be out of action, at least for the time being.

The prisoner! In the excitement, he had forgotten him. Toby moved quickly to the makeshift cage. The man had risen to his feet and was clinging to the bars. There was an old fashioned hasp and a key lock holding the door. No time to look for the key.

"Stand back," Toby motioned to the man to get away from the lock. He held the muzzle of the Thompson six inches from the lock. At the shot, the lock burst into a hundred pieces.

"Carter!"

Toby was startled at the sound of his name; it had been weeks since he had heard it pronounced. Who the devil...? Then he recognized the man.

"Captain Preston!" It was strange to hear his own voice.

"I will be damned, Toby. What the devil are you doing here?"

"I'll explain later. Can you walk?"

"I think so. It's been so long since I've tried."

"Here," Toby handed Preston his flashlight. "Take this, go into the cave a hundred yards or so then wait for me."

"You come with me."

"I've got something to do, first. You go on, I'll be along in a few minutes."

"What if some of them are still alive? Shouldn't I cover you?"

Toby thought about that for a few seconds. "That might not be a bad idea. Can you still handle an M-16?"

"I can sure as hell try! What are you going to do?"

"I'm going to try and disable that gun. All I've got are a few hand grenades. Have you got any ideas?"

"All I've been doing for a month now is thinking of ways to get rid of that damn gun. That's the one that brought us down, you know."

"Yes, sir. I know."

"About the best thing you can probably do is set-off one of your grenades in the breech. The barrel is too small for it to fit into or you could drop the thing down it."

"What about setting off a grenade in the ammo box?"

"That just might work. But you would have to run like the devil to get away from it."

"I've got some five-fifty cord. I could rig a line to pull the pin."

"Good idea. Rig two of them, one in the breech and the other in the ammo. Where did you find grenades, anyway? And that submachine gun?"

"Tell ya later, first we need to take care of business."

Toby quickly rigged the two grenades, tying one in the breech of the gun and the other in the ammunition box on the carriage. He tied a length of cord to each after making sure the grenades were anchored with similar cord. After tying the two improvised lanyards together, he attached his ball of 550 cord to them.

"Okay, let's run like hell and get around the corner."

"Don't get in my way!"

When they were about a hundred feet away Toby pulled the cord, then jumped behind a rock. The two grenades went off almost simultaneously. They couldn't see how much damage was done to the breech of the gun, but fragments from the second grenade set off a shell in the metal box. A few seconds later the round exploded, setting off other rounds. The walls of the cavern reverberated with the sound.

"Let's get the hell out of here, quick." Toby pulled off his cap and struck the striker of his carbide lamp. A blue and yellow flame shot out from the tip.

"Where are we going?"

"We're going to get as far from this place as we can. How do you feel?"

"My legs are a little stiff, but I can walk okay. Have you any water?"

"Sure." Toby pulled out his canteen and handed it to the pilot. "When we get far enough away from here, I'll give you something to eat."

"Food! Man, I'd give anything for something to eat. Those bastards haven't fed me anything but pumpkin soup since they captured me!"

"It's not much. C-rats."

"They'll do. I'm so hungry I'd eat almost anything."

"Here," Toby reached in his pack. "Try this cereal bar. But watch it, they're pretty hard. You can munch on it while we get out of here."

"Anything is better than what I've been getting the past few weeks, which is not much."

"How's your strength?"

"Good question. This is the first time I've been able to do anything other than pace around that cage in a long time. Right now my adrenaline seems to be keeping me going. I don't know how long that can hold up."

"I hope it holds up long enough for you to climb an eighty foot breakdown pile. Do you have any rock-climbing experience?"

"Rock climbing? Sure. I was in the Alpine Club at the Academy. We used to go up into the Ramparts nearly every weekend." Toby almost halted in his tracks at Preston's revelation. Here he had been worried sick about getting the man up the breakdown pile, now he finds out he's an experienced climber! Now the question was whether or not he would be up to the climb.

They were silent until they were deep inside the cave. When Toby estimated they were more than a mile from the entrance, he signaled a halt.

"How're you doing?"

"Holding my own. How far do we have to go?"

"It's about two miles to the climb. Once we get up, we'll be safe. We can rest there and I'll fill you in on how we're going to get out of here."

"Get out of here? Do you mean you've got rescue coming after us?" Preston made no effort to conceal his excitement at the prospect of rescue.

"In a manner of speaking. I'll fill you in on the details but let me say this much; if everything work's out, we'll be eating breakfast in a GI mess hall tomorrow."

"I never thought the prospect of eating in a chow hall would sound like heaven, but it does!"

"It does to me too, but first we have to get out of here. We better press on to the climb."

Preston was weak from his captivity but adrenaline filled his veins, giving him an energy that was almost equal to that of Toby Carter. When they reached the climb, Preston surveyed the rock pile then remarked, "I could free-climb that."

"I don't think that's a good idea. Let me go up first, then tie the rope around your waist. I'll get up on the upper level and give you a hand. Sling the rifle over your shoulder; it'll ride okay that way."

Toby was still fearful that Preston would have problems, not without some justification, considering the man's condition. But the young officer was possessed of the same will to live that had allowed Toby to survive for so long; he made his way up the pile of rocks almost without assistance. Toby reached down and helped him up the last pitch to the upper level.

"Well, the hardest part's over. Now all we have to do is wait for our chariot of fire."

"Chariot of fire?"

"A figure of speech, out of the Bible. You remember when Elijah went to heaven? He was taken up in a flaming chariot of fire."

"What's the significance of that?"

"We're going up in more or less the same way, although not in a chariot. And it won't be on fire, at least I hope not. Do you know anything about the Sky Hook program? The Fulton Recovery System?"

"You mean the new 'snatch and grab' thing that Rescue is using? I thought that wasn't operational."

"We're not going to be picked up by Rescue."

"Who then, Air America?"

"No, sir. I've got an in with some people. Hey, listen. How about some chow? How would a hot meal sound?"

"A hot meal? You're kidding! As long as it's not pumpkin soup."

"No, it's not soup. Actually, you'll have a choice."

"Oh, you mentioned C-rations before."

"They're not half bad if they're heated up. I've got an alcohol stove. It works pretty well. I've got that stuff stashed not far from here."

"Where did you find C-rations, and that Tommy gun?"

"You may find this hard to believe, but I found everything in the cave. I was exploring one day - there was nothing else to do - and I came across an old airdrop bundle, from World War II I guess. It had fallen into a surface pit and dropped into the cave. The parachute was still attached. I have everything hidden away since we're going to be leaving. Anyway, when I opened the bundle I found a bunch of weapons, ammunition, grenades and rations. It must have been supplies for an OSS team during the war."

"I'll be damned! Let's go get some of that chow. I'm starving - literally."

Toby led his pilot to where he had left the stove and enough rations to get them by until the rescue plane could come. Preston picked a beefsteak and potatoes; Toby opened the can and put it on the fire. While Preston ate he boiled water for hot tea and coffee.

"How did you manage to keep from getting captured?"

"By a stroke of luck I came down on top of this ridge. I landed in a clearing on top of a huge limestone slab. Then I discovered a sinkhole with an entrance leading into the cave. Once I was in the cave, I was home. But I had no idea how I was going to get out of here."

"Why didn't you just call for a Jolly Green? You've got your radios." Preston could see the radios in Toby's mud-covered survival vest.

"I thought about that, but the ridge is on the wrong side of the valley. A helicopter wouldn't have a snowball's chance of getting in here. Then I came across the airdrop bundle. There were a couple of Springfield rifles in it. I decided to declare war on the gooks."

"So you're the one that's been causing them so much trouble! They asked me about that in one of their interrogations. One of the women spoke excellent English. Turns out that she had been educated in a missionary school. But she is a real bitch, even if she does have a body out of Playboy."

"Wait a minute, do you mean the one with the big boobs?"

"That's the one, she's a real knockout. How did you know about her?"

"Yesterday I went on a reconnaissance on the hillside, trying to find out about the entrance. I thought I might could pull my raid from outside. I came across several of the women swimming in the river. They didn't see me, though. But I saw them; they were all buck-naked."

"So you got a look at her then?"

"Not exactly. I started poking around and came across this girl and a Vietnamese, a real stud I guess. They were going at it on a boulder. She was a greedy little bitch, from what I saw."

"She's that all right, and a real prick teaser, too. During one of our interrogations she unbuttoned her blouse, reached over and started fondling me! Then, when she saw that I was fully aroused, she made like she was going to make it with me. She pulled down her slacks, then laughed in my face. I could have shot her!"

154

"She was really giving that gook what for yesterday, that's for sure. There was no doubt that she was in charge of what was going on."

"Not to change the subject, but what about the rest of our crew? Have you seen anyone else?"

"No, but then I really didn't expect too. They had all jumped before you came down out of the cockpit. My guess is that it was at least five minutes between the time Captain Danson jumped and I did."

"In five minutes we could have gone twenty miles or more."

"Exactly. Evidently we turned east after they jumped."

"The damn thing was flying right wing low. The auto-pilot couldn't keep it level."

"I imagine they jumped far enough to the west that they were able to be picked up. They're probably all back at Naha by now."

"Maybe we'll be back there soon ourselves, if your Sky Hook trick works."

"It will, or at least I think it will. I've been in contact with Moonbeam; I asked them for a Sky Hook tomorrow morning at 0400, while it's still dark."

"How long is that from now? The gooks took my watch, along with everything else I had."

"A little over eleven hours. It's 1635 now."

"You know, Carter. I hope your grenades did put that gun out of commission. Those gunners have done a lot of damage in the past few months. Two '130's, a couple of F-4's, an A-1E damaged and an A-26 shot down. That's the ones I've heard about; no doubt there were more."

"I never realized just how hard it is to knock out a gun. You can kill the crew, but someone else will just take their place unless the gun itself is damaged beyond repair."

"My guess is they'll have somebody working to fix the gun as soon as word gets out that its been knocked out. At least you took care of the crew. Maybe it will be some time before they can get as good a crew in there as they had. At least you got that bitch; she was the crew chief."

"Which one?"

"The one with the beautiful boobs. She was in charge of the crew. You took her out, I saw you standing over her body."

"You mean the one I hit with the gun butt?"

"Was that how you killed her? I thought you shot her."

"No, I hit her with the gun stock. But she wasn't dead. She was still breathing when we left."

"You should have killed her when you had the chance. If she's still alive, they'll just use her to train another crew. That girl was the number one gunner. She was the one who shot us down. She told me so herself."

"Damn!"

"Don't worry about it. You've done enough, for God's sake. After all, you got me out of there. If you hadn't, I would have been on my way to Hanoi by now. They were getting ready to move me up north."

"You're sure?"

"That-s what they told me. They were waiting for a squad returning from the South to take me back north with them."

Toby's thoughts turned to the woman. So she was the gun crew commander? Damn! And he had had his chance to kill her, but because she was so beautiful he had let her live. He had to make a choice - he could leave well enough alone and get out of Laos tonight and hope the gun was beyond repair, or he could go back and make sure the woman was dead. He had almost twelve hours before his ride to freedom was due to contact him. That was plenty of time to allow him to get to the mouth of the cave and back again, as long as everything went as smoothly as his past journeys had gone.

"Captain Preston, I'm going to have to go on a little errand. But first, I need to put you somewhere where you will be safe until I get back. We're going to have to do a little crawling; can you handle that?"

"Carter, after what I've been through the last few weeks, I can handle anything. Lead out."

"Come on, Captain. Let's move on to the sinkhole. That's where I plan to signal the Sky Hook from. Take a couple of C-rats with you, leave everything else here. This is as good a place as any to stash everything. No one will ever find it anyway."

The two men quickly stowed the remaining C-rations and camp stove. Toby didn't know why he was so careful to insure that the food was placed so the containers would stay dry. It was not like he planned to ever come back to the cave. No one would ever need the food or the weapons, not that he could foresee. When everything was in place Toby led the pilot down the passageway toward the sinkhole.

Preston was put-off a bit at the thought of crawling through the narrow tunnel leading toward the sink, but when he realized that was the only way to safety he overcame his reservation and followed Toby's light. He was glad enough when they came out into the larger room near the entrance.

"Captain, we're almost to the entrance." They could see daylight up ahead. "Right up there is the top of the ridge. The sinkhole opens up right in the edge of a clearing. What I plan to do is have the Sky Hook drop their equipment as close to the entrance as possible. They can make the pickup from just outside the entrance."

Toby handed Preston one of his radios then removed his wristwatch and handed it to the pilot. "Take this. I'll keep the other one - and I won't need my watch. If I'm not back here by 0400, call Moonbeam yourself and arrange for the pickup. They may need to authenticate. Tell them I got lost or something. They won't be expecting you."

"Where are you going?"

"I've got some loose ends to tie up. If everything goes right, I should be back in plenty of time. If not, it won't make any difference."

"Are you sure you have to leave me, Toby? What is there left to do?"

"I'm sure. Don't worry. You'll be all right. I should be back soon. Why don't you try and get some sleep? No one will bother you here. Just stay inside the cave. You've got my M-16; I'll leave the Thompson as well. See you!" With those words Toby Carter disappeared back into the depths of the cave.

Chapter Seventeen

"Come on in, Colonel. You too, Captain. General Momyer called and told me to expect you. Have a seat." The tall Air Force colonel motioned toward chairs in his office in the building with the sign out front that read 14th Air Commando Wing. Like Loveless and Jester, he was dressed in the summer weight polyester tan 1505 uniform. Over his left breast were tiny command pilot wings; over the left pocket was the standard Air Force blue name tag with his name "Nelson" embossed on it in white letters. "Excuse me a moment." He reached for his phone.

"Bill, call Colonel McLean. Ask him to report to my office. Also, why don't you call Colonel Hempstead. I'd like for him to be in on this, too." He placed the receiver back on its hook and looked first at Colonel Loveless, then at Captain Jester. "Before we get started, I'd like for two of my associates to sit in. Colonel McLean is the Special Forces representative. Colonel Hempstead is our fixed-wing operations officer. While we wait, how about coffee?" Both men nodded in the affirmative.

"How are things in Thailand? That's right, isn't it; you're from Udorn?"

Colonel Loveless answered, "Right. I'm chief of intel for Seventh/Thirteenth. Captain Jester is my chief photo-interpreter." The door opened and a massive figure wearing starched jungle fatigues came through; a green beret was tucked under an epaulet. There was no mistaking who this man might be! Behind him came an Air Force lieutenant colonel, also dressed in jungle fatigues.

"Good! Colonel McLean, Lieutenant Colonel Hempstead. Meet Colonel Loveless and Captain Jester. They're from Udorn. General Momyer sent them up this way. It seems they might have a mission for us. Colonel, why don't you fill us in?"

Like Nelson, Loveless was a full colonel. He did not preface his remarks with "sir."

"Gentlemen, it seems that a little over a month ago one of Captain Jester's airmen happened to spot something on an aerial photograph. Show them the photo, Jester." The Captain reached into a portfolio marked "Top Secret" and pulled out the picture.

"Sirs, this photograph was taken several weeks ago along a ridge overlooking the infiltration routes in Laos. If you look right here," he pointed with a finger, "you can see what appears to be a tent with a person in it." Jester reached into his portfolio and pulled out another photograph, the enlargement of the section with the tent-like object. "This enlargement reinforced our opinion. There is little doubt but that this is a shelter made from a parachute and there is a person in it."

"How do you know you're looking at an American and not a Vietnamese?" Colonel McLean asked the question.

"We can't sir, not with one hundred per cent accuracy. But there is every indication that it is. For one thing, the shelter is very similar to those taught to Air Force aircrew in survival courses. And it is undoubtedly made from a parachute."

"Couldn't the NVA get one of our parachutes? There must be hundreds of them scattered along the Trail, from flares and what not as well as those from pilots who were shot down."

"Colonel, the parachute shelter is the least of our reasoning." Colonel Loveless took over from Jester. "If you look to the left in the photograph you can see a shadow. We've identified it as a sink-hole, a depression in the ground that is common in limestone areas. We've further analyzed this particular picture - show the other slide. It appears that this particular sinkhole has an entrance to what is undoubtedly a cave in it."

"A cave? What does that have to do with the man in the shelter?"

"I'm glad you asked that, Colonel McLean. It has everything in the world to do with it. About a week before this photograph was taken, a C-130 flareship was shot down in this same general area. All of the crew was rescued but two men, the pilot - a Captain Preston - and the loadmaster who just happens to be an experienced cave explorer."

"Toby Carter?" Colonel Hempstead interrupted with glee as all eyes turned toward him.

"You know him." Although Loveless said the words as a statement, he was asking a question.

"Sure, I've flown with him. A good kid and a damn fine loadmaster. Everybody in the seven, seventy-ninth at Pope knew about Carter and his fascination with caves. He always carried a special survival kit with him; he called it his 'cave pack.' It was a big joke in the squadron. He was supposed to go into Sky Hook, but got special assignment rush orders to Naha and shipped out before we had a chance to have them canceled. His old crew is here at Nha Trang - Captain Shoemaker."

"That is certainly ironic, but then this whole situation is filled with ironies, remarked Colonel Loveless. "Let me fill you in on the rest of the story. When Captain Jester's men spotted the man in this photograph, he came immediately to me. We had a conference with air rescue and decided there wasn't anything we could do until the survivor - if it was indeed a survivor - contacted us. All we could do was wait.

"But then about a week or so later, my office picked up an intelligence brief about an intercept by one or our Security Service crews. It seems that the Viets had suddenly become very excited about a sniper who was picking off their antiaircraft gun crews one by one. Evidently the sniper was a crack shot; every victim was hit in the head."

"What's that got to do with this, Colonel?" The Army colonel made his first comment.

"Just that the area where the sniper was, or I should say 'is' working is the exact same area where these photographs were taken."

"Go on, Colonel." Colonel Nelson made a "proceed" motion with his right hand.

"This man, Carter, is from Tennessee. You know what they say about Tennesseans. I'm from Texas where the Rangers have a slogan 'Ride like a Mexican, trail like an Indian, shoot like a Tennessean and fight like the very devil' as their self-descriptive goal. Airman Carter is the real item. We had an intelligence officer from Sewart go by and talk to his parents. One of the things he found out is that Airman Carter is not just a crack shot; there probably aren't very many people in the world who can out-shoot him. His father produced an old target from 4-H camp. Ten shots were right in the center of the bulls-eye, you could cover them with a dime."

"We've got men in Special Forces who can do that."

"I'm sure you do, Colonel McLean, but are they eleven years old?" McLean's eyes grew wide with amazement, but he didn't answer the question. Loveless continued with his briefing.

"Two nights ago he made contact with a Blind Bat flareship that was working the area. Then last night he called again. He wants to be picked-up and he wants a Sky Hook."

"That, Colonel Hempstead, is where you come in," Colonel Nelson took charge of the conversation. "General Momyer wants this young man brought out of Laos, and he wants us to do it. 'If it's a Sky Hook he wants, then a Sky Hook we'll give him,' those are his exact words."

"Sir, if I may interject."

"Go right ahead, Colonel Loveless."

"Last night Airman Carter - it definitely is Carter, we've identified him through his personnel authenticator - anyway, he requested a pickup for 0400 tomorrow morning."

Nelson looked at Hempstead. "Can we have an airplane ready for a pickup then? What's the status on your birds?"

"Well, sir. We've got a supply drop scheduled 'up north' for just after midnight. Captain Shoemaker's crew, in fact. The other airplane is at CCK for periodic maintenance. I guess we could have them drop in at Da Nang and refuel, then fly another mission."

"Couldn't they carry enough fuel to remain airborne after their drop?"

"We're talking about four hours. They would have to climb to high altitude to do it, and that might compromise our whole operation. They'll be less than an hour out of Da Nang when they make their drop, then it's about the same distance to the area you've indicated. It should be no problem. Besides, I'm sure Shoemaker and his boys would bust their butts if they know who they're going after. They'd do it for anyone, but especially for a buddy."

"Where do I fit in here, this seems to be an Air Force show?" McLean asked.

"I thought you might want to have a talk with the young man after we get him home. From what Colonel Loveless told General Momyer, it seems one young airman has been doing more damage to the infiltration routes then the whole 7th Air Force and Special Forces combined. Maybe you can pick up some pointers."

McLean's face became as red as his hair. Then he realized his Air Force counterpart was not needling him; he was dead serious.

"I didn't mean to touch a nerve, Doug." Nelson's voice was softer than normal.

"That's okay, Mitch. I know what you mean. Of course I'd want to be part of the man's interrogation, especially if he's been on the ground in Laos as long as you say. I'd be glad to send in a ground team, for that matter, to bring him out."

"If it should come to that. Although it seems that won't be necessary, at least if everything goes well tonight. Listen, men, we don't have a whole lot of time to get this thing set up. Gene, why don't you sit down with Colonel Loveless and Captain Jester and get the skinny on this whole operation. Then you can get together with your crew and figure out how you want to run the mission. Don't get them out of crew rest, though. They're going to have a long night ahead of them."

Four hundred miles away, on the other side of the Annamite Range, Toby Carter was preparing to set out on one last expedition into the depths of the huge Laotian cavern. He decided to take the Browning Automatic Rifle this time, to hell with any ricochets. They just might work in his favor, anyway. He stashed his trusty Springfield with the rest of the equipment from the airdrop bundle. The Browning was going to be heavy enough by itself. Preston had the M-16 and Thompson, along with all the ammunition for them, and both the radios. He still had his cave pack and was wearing the vest, mainly so he could carry his revolver and knife.

He would have to hurry as fast as he could to do what he had to do, then get back to the sinkhole in time. Toby set off down the passageway at a trot, moving as fast as he dared on the uneven terrain. He was out of breath by the time he reached the drop to the lower level, but had no time to rest. Quickly, he lowered himself through the slot, then made his way down the breakdown pile. Without his watch and in the depths of the cave, he had no idea of time. All he knew was that he had less than ten hours to get to the mouth of the cave and back to the sinkhole.

The river was as loud as it had been earlier when he made the same journey. Then he had been almost reconciled to his fate and only half expected to be able to return again the same way he had come. Now he wanted to live; he wanted it with all his heart. He wondered - had he gone mad; what kind of idiocy would make a person want to jump right back in the middle of quicksand when they had already gotten out of the quagmire once, and when rescue was just over the horizon?

How long had it been since he came back this way with Preston? Four hours? Three? Whatever, it seemed like an eternity and it was very hard to believe he had freed his pilot from a tiger cage and now the man was hiding in the sinkhole on top of the ridge. What was he going to find when he got back to the mouth of the cave?

He knew what he hoped to find, that the gun crew was all dead, including the woman, and the gun was permanently out of commission. This time he intended to make certain, if at all possible. There were more grenades in his cave pack. He planned to use as many as it took to render the gun completely out of commission.

As he neared the mouth of the cave, he heard a new sound; some kind of gasoline or diesel engine was chugging away. The generator! Someone must be around the gun after all! A mixture of despair, relief and eagerness swept over the twenty-year old boy from Tennessee. Despair that someone was in the vicinity of the gun, coupled with relief that he now knew there were people there and eagerness to get on with the job. Adrenaline rushed through his veins as he hurried toward the light around the bend.

In his excitement, Toby came within a hair's breadth of forgetting to kill the flame on his carbide light. He remembered it only as he was about to round the final corner that would bring him into full view of the cave entrance. His mind had only an instant to register the scene at the entrance before he went into action. Someone had removed the bodies from his earlier carnage. A crew was working on the gun with an acetylene torch while others stood guard with AK-47s at the ready. And, overseeing the whole shebang was the woman.

Toby strode purposefully toward the scene with the BAR clutched securely by his right side with the muzzle pointed toward the crew on the gun. He was still in darkness; no one had caught sight of the madman coming from the depths of the cave. He wanted to get as close as possible before opening fire. And he hoped the damn gun worked! He had never fired this one.

The gun worked. When Toby squeezed the trigger, a flame two feet long leaped from the barrel in the semidarkness. He held the trigger down, pouring round after round of .30-caliber steel-jacketed bullets toward the crew on the gun. Every other round was a tracer; all he had to do was walk the rounds toward his targets. Red balls of fire were shooting all over the place, looking like shots from a roman candle, as the bullets ricocheted off of rock and metal. A muzzle flash told him one of the guards was shooting back; Toby swung the muzzle of the BAR toward the flash. A round of tracer extinguished the flame. An explosion rocked the cave. What the devil? Then he remembered the men with the acetylene torch. A round must have ruptured their tank. A click told him the magazine was empty. He dropped behind a rock, then pulled the old magazine out and turned it around so that the full one he had taped to the one in the gun was now in place. Then he stepped out from behind the rock, his BAR blazing.

There were still people alive in the glow of the light from the generator so Toby swept the area with fire. There were no tracers in this clip so he aimed by instinct. When there were was no one left standing, Toby turned the BAR on the generator. One well-aimed burst ruptured the fuel tank, pouring hot fuel onto the exhaust. Just like the trucks he had shot up, the generator blew up, plunging the interior of the cave into darkness except for the glow from the burning gasoline. Night had already fallen outside; once the fire burned out, everything in and out of the cave would be immersed in darkness.

Toby listened for sounds of movement over the roar of the river. He heard nothing but running water, but then the roar of the river was so loud he wasn't sure if he would have heard anything or not. He squeezed off a short burst with the BAR, and watched for muzzle flashes of returned fire - nothing. He waited.

Toby stood perfectly still for several long minutes, watching for any sign that someone might still be alive around the gun. When he saw no lights or any other sign, he decided to risk a light of his own. He snapped on his angle-head, being careful to hold the flashlight far from his body. His eyes had adjusted to the semidarkness; the red glow from the flashlight seemed as bright as sunlight. There was absolutely no response from anyone. Still, Toby was hesitant to reveal himself further, but there was no choice. He had come to destroy the gun completely this time. He flashed the light here and there. Bodies were scattered like worn-out rag dolls. Where was the woman? For the first time since he began firing, he remembered her. She was nowhere to be seen.

Stealthily, Toby worked his way around the cave entrance, checking the bodies for signs of life. He had already made up his mind that no one was going to be alive when he left this time. He couldn't believe he had been able to get away with two stunts like this, at the same place, against the same people, using more or less the same tactics and within twelve hours of each other! Just a few minutes more and he would be able to start back toward the sinkhole - and impending freedom.

When he was satisfied that every one of the people around the gun was dead, Toby reached into his cave pack for a grenade. He could see that the gun's breech had been damaged by the grenade he had set off in it earlier but maybe it was repairable. He put two in the same place this time and taped them securely with the roll of duct tape from his cave pack. He ran a length of nylon string through the pins of the grenades, then played it out as he made his way to a rock behind which he could take shelter. The two grenades went off almost simultaneously, close enough together that the explosions sounded like a single blast. Toby heard debris striking the other side of the rock; he hoped it was pieces of metal from the gun. He waited for the dust to settle before he would move out from behind the rock to take a look.

Toby was pleased with the results of the two grenades. The gun's breech was twisted beyond repair; the only way this gun could go back into action was if it were put through a complete restoration, a process the Viets could never perform here, regardless of their legendary resourcefulness. Before coming out from behind the rock, Toby lit his carbide light. He sat it in the gunner's seat on the gun, then hefted the BAR onto his shoulder in preparation for setting out back upstream, the task he had come here for completed. He was disappointed that he had not seen the body of the woman, there was no doubt she had been supervising the work crew at the gun. Maybe she had crawled off somewhere to die. She obviously was strong of countenance.

The BAR saved Toby Carter's life. When the blade of the knife came down toward the base of his neck, the point was deflected by the barrel of the gun. Toby felt intense pain on his left shoulder as the knife ripped open the flesh over the muscle. He swirled around to peer into the eyes of hell itself.

"Hell hath no fury as a woman scorned," so goes the old proverb. The woman Toby saw had not been scorned, but she was plenty mad at the one who had now destroyed the one object that had obsessed the young Vietnamese woman for the past six months. As commander of the antiaircraft crew, the gun was her responsibility. It had been the power of that gun that led to her incredible sex drive, an attribute she had never possessed before she became an officer in the Army of the Peoples Republic of Vietnam.

The woman had driven the knife at Toby Carter's spine with all the strength she could muster, a strength increased four-fold by the same adrenaline that had caused her quarry to walk right into her realm of responsibility, not once but twice, and to rather blissfully shoot down every one of her companions, including Ky, the stud upon whose services she depended to relieve the yearnings of her young body. Her blow had been so powerful that the vibration caused by metal striking metal coursed up her arm and caused her to lose her grip on the hilt of the knife. When Toby grabbed the woman's wrist, the knife slipped from her grasp.

Although momentarily stunned, the woman quickly regained her composure and began battling the American with all her considerable strength. He may have outweighed her a good fifty pounds, but the young woman had a strength that had been honed from carrying nearly her own weight in ammunition for this very gun during her own trek down the Trail to this place. Toby gripped her right hand with his left; with his right, he reached for the left hand that was pounding on his chest. Then he felt the firmness of her breasts pressing into his chest. He felt himself growing hard. They fell to the ground, with him on top. The girl continued her struggle.

The Vietnamese girl was wearing cotton slacks and a shirt while Toby was still wearing the same jungle fatigues he had been wearing for more than a month. His under-shorts had long since fell apart and been thrown away. Only two layers of tropical weight material separated the two; she felt his arousal as certainly as he could feel her breasts. The girl wriggled her hips; she was becoming as aroused as he!

Toby was in an absolutely incongruous situation. Here he was, lying right on top of a young Vietnamese woman whom he had gone to great lengths to come to this very spot to kill, and who had tried to kill him only seconds before. Now this very same woman, an enemy who had tried to kill him, was giving every indication that she wanted to make love with him!

For them to get together, Toby had to release one of the girl's hands so he could reach down and undo their clothing. Even though she was making seductive motions - she had yet to say anything even though Preston had said she spoke English, if this was the same one - Toby didn't quite trust her. He remembered what Preston had told him, how this same woman had used sex to torment him. "She's the power behind that gun, Toby. If there are witches, she's one." She pressed up against him. Her motion influenced his decision considerably. He released her left hand and raised up as he brought his right hand toward his body.

Then, in the light from his carbide lamp, he saw it; the shiny blade of the knife with which the girl had tried to kill him but moments before. She had seen it too; her hand was reaching to grasp the hilt. She was fast but Toby Carter was faster. His right hand came right across her chin and kept going, right to the hilt of the survival knife strapped to the left front of his survival vest. He knew exactly what he was doing; in an instant of time the knife was out and Toby had plunged the blade into the girl's body, the point penetrating the soft flesh below her left breast and plunging between two ribs. He knew the blade had found her heart as she shuddered once and lay still. He gave the knife a twist, then withdrew it. Warm, bright red blood gushed from the wound and flowed over his hand.

Toby stood up, keeping close watch on the girl as he did. All thoughts of lovemaking had vanished; she was once again his enemy. This time he was going to make certain this gun crew was not resurrected. He pulled his .38 out of the holster behind his left kidney, pressed it against her left temple, and pulled the trigger, sending one each .38 caliber bullet into her brain. Pieces of flesh and bone flew all over the place. The whole ordeal seemed like one really bad dream!

Unfortunately, this was not a dream, although this was definitely the stuff nightmares are made of. This was real, and he really had to get out of here. He had been impervious to the pain of his wound during the struggle. Now, it was nearly debilitating. There was no way he would be able to carry the BAR back. The river! That was it, he would throw it in the river where it would be of no use to anyone. His carbide lamp and cap were still on the gunner's seat on the gun. He put the cap on his head, took the BAR by the barrel and started toward the stream some twenty yards away. He didn't look at the woman's body. That she was dead was beyond doubt this time. No one could survive a bullet in the brain fired at pointblank range, especially after it had blown out the side of their head.

Toby threw the Browning into the river, thinking as he did so that it was a damn shame to waste such a beautiful weapon in such a way. He pondered for an instant the correlation with the death of the beautiful Asian woman. Then he started back the way he had come, yet knowing it was doubtful, considering his injured condition, that he would be able to climb back to the upper level of the cave.

Chapter Eighteen

The sun had just gone down behind the mountains overlooking the city of Nha Trang when Staff Sergeant John Carmichael walked out of the door of his hooch on the air base. There was just enough time to get to the mess hall and grab a quick bite of supper and still make it to the flight line in time for briefing. The other enlisted men had long since gone to the chow hall; Carmichael was finishing up a letter to his wife back home in Spring Lake when they left. Neither Dilday or Potter, the two loadmasters on the crew, were married. Neville, the radio operator, was divorced.

Carmichael had hoped to catch up with the other three airmen in the mess hall, but they had already finished and left for the flight line by the time he got through the serving line. He wished he could have eggs and bacon but the chow hall at Nha Trang was as yet not progressive enough to offer breakfast-type meals at all hours for those whose day was just beginning. He would have to make do with roast pork and mashed potatoes. After all, it could be worse. He could be eating C-rats out of a can!

"Guys, we've got a little twist tonight." Colonel Hempstead began the briefing. "You're going to have to fly two missions tonight instead of one." Groans went up from the other eight men in the room.

"I know, I know, but I think, once you hear the purpose of this mission, not a man in here will regret the second trip. First, let's get our primary mission out of the way.

"You'll be taking off at 2300 local as SPEAR 101. The mission calls for you to deliver 2,500 pounds of cargo to a team working here," Hempstead pointed to a spot on the map in the mountains west of Hanoi. It's a standard load; ammunition, rations and medical supplies. Your route will keep you well clear of all known flak positions and there are no SAMS this far west that we know of.

"Once you've made your drop, you'll egress the same way you came in but, instead of returning to Nha Trang, you'll be going to Da Nang to refuel. You'll take-off again at 0230. The second mission will be a Sky Hook; you're going to make a pick-up, a real one, in Laos. There will be at least one person and possibly two.

"Now guys, this is not a bunch of snake-eater Green Beret types you're picking up. This is one of us, a trash-hauler, one of the loadmasters on an A-model that was shot down over Laos several weeks ago. In fact, this is not just any loadmaster. This young man has been hiding out in a cave, now he's ready to come home."

"You're shitting me, Colonel! Not Carter!"

"Right you are, Carmichael. The one and only Tobin Carter. I know that name may not mean a lot to Neville or Captain Binghamton, but the rest of you know him."

"Damn right, Colonel. He used to be on our crew."

Hempstead ignored Carmichael's second outburst, "Marve," he addressed the aircraft commander, "this thing could be dicey, to say the least. There are a ton of guns not more than a mile and a half from the pick-up point and one of them is a big mother, a 100-MM, that's already claimed half a dozen airplanes - including two C-130s. That's the main reason we're sending you; there's no way a rescue helicopter could ever get in there and out again in one piece."

"Colonel, If we're going after Toby Carter, we'll take our chances," Marve Shoemaker replied.

"I thought YOU would, especially considering who's involved. But for the record, General Momyer personally ordered this mission. In fact, if we weren't afraid of pissing off the Army, we'd cancel the first mission and reschedule it for tomorrow night, or next week. As it is, I hate to send you guys out on two potentially dangerous missions on one night, but you're all I've got with the other airplane at C-C-K for maintenance.

"Besides, considering who we're picking up, I thought you guys would want to do this one."

After the briefing was over, Carmichael and the other enlisted men filed out of the room, down the hall and out into the fading light.

"Just what is the deal on this guy, Carter, anyway?" asked Neville to no one in particular.

"Yeah, just who is he? I know I've heard Captain Shoe and you and Ellison talk about him, but he was before my time in the squadron," said Potter.

Dilday commented, "Wasn't he on the crew before the squadron switched over to Sky Hook?"

. Yeah, Carter was our loadmaster. We flew together - Captain Shoemaker, Captain Cornelius, Captain Ellison, me and Carter - for almost two years. For Ellison - he was a lieutenant then - Carter and me, this was our first crew ever. We had a lot of good times flying out of Evreux, Kadena, Mactan. He was with us on DRAGON ROUGE. The whole crew was scheduled to go into Sky Hook together but when we got back from Mactan, Carter got orders to Naha."

"What's Blind Bat? I've never heard that term before," asked Dilday.

"Who the fuck knows? There are so many different things going on in this war. Colonel Hempstead said something about Toby being on a flareship. I didn't know anybody was flying flare missions in C-130s but us.

Since he's across the fence, I guess there's something going on over there we don't know about."

The four enlisted men climbed into the two seats of the Dodge "six-pack," a pickup truck with two full-sized seats in the cab. Operations was right on the flight line; the ride to their airplane was short. The driver pulled up before a C-130, one could tell at least that much by the high wings, turboprop engines and huge sail-like tail. But while this airplane was definitely from the Lockheed C-130 lineage, to even the most casual observer that this was no ordinary transport was readily apparent.

In general profile, size and shape, the airplane was virtually identical to the airplanes in which Toby Carter had been flying his Blind Bat missions as well as the dozens of routine "trash-hauling" trips around the Orient. But this airplane was an E-Model, the same model of the Hercules he had flown with Shoemaker's crew back at Pope. But even then, this was not a typical C-130E. The familiar porpoise nose profile was changed; this airplane looked more like a giant beetle than a denizen of the deep! Two large, metal probes were extended in front of the nose at a sixty-degree angle to one another. There were also several air scoops and antennae on this airplane that were not present on other C-130s. But the most curious feature of the airplane was the camouflage; instead of the familiar green and tan with a gray belly, this airplane was painted green and black with a special radar-absorbing paint. There was only one word to describe the appearance of this strange, generally black airplane - sinister. It was a C-130E-1 "Sky Hook," also known as COMBAT TALON but generally known by those in the C-130 world as "Blackbird."

They weren't scheduled for take-off until 2200 hours, but there was a lot to be done before they could depart Nha Trang for their airdrop mission. Airdrop missions were a regular part of daily operations for all C-130 crews anywhere in the world, but this one was different. Shoemaker's crew would be dropping supplies to a ground team operating two hundred miles north of the 17th Parallel, the imaginary line that separated the two Vietnams. They would be doing what they had been specially trained to do, making a night low-level penetration deep into enemy territory.

Toby Carter hurried as fast as he could into the depths of the cave, partly to place himself far enough from the entrance that he would not be detected in the event someone came in from outside, and partly just to get away from the carnage he had perpetrated. Never before had he killed anyone other than with a gun, except for the lucky knife throw up on the ridge. Feeling the knife penetrate the soft flesh, coupled with the warmth of the life's blood of the victim, was an experience he had never visualized. That the person he had killed was a woman left him with a feeling of guilt he might not have had had he killed another man. She was an enemy, one responsible for the deaths of several of his comrades and who knew how many others. Such rationale didn't make him feel any better about what he had done. Then there was the bizarre sexual aspect of the event; he had actually enjoyed the struggle, had become fully aroused. He would never know whether the woman was as aroused as he, or merely using her charms as a diversion so she could plunge her own knife into him, to rectify the mistake that had allowed him to live when her knife was deflected.

When he was well out of sight of the entrance, Toby stopped to check his wound. His already decrepit fatigues were covered with blood. How much was his and how much was the woman's, he could not tell. His shoulder hurt like the devil; the wound was on his back. There was no way he could even see it, much less attend to it. His back felt sticky, but then it had been feeling sticky since at least the second day after he was shot down. He had been wearing the survival vest. The knife would have had to slash through the nylon material, as well as the cotton jacket; perhaps the wound was superficial in spite of the pain.

By the time he had gone a mile from the entrance, that he was losing an undetermined amount of blood was obvious. He was losing some of his strength, but then that could be the normal result of decreasing adrenaline in his blood stream. He always felt drained after an encounter that placed him in danger, whether it was taking flak over the North, hearing the impact of bullets all around him as he climbed the limestone face of the cliff, suddenly finding himself facing a dozen enemy troops or rushing into what appeared to be certain death. Whatever the event, he always felt weak afterwards.

This was no time to feel weak. Toby knew that he was facing an eighty-foot climb when he reached the waterfall, and his left arm was going to be practically useless. Even without the extra weight of the BAR, just getting to the top of the pitch was going to be a real challenge. He had worried about Captain Preston making the climb; now he was full of doubts about his own abilities after his injuries.

He hoped he wouldn't be pursued. Apparently no one had escaped his fire, but then who knew who might be outside the entrance of the cave. Only the roaring of the river gave him assurance that perhaps the sound of the firing and the detonations of the grenades had not left the general area of the entrance. Had there been anyone in the immediate area, no doubt they would have made an appearance shortly after he began firing. Or at least after the grenades went off.

In any event, Toby did not want to meet up with anyone in the depths of the cave. Without the BAR, he had only his .38 and the survival knife. The pistol was better than nothing, but it lacked the accuracy of a rifle and he was a far better shot with a rifle than with a pistol. Not that he couldn't hit with the short gun, he could, but with a rifle he was deadly. As for the knife, ironically, he had killed two people with it. Yet he knew that in both instances he had been very lucky; there was no other way to explain his success.

What time was it? Without his watch, Toby had no way at all of telling time, not in the pitch-black darkness of a cave. One loses all track of time in a cave, even with a watch. All he could do was hope that he would be able to get back to the sinkhole in time. Without an injury, he had never really doubted but that he would be able to get back with time to spare. Now he had his doubts.

At the sinkhole, Captain Bob Preston was having a hard time sleeping. That he was finally free of the cage was an overwhelming thought; he had expected to end up in a similar cell in a North Vietnamese prison camp in Hanoi, or worse still, in Laos in the hands of the Pathet Lao. Now he was out of the cage and free to do what he wished, within the limits of his circumstances. Those circumstances looked pretty good now, especially considering what Toby had told him before he pushed off again into the depths of the cave. What the hell was Carter doing anyway? They were free; a rescue bird would be coming for them in the wee hours of the morning. All they had to do was ride the winch to safety. That was something he did have second thoughts about, but if the Air Force trusted the system, then he should too. After all, it was the only way to real freedom and the loving arms of his wife and family.

Carter hadn't said what he was going to do, only that he had some loose ends to tie up and that he would be back well before the 0400 when the rescue ship was expected to make its appearance. He hoped the idiot hadn't gone back to make sure that damn gun was out of commission! Good Lord, the boy had already carried out a superhuman feat as it was. He'd risked his life to knock out the gun crew and rescue him. When they got back, he was going to recommend him for the Medal of Honor. If anyone ever deserved it, Toby did.

He looked at his watch, Toby's watch, really - it was nearly midnight. Only four more hours to go. Where was Carter?

As Preston was looking at his watch, two hundred miles to the northeast, Marve Shoemaker's crew was nearing their drop zone. The veteran pilot had brought SPEAR 101 six hundred miles from Nha Trang to the vicinity of their drop zone where a special operations team made up of five Vietnamese and two American Special Forces types would be awaiting their delivery. A week ago they had dropped that same team from 30,000 feet onto a drop zone twenty miles south of where they were expecting their supplies tonight.

He scanned the instrument panel, as he had been doing ever since they dropped down to "nap of the earth" altitudes nearly an hour before. The needle of the radar altimeter hovered right at fifty feet; the 140,000 pound airplane was zooming along at 250 knots less than the height of a tree above the tops of the trees that covered the hills of the Annamite Range beneath them. At this altitude, under the cloak of night, they could barely make out the outline of the ridges on either side of the specially modified Hercules. Shoemaker and every member of his crew knew their lives depended on the accuracy of the terrain avoidance radar and the low tolerance auto-pilot to which it was coupled. They also knew that the low altitude the radar/auto-pilot combination afforded was their best insurance against detection by the hundreds of radar sites that dotted the North Vietnamese landscape.

On his right Captain C.J. Cornelius monitored the terrain avoidance radar from the copilot's seat while behind them while Carmichael kept close watch on the airplane's systems. No matter what the configuration, the job of flight mechanic on a C-130 always remains the same - monitor every amp of electricity, every pound of hydraulic pressure, every ounce of fuel. Behind and to the right of Cornelius, Captain D.J. Ellison was keeping track of their position on the maps spread on the tiny table at which he sat. D.J. had his own radar monitor; he used it to pick out landmarks on the earth beneath them.

In a special compartment behind the cockpit, Sergeant Terrence Norville monitored the frequencies of the array of radios at his disposal. In the modern world of channeled radios, the skill of the airborne radio operator was a vanishing art; only certain special mission aircraft still carried them, even though a decade or two before, every multiengine airplane that flew carried an R/O as part of the crew.

Beside Norville, Captain Larry Binghamton monitored his own panel, an array of switches and cathode ray tubes that controlled and monitored the tools of his trade - an electronics warfare package. As an EWO, Binghamton's job was to be on the lookout for North Vietnamese radar defenses and SAMS, and to throw out an assortment of special signals that would fool or completely disable the radar signals that were the eyes of the North Vietnamese air defenses. No other C-130 crews included EWOs, most were either part of SAC bomber crews or flew aboard special electronics counter-measures aircraft. The Blackbirds carried EWOs because of where they operated - deep in the heart of enemy controlled territory.

Back in the cargo compartment the two loadmasters, SSgt Freddie Potter and Airman First Class Doug Dilday, went about their task of completing the final checks of their airdrop system, just as other loadmasters did on other transports. But the system they were using was different; if featured an overhead trolley system similar to that used on the old C-119, the "Flying Boxcar" or "dollar-nineteen" of Korean War fame. American C-119s had flown airdrop missions over Dien Bien Phu back when the French had been battling the forerunners of today's North Vietnamese. The first Americans to die in Vietnam had been civilian pilots employed by a clandestine airline known in those days simply as C.A.T. C.A.T. was still around, but now part of a larger clandestine airline system run by the Central intelligence Agency and known by all who flew in the Far East as Air America. James McGovern and Wallace Burford, the two C.A.T. pilots, had died after an airdrop over Dien Bien Phu the day before the outpost fell. Dien Bien Phu wasn't too far from where they were tonight.

"Ten minute warning," the Blackbird was only ten minutes from the drop zone. Instead of slowing down and popping up for the drop as was the practice in conventional airlift, Shoemaker would maintain his airspeed while the loadmasters opened only the cargo door, leaving the ramp retracted. The aerial delivery rail would be extended over the gaping hole left by the open door and the bundles would drop from the trolley. Since they did not slow-up or pop-up, anyone on the ground who might by chance be observing them by radar would never know where the drop had been made.

At the appointed place, Ellison called out the words that had been sending paratroopers and airdrop loads on their way since World War II - "green light." Five 500-pound bundles were then sent on their way, each with only a small pilot chute trailing behind to insure that they landed upright when they hit the ground. Fortunately, Cornelius had spotted the tiny white strobe-light operated by one of the Special Forces types on the ground at the right time. They were able to drop on the first pass.

"Okay, guys. Let's clean her up and head for Da Nang."

At 0110 hours the black camouflaged C-130 touched down on the long runway at Da Nang.

As Toby Carter made his way through the huge cave, he became more and more apprehensive about the possibilities of making the climb that lay in store for him. The wound in his shoulder was throbbing; his left sleeve was now soaked in blood. There was no doubt but that he was losing blood - and strength he would need to get through the rest of the night. Finally he came to the huge breakdown pile that was his only means of getting to the upper level of the cave and on to safety. What was he going to do? Toby tried to climb with one hand, using his feet to propel himself upwards. He met with limited success but got only about ten feet. Although his shoulder ached immeasurably, he tried to use his left arm. The pain became unbearable; he screamed in spite of himself. Despair almost overwhelmed him.

If there was one thing Toby Carter had learned in the twenty years he had been on this earth, and especially in the preceding weeks, it was never to give up, but to keep looking for a way. Then, an idea struck him. He was perched somewhat precariously on a boulder about ten feet above the floor of the passage - with at least seventy feet above him yet to climb. Toby reached into his cave pack and pulled out the coil of nylon 550 cord he had been carrying since he first came up with the idea of a cave/emergency survival pack in the first place. Five-fifty cord was the loadmasters number one tool; it was used as a safety to keep extraction parachutes from releasing prematurely and for tying loose equipment so it would be out of the way of airdrop loads. Some guys used it for shoe laces, Toby included.

With his knife, Toby cut a length from the coil of about five feet. Using a surgeon's knot and a locking knot, the standard knots used in parachute rigging, he tied the length into a loop. Toby took the nylon loop and wrapped it twice around the rope he had braided, the rope that was his only hope of salvation from his ordeal. He then pulled the loop down over his shoulders and around his chest. He leaned back so that his body weight was contained by the loop. Then, taking the resulting Prussik knot in his right hand, he pushed the knot up the taut rope as far as he could.

Leaning back in the loop, he walked his feet up the boulder until they found foot holds. Then he repeated the procedure. Toby's improvised climbing technique would have brought gasps of dismay from those who fancied themselves to be experienced "vertical" cavers, but then they had never been in a situation where their lives depended on climbing a hand-made rope with one arm totally useless, and bleeding like a stuck hog to boot! Regardless of what cavers would have thought, the technique worked and Toby managed to climb out of the lower level of the cave. When he got to the top, he collapsed in a heap while he gathered his wits and gave his body an opportunity to reconstitute itself.

For a moment, Toby was on the verge of slipping into unconsciousness. His now-damaged body had been pushed to the very limits of endurance - and there was still more than a mile to go. He managed to shake the impending darkness of his mind, at least temporarily, and set out down the upper level of the cave toward the sink-hole. Now he was walking again, and in passage that featured fairly smooth floors, even if he was negotiating a constant uphill grade. Yet in spite of the relative ease of movement *in* this passage, Carter felt his body growing gradually weaker, while the pain was still there, as intense as before. At least on this level he shouldn't have to worry about running into any Viets.

Toby had thought the climb would be his worst obstacle. It wasn't; he had forgotten about the crawl-ways leading to the sinkhole. When he reached the tiny passage, a sense of well-being came over him. The sinkhole entrance of the cave was less than two hundred feet away. All he had to do was crawl a little ways, then he would be home free. But when Toby dropped down to a hands and knees position, his left arm gave way under his weight. There was no way he was going to be able to crawl on hands and knees.

He had only one choice, to slither along on his belly like a snake! He could push himself along with his toes and use his good hand to pull, but with only one good arm, belly-crawling was going to be a real chore. Stlll, he had to do it, if he wanted to live.

Chapter Nineteen

Bob Preston looked at Toby's watch. It was 0345; in fifteen minutes it would be time to make contact with the rescue plane. Where the hell was he? Preston knew that without Carter the rescue crew was not going to attempt a pickup tonight, not without authentication. They had already identified Carter; he had told him that much before he left. But, unless they happened to have his own personal authenticator information with them, the crew would have to call for the data. By the time they got it, it would be daylight and too late for a pick-up. He would have to spend another night in this God-forsaken cave!

Were his ears deceiving him, or did he hear something? He thought he heard a sound, like something - or someone - scraping a rock, coming from somewhere within the cave. Could it be Toby? He was tempted to call out, but remembered that Carter had warned him not to do just that. There was always the possibility someone might be on the surface. Then he heard it again; something was definitely moving around n the passage below him. He heard another sound, a groan, as if someone were in pain.

Toby Carter was very slowly but surely worming his way through the low passage, crawling on his belly like a snake, inching his way forward mere inches at a time. His wound felt as if someone were holding a hot poker to his shoulder, the hurt was that bad. Several times he lapsed into semi-consciousness and collapsed in a heap in the crawl-way. Each time he revived himself solely by sheer willpower and the desire to live. He wanted to see his folks again, his parents and his brothers and sisters. Then, finally, he pushed through the crawl-way and into the sinkhole entrance. He didn't know how he did it, but he managed to stand up.

"Damn, Carter! I had just about given up on you! Do you have any idea what time it is?"

Toby, by this point, was so relieved that he had made his way through the cave that he had completely forgotten why it was so urgent that he get there! Then he remembered, and a new rush of adrenaline filled his veins, bringing with it a new vigor.

"What time is it? It must be getting close to time for Sky Hook to appear."

"It's five minutes to four. You got here right in the very nick of time, buddy."

"Hand me the radio. They'll be calling any minute."

Toby stuck his head out of the entrance in the sink-hole. He looked up; thank God there were stars! If there had been fog, the pickup would have had to be postponed. He reached in the special pocket on his survival vest for the strobe light that every aircrew member carried. The blue glare shield was in place; without it, the flashing light would look like a muzzle flash from a heavy machine gun. He placed the strobe on top of a rock and pushed the button that activated the flashing light. It worked, but he knew it should. It had worked when he tested it two days before.

Seven thousand feet above the ridge SPEAR 101 was maintaining a lazy orbit, flying loose formation with BLIND BAT, following the procedure that had been worked out earlier in the day. The Blind Bat crew had been working the area since before midnight, running air strikes against targets, real and imagined, all along their section of the Trail. Shoemaker's crew had been on station with them for the past thirty minutes, orienting themselves with the area and making note of the heavy concentrations of flak along the walls of the gorge. It was odd that the atheistic North Vietnamese only put guns on one side of the gorge, believing that the other ridge had some kind of sacred significance. At least that was what those intelligence folks from Udorn said.

As the black camouflaged C-130 circled lazily in the early morning sky, Marvin Shoemaker thought about the young man who was somewhere on - or beneath - the ridge below. It was hard to believe that they were here to pick up his own former loadmaster. This whole Sky Hook thing had been developed for use with Army special operations people, not downed airmen. He had had no idea that Toby Carter had been flying spook missions over Laos, or even that there was a C-130 forward air controller mission. But then there were so many sneaky-Pete missions in this war; his own crew was part of the sneakiest of them all!

Shoemaker thought about the young man from Tennessee who had turned up on his crew back at Pope in the summer of '64. That was only two years ago but seemed like at least a decade, so much had happened in the intervening months. He'd had some doubts about having such a green crew; Carmichael, Ellison and Carter had all been fresh out of initial training for their respective positions. At least Carmichael and Ellison had a little bit of maturity about them, both were in their mld-twenties at the time. Carter, on the other hand, was still a teen-ager in 1964. Hell, he couldn't be much more than twenty now!

But looks can be deceiving and Toby Carter had proved to be a quick learner, with a maturity of his own. At least he wasn't like some of the other enlisted men who got drunk and missed flights. Heck, the only time Garter had ever gotten in trouble with the Air Police, he had been with him and Carmichael! They had gone to an off-limits bar in Cebu City while they were at Mactan, and after curfew at that! Colonel Newbold had let him off on that one, knowing guys had to let off steam once in awhile. That Carter was only an airman second class while he was a captain could have gotten

177

him in real trouble in some squadrons, but, what the hell, they were all part of the same crew and rank didn't matter.

What kind of condition would the kid be in; that was a question that had been raised by everyone from Colonel Nelson on down, as well as the two intelligence types from Udorn. After all, it had been nearly two months since the flareship went down. Unless Carter was thoroughly adept at living off the land, chances were he would be suffering from severe malnutrition. But then again, he was a Tennessee country boy, a hunter at that. Shoemaker knew all about growing up in a rural environment; after all, he was from southwest Virginia himself. There were a lot of things out in the woods that might not be gourmet delights, but they were nutritious enough if one were able to separate the good from the stuff that would kill you.

At any rate, one of the guys from the flight surgeon's office was flying with them tonight, Sergeant Wooley. Wooley had been at Pope and, by coincidence, had known Carter. He had been TDY with the squadron at Mactan and had flown a number of missions with their crew then. Hell, this was going to be like old home week, once they got Toby in the airplane!

"Hey, look at that!" Cornellious was pointing at something on the ground below. "There, at one o'clock. A flashing bluish light! That must be Toby's strobe light."

"Yeah, I see it. Get on the horn and give him a call."

"BLIND BAT LOADMASTER FIVE, this is SPEAR 101. If you read, come up voice," the co-pilot spoke into the boom mike in front of his mouth.

Seven thousand feet below, the words from the modified Hercules came through the receiver on Carter's survival radio. The voice sounded familiar - who was it? Hey, that's C.J.; C.J. Cornelious! Carter could barely contain his excitement when he answered, *Roger SPEAR 101, this is BLIND BAT LOADMASTER FIVE, I read you five by, over."

"Roger that, BAT FIVE, we read you five by also, and we've got your light. Where do you want the package?"

"Drop right on the light, and I'll need two suits. BULND BAT ONE is with me."

Shoemaker looked across the console at Cornelius; damn, somehow or other he'd found his pilot! As far as they knew, Carter was the only one they were to pick-up. "Better notify CROWN," said Shoemaker to his co-pilot.

"Roger, BAT FIVE, we understand BAT ONE with you. Stand by for drop in five minutes."

Shoemaker pulled the power off on the Hercules and began a diving descent well clear of the gorge. He didn't want to alert the gun crews along the sides of the gorge of his intentions. There was no doubt but that they knew the airplane was there, but he hoped they thought it was just another flareship. In the back of the airplane, the two loadmasters, Potter and Dilday, were preparing to drop the Fulton kits. Two bundles hung from the trolley on top of the cargo compartment, ready to be sent on their way.

On the ground Toby Carter ignored the difference in rank in his glee and punched Bob Preston on the shoulder. The recently freed pilot returned the favor, hitting Carter's left shoulder with a balled-up fist. Toby clinched his teeth from the pain, but kept silent about his wound. It was almost a minute before he could say anything. Finally he regained his composure.

"He'll be descending to drop altitude. In a couple of minutes they should be dropping the rescue kit. There should be instructions in it on how to set the thing up." After that statement, Toby was silent, as was Preston. The two men kept their ears cocked, listening for a certain sound. And then they heard it, the high-pitched whistle of four Allison turboprop engines. Almost immediately a huge black shadow swept across the clearing. They could see the red lights in the open cargo door turn to green. Two tiny lights dropped from the airplane, then grew larger and larger as they fell almost on top of them. THUNK, followed by another THUNK, as the Fulton kits landed on the limestone slab right outside the sinkhole, not more than twenty feet from where the strobe light gave off its signal.

"Good drop, SPEAR 101. We have the goodies."

"Roger that, BAT FIVE. We'll be gone for awhile. Give us a holler when you're ready. We'll have to make two trips."

"Will do, 101. Don't stray to the west. There's briars in the bushes over that way!"

Toby knew what Cornelius meant by "two trips." While the Fulton Recovery system was capable of picking up two people at one time, for some reason SPEAR 101 was going to have to make separate pick ups. He ran from the sinkhole to the first bundle. It was connected to the second by a length of 550 cord. He opened the bundle and pulled out a padded, hooded suit, a length of nylon rope and another container filled with something made of a rubbery material. He knew what it was, a balloon. A metal canister in the kit was filled with helium.

Preston had followed him up the sloping sides of the sinkhole. "Do you know how this thing works?" Toby asked.

"No, I've heard about it, but I've never seen it. You zip yourself into this suit. We hook one end of the line to this V-ring here; the other goes to this one." He held the end of a line attached to the balloon in one hand. "We run the balloon up into the air, you sit down and wait. Then you get a ride in an elevator."

"You're shitting me! They're going to come by and snatch me off the ground in that fucking suit?"

"Either that or you stay in the cave."

"I'll be double damned. But anything is better than that cage those gooks had me in. Have you got a coin? We can flip to see who goes first."

"You go first."

"No, you go first, that's an order."

"You go first. I know how to set up the equipment, you don't." Preston didn't respond to the convuluted logic of Toby's statement. After all, the instructions were in the bag!

"Put on the suit, I'll start inflating the balloon."

The pilot put on the bulky orange suit; they could tell the color in the glow of Toby's carbide light. Toby connected the end of the inflation hose to the helium cylinder. Within seconds the material began assuming the shape of a miniaturized World War II barrage balloon. By the time Preston was finished securing himself in the suit, the balloon was ready to be launched. The whole process had taken less than fifteen minutes.

"Are you ready?" Toby asked.

"As ready as I'll ever be," the grounded C-130 pilot replied, "But I'm not at all sure about this."

"It works."

"How do you know? Have you ever done this before?"

"I've seen a film."

"A film! Oh, great!"

Toby picked up the radio and spoke into the mouthpiece, "SPEAR 101, BAT FIVE, we're ready. You'll be picking up BAT ONE on the first pass."

Cornelius' voice came through the receiver, "Roger. What are the winds down there?"

"Dead calm."

"Understand - calm. In that case, we'll be making our approach from the south, parallel to the ridge. Have him sit facing south."

"Wilco."

Preston sat down near the edge of the south side of the clearing. Behind him three hundred feet of nylon cord played out into the atmosphere as the balloon ascended toward the heavens. Toby could still see the opaque plastic balloon even after the last coil of the rope unfurled, indicating it had reached the end of its length. He took advantage of the lull as SPEAR 101 repositioned for the pickup to lay out the materials of his own kit. Five minutes later they again heard the whine of the turboprops. Preston grimaced at Carter; Toby flashed a thumbs-up. Then, he was gone. In a flash the silhouette of the special operations Hercules passed overhead, the outstretched beetle-antenna directed the nylon line toward a special retaining device on the nose, and Preston was on his way!

The sound of the departing airplane was beginning to fade when Carter heard Cornelius in his receiver, "Go ahead and set up. Give us a call when you're ready."

Carter responded to C.J.'s transmission, then remembered there were a couple of things he needed to take care of. It was obvious he wasn't going to be able to carry the M-16 or Thompson with him. He also realized he was going to have to leave his cave pack behind. He bundled everything up and put it in one of the bundles in which the recovery kits had been dropped. He then took the bundle into the cave entrance and stashed everything in an inobvious grotto. Why he did it, he did not know. There was no way he would ever be back this way again but he did not want the gooks to find the stuff, yet at the same time he didn't want everything to be destroyed by the elements.

The last thing Toby put into the bundle was his trusty carbide light and cab. He even went to the trouble of dumping the old carbide and washing out the reservoir with water from his canteen so the copper wouldn't be eaten up.

He would use the angle-head to get back to where his recovery kit was awaiting his return. He hated to leave the lamp, it had been so much a part of his life, yet for some reason he felt it belonged here, that it should remain in the cave. Perhaps someday in a more peaceful time some cave explorer would find it and know that someone had been here before.

When he was certain he had covered everything and left no loose ends, Toby climbed out of the sinkhole and put on the suit. Then he inflated his own balloon and sat down facing the direction from which the airplane had last come. He pulled the radio out of the pocket on the suit where he had placed it, then notified SPEAR 101 that BAT FIVE was ready. Then he sat back to wait.

He didn't have to wait long. In less than five minutes he heard the whining turboprops as Shoemaker approached the pick-up zone in SPEAR 101. This time the roar of the engines did not fade as the airplane passed overhead; as the C-130 went on its way, Toby Carter trailed right behind! He had thought his parachute descent onto the ridge was the thrill of his life. He was wrong, this was something else!

SPEAR 101 was only a hundred and fifty feet above the treetops when Marve Shoemaker brought the black and green C-130 across the tiny clearing on top of the Laotian Ridge. Behind him, D.J. Ellison had the outline of the miniature barrage balloon on his radar; special radar reflectors bounced back the airplane's signals. He gave the pilot headings to fly so that the beetle antenna would contact the nylon rope somewhere below the balloon. Should he miss, steel cables would deflect the line off the end of the wings. But Shoemaker didn't miss.

When the pickup rope caught in the special catch, the balloon broke away, leaving only the pickup rope fastened securely in the vise-like snare. Immediately Toby Carter was lifted off of the ground and one hundred feet straight up into the air, then he swung out behind the low-flying C-130 as Shoemaker nosed the airplane into a steep climb to be sure the man swinging behind cleared the trees.

In the cargo compartment of the C-130, loadmasters Potter and Dilday stood on the ramp; in his hands Dilday held a long pole with a hook on the end. As Shoemaker began his climb, the nylon pickup rope swung right up beneath the belly of the airplane, close enough that Dilday was able to snare it with his pole. Carter was now having the ride of his life, literally flying through the air tethered to a long nylon line. As Dilday pulled that same line above the level of the open cargo ramp, Potter reached out and clamped another line to the pickup line. This second line was connected to a winch that was part of the Fulton System. When the line was definitely secured to the winch cable, Potter notified the cockpit via his interphone. Cornelius released the catch holding the pickup line and Potter and Dilday began winching the man swinging behind and below them into the cargo compartment of the airplane.

The entire pick-up procedure had originally been developed for airborne retrieval of satellites, then adapted for personnel recovery of downed airmen by Air Rescue Service and special operations teams by TAC. Now, it was being used to retrieve Toby Carter from Laos.

Toby was so glad to be on his way to safety that he forgot about being scared while swinging a hundred feet behind a C-130 flying five hundred feet above Laos and climbing higher and higher. Still, he was glad when he realized that he was swinging over the open ramp and into the familiar confines of the cargo compartment of a Hercules, even if this one was somewhat different than those he was used too. He had seen the insides of a Sky Hook airplane before. Once he was on the ramp, Potter began closing the ramp and door, using the switches on the ADS panel behind the left paratrooper door. Toby Carter was home again.

When the doors were closed, Potter and Dilday unzipped the bulky pickup suit and helped Toby Carter from it. Although they knew the man they had picked up - at least by reputation - after more than two months on the ground in Laos, much of that spent crawling around in a damp cave, Toby was completely unrecognizable as an individual and almost as even a human being! His stench was overpowering, even more so than had been that of the pilot they had brought in on their first pickup.

As soon as he was out of the suit, Chuck Wooley led Toby forward. He stripped the nasty remnants of the jungle fatigues off of Carter's body. When he cut away the survival vest and muddy fatigue jacket, Wooley realized that much of the mud was mixed with blood. Under the jacket Toby Carter's body was covered with blood, some dried and some fresh. Then he saw the wound.

"We've got to get this man to a hospital, pronto!" Wooley motioned Potter over and told him to advise the cockpit of the condition of the survivor.

"Hey, boss. Wooley says Carter's hurt bad and needs to get to the nearest hospital."

"Roger that, Potter. D.J., what's the closest military base with a hospital? Would it be Da Nang or somewhere in Thailand?"

"Stand-by one," came the reply. Then, "It looks to me like our best bet would be to head for N-K-P. That's the closest base, besides, they've got rescue choppers based there. They should be able to handle casualties."

"Roger, C.J. notify CROWN that we've got BAT ONE and FIVE aboard and are taking them to N-K-P. Tell them BAT FIVE has injuries. By the way, Potter, what kind of injuries does he have?"

"Wooley says it looks like a knife wound, his left shoulder is slashed open. Looks nasty."

"Okay, tell 'em he's got a knife wound. D.J., what's our ee tee aa?"

"It's only about seventy-five miles; we should be there in twenty minutes. Make that 1845 Zulu."

"Tell them to have an ambulance standing by."

"Load, pilot; how did he get a knife wound?'

"Beats me, sir. Wooley asked the other guy, he didn't know anything about it. Said he had no idea he was injured. Just that Carter had crawled off several hours ago, then came back just before he made contact with us."

To get to Thailand, Shoemaker would have to turn the airplane west, across the infamous Ho Chi Minh Trail that ran in the valley just to their right. The best approach to the problem would be to climb-out straight ahead, over the mountains, or even turn back to the east, to gain altitude before turning west toward the guns that guarded the infiltration routes. But Shoemaker knew they didn't have the luxury of a leisurely climb-out to get above the effective range of the guns. They would just have to take their chances.

Seven thousand feet above them, BLIND BAT TWO had been keeping a close eye on the proceedings beneath them. The crew of the A-model flareship was under the command of Captain Steve Danson, back at Ubon with the rest of Preston's crew, along with a new co-pilot and loadmaster to replace the two missing crewmembers. Danson heard Cornelius advise CROWN that they were going to take the survivors to NKP. He knew the special ops crew was going to have to over-fly the gorge to go to Thailand, and he was well aware that such a move at so low of an altitude could be disastrous. Danson knew there were six flares loaded in the chute back in the cargo door. They had been there for the past thirty minutes; he had ordered them loaded in the off-hand chance they might be needed during the rescue pick-up.

"Hold on!" Danson almost shouted the words into his microphone as he racked the C-130 into a tight right turn and began a dive toward the gorge below. There was no time to brief the crew; he would have to let them in on his plans as he carried them out.

"Loads, pilot. Get set to drop all six on my command, one at a time. We're going to make a high-speed low pass down the gorge to create a diversion. Where in the hell are the damned fighters when you need them?"

Shoemaker had made his decision; he banked the Blackbird to the left, in a climbing turn toward Thailand, knowing his airplane would be especially vulnerable to ground fire during the climb. The black, bulbous nose of the C-130 was just passing over the edge of the gorge when a burst of flame caught the pilot's eye. Oh, shit! Here it comes, Shoemaker thought to himself. No! Wait a minute, that's not ground flre7 What the fuck is it?

One, two, three, then six separate fires erupted in the valley below, each burning with a brilliance that could only come from magnesium, or maybe phosphorous. Hell, those looked like flares! Whatever they were, the diversion apparently worked because SPEAR 101 passed over the gorge without a single shot being fired at the Hercules. Who was it? Then he knew - Blind Bat.

"BLIND BAT, this is SPEAR 101. Thanks a lot."

"Glad to be of help, SPEAR. Just get our guys home."

Toby Carter was out cold when SPEAR 101 touched down on the PSP runway at Nakonphanom. He never saw the members of his old crew, never had a chance to say even hello. Part of his condition was due to loss of blood, but as much or more was the result of pure exhaustion.

An ambulance picked up the two survivors aboard SPEAR 101 and rushed them to the base dispensary. A young flight surgeon cleaned and sewed up Carter's wound and checked Preston over. Then the two men were once again loaded aboard an aircraft, this time a HH-3 helicopter, for airlift to the hospital at Udorn some thirty miles away. Toby Carter didn't wake up for three days.

Chapter Twenty

An April sun shown down on the concrete parking ramp apron. It was a Saturday morning at Naha Air Base, Okinawa, a time when the four hundred young men assembled in front of Base Operations would just as soon have been snuggled up in their beds, recovering from their hangovers from the night before. Either that or still in bed with their niessen down in Naumenoui. But the brass had other plans for them this morning. After all, it wasn't every day that the Chief of Staff came to Naha, nor was it every day that they had a parade. Parades have long been a tradition in the military, but more so for the Army and Marine Corps than for the Air Force. In the Air Force, parades are held only on very special occasions, such as when a high ranking officer or senior enlisted man is retiring, or when someone is to receive a decoration.

"PAAARADE,   ATTEEENNNNNNNNHUTTTTTTTT."   The Sergeant at Arms called the assembled formation to attention. Then, as the first strain of John Philip Sousa's "Stars and Stripes Forever" swirled out over the flight line, the 400-man formation stepped forward as one, each man's left foot striking the ground in nearly-perfect unison with the thud of the big bass drum. Toby Carter stood at attention, his heart thrilling to the strains of the Sousa march. Toby had loved marches as long as he could remember. Sousa had especially appealed to him ever since he saw a movie about the life of the Marine Corps Sergeant Major who led the Marine band, then went on to become America's most notable and best loved composer of martial music.

Although as a junior enlisted man Toby would ordinarily have been part of the formation, today he wasn't. He was standing on the platform behind the base commander, the 374th wing commander (the 6315th Operations Group had been upgraded to a wing and re-designated back in August), the commander of the 51st Tactical Fighter Wing, the military governor of Okinawa and about two dozen other dignitaries representing various organizations from throughout the island. The commander of the First Special Forces Group was there, along with several high ranking officers from the base up-island at Kadena. After all, it wasn't very often that the Chief of Staff of the Air Force came to Okinawa to award the nation's second highest award for valor. And it wasn't every day that the recipient of that award was an airman first class. From his vantage point in front of the reviewing stand, Toby could see the mass of men moving as one, arms swinging and legs moving in perfect unison. Blue garrison caps moved along on top of rows of khaki as the formation moved out from in front of the base operations building, then down the flight line past the black, bulbous noses of parked C-130's.

The parade commander, a major from the 817th squadron, led the formation parallel to the parking ramp, then upon passing a chalk mark on the concrete, executed a perfect left face. As each rank of eight men reached that same spot, each man pivoted behind the man to his immediate left. Just when they pivoted depended upon how far from the left side of the formation they were. The second man took two steps before executing the pivot, the third took three and so on until the last man on the right took eight steps before turning ninety degrees to the left. To the observer, the formation appeared to turn one corner of a perfect right angle. Then, at another identical mark, the commander led the formation into another left turn then turned right and continued marching in place as four hundred men moved into place behind him, the entire process executed in time to the beat of the bass drum as the band played first one Sousa march, then another.

When the formation was in place before the reviewing stand, the commander ordered "Right Face," followed by "Formation, halt." The marching men stopped and came to attention even as the Fifth Air Force Band, flown down from Yokota for the occasion, continued playing "The Stars and Stripes Forever." As the sounds of the last bar died away, the parade commander ordered the formation to "parade rest." As one, four hundred men clasped their hands behind their backs and spread their feet exactly thirty-six inches apart. And then the ceremonies began.

Several men were to be decorated that day, everyone of whom was higher in rank than Toby Carter. A full colonel from the 51st Fighter interceptor Wing was to receive the Legion of Merit for his outstanding work as Director of Material. A major from base finance was to receive the Meritorious Service Medal for doing a superior job of dispersing the government funds under his control. A captain from the 51st was to receive a Distinguished Flying Cross for dead-sticking his F-102 to a landing after the single engine fighter flamed-out during a training flight out over the Sea of Japan. Then there were the DFCs and Air Medals going to officers and NCOs from the 374th, men like himself, who had earned their awards flying trash-hauling missions "down South" or out over The Trail or "up north" With BLIND BAT and LAMPLIGHTER.

Quite a lot had happened in the war in the several months since SPEAR 101 plucked Toby Carter and Bob Preston off of the Laotian limestone ridge. Although it would be years before historians would recognize the war's divisions, the Vietnam War had moved out of the "advisory" stage and into a full-scale ground war. North Vietnamese divisions had begun operating throughout South Vietnam, while the Viet Cong had moved away from their "farmer by day, guerrilla by night" image and began fighting in a more conventional manner. In response, the U.S. forces had become more aggressive in their efforts at halting the communist onslaught in South Vietnam. As a result, things had gotten very hectic for the airlifters.

Only a few weeks before, back in February, the 173rd Airborne had moved into War Zone C in a full-scale assault into the region along the Cambodian border. Operation JUNCTION CITY had begun with a battalion-sized airborne assault onto a drop zone near the village of Katum. The troopers were supported with supplies airdropped by C-130s and C-123s. For the first time in the war, American troops were waging war much like they had practiced in countless exercises back in the States.

Toby Carter was back in the war in the South, and far removed from the activities along the Ho Chi Minh Trail. Like everyone else in the 374th, Toby was spending sixteen days at a time operation out of Cam Rhan Bay, either flying with a crew or working as duty loadmaster. The routine was occasionally broken by a tour in Thailand, flying logistics missions out of Bangkok. And back in February Toby had taken an airplane back to the U.S. for extensive modification at the Fairchild factory in Clearwater, Florida. It was during that trip that Toby Carter discovered that his experience in the cave had left him with lasting scars of a sort he never even knew were possible.

Christine, that was the girl's name. She was from near Ashland, Kentucky, but had been visiting her grandmother in St. Petersburg. Nineteen years old, and with a body that would not have looked out of place on the pages of "Playboy," Christine Salyers had checked into the Seafarer Motel for "a few days away from the old people" as her grandmother had said when she handed her the key to room 103. Toby Carter was staying a few doors down, in room 108, while waiting for word that the airplane they were to take back to Okinawa was ready to be picked up.

Toby had spent two weeks in Tennessee, visiting the folks at home, then had flown to Tampa because an airplane was supposed to be ready for the trip back across the Pacific. But when he got there, he found that there were maintenance problems, problems that could take as long as a week to fix. The rest of the crew had gone here and there but Toby had decided to stay in Clearwater. On the second day there, he ran into Christine when he stepped out of his room on his way to the pool.

It was nine o'clock on a Tuesday morning; the motel pool was deserted except for them. With no one else there, they soon began talking. Before long it was time for lunch. They ate together in the Oyster Bar next door. After lunch they walked down to the marina to look at the boats. That evening they went into the lounge for a few drinks. At nine o'clock Christine, only slightly tipsy after three gin and tonics, whispered into Toby's ear, "Let's go to my room!"

Christine Salyers was a beautiful girl, but with a handicap - she had worn thick glasses since first grade. "Four-eyes" had been her nickname throughout elementary school. Even after she began to blossom in the eighth grade, boys tended to ignore her as if there was some stigma attached to her. She had managed to lose her virginity at age seventeen, but that had been while she was away at camp, with a boy she had not known since childhood. She had thought the experience was "kinda nice," but had not been able to repeat it. This particular boy was from Paducah, on the other end of the state from where she lived. She hadn't seen him since the last day at camp.

Christine might wear glasses, but she was one of those girls with a body like the proverbial brick outhouse. She wasn't tall, nor was she especially short. In an earlier time she would have been described as having an hour-glass figure, with prominent breasts - very prominent - a thin waist and hips that curved in harmony with her bust. Some would have described her as voluptuous. Toby Carter had been aware of that body all day; besides, like the boy who had sampled her charms over a year before, he had seen her without glasses at the pool. Her bathing suit had barely covered her best assets; then she had gone to the nightclub in slacks and a tight jersey. He had gotten a powerful erection while dancing with her; it was when she pressed against him and felt his maleness pressing against and into her that she had suggested they go to her room.

It had been a long time since Toby had been with a woman, not since Sharon Craft, and he was afraid he might not be able to hold himself back long enough to give Christine a good time. But when he mounted her, to his surprise he did not come immediately. In fact, he had no trouble holding back his come. Something strange happened to Toby Carter as he was making love to the beautiful young Kentucky girl, something scary. A feeling came over him that she was his enemy, and he was stabbing her with a knife. Perhaps it was her breasts; they were as lovely in the light from Christine's open bathroom door as had been those of the Vietnamese woman he had killed in the cave. Whatever was responsible for the feelings that came over him, instead of making gentle love to a very beautiful young woman who was as attracted to him as he was to her, Toby Carter was using his penis as a weapon, repeatedly stabbing into the girl's tenderest flesh with all the power he could muster.

Had it not been for her well-lubricated vagina, Christine might have found the experience painful. Instead, she was undergoing the most intense pleasure of her life. Sounds were coming from her throat that Toby thought were grunts and screams of pain, but which were the cries of a woman in ecstasy. He wondered why the girl he was trying to kill had not expired, then he felt her entire body become rigid and arch up toward him with superhuman strength. Then, her eyelids fluttered as she sank back onto the bed and lay still. It was only then that he realized he was not in the cave, that the girl lying motionless beneath him was not the Vietnamese. What have I done?!!, he thought.

Then he felt soft, gentle hands on his cheeks as Christine drew his face down to hers. Her exploring tongue inside his mouth made Toby realize that he had not killed her, that she was gripped by passion, not pain. Then he became aware that he had not yet came, though his loins ached with a desire for release. Toby resumed his thrusting, but this time in an attempt at gaining release, not as if he were wielding a knife. Christine sighed her pleasure.

Soon Toby's movements were as vigorous as before, and again Christine was enraptured with passion, but now the young man was fully conscious of who he was with and where. He was thrusting into the girl with all his might, not to bring her pain, but to bring himself release, a release that would not come. For what seemed like hours, Toby Carter pushed his pelvis against that of Christine Salyers; his loins ached to be relieved, but the release just would not come. Finally, after Christine had again collapsed against the pillow, Toby lay still, his testicles aching.

For several minutes they lay together, Christine's head upon his chest, as he caressed her body. Then Christine began exploring, to find that he was still erect. She threw a leg over his waist, then pulled herself over even as she settled down upon him, bringing him into her velvety sheath. With a slow, sensual, rhythmic motion that seemed almost like an afterthought, the girl moved herself up and down the length of her newfound lover while Toby kissed those lovely breasts. He felt it begin in his loins, then spread through his entire body as he finally came, a release that caused Christine to cry out as she felt him burst inside her. The feeling was so intense that the girl stopped her motion; she lay clinging to Toby Carter, as they both savored the rapture of the moment.

Christine had spent the next three days with Toby, until their airplane was finally ready and he began his journey back to the Pacific. They had made love several times but he had not again felt the enmity toward her that he had felt that first time. But, he had discovered that he could not come when he was on top of her, or even from behind. The only way he could find release was for her to make love to him, to control their motion. Whenever he was in control, his release just would not come. Yet, whenever she assumed the superior role, it always did.

At first he had thought it was the lovely sight of her hair plastered against her face, and the drops of perspiration running down her neck and into the valley between her breasts that caused him to turn loose. But then he had realized it wasn't that, but rather it was that he had surrendered control to her; she was the one responsible for their loving, not him. And only when he was no longer in control could he climax.

That had been more than two months ago. Their airplane had finally come into commission and Toby had winged his way across the United State to California, then up the coast to Alaska, and finally out over the northern Pacific to Midway island and finally on to Naha. The route had been circuitous; the original plan had been to leave California bound for Hawaii, then on to Wake. But the late February winds had been well over 100 knots across the Pacific; too strong to allow the short-legged A-model to cover the wide expanse of Ocean between the West Coast and Hawaii and arrive with enough fuel to go to a safe alternate if the weather were bad. So, instead of the balmy breezes of Honolulu, they had endured the 40-below temperature and snow of Anchorage! Even when the winds subsided, they had to take a circuitous route back to Okinawa, by way of Adak, Alaska, Midway Island and Guam.

Toby continued his daydreaming while the Chief of Staff decorated each man after the adjutant read the citation to go with the decoration he received. He thought about the creamy flesh of Christine Salyers - Sharon Craft was no longer in his thoughts. (There had been no letter from her waiting when he got back to Ubon and he hadn't written her before he was shot down. Her address had been in the things that were in his locker at Ubon and had been lost in the shuffle as they were packed into boxes.) And he thought about the cave, and the woman he had killed. Not a day had gone by since he left the cave that he had not relived the experience in his mind. Would he ever be relieved of the memory? At night she came to him in his dreams. Had she really intended to kill him? Or was she merely stretching to prepare to receive him as Christine had done, and Sharon before her? Somewhere deep inside he knew the answer, but the doubts in his mind just would not go away.

It was 1967 - his enlistment would be up in a few months. A lot of people had been putting pressure on him to reenlist - and to extend his tour on The Rock. The folks from the new special operations unit down at Nha Trang were after him to volunteer for the Black Birds. At the same time, the Army's Special Forces people wanted him to work with them; no one else had the knowledge and experience in that section of Laos that he had. Even Air America was after him; the station manager from their office on the north end of the airfield had called him down for an interview. He was thinking about jump school - the Green Beanies ran one up the island at Sukiran. Of course that would be if he re-upped and stayed at Naha.

Finally, it was his turn. The Chief of Staff stood before him, looking right into his eyes as the adjutant began reading the first citation:

"Airman First Class Samuel Tobin Carter distinguished himself as a C-130 loadmaster during the period between 15 June and 10 September, 1966. After Airman Carter's aircraft was shot down, he managed to evade capture for more than three months. During his time on the ground, Airman Carter managed to inflict great damage upon the enemy forces within his area, causing much confusion. When Airman Carter discovered that another American was being held prisoner near his position, he selflessly placed his own life in danger to free that prisoner and bring him to safety. For gallantry and heroism in action, Airman First Class Carter is awarded the Air Force Cross. Airman Carter reflects great credit upon himself and the United States Air Force."

The Chief of Staff took the light blue and red ribbon with it's gold cross from the officer who followed behind him, then pinned it on Toby Carter's chest. The four-star general stepped back and saluted the three-striper airman as Toby returned the salute. Then the adjutant began reading again:

"Airman First Class Samuel Tobin Carter distinguished himself as a C-130 loadmaster on 19 August, 1966. While evading capture after his aircraft was shot down, Airman Carter discovered the location of a concealed antiaircraft gun that had been doing great damage to the allied air effort in Southeast Asia. Airman Carter placed himself in great personal danger by attacking and destroying this gun and in the process freeing a fellow airman who was being held prisoner. For gallantry in action, Airman First Class Carter is awarded the Silver Star. Airman Carter's actions reflect great credit upon himself and the United States Air Force."

Again the Chief of Staff took a medal, this time a red, white and blue one with a silver star suspended beneath, and pinned it on Toby Carter's left pocket, just beneath his silver aircrew wings. Again, the airman and the general exchanged salutes. Then the adjutant began reading again:

"Airman First Class Samuel Tobin Carter distinguished himself as a C-130 loadmaster on 14 May, 1966. When his aircraft was hit by ground fire, Airman Carter supervised the jettisoning of hazardous cargo. As senior loadmaster, Airman Carter remained aboard the burning aircraft after everyone had jumped but himself and the pilot. Airman Carter placed himself in great personal danger by waiting in the airplane until he was certain his aircraft commander was going to able to exit the stricken and burning aircraft. For distinguishing himself while in aerial flight, Airman First Class Carter is awarded the Distinguished Flying Cross. Airman

Carter's actions reflect great credit upon himself and the United States Air Force."

Again the Chief of Staff took the medal that was handed to him - a red, white and blue ribbon with a bronze cross in the shape of a propeller suspended beneath - and pinned it on Toby Carter's shirt. Then, the adjutant began reading again:

"Airman First Class Samuel Tobin Carter distinguished himself while evading capture during the period of 15 June to 10 September, 1966 after his aircraft was shot down in a classified location. During the time Airman Carter was on the ground, he placed himself in great personal danger to gather valuable intelligence which he later provided to U.S. Army special operations forces. For his actions, Airman First Class Carter is awarded the Bronze Star with combat V for valor. Airman Carter's actions reflect great credit upon himself and the United State military services."

The Chief of Staff was handed another red, white and blue ribbon with a star suspended beneath, though in bronze instead of silver. The Bronze Star award had come from the Special Forces people at Nha Trang. They had also wanted to give him something else - the coveted blue and white combat infantryman's badge - but had been prevented because Army regulations stipulated that the award could go only to personnel who were assigned duty with the infantry.

After the Chief of Staff pinned the last medal on his chest, the general turned around to face the men standing before him. "Paaaassssssssssss innnnnnnn reeeeevieeeewwwwwwwwwwwwl"

The adjutant ordered the parade into action. The parade commander called the men back to attention, then, as the band began the Air Force marching song, the mass of assembled men stepped out as one. Toby Carter's heart thrilled to the music, as it always did when he heard the familiar tune. He even knew most of the words; they had been published in the American Legion magazine his grandfather got when he was about fourteen years old.

As each company passed before the reviewing stand, the company commander ordered his men to "Eyeeeeeeeees, Righttttttt!" Then the officer saluted the men on the platform on behalf of those under his command, a salute which he held until his entire company had passed before the stand. All of the officers and enlisted men on the stand returned the salute.

When the parade ended, being a Saturday, the duty day was over. Many of the officers and NCOs retired to their respective clubs for Bloody Marys before lunch. Some of the airmen did likewise, but most ended up in the barracks. That evening several of the guys went into town, stopping first at Jack's Steak House for one of the mouthwatering sandwiches they would remember for the rest of their lives, then heading for a bar. Traditionally, each of the four squadron's had its own bar and each member always, without fail, stopped in to have at least one drink. In the case of the 35th, the squadron bar was the Sunflower Club. That was where Carter, Cavendish, McDonald, Kelly and several other guys started out. But before the evening was over, or actually after it was, since it was past the midnight curfew, everybody ended up at the New York Bar.

By the time Toby staggered up the steps of the barracks to fall into bed, it was well into the wee hours of the morning. His mind had been racing all evening, no doubt prompted by the day's events and the resurrection of so many memories. Everybody wanted to know just what really did happen to him; he managed to remain generally vague in his answers. He had told no one about the woman. Even Bob Preston did not know all the details of the final battle in the cave.

In spite of his inebriated condition, Toby did not fall asleep right away. He said his prayers, as always, then lay with his head on his pillow staring at the ceiling above his top bunk. There were just so many questions in his mind. He had to come to some decision within the next few days as to whether he would reenlist or not, and whether he would extend his tour on The Rock.

What about Christine? There was no doubt but that the girl was enamored with him, but then she was going to be enrolled at the University of Kentucky this fall. She wanted to obtain a degree in corporate law, and work for an oil company. Marriage was not in her immediate future, or so she said, though she had indicated that she was always open to a roll in the hay with him, should he come around.

Had the gooks ever replaced their gun? He was through with Blind Bat; neither he nor Preston had gone back to Ubon after their rescue. They had not been allowed too, under the assumption that both knew too much to be placed back into a possible situation where they might be recaptured. Even though the North Vietnamese didn't go by the Geneva Convention, they would certainly use it to their advantage should it suit. None of the other guys had said anything about The Big Gun since he came back, so it must not have gone back into operation.

But the one question Toby Carter had on his mind as he finally drifted off to sleep would seem trivial to most, yet it was very important to him - "Whatever happened to my carbide light?"

Even as Toby Carter finally drifted into slumber, on the other side of the South China Sea two time zones away, the folks in Special Forces at Nha Trang were burning the midnight oil.

"Colonel, how would you propose we do away with this Colonel Yang?" An Army major by the name of Jenkins sat across the table from a big man wearing combat fatigues with a green beret tucked under an epaulet.

"Well, major. This Chinese colonel seems to be quite elusive. Yet his influence is being felt throughout II Corps. I propose that we assassinate him."

"But how are we going to do that, sir? We know that he makes his headquarters in a cave, and that he is always surrounded by a couple of dozen bodyguards."

"We send in an assassin, someone who knows their way around a cave and who can shoot out a gnat's eye from 1,000 yards."

"But that's an awfully tall order, Colonel. We couldn't use any of our people in that kind of a situation. No doubt the gooks keep close tabs on everyone in our operation, even if we did have someone who could get close enough to do the job. They would know they were coming."

"You're right, Jenkins. No, I have something else in mind. We find a man who can jump out of an airplane, who knows how to operate alone and who can find his way around in the darkness of a cave. Maybe someone who is not one of us. Someone who knows how to shoot."

"Do you have someone in mind, Colonel?"

Colonel McLean leaned back in his chair, "I sure do, major. I certainly do."

THE END

About the Author

Sam McGowan is a retired commercial pilot, an author of numerous magazine articles on military and other subjects. During the Vietnam War he served as a crewmember on USAF C-130s flying highly classified missions over North Vietnam and Laos. A Tennessee native, he currently resides in the Houston, Texas area.